Dragon's Justice 3

Bruce Sentar

D1528410

Cover by Yanaidraws

CONTENTS

CHAPTER 1

I scribbled in the last answer on the biology test, not even caring if it was the correct answer. I was ready for it to be done. It was the last thing standing between me and flying off to Switzerland with Jadelyn and Scarlett.

Jade had pulled some strings so that we could all take our finals a week early. It had been two days since the knockout fight with Nat'alet and Morgana's disappearance, and I was antsy to go find Morgana.

My hand tensed just thinking about it, and my number two pencil crushed its tip against the page and then snapped in half. I grumbled. My new strength was great most of the time, but sometimes, it was just a pain.

The beast inside me smiled, pleased with the crushed pencil. But it thought I should just let my strength out in a mad rampage, smashing everything in sight, then burn it to cinders and piss on the ashes.

To put it gently, the beast had been extra frustrated the past two days, straining to get free and go after Morgana. I was pretty sure it would not have been okay with sitting for months before it could go after her.

"Are you okay, Mr. Pendragon?" Professor Vandal asked, breaking me from my little spat with the beast.

"Fine. Sorry, I'm just in a rush." I did my best to smile.

"I can see that."

I waited until he looked back down at the stack of papers on his desk before shifting my finger into a razor-sharp claw. With my golden, glittering claw, I shaved one of the broken halves back to a point and scribbled furiously, wishing I could write faster.

Jadelyn was much more composed. She sat near me, calmly scribbling on the paper. She was leaning over, her face nearly pressed against the page as she focused intently. I smiled, watching her bite her lip just a little as she tried to puzzle through the problem on the page.

Looking back at my test, I finished the last of the questions and slapped my pencil down, breaking it again. Since I was already done, I didn't care, dropping the broken pieces into my bookbag.

I stood up, realizing Professor Vandal was staring at me, a skeptical frown on his face as he stared at where the pencil had been.

I quickly started moving, not wanting to give him too much time to think about it, handing him my test.

"Well done, Mr. Pendragon. You're free to go."

Jadelyn looked up and then back down at her own test. She gave me a nod to wait a moment as she finished it up as well. Then she neatly put away her supplies into her bag and handed in her test. As she walked by me, I snagged her bag, throwing it over my shoulder as well.

"Both of you have my condolences. Please be well."

"Thank you again, professor." Jadelyn gave him a sweet smile that could charm just about anybody we met, woman or man.

As we walked out, I lifted an eyebrow in question. "What did he think was the reason that we were taking the exam early?"

"I don't know." Jadelyn shrugged. "One of my men arranged it for me."

I nodded. From what he'd said, I was guessing the professor thought somebody had died? But it didn't matter much to me. We were free, and my dragon was roaring to be off in search of Morgana.

As we approached the edge of campus, a black SUV pulled up, and two suited men popped out of the car. One of the men scanned the surroundings while the other opened the door for us.

I still wasn't used to the security teams, but now that I was married to Jade, I'd have to get used to them. They were officially part of my life.

The beast in me did not see the need for their protection of Jade. I could become a several-ton, gold or silver dragon-scaled tank at will, or at least, that's how I thought of myself. In reality, I was a dragon, and I felt pretty sure that I could protect her just as well, if not better, than the small army of men they called guards.

The gold or silver part still had me a bit baffled. Somehow, I was both, which was apparently impossible based on every book I could find in Jadelyn's library.

If I could read a few dozen languages, I would have been able to use Morgana's library as well. But that would have to wait until I wrangled my wayward partner.

"Airport please," Jadelyn said as the men hopped back into the car.

Scarlett turned around from the driver's seat. She wore a hat, with her orange fox ears sticking up through the top. I'd learned by that point that people liked to explain away the oddities. They'd most likely think they were a prop. But her ears twitched as she scanned the surroundings quickly. As Jadelyn's guard, she was currently on duty.

"On it!" Scarlett said.

I was pressed back into my seat as Scar tore forward. "You almost drive as poorly as Morgana." I grumbled.

"Oh, really? Remind me... who was the one that wrecked Morgana's car?" Scar took a hand off the wheel to tap her lips in thought.

"I'm never going to live that down, am I?"

"Nope. But at least you didn't wreck any last time," Jade pointed out.

"There's always next time." Scar said, far too peppy for the topic.

I made sure my seat belt was fastened as she turned through the bar street just off campus. It was still busy despite it being the middle of the day.

We whizzed by a bunch of people who had no idea that the world was filled with paranormals. Not long ago, I would have been among them. It had taken confronting a werewolf asshole for me to even realize that I wasn't human.

"Do you have everything you need? You didn't pack much," Jadelyn asked, scooting closer to me in the back seat and intertwining our fingers.

I pulled out a foam pad from a bra, holding it up for them. "I have what I need right here."

The entire car looked at me as if I'd gone crazy. I just smiled, enjoying their confusion.

"It's Morgana's," I said, helping them understand.

"That just makes it creepy. That's from her bra?"

Laughing, I decided showing them would be better. "And so much more."

I stuck my hand into the bra pad, or more precisely, into the spatial pouch inside of it.

When she had left, I had looked through her room a few times for any hints of where she had gone, using my dragon eyes to sense magic. And while doing so, I had come across the bra pad in my hand.

It all made so much more sense now. Morgana was always pulling things out of her bras. With how tight her clothes were, I'd never been able to figure it out. She'd apparently used her spatial abilities to create additional storage.

Pulling the silver templar sword halfway out of the bra pad, I gave both girls a big smile. "See?"

"Holy shit." Scarlett's eyes were wide in the rearview mirror as she watched me rather than the road. "That's a bag of holding."

"Maybe tell us that first before proclaiming all you need is Morgana's bra. I thought you planned to use it for her scent or something." Jadelyn rolled her eyes at my antics.

Shrugging, I put the sword back into it and placed the pad back in my pocket. "I don't know. I liked it my way. It was funny to watch your faces. And this has a dual purpose. It makes it easier to carry and lets me bring a sword through customs."

"We have a private jet—there are no customs." Jadelyn looked confused.

I stared at her for a moment. I'd never ridden on a private jet before. It hadn't occurred to me that they'd travel in style, but now that she had said it, I wasn't very surprised.

"Sweet," I replied slowly. "I guess we have a direct flight then to The City in the Shade. What's it like?"

"It is absolutely beautiful," Scarlett said from up front. "The city is run by the royal family of the high elves. They also maintain the enchantment on the city to keep it hidden."

"How exactly do we get to a secret city of supernaturals? I mean... there's got to be some sort of catch."

As soon as I said that, Scarlett snorted, barely keeping in her laughter.

"What?" I could tell that I was missing something.

"Nothing." Jadelyn couldn't hide her blush, though. "There's a secret platform in a Lucerne train station."

"Kind of like—" I started, but Scarlett burst out laughing, interrupting me.

"Yes, exactly like it. You should have seen Jade when that scene happened in the movie. She was screaming for her father, that the humans know about the Shade Express. She was convinced that our secrets had been spilled."

Jadelyn's face was turning bright red all the way to the tips of her ears. "Sometimes fiction mirrors reality. Plus, I was, what, eight when that movie came out?"

I laughed along with Scarlett, imagining little Jade running around the house, sounding the alarm that the humans were coming for them. Although, I realized her panic had been created because of the immense fear pushed onto children that the paranormal world cannot be found out by humans.

"I think it's cute." Running my hand through her hair, I pulled Jadelyn close and kissed her. I went to pull back, but once wasn't enough, so I leaned in again, sucking on her lips and letting my other hand roam her curves.

Scarlett coughed politely up front before we were suddenly blasted with cold air conditioning. "Sorry, I needed to cool it down back there if I'm to maintain my focus."

"I'll remember that," Jade warned with a frumpy set of her shoulders as she lay back against her seat.

"Don't worry. I'll help you get payback for it." I glared at the back of Scarlett's head until her ears twitched. "Anyway, so we take a secret train to the city? That's pretty cool."

"That's just the tip of the iceberg," Scarlett said, feeling safe to rejoin the conversation. "The city itself is quite literally magic. You just have to see it to believe it."

I couldn't wait. I was so ready to explore the paranormal world, but I was even more ready to hunt down Morgana.

The only real friend in town I'd ever seen with Morgana was T. He knew that, if Morgana left, she would go back home, and he was likely in contact with her.

T was an ancient elf who was wanted for having performed forbidden magic. Yet no one seemed interested in going for him directly; instead, his daughter was the one everyone was after. She was his most guarded secret.

Yet T had given me instructions on how to contact his daughter, including secret messages disguised as fliers. A stack of them was printed up and stored in the spatial bra pad.

I was starting to wish Morgana had enchanted something else. It wasn't the most convenient thing for me to carry around.

Checking once more that the fliers were in there, I relaxed again.

We had a plan. We would get to the city and post up the fliers. Hopefully, T's daughter would then get in touch with us. She was our best hope. It seemed likely that if Morgana had in fact returned to The City in the Shade, she'd be in contact with her oldest friend.

If she was T's daughter, I hoped she'd be able to help Morgana, because besides just catching up, Morgana needed healing. Though that didn't explain why she had run without planning to return.

During the fight with Nat'alet, I'd learned enough to know that she'd been essentially poisoned by celestial magic during the seventeenth century war, four hundred years ago, between the Church and the paranormal. Her special champagne was actually angelic blood, which she drank in an attempt to hold off the damage.

But the fight with Nat'alet had pushed her to the point that she had had to use her hidden affinity with angels, transforming into some strange vampire/angel mode and wrecking Nat'alet before being overcome with her affliction. And she'd done it to help save me.

I was still mad that she'd run off. She needed healing just as much as I had. But she wouldn't have handed off Bumps in the Night, her nightclub, if she wasn't serious about staying away. So I was off to find her.

"Hey, broody mcbrooderson," Scarlett called to get my attention. "Tone it down—you're growling. We'll find her."

"Thanks."

She could read me like a book and had been a big help during the past two days in trying to stay grounded and focused on the solution rather than getting lost in my thoughts.

"Besides, we are almost there." Scarlett pulled up to a booth, and I realized we were at some private entrance for the airport.

She flashed her ID and was let through without much fuss, driving out past a few dozen private hangars and into one that had a small ground crew working.

I'd expected them to be in the grungy jeans and reflective vests I was used to at the airport, but instead, they wore clean black slacks and blazers.

Scarlett pulled up, stopping the car to the side of the hangar as the three security men bailed out and did a sweep of it.

She whirled around in her seat to talk to us as I reached for the door handle. "Just a minute. They have their jobs to do."

It was all routine, I told myself as they calmly checked the place, one using a little fold-out wand to scan the underside while another stepped inside to check it as well. The third stood at the nose of the jet on watch.

When he tensed up and drew his weapon, I knew something was wrong.

"Stop where you are!" he shouted, sighting down his gun.

I didn't need another warning. The car door crumpled under my strength as I tore it off in my haste to get out of the car.

"Zach! Let them do their jobs!" Scarlett shouted after me.

I ignored her. I had energy to burn off.

When I saw a shifted werewolf sprinting towards the hangar with a large duffel bag hung over their chest, my vision went red and I roared, shifting into my dragon form and pouncing over the guard.

The werewolf tried to stop, its claws skidding on the smooth ground and losing traction.

I landed on top of the werewolf, my size making the hangar shake. Fully transformed, I was but a whelp compared to many dragons. I didn't even have my wings yet.

But that didn't mean I wasn't a giant, four-ton wrecking machine.

I leaned down, pinning the werewolf under my claws.

"Stop!" Scarlett was screaming from behind me, and the panic in her voice made me pause. I had the werewolf under control—why was she concerned?

My dragon brain was often processing things I hadn't given conscious thought yet, so I did pause.

And in that moment, the werewolf shifted back into its human form.

Soon my claw was holding a very naked Kelly. She was holding a duffel bag almost as big as her to her chest.

"Hi?" she said tentatively.

I let out a deep grumble from my throat and shifted back, standing naked over her. Before I could speak, Scarlett was there, grabbing Kelly by the collar and hauling her up while yelling at her.

"What are you doing here?! Did you not think about the fact that we have a fucking pissy dragon here to keep in check? Do. Not. Startle. Him." She scanned the rest of the hangar, nodding to her men to put their guns down.

"Fuck," Scarlett cursed, dropping Kelly, who at least looked ashamed. "Men, finish your sweep of the plane. Jonny, get a cleaning crew to make sure we wipe any footage. We don't need others seeing golden boy here."

Once they confirmed their orders, Scar whirled on me. "Calm down. I know you are tense, but jeez! Didn't you recognize Kelly?"

A little ashamed of myself, I looked down at Kelly as she got to her feet and swung the bag over her back, comfortable in her nakedness. "Just the tension of the situation, I uh…"

"Went crazy," Kelly coughed. "I mean, dear god. I've never been so afraid for my life."

"You"—Scarlett glared at Kelly, silencing her—"don't get to speak besides telling me why you are here."

Kelly rolled her eyes. "Duh. I'm here to go get the blue bitch."

"Don't you have a pack to manage?" I frowned. When I'd last left her and the pack, she was barely holding onto her status as alpha.

But she just waved away my question. "It's under control. Took a day of beating the boys senseless, then hiring a coach back for the team and getting some number twos established, but it's handled. It'll be good for me to be absent a little. They can cool off, and then I'll come back and beat them senseless again. You know, really drive it home that they have no choice in the matter."

I knew nothing about pack politics or even the magic that tied them together, but I shifted my eyes to look at her magic.

A brilliant orange web spanned out from Kelly, stretching mostly in the same direction. It appeared to be very stable.

Staring at it, I didn't have a good reason she shouldn't come with us. "What do you think, Scar, Jade?"

Kelly gave Jade a pair of puppy dog eyes.

"Don't you dare." Scar grabbed her by the ear.

"I think she can come. You were saying we were light on security, anyway," Jadelyn said.

Scarlett stomped her feet. "Damnit."

"Are we not bringing the guys?" I asked, looking at the team doing a sweep of the plane.

"There's a team at the Scalewright's home in Sentarshaden. We won't have a detail, though. I figured that, with you and me, we could handle any surprises as long as we flew under the radar." Scarlett chewed the inside of her lip as she looked Kelly up and down. Her face turned stern when she finally spoke. "While we are on this trip, you listen to me, got it?"

Kelly perked up. I had a feeling that if her tail was out, it would have been wagging. "Yes, sir." She gave Scarlett a cheeky salute.

Scarlett scoffed, not believing a word of the world's only female alpha. Like she'd listen to another. "Fine, then get on the plane."

One of her men was giving Scarlett the all-good signal as he finished sweeping the tail of the plane.

"And get some damn clothes on," she added.

A tap on my shoulder made me turn.

"Here." Jadelyn held up a pocket from my torn clothes with the bra— er — spatial artifact inside it.

"Thanks." I wasn't quite as comfortable as Kelly in the nude, but the appraising look that Jadelyn gave me made me feel far more comfortable.

"Least I could do for my big, scary protector." Jadelyn sashayed in front of me and walked up the steps to the private jet, swinging her hips and trailing her fingers along the banister.

It wasn't like I needed her to ask. I chased after her; the beast inside of me was already trying to break his way out of my chest.

But even the beast paused as I got to the top and got a peek inside the plane. The interior was a soft, tan suede leather, with half a dozen swivel chairs throughout. Two beds sat in the back, and a full bar peeked around the corner.

"I said get some clothes on," Scarlett yelled as Kelly rushed up the steps and slammed into me from behind, knocking the two of us down on the floor, still naked.

Jadelyn turned back and lifted an eyebrow curiously. "Kelly. Please do get your clothes on. Zach, please leave them off."

"Not fair," Kelly whined.

Scarlett stepped over both of us. "Deal with it."

The door closed, and two pilots made their way to the cockpit. Both of them professionally ignored the two naked people on the floor.

Pushing Kelly off of me, I got up and scooped Jadelyn up, carrying her to the bed in the back.

She put her lips to my ear and let out a single note that made my eyes close as I squeezed her tight, careful not to tip over as her siren song drove me wild.

"I'll handle this one." Scarlett closed a curtain and dragged Kelly away. "But don't think I'm going to be left out. I want to join the mile-high club too."

"I expect you as soon as we hit a mile in the sky, then," I said as I threw Jadelyn onto the bed.

The lovely siren arched her back and gave me a come-hither look, beckoning me with her finger while her eyes smoldered.

She had been using sex as her own way to distract me the last two days, and it had been working. I had yet to tire her out, but we had a transatlantic flight for me to give it another go.

CHAPTER 2

"There's only a half an hour left on the flight. If you need a moment to get cleaned up, please do so," the pilot announced over the intercom.

I guessed we hadn't been very quiet.

Jadelyn was flush in the face and breathing heavily, a broad grin stretching across her face. "Hope I didn't wear you out."

"Never." I threatened to roll back on top of her, but she patted me on the chest.

"We are about to land, and we can't take up much time on the tarmac without getting in trouble."

"You two," Scarlett groaned from off the edge of the bed.

I peeked over the side to see my favorite kitsune liberally coated with sweat, semen drying on her breasts. "Us two what?"

"One day, I'm going to learn your secret, Jade," Scarlett vowed, shaking a fist in the air.

Jade pulled me back from the edge of the bed with a few kisses. "I'm literally made for sex with him now. That and, of course, plenty of practice. Frequent practice is definitely necessary." She snuggled into me.

Jade could also make enough lubrication that we could have sex under water, and that helped considerably as well. But I let that go unsaid.

Rolling off the bed on the side Scarlett wasn't occupying, I grabbed my spatial artifact and ducked into one of the two mid-cabin bathrooms. I turned on the shower. The water was still heating up, but the cold didn't bother me. I dipped under the spray and washed myself clean, scrubbing between my legs thoroughly to get off all of Jade's juices.

Even as my shower kicked off, I could hear the other one running.

Pulling a fresh set of clothes out of the spatial artifact, I got dressed and decided to check on Kelly.

Up in the front of the cabin, Kelly lay sprawled out on an egg-shaped swivel chair. Her pants were pulled down and an empty whiskey bottle was on the floor.

"Kelly, wake up. You can use the shower on the left." I nudged the horny and drunk werewolf awake.

"Huh? Is it my turn yet?" she asked groggily before she blinked away her sleepiness and cursed. "You're dressed. That means I missed my shot."

"There was no shot, at least not right now." Jadelyn came out of her bathroom with a towel wrapped around her head. "Plus, it looks like you made yourself plenty comfortable."

Kelly gave her a deadpanned look. "Do you realize how loud the three of you are? Fuck, it drove me nuts."

Jadelyn just shrugged and pulled a change of clothes out of her bag. She put them on right there in the middle of the cabin.

I was tempted to take them right back off, but the sound of the landing gear coming out below us reminded me that we were out of time. It also meant that we were one step closer to finding Morgana, and I felt my adrenaline surge.

Walking over, I settled for a simple kiss on the cheek for Jadelyn and opened the door to the bathroom to kiss Scarlett and remind her, "Might want to get in a seat. I don't think standing in the bathroom is going to go over well when we land."

She ducked under my arm, still naked, and dove into a seat, buckling herself in while still drying herself off with a towel.

I joined her. We were all seated in the swivel chairs as the plane bumped down on the runway.

It was far less jarring than I remembered.

"Smaller plane," Scarlett answered. "And better pilots."

She unbuckled her seat as soon as we were on the ground and wiggled herself back into a pair of tight jeans and a leather biker jacket.

When the plane stopped, Scarlett held up a hand for us to wait and opened the door, jumping out on her own to do a sweep of the area.

"Thanks for flying with us." The pilots came out of the cockpit.

The copilot looked at the mess behind us with a strange expression before looking at me in complete disbelief.

I just shrugged and smiled. "Dragons have stamina. It lets us keep up with all our women."

"Don't worry—we have a cleaning service coming," Jadelyn told them both.

"Do you know when exactly your return trip will be?" the pilot asked.

"Not for a few days. You both are on paid standby for the next week," she answered the question she knew they'd be asking next. "So kick back for two days. By then, I'll hopefully have a better understanding of what our schedule will look like."

The pilot nudged the copilot with a wink. They seemed happy enough with that plan. I was curious what they were going to do with their free time given that they looked so excited, but I figured I'd just leave them to it.

Scarlett poked her head back into the plane. "All clear—let's go."

I grabbed Kelly's bag on the way out, slinging the massive thing over my shoulder. "By the way, where are your bags?" I asked Jadelyn.

"Shipped to my place in Sentarshaden," she replied. "I just keep a few things on the plane."

"Damn." Kelly looked at her bag. "Here I am, traveling with everything like a pleb."

"Don't worry, I have all of my stuff with me, too," I said.

Kelly looked me up and down and then back at the plane. "Where?"

"Right here." I pulled the spatial artifact from my pocket.

"Is that a bra pad?" Her jaw nearly dropped. "Perv."

"No." I waved my hands to stop her. "It's a spatial artifact," I corrected her.

"That also happens to be a bra pad," Scarlett snickered as she led us across the tarmac to a black SUV that had been waiting.

The driver stepped out of his car in a thick coat and held a sign that said, 'Golden Boy'. "Are you Golden Boy?"

Scarlett looked back at me, waiting for me to answer. The joy in her eyes told me she was enjoying that moment.

I sighed, deciding it was best to play along. "Yep, that would be me."

"Great. Then come on in. I'll get you all to the train station."

The four of us piled into the back two rows comfortably. I had a momentary pause, realizing that, if the group of girls I surrounded myself with got much larger, we would have to start taking more than one car.

"So, what are you guys doing in beautiful Switzerland?" the driver tried to make conversation.

"Vacation," Scarlett answered quickly. She shot me a look, and I nodded at the unspoken communication. The driver didn't know about paranormals.

"It is beautiful this time of year."

Everything but the roads was coated in a heavy snow. The homes were picturesquely decorated in the white, powdery snow.

"It really is." My breath fogged up the window, and I had to rub at it to keep it from hindering my vision.

The world was different to me now. Rather than just fields of snow, I couldn't help but wonder if there was a paranormal out there enjoying it. I wondered if Yetis were an actual thing, but I couldn't ask the girls in front of the driver without sounding crazy.

Another thought hit me, but I'd have to ask the girls later. If this was a city of paranormals, what were the chances there was another dragon in the city?

I knew that there weren't many dragons, but it seemed likely a big paranormal city would have at least one. One that, unlike the Bronze King in Dubai, might try to keep a low profile like me.

I was still doing my best to keep my powers under wraps. I wasn't strong enough to hold my own against the kind of groups that would want to use my body parts.

I shivered at the thought.

"Hey, Kelly, with you out here, who's stopping the rest of your pack from spilling my secret?" I suddenly asked.

"Uh..." Kelly stalled. "I don't know if I could have stopped them all, even if I was there. Sorry, but two hundred college kids are like a gossip machine."

I had already realized that they were a massive flaw in my ability to stay under the radar, but I couldn't bring myself to kill all of them.

"It had to come out eventually," Scarlett reminded me, shrugging. "Plus, random rumors without some solid support to back them might just fade away."

"Yeah. We'll run damage control when we get back." Kelly jumped on Scarlett's idea, agreeing and trying to comfort me.

I nodded. Now that I could shift, I felt far less vulnerable, but I was sure that there would be consequences when my secret got out.

At least I was getting used to change. I'd managed to go from a geeky kid pursuing med school to a mercenary in the paranormal world. And I was getting better at taking on what came my way. I'd even managed to take down a god with a bit of extra help.

I tried to pump myself up so that I'd focus less on the massive threat of my secret getting spilled.

But as I looked at my two beautiful women, and thought about the third I was about to hunt down, I only wanted to press forward into the paranormal world. I'd just have to handle what came at me.

"We're here," the driver announced as he pulled up to a large concrete building.

"Thank you." Jadelyn handed him a hefty tip. "Have a good day."

"You too," he said excitedly before fishing around in his coat pocket. "If you need a driver anytime, just call me."

"Will do." Scarlett took the card for Jade.

Closing the door behind Jade, who was the last to get out, I looked up at the extensive building with a fancy concrete arch welcoming us to Switzerland.

"Come on, we better hurry." Scarlett checked her phone for the time. "Next train is in fifteen minutes."

"How often does it run?" I asked, walking briskly to keep up with her tiny legs as she hurried.

"Four times a day. We'll wait for hours if we don't hurry." Scarlett kept up her fast pace, and I snagged Jadelyn, helping her keep up.

Kelly had no problem speeding through the area, bouncing beside us with her massive pack over her shoulder.

***

The massive stone archway welcomed us into the train station.

Beyond the old arch, the station was actually quite modern. Crowds passed us by as we pushed our way into the station. Everybody was in a rush, working to get where they needed to go.

"So, where is this secret station?" I asked, looking around and not seeing the obvious answer. There wasn't even space between stations 9 and 10.

"Secret station?" Kelly asked. "Like H—"

"Exactly like it," Jadelyn interrupted her and smacked Scarlett as she opened her mouth to once again tell the story of little Jadelyn.

Jadelyn then pivoted to look at Kelly. "Have you never been to Sentarshaden?"

"Nope. My dad was a local kind of guy. We drove to any vacations." Kelly hugged her bag tighter at the mention of her old man. She still needed time for that wound to heal.

Wanting to leave that conversation as quickly as possible, I nudged Scarlett forward, and she took the lead once again.

"Just follow me." She took a big step forward and started her charge across the station.

An idea came to me, and I pulled a pair of sunglasses from my spatial artifact. I put them on to hide my eyes as I shifted them. Everything came into a higher clarity, and several people walking around lit up with magic on their person. But what surprised me most of all was that the wall at the far end of the station was an illusion. And it was what Scarlett was charging towards.

"Can you see it?" Jadelyn asked, peeking around my glasses.

"Yeah. We just walk through it?"

"You have to take it at a run, or you'll bounce off it," Jadelyn informed me and Kelly.

Kelly squinted her eyes at Jadelyn. "You first."

I laughed. It would be like Jadelyn to get Kelly to charge into a wall.

"I'll go first." I said.

The wall was only about five paces away when I kicked into a jog. Despite seeing the magic with my dragon eye, I still closed my eyes, bracing for impact.

But the impact never came. I ran right through the wall.

Kelly came barreling behind me, knocking me over and landing on top of me.

"Oops." But she said it in a way that didn't sound like a mistake.

Grabbing her and rolling both of us to the side, I stood before Jadelyn, and Scarlett trampled over us.

"That wasn't so bad." I dusted off my coat.

"What keeps people from seeing everyone run at a wall?" Kelly asked.

"More magic and wards. The station has paranormals in the management, so the cameras don't catch the right angle either," Scarlett explained.

I broke from the conversation and looked at the platform. A werewolf was just standing there on the platform, partially shifted, its gray fur on full display.

"Some of us are more comfortable showing what we are," Jadelyn said by way of explanation. Her mermaid ears had come out, and I could see scales peeking out of the collar of her coat.

Scarlett's ears and tails popped out as she stopped covering them with illusions.

I looked over at Kelly, watching as she let her wolf ears pop out. But otherwise, she stayed human.

"You could just take off your sunglasses and show those eyes of yours. No one will realize what you are," Jadelyn encouraged me.

It was a very strange moment for me as I pulled the sunglasses down and let my paranormal flag fly for the first time.

I was different, and... no one cared.

Nobody stared at me. Not the werewolf, the vampire, or even the elf waiting on the platform spared our group another glance as we walked up to wait for the next train.

"This is..."

"Awesome," Scarlett filled in for me, smiling. "I know. I hate hiding my tails. Everything feels so much better when I can let them out."

Her soft, fluffy tails batted at my chest, absorbing some of the mana I was giving off. As a dragon, I was one of the few paranormals that actually produced mana rather than just consuming it.

Mana was a vital resource for the world and paranormal kind. It gave most paranormal creatures their various abilities. Which meant that dragons were an openly protected species, as the world was being depleted of mana. But it also meant that we were valuable and could be hunted. Since our bodies were flooded with mana day and night, that made me and the rest of dragon kind precious. Our bodies were literal treasure troves.

When I had visited T, he had been giddy over just a few nail clippings and had bargained for a lock of hair.

The old alchemist was wanted by all elven kind and was a friend of Morgana's. I trusted him in general, but I was still antsy about what he was going to do with the bits of me he was collecting.

Scarlett bumped my hip. "You're staring."

"Oh." I quickly looked away. I had been staring at an elf while I had been thinking.

"She's a cute one. High elf for sure," Jadelyn said from my other side.

"How can you tell?" I wondered what set the elven races apart.

Morgana had been a bit of a dead giveaway with her blue skin, but the elf here had pale skin that would have blended in with any of the other Switzerlanders in the middle of the winter. She had blonde hair and pointy ears that poked out of her hair.

"The eyes," the two of them said together.

Careful not to seem like I was staring again, I looked back and realized with a shock that her eyes were an almost magical violet and blue. The colors swirled together like they were alive with some undercurrent.

"Yep, there are a lot of high elves in Sentarshaden. The ruling family are high elves, after all," Scarlett continued to give me details about the city.

I nodded, absorbing the information. "What kind of elf is T?"

They looked at each other.

"I'm not really sure," Jadelyn said first. "He certainly isn't a dark elf, but he barely opens his eyes, so I'm not sure if he is a high elf either."

"What other options are there?" I pushed for more information.

"Wood, mountain, desert, high, and drow." Scarlett quickly ticked off a list on her fingers. "Desert are super tan, and drow are blue. High, wood, and mountain are all more normal skin tones. Though wood often have a golden tan to them, and they generally have green hair."

I nodded, keeping track of their differences. "So do mountain elves have any defining characteristics?"

"Short. The rest are kind of tall and lanky, but not the mountain elves."

Glancing down the platform, I waited to see if I could spot any of the other elven varieties. There was one green-haired man a ways down; I assumed then he must have been a wood elf.

I smiled, happy at the new information I'd already gotten.

While I was busy scoping out the platform with all its oddities, a heavy plume of smoke trailed towards the platform, and a heavy red and white locomotive careened into the station.

"Jadelyn, that thing looks like it isn't going to stop."

"Oh, don't worry. It's something you need to get used to. Here, paranormal kind can actively merge technology and magic."

I stared at the train barreling towards the platform. It had to be going a solid eighty miles an hour at full steam when it made it to the platform. But when it reached, it decelerated smoothly, without the screeching of metal.

It stopped, perfectly aligned to the platform.

"That was..."

"Incredible," Kelly finished for me. "What made that work?"

"Magic," Jadelyn answered with a laugh, like she'd been holding that one in.

It didn't matter what made it work; I was thoroughly impressed. And I was excited. I had a feeling that Sentarshaden was going to provide a wealth of new experiences for me.

People poured out of the train cars in an assortment of clothes, looking like everyday travelers.

So many of them were shifting their hair to hide their ears, putting on illusions, or shifting back to fully human as they crossed the platform and streamed back out into the regular portion of the station.

"Come on, stop staring or you'll miss the train." Jadelyn hooked her arm around mine and pulled me into the now empty train.

I could tell that she was excited too as she pulled me through the doors and down a little hallway where each of the cars was lined with eight small private rooms.

I knew this wasn't new for her, so I tried to figure out what was exciting her so much. But then I figured it out. "Jade, how often do you travel without guards?"

She paused, smiling up at me sheepishly. "Never. My mother only let me go with just you and Scarlett because of what you are. She's sure you'll keep me safe."

Jadelyn gave me a winning smile, and she dragged me down to sit in the seat with her.

Scarlett narrowed her eyes at me as she slid into her seat across from me. "So no running off. You need to keep Jade close to keep her safe. Same goes for you, wolfy."

Kelly stopped looking around, marveling at the train. "Not a problem. Keep Jade safe. I can do that." She nodded to herself, as if something else had just occurred to her.

Stuffing her bag in the space over her head, Kelly sat down with a big grin. "If I save Jade, does that make me valuable enough to keep around?" Kelly pointedly asked Scarlett.

My lovely Kitsune mate's tails thrashed angrily behind her. "We'll see. Let's just hope no one recognizes her."

CHAPTER 3

As soon as we'd all been seated, a light knock sounded on the door to our little room.

Kelly looked over at Scarlett, who nodded. Getting up, Kelly opened the door, an eager elf standing on the other side.

Kelly stared him down. "Can I help you?"

"Is that Jadelyn Scalewright?" The elf pulled out a notepad. "I have a few questions for the Shade Times."

"Get lost," Scarlett growled. "We are just passing through."

"But if I could—" The rest of the elf's question was cut off as Kelly slammed the door with a smile on her face.

Jadelyn sighed. "I'm sorry. They bother me everywhere I go."

"Don't be." I pulled my lovely siren closer. "If it gets too bad, I'll just eat them all."

She gave me a wry chuckle and then shook her head, making her platinum blonde hair spill over her face. "Don't do that. Then everyone will know you are a gold dragon, and we'll end up even more swarmed by the press."

She nuzzled into me.

"That bad?" I asked.

Kelly jumped in. "Oh definitely. You'd become extremely famous. Just think about how much everyone talks about the Bronze King in Dubai. If there was a known gold running around Philly, you'd... well... you'd probably have reporters and an army of women chasing after you," Kelly agreed with Jadelyn.

"Army of women?" I snorted.

Scarlett glared at me. "Don't forget all the perks. I mean, we don't do much about it, but they could waddle away with a hundred thousand dollar payday if they scooped your seed out and sold it."

I shook my head, still a bit unsure how I felt about my seed's value to paranormal alchemists. I was just glad I'd found women who didn't use me for that money.

"Okay, I'll try not to eat anyone." I took their caution to heart. Unless they were truly in danger, I'd keep it under wraps. I couldn't make any promises if I felt it was needed to keep them safe. They were mine.

The beast growled in my chest in agreement.

Movement caught my eye, and I realized the elf reporter was lurking just down the hall, scribbling in his notepad as he watched us.

I stood and pulled the blinds down on our little room. It would make it feel a little cramped, but at least we wouldn't be watched like some sort of zoo animal.

"Thank you," Jadelyn said.

"Let's focus on other things." I watched out the window as the landscape passed us by. "How long of a train ride is this?"

"A few hours. Sentarshaden is hidden among the Alps." Scarlett pulled out her phone and started tapping away. "There are some paranormal apps you can get now that we are close, though."

"Like what?"

She held out her phone for me, and 'Shade Times' ran across the top in scrollwork letters. "They have a few newspapers there, dating apps, maps, and really anything you can think of. It's a bustling city with just as much opportunity as any other city."

Jadelyn butted in, "Only everything has to be kept secret. You can only pick up the apps when you are in range of the city, lest some normal person suddenly find a dating app full of werewolves."

I looked out the window as we left the city and started passing through snow-covered hills. Watching the scenery pass, I raised a question that was on my mind. "This can't be the only city like this, can it?"

"There are others. El Dorado in Mexico is run by dwarves. They do love their gold," Scarlett laughed. "Another in China, the Yangze Valley. You have to be invited there, and Jade's family is not well loved by her Chinese rivals. We've never gone."

"Security issues," Jadelyn air quoted, rolling her eyes.

"It really is!" Scarlett took offense. "Do you realize how dangerous it would be for you to go there?"

"But you are a kitsune," Jade pointed out, as if that was supposed to make a difference.

I thought that Scarlett's head was about to explode.

"I'm fucking Irish, not one of those crazy fucking Asian foxes that trick you to eat your own heart with a smile on your face. You know this." She squinted dangerously at Jadelyn.

"I still really want to go one day."

"Maybe they'll invite golden boy one day when he's out. They'd probably make a deal given that you are married to him," Scarlett pointed out.

Jadelyn turned to me with dreamy eyes full of hope.

"Nope. Not unless Scar gives the trip the all-clear. If anything happened to you, I'd..." Images of the world burning down to ash came to mind, but I decided to keep those thoughts to myself. "... let's just say things would get bad."

Jadelyn was studying me, a bit of concern on her face as she ran her hand along my face in a soft motion. "Nothing will happen to me. I don't want you to worry."

She let out a small little note into my ear that helped wash away the momentary anxiety that had reared its head at the thought of her death.

I looked around and saw Kelly bracing.

But she relaxed as I relaxed, letting out a small whistle. "Damn. I thought this train was going to explode for a moment. I'll bet you just scared off that reporter, though."

I frowned, noticing Scarlett was also staring at me. "What?"

"You just put out a terrifying aura," Scarlett informed me. "If I wasn't so comfortable with you, I might have been scrambling to get out of this booth."

"Oh. Uh... that's new," I said, confused. "I'll try not to do it again. Just the thought of something happening to my mate..."

The same thought triggered in my mind, and I could feel it wash out of me again.

"Okay." Jadelyn put her hand on my shoulder again. "Let's just drop the thought. But it seems you are still growing."

"Growing quickly, too," Scarlett said. "I thought your gold dragon form looked a little bigger when you pounced on Kelly earlier."

I didn't know. It was hard to get a good measure of my dragon form besides estimates. But I knew that, as far as dragons were concerned, my dragon form was considered quite young. It didn't even have wings yet.

If Morgana was right, my dragon was playing catch up from being sealed for so long.

"Let's focus on happier topics. What are you going to do to the blue bitch when you see her again?" Kelly laughed.

"Pin her to the wall and get answers," I growled. "I can't believe she ran out on me."

My comment caused a lull in the cabin, and I let it sit. There were answers that Morgana owed me, and I was determined to get them out of her when I saw her next.

***

The landscape continued to blur by us until the train reoriented itself straight for a mountain.

"Uh. Jadelyn. The train looks like it is about to crash." Even though I knew that one of these mountains wasn't real, it was still hard to watch the train continue on a collision course.

"Breathe." Jadelyn held my hand. "The first time is the worst."

"Just close your eyes," Scarlett said, her own eyes closed.

I did so, still bracing for impact... that never came.

"Open them!" Jadelyn excitingly stated.

Cracking my eyes open, it was suddenly brighter, but not the blindingly white glare off of snow. It was a warm light.

Welcome to The City in the Shade, Sentarshaden." Jadelyn gave me a winning smile that distracted me from the window for just a moment.

The train turned, curving its approach towards the city, and my breath caught.

A tree larger than any I'd ever seen or even imagined could exist stretched upwards where the mountain would have been.

"That's where it gets its name. Sentarshaden is the elven word for it, but that tree is the root tree of the royal high elf family."

I'd heard about root trees several times in conversations between T and Morgana, but I'd never imagined they would look like this tree. "Are they all that big?"

"Not at all," Scarlett informed me. "That one is utterly massive, and it's why high elves are known for their magic. It helps provide enough power for the illusions over the city, and rumor has it that the tree itself is enchanted out the wazoo."

I noticed little sparks up in the tree's leaves. I stared at them, trying to puzzle through what they were, when I realized that they were some sort of burning magical beasts living in the limbs.

The tree's scale was hard to comprehend. It managed to shade the entire city.

Skyscrapers poked up around the roots. I knew those buildings had to be almost a hundred stories tall, but they looked tiny under the mountain sized tree.

I put down the window a crack, realizing we'd left the snowy tundra. The tree seemed to be giving off a warmth, making it feel like a brisk fall day.

The train wound its way to the city, bringing the city into and out of view as it curved. But I couldn't take my eyes off the city, wanting to see every detail as we got closer.

"It's beautiful, isn't it?" Jadelyn snuggled up close to me. "There's about two million people in the city, all of them paranormal."

"Seems like the Church's inquisition didn't thin out paranormals at all," I commented.

"There have always been a lot of them, and during the wars, a nice hidden sanctuary like this has only blossomed." She watched the city with me.

It was truly awe-inspiring to see the massive tree. If it were known to the world, it would fit right up there with the pyramids of Egypt as one of the world wonders.

And if the tree wasn't impressive enough, the city was massive. I stared at all the buildings, knowing I had little chance of finding Morgana without help, especially if T's daughter was going to be hard to find. I needed to find T's daughter.

I stuck my hand inside the spatial artifact and pulled out a leaflet.

T had given me instructions on how to communicate with his daughter. The flier in my hands was for 'once in a lifetime alchemy lessons', along with tomorrow's date at noon at Gnombold park. There were even a few random splotches in the corner that T had said really meant for them to meet at a bar. But the time would remain the same.

I thought the whole thing felt like overkill, but my goal for the rest of the day was to post these fliers everywhere I could.

T said the train station would work well, and to also put them outside a few coffee shops. But I planned to plaster them everywhere. I wasn't exactly willing to sit around, losing days in finding Morgana.

While the misdirection seemed like a lot, I respected that T wanted to keep his daughter safe. He'd sent her into hiding. T had somehow angered the elves and made them want to find his family's root tree. For whatever reason, they didn't go for him directly, but his daughter was in danger if they found her. Looking at the massive tree, I was starting to understand the resources the high elves might have at their disposal.

"Sentarshaden station," a voice proclaimed over the loudspeaker as the train came to a gliding, smooth stop.

It was far less concerning on the train than watching at the station. I was impressed with how smooth it felt, knowing that we had just gone from eighty to zero in under four seconds.

"Time to face the music." Kelly pulled the blinds up. Behind them, several elves were waiting with cameras. It appeared that the first one had had a big mouth.

Flashes began outside the window as they started taking pictures. There was a small army of paparazzi amid the dazzling flashes that bombarded our train.

Pausing for just a moment, I drew back on my feelings of worry for Jadelyn's safety. But then I got just a bit angry at them for messing up her trip. As the anger rose, I felt an aura ripple out from inside of me.

The cameramen nearly dropped their livelihoods as they ran, making me smile. But the people in the train cars also panicked, pushing and shoving each other as they scrambled to get out of the way.

I turned to Scarlett, the smile leaving my face as I took in her disapproval.

"Maybe don't do that again..." Scarlett watched all the people fleeing. "I understand that you don't like them, but we can deal with them in less disruptive ways."

"Damn. Warn a girl before you do that." Kelly was straightening back up. She slung her bag over her shoulder and led the group out in a much more orderly manner than the rest of the train.

"My bad. What does it feel like?" I asked, curious.

Jadelyn paused, playing with her lips. "Like someone just opened up my head and poured a cup of fear into it. It isn't necessarily about anything, but the mind seems to try and latch onto things. Knowing it's coming from you is the only thing that lets me block it out."

I smiled, glad they trusted me enough to be able to ignore the feeling.

But Scarlett was right. I needed to learn to keep it under control.

"Let's get going." I pushed past Kelly, charging across the platform before tacking fliers on several cork boards we passed.

"This way—we have a ride." Scarlett pushed me in a different direction.

Looking around, I realized the paparazzi was regaining their courage and coming back toward Jadelyn. Although, a few of them had pivoted their attention to interviewing the people on the platform.

I grimaced as I realized the story of my aura would likely be plastered across city news that evening.

We kept moving, breaking through the crowd at the edge of the train station. Two black SUVs were waiting. And there were four burly looking sirens who were not hiding their nature.

"Miss." One of them spotted us and parted the last few travelers to make a path for Jadelyn. "We'll take you to your home."

Then he looked at Scarlett. "Boss. Hope you had a safe trip."

"Thank you." Jadelyn hopped in, followed by the rest of us.

Scarlett paused outside, getting a report from the men before joining us in the car.

"We'll take a long way home, stopping so you can post up your fliers," Scarlett informed me, and I appreciated her all the more. She knew how important it was to me to find Morgana.

The driver and extra guard took the front seats, so the four of us had piled into the back two rows of the SUV.

"So what are the fliers for?" Kelly asked.

"Secret communication with one of Morgana's friends," I answered, realizing she hadn't been part of the conversation with T.

"The blue bitch has friends?" Kelly said, gasping for effect.

"Wait until you see her to tease her; she's not even here to defend herself," I grumped.

Jadelyn gave me a questioning look, and I crossed my arms, turning to look out the window. I felt so close yet so far from finding Morgana and getting some answers.

"Anyway," Scarlett said slowly to break the tension. "Morgana has one childhood friend here in the city that is the most likely person to know where she is."

"Got it. The fliers get us to her, she gets us to Morgana, then we get to see golden boy rail the blue bitch until she begs to come back. Did I get that right?" Kelly said it in such a cheerful tone that it was off-putting, and her wolf ears didn't lie as they sat perky on top of her head.

"Not quite," I said. "She was a mess when she left. I'm worried that she is in more trouble than she knows what to do with."

"So we dig her out," Scarlett said with confidence.

I nodded. Morgana, while not exactly great at showing she cared, had helped and supported me through my transition into the paranormal community. If she needed my help, I'd be there in a heartbeat to return the favor.

"Boss, we have some stopped traffic coming up. There's a celebration today. I swear this street was open on the way over," the driver informed Scarlett, sounding a little like he was beating himself up.

"Celebration?" I asked.

The driver bobbed his head, keeping his eyes on the road. "It's a week-long celebration of the elves' root trees. Which means, around Sentarshaden, it's near constant parades and parties this week. At the end of the week, they give offerings to their tree. Generally some mix of magic and simpler things like fertilizer. Whatever they can do to care for the tree."

I looked up at the massive tree as we passed under one of the roots. Just how much damn fertilizer did a tree like this take?

"So, what's the traffic?" I asked.

The driver peered over his steering wheel. "Looks like it might actually be the Highaen family."

Scarlett let out a small whistle. "Maybe steer clear of the parade. No doubt the whole area is on lockdown."

"Would it be easier to walk through?" Jadelyn asked. "It's just a few miles to my family's house."

Scarlett bit down on her thumbnail in thought. "George, radio Mike. You two are going to split up and go post some fliers for us."

"You sure, boss? That's a packed crowd." The driver looked back at her to confirm.

"Yeah, but it also has Highaen security crawling all over it. Look up there." Scarlett pointed to a rooftop that nearly brushed the massive tree root that came down a few miles from us.

I didn't see it at first, but then a glint caught my eye on top of the ten-story building. There was a sniper posted for security. They weren't messing around.

"They have the entire area on lockdown. We'll be fine."

"Alright, boss. Hop on out." The driver put the car in park and flipped the locks. "Give me those pamphlets."

I handed him a stack, knowing he'd split them up with the other driver.

We piled back out of the car and started moving through the stopped traffic towards what looked like some sort of street fair. Several parade floats could be seen on a parallel street through the buildings.

"Looks like the celebration has just overflowed," Scarlett said as we made our way through the stopped traffic.

Soon the traffic transitioned to foot traffic. People were out in the streets dancing and celebrating in a way I'd never seen before. They didn't give two shits about the traffic they were holding up. Elves everywhere were in full-blown celebration.

"It normally isn't like this," Jadelyn said, staring around. "Normally, it's more like you'd expect of any city."

"The elves love to celebrate their root trees," Kelly said by way of explanation. "I'm sure back home the elves are cloistered away, celebrating their own."

My dragon eyes looked toward where the root closest to us seemed to dig into the ground. It was the focal point of the celebration, and the amount of magic that covered that root was amazing.

I remembered seeing the elven community when we were hunting trolls. Their neighborhood had looked like a magical fortress, and now I was seeing several times that level of protection covering the entire root. I could only imagine what was on the tree itself.

"Might as well let you see the Highaen family for yourself," Scarlett said. "After all, they are the rulers of the city."

"That sounds lovely." Jadelyn pulled my arm between her breasts. "Tyrande is always so nice when she visits."

I looked back but couldn't spot the guards anymore. But Scarlett had given them orders. They'd plaster up the fliers, which meant I did have some time to kill.

Turning back, I gave Scarlett and Jadelyn smiles as I grabbed their arms and pulled them through the crowd. We might as well have a little fun and sightsee while we waited.

CHAPTER 4

As we walked through the streets, the festival area was alive, with gold and green everywhere. I assumed that must be the colors of the high elf family.

"Which way is your home?" I asked Jadelyn.

"Straight through. It's maybe a few streets over, towards the parade." She pointed off into the distance, but her finger meandered around in just the general direction. Jadelyn was doing her best to keep her head down as well.

I heard a scoff and turned to Scarlett, who spoke up.

"The house is four streets over and just over a mile north." Scarlett reached over, grabbing Jade's swirling finger and pointing it more directly.

Jadelyn puffed out her cheeks. "I know where my house is."

"Sure." Scarlett gave her a broad smile that diffused any more arguments.

"Look at that float!" Kelly pointed between the buildings, where a mock version of the tree over the city was rolling past. Two lovely ladies stood at the crown of the tree.

I stared at them, my draconic eyes able to take in details I wouldn't normally be able to see. I might even have better vision than an eagle. Even from several streets away, I could see them clearly. They were both gorgeous elves, wearing the Highaen family colors.

"Can't see them from here." Scarlett shaded her eyes. "But given the float, I'd guess that's the daughter of the Highaen family. I'm not positive about the other."

"Their adoptive daughter," Jadelyn said with surety.

I turned to her, wondering why she knew.

"What? The Highaen family is on the same level as the Scalewrights. I keep up. Tyrande visits anytime I'm in the city," she defended herself.

Kelly perked up. "So they are princesses too? Why adopt?"

Jadelyn looked unamused at the princess title, but she ignored it and shrugged. "Something about her having insane magic potential. I haven't met her personally, though."

They had my beast's attention, though; something about the adoptive daughter bothered it. The beast started to bump against my chest, demanding to get a closer look.

The lump of draconic instincts that I called the beast hadn't led me wrong yet, so I was not about to ignore the warning. "Let's get closer. I'd like to see more."

"She's hot, isn't she?" Kelly frowned. "No chasing after hot elven heiresses. How am I going to compete with that?"

I paused and grabbed Kelly, looking straight into her eyes. I was tired of her constantly being so needy. "Kelly, you are the first female alpha. Act like it."

Sometimes Kelly acted so docile around me, like she was still recognizing me as her alpha, even if I hadn't claimed that right in an official capacity. Or maybe it was a wolf thing that I didn't understand.

She pulled back in shock, swallowing. "Right. You got it."

"Good girl." I ruffled her hair between her ears, and she blushed. But then she straightened herself, taking on an air of strength.

I nodded to her. That was better.

Kelly started moving, letting out a growl.

"Tone it down." Scarlett jabbed her in the side. "Please don't show aggression out here with all the security."

Kelly nodded, relaxing a touch and finding the right balance.

We pushed through the crowd until we could see the parade clearly.

A band of some sort of bird paranormal was singing some springy, dual-tone song. The haunting dual tone wafted through the air, entrancing all that had heard it. What they were doing would have been impossible for humans. I stared, watching as they danced and twirled, completing complex choreography while they sang and flew.

The parade was all a strange blend of familiarity and newness. Much of it was the same as what I'd experienced, but it was all done with some sort of extra twist or flourish.

A massive truck decorated as a pinata came by as two elves threw candy into the air. The candy all caught on the breeze and sprinkled itself out onto the crowd.

It was magical.

We caught up to the Highaen float just as it reached the base of the root. I noticed that mounds of gifts and stacks of bags were already placed around the root, like some sort of dedication.

As they reached the root, the two elves on top of the float bowed in all directions to the crowd, then lifted their hands into the air.

"Damn, they really are hot, like two little flowers," Kelly said from my side.

But I was stuck staring at the adoptive daughter and the magic that was weaving into the air.

Their magic seemed to be tapping into existing enchantments on the root itself. Colors began to swirl in the air, even on the visible spectrum. But I could see more with my dragon eye. I watched as the colors shifted and seemed to seep into the tree.

The tree was actually absorbing all the gifts through whatever spell the two women were completing. The magic began to swirl, and the gifts lifted off into the air, spinning around the tree. They blurred and dissipated as they became one, absorbing into the tree as they swirled.

"I guess that's how you fertilize a massive magical tree," Jadelyn said quietly, watching the display.

While everything else was feeding the tree, the tree seemed to feed back into the two girls, pouring a small amount of mana into them.

It was incredible to watch the symbiotic relationship between the root tree and the elves firsthand. The elves cared for the tree, and it in turn, the tree nourished them with mana. I would almost call the root trees a paranormal creature, given its part in the relationship.

"Are there specific types of trees that are root trees? Or do they have special magic properties?" I asked the girls.

"That's a question for Morgana, but as far as I know, it can be any type of tree." Scarlett pushed us forward, continuing towards Jadelyn's home.

BANG.

An explosion startled the crowd, myself included.

I wrapped my arms around Jadelyn and Scarlett, nearly shifting as the beast rose up to the front of my consciousness. It was ready to help the second it was needed to protect my women.

"Calm down. That was blocks away." Scarlett rolled out of my arms and pointed. She took one look at my face and grabbed it between her hands. "We are fine. Relax. You can't shift here."

Her eyes darted around, taking in the crowd before they returned to me with a plea in them. I took some deep breaths, doing my best to relax as I still scanned for the threat.

The Highaen family was coming out of the woodworks, heading towards the explosion.

I kept working on my breathing. I was having a hard time halting myself from shifting as my muscles began to swell and my clothes bulged with new mass.

The beast rode at the front of my mind and let out a roar of frustration. As it roared, I felt a pulse in my chest, and I looked down, trying to figure out what had just happened.

But the pulse stopped, and everything settled down. I pulled myself back together.

"Did you guys feel that?" I wondered if it was something like the fear aura from before.

"No?" Jadelyn asked, confused.

But another commotion drew my attention before I could ask more questions.

There on the Highaen float, the adoptive daughter of the Highaen family bubbled up. An emerald green sheen covered her as she grew into a large green dragon, whipping her head every which way, like she was searching for something.

Though, the crowd below screamed in a mix of awe and confusion at her appearance.

"Did you do that?" Scarlett asked angrily.

"How am I supposed to know?" Damn beast.

Scarlett grabbed Jadelyn and hurried her out of the agitated crowd. I followed close behind, not wanting to lose sight of either of my mates. That was enough to pull my focus from the beast trying to shift.

I was pretty sure that I was, in fact, responsible for whatever had just happened. It was too coincidental that my beast had pushed himself forward to send out that pulse at the same time that the Highaen girl had shifted.

We hurried down several streets before we broke from the crowd. Scarlett only spared a glance over her shoulder to make sure Kelly and I were following her as she hurried Jadelyn away.

"Scarlett, what's the rush?" I caught up to her.

Kelly was on my heels; her legs had shifted so that she could keep up.

"Kidnapping playbook rule one: cause chaos. Step two: abduct the target. We need to get Jadelyn clear and to her home ASAP."

I shut my mouth. Scarlett was clearly in work mode. Even though I thought the chances of Jadelyn being the target were minimal, she was doing her job. The explosion had triggered a protocol.

Scarlett continued to push Jadelyn forward. Jadelyn seemed to accept her role with a resigned sigh. We both knew there was no arguing with Scarlett when she was like this.

I stayed alert, but the only people who paid us any mind were a few of Highaen's security. After one look at Scar and Jade, they walked on by.

Scarlett beelined for a specific building, and I assumed that must be Jadelyn's house. Sure enough, as we approached, there was a security team in place nodding to Scarlett and Jadelyn.

The home was, of course, beautiful. A rough-cut stone exterior made it feel a little like a castle, but the shape was a modern home. It wasn't an unpopular style from what I'd seen in Sentarshaden so far.

As we stepped inside, we were in a grand entrance, with eighteen-foot ceilings and plenty of space.

"Where do the guards stay?" I asked.

"Attached bunkhouse," Jadelyn said, winding her way into the kitchen, more relaxed now in the safety of her home. "Would you all like anything to drink?"

"Just water," I said, sitting on a bar stool at the island as she went about playing hostess. "So, any idea what the explosion was?"

I spotted a TV and wondered if there were any local stations.

Kelly beat me to it, snatching up the remote and turning it on as her heavy bag thumped on the floor.

"Today's excitement isn't over yet. With the big reveal that the Highaen family's adoptive daughter is a dragon, there are many questions being raised. Where did she come from? Did the family know? How has she hidden it all these years? Back to Tom at the station," the reporter sounded off. Tom seemed to repeat the same exact information. It didn't seem like they knew much else.

Kelly started rapid fire changing channels, but sure enough, every news station was talking about the same thing. The green dragon. Everyone was giving their opinions, which ranged from conservation of the dragon species to manufactured out-rage at the Highaen family hiding one from the public.

One thing was consistent: everyone want-ed to speak to the dragon.

"Is it that big of a deal?" I asked, shocked that the dragon reveal was completely over-shadowing the explosion.

"Huge," Jadelyn said. "When you finally spread those wings of yours and become known, my family is going to have re-porters trying to get hired on as cleaning staff just to try to get a scoop."

"We screen them better than that," Scar-lett grumbled, crossing her arms.

"I said 'trying'." Jadelyn rolled her eyes as she put down glasses of water for each of us.

The TV kept changing channels as Kelly clicked the button. Everyone was in awe of a dragon in the city. There were al-ready conservationists making their posi-tion known on the channels, demanding she be freed or protected by their groups. Others were speculating about the risk of militant groups going after her and how she'll be closeted away.

In general, everyone was shocked that the Highaen family had adopted a dragon, and her past was now the topic of gossip.

Kelly finally turned off the TV. "So, what do we do now?"

"Wait and keep a low profile," Scarlett said. "My guys will finish putting out the fliers.

And then tomorrow we'll go and see T's daughter."

I had a slightly different plan. "I'll see T's daughter alone. It is best if we don't all go to the bar to meet her. Last thing I need is to spook her."

"We'll be fine," Jadelyn tried to argue, but I gave her an unamused look.

"No offense, Jade, but you can't really do subtle. You're too beautiful for it." I turned on a little charm.

She blushed bright red but nodded in agreement.

Kelly snickered into her water. "I'm not sure which of you has the other wrapped around their finger, but you two are cute."

Scarlett sat down next to us, finally seeming to relax out of her guard role. "I think sending Zach in first will work fine. There's not much he can't handle, but be careful. The last thing we need is you shifting here in the city."

Her eyes flicked back to the now dark TV.

We were all thinking the same thing. I'd had a sneak peek at what would happen if my dragon became known to the world, and it would be worse since I was a gold dragon. I would become an instant celebrity, and my life would never be the same once it got out. It wasn't something I wanted.

"Alright, I'll do everything I can to keep myself from shifting." I took another sip of water as a knock sounded at the door.

One of the security guards was talking to someone, and then fast-moving footsteps headed our way.

At the speed of the steps, Scarlett stood up, once again resuming guard mode.

"Miss, Tyrande Highaen is here to see you." The guard looked a little anxious.

"Let her in," Jadelyn said with a kind smile as she stood up straight.

I was expecting her to be more flustered with the high elf family coming to her door, but Jadelyn was perfectly composed. Then again, important guests were something she dealt with on a regular basis.

I wondered just how the Scalewright and Highaen family compared.

"Jadelyn." Tyrande strolled in with her adoptive sister right on her heels.

When I saw the sister, I stuffed the beast down as deep as he would go.

And it was just in time. I could feel him start to rear his head at what I now understood was another dragon. The stupid beast was apparently territorial or horny, and I didn't want to find out which.

"Tyrande, lovely to see you. It's been years. We were just coming to the city for a little honeymoon. I wasn't expecting all the excitement today." Jadelyn smiled, moving over to the cupboard to pull out two more glasses. "Water? Or would you like something stronger after today?"

"Something stronger would be nice. You don't happen to have any tequila and shot glasses, do you?" Tyrande pulled another of the barstools out and sat down, turning to her sister and frowning. "Yev, what's wrong?"

Yev was staring at me like she wanted to pull me apart and put me back together. "There's something about him." Her voice was a little deeper than I had expected from her slight frame.

"Meet my husband." Jadelyn graciously gestured to me. "This is Zach."

"Pleasure." I held out my hand to Yev.

"Yevanandra, but most people just call me Yev. Though maybe that'll change now." She let out a heavy sigh, seeming to release whatever tension was within her. She sat down on the last barstool.

Jadelyn was opening cabinets and checking them for shot glasses. "What brings you two here today? I thought you'd have bigger problems to handle, what with the explosion and all the excitement."

She finally found the shot glasses and put them down on the island. Then she moved to fetch a bottle of tequila.

"I heard from my security detail that you were in the city, and we needed a place to hide out anyway." Tyrande gave Jadelyn a cheeky wink. "Hope you don't mind. You know we'd normally come to welcome you, but I'll admit this time it's also a bit selfish. We could use the breather." Tyrande gave her a shaky smile.

It was clear she was still riled up by the day.

"Not at all. You're welcome anytime either to say 'hi' or hide out from the news," Jadelyn dismissed it easily. She knew what Yev was feeling just about now.

"I thought the parade and ceremony at the root was fascinating," I said, trying to add a positive light to it all.

Jadelyn poured Tyrande a shot and the elven heiress downed it in a single gulp.

"Yeah, it's cool the first time you see it," she said noncommittally.

Yev rolled her eyes, leaning over to explain to me. "Maintaining the tree is something that the family has had to keep up for generations. At some point, they have grown numb to how beautiful it is. But the magic of the act is truly beautiful. I wish more could see it as I do."

I nodded along with Yev, and the beast used that moment to try and rise back to the surface. It was like it wanted to take a bite of Yev. Freezing, I had to wrestle the beast back down.

Jadelyn was thankfully intuitive enough to fill in my pause in the conversation. "So, what plans do you have now that your nature is out in the open?" she asked Yev.

Yev looked at Tyrande in question.

Tyrande waved the concern away, down-ing another shot. "She's an old friend. Whatever you say here will be kept within this group."

I was surprised with how comfortable Tyrande was with Jadelyn. Then again, be-ing a shipping giant might make you fast friends with a city's ruling family, especially since normal human companies probably didn't deliver here.

Yev sighed. "I want to find the other drag-on in the city. The bastard needs to pay for startling me today."

Scarlett and Jadelyn were controlled enough to keep their heads looking at Yev, but I saw the slightest reaction on their faces. I was glad the women had such great poker faces.

Kelly, on the other hand, was not so sub-tle. She gave me an odd side-eyed look, but based on where she was seated, it luckily wasn't obvious to our guests.

Yev continued. "But I expect that, now that word is out, the bronze dragon is going to summon me. And he'll try to marry me off to breed more dragons, like some sort of racehorse." She let out a heavy breath. "I would rather have done all of this on my own timing."

"I always thought dragons were fascinat-ing." Jadelyn leaned forward on her elbow. "But how do you know there's another dragon?"

Yev glared angrily at no one in particular. "He made his presence known. Bitch slapped me with his presence. He's an old and powerful one." She gritted her teeth in anger. "Why the fucker decided to do it when I was in a crowd, I don't know. But I plan to ask when I find him."

"You know it's a he?" Jadelyn continued to ask questions on my behalf.

Yev seemed to be growing so angry that she was having trouble speaking.

Tyrande put a hand on her shoulder to calm her sister and spoke for her. "Apparently, what he did was some sort of attempt to claim her, and it nearly worked."

A new tension began to build in the room, and it was coming from Scarlett and Jadelyn. I did my best to give them subtle looks to say that I didn't mean to do it.

I scolded my beast internally, coaching it that forcing itself on others was not okay. She may be a gorgeous dragon, but it was going to get me in deep shit if it kept just claiming women.

I was glad that Yev was so angry at the hypothetical old, powerful dragon and not looking at the people in the room closer. If she was paying more attention, I was sure she'd spot the mark I had put on Jadelyn's shoulder.

If she looked for it, it would be easy to find. I always noticed it, enjoying my mark on her.

"Enough of that. I'm curious to know more about Jadelyn's husband! I didn't even know you were seeing someone," Tyrande changed the subject and turned to me. "And I can't believe that you managed to keep it from the tabloids."

"Ha. Please tell me that's not where you get your news about me," Jadelyn snorted and poured the two elves another shot.

Tyrande and Yev downed their shots. "No, but they're fun to read when they're not about you. Although, that tool you were engaged to before didn't seem like much. Glad you could get out of that." She smiled before looking me over once more, confusion on her face. "I just can't place you, though. What big family do you belong to?"

"None. I'm actually a lost one." I helped Jadelyn line up the shot glasses.

"A lost one, aye?" Tyrande looked at Jadelyn in surprise. "Your father agreed to it? I don't believe it."

"Zach won my mother over, and she pushed it forward," Jadelyn said with a smile as she ran the bottle over the line of glasses, spilling a fair amount of tequila on the island.

Tyrande bounced in her seat, seeming far more alive after just two shots. "I want to hear the story. It's been forever since we had a chance to catch up, and now you surprise me with a husband."

Jadelyn started from the beginning, telling the story about how her then fiancé, Chad, had gotten territorial and attacked me. Then he'd been leading a plot to harm the packs using dark magic before I was able to stop him and save them.

She painted me in quite the heroic light before she went on to describe my mercenary work with Morgana.

I was surprised to see that Tyrande didn't even bat an eye at the mention of the elven outcast. I'd expected some sort of reaction given the way Morgana described her relationship with the other elves.

Shots continued to go around, and the gathering turned more celebratory. Toasts were made and stories were shared as Jadelyn and Tyrande caught back up.

I did my best to avoid Yev, but things wound down after the second bottle of tequila dried up and Tyrande excused herself, Yev going along with her.

Scarlett waited until they were long gone before turning to me, a little drunken glaze to her as she squinted at me. "Tried to claim that dragon ass, did you? After all that on the plane, you still need more?"

"I swear I'm not going dragon hunting while we are here." Though, the beast butted against my chest, disagreeing with me. The greedy, insatiable dragon instincts of mine wanted more wives. It always wanted more.

"Well, I'm going dragon hunting." Scarlett grabbed my hand and pulled me back to the bedroom.

CHAPTER 5

The next day, I was wide awake early, prying myself out of Jadelyn and Scarlett's limbs. Both of them were hardcore snugglers, so I found myself completely smothered whenever I'd wake up in the morning.

Particularly Scarlett, who wrapped her tails around my chest. They needed to be taken off delicately, though the fluffy limbs often refused to part with my chest.

Slipping out of their embrace, I threw on a pair of pants and padded my way out to the kitchen.

Kelly was already there, making a mess of the kitchen as she hunted through the cabinets. Already, several things had been deposited on the counter in her hunt.

"Anything I can help you with?" I asked.

A very cranky looking Kelly glared at me and spoke one word, "Coffee."

"Use your nose. It can't be that hard, can it?" I teased her.

She squinted at me and pointed to a fancy canister of coffee. "Found the grounds. Need filters. Damn filters," she grumbled as she continued ransacking the cabinets.

I poked at Jadelyn's spiffy coffee machine, opening the compartments up and seeing that there was a wire mesh inside. Taking the grounds, I went ahead and poured them in without a filter, taking a chance that it didn't need it.

"What are you doing?"

"Making coffee," I said. "Unless you don't want any?"

Kelly slammed the cabinet door and growled at me as she got low, like she was going to pounce.

"Kidding. Calm down. Damn, you are testy before your first cup."

Kelly nearly sat down on the floor as she crouched, waiting somewhat patiently. But when the first few drops fell into the pot, she was alert again. That nose of hers lifted up, sniffing the air.

She moved her face within an inch of the pot, breathing in deep breaths through her nose. "I think I love you."

"If that's all it takes, we can take you down to a coffee shop. I'm sure they have one somewhere around here. We can see how many men are willing to buy you a cup so that you have lots of options."

"No," she grumbled but didn't stop hovering over the pot of brewing coffee. "You are the only guy other than my father that's been able to stand up to me. I want you and no one else."

It was a little early, and I wasn't sure if in Kelly's pre-coffee mind that she just realized how that sounded.

After a moment of silence, I spoke, "You know I have a lot going on, Kelly. More things seem to be rearing their head every day."

"Like trying to claim a dragon hussy the second you see her?"

I let out a heavy breath. "Yeah, like my beast trying to claim a woman just because she's a dragon."

"Your 'beast' isn't really anything other than your instincts. You still did it."

I didn't argue with her. It had always felt like another, more separate part of me. But I had to admit, the more I embraced it, the less it felt separate and the more it did feel like some sort of inner instinct.

"Doesn't seem to stop it from doing its own thing."

"Maybe, if you spent more time with the pack, you'd learn a thing or two." She smiled at me. "There's a reason that we let ourselves shift and go for a run in times of stress, or at least once a month. You can't keep that part of you bottled up."

"Yeah, let me just go for a run in the street here and shift. I'm sure that won't cause any problems." My voice was dripping with sarcasm.

It earned me no points with Kelly as the non-caffeinated grouch turned to me, unamused. "Work with me. Find a chance and take it out for a spin. Maybe the beast will settle down."

She started bouncing on her feet as she watched the coffee trickle into the pot.

"Fine." I held my hands up in surrender, noticing the coffee pot might have enough for a cup.

Sure enough, Kelly was already moving, pouring herself out a mug while some dribbled on the hot plate. But she somehow had the pot back in place in record time. Paranormal reflexes were good for something.

"Ah," Kelly let out the most contented sigh I'd ever heard as she curled herself around her warm mug of coffee, inhaling the steam in between big gulps. She was off in her own little world for the moment as she powered on for the day.

I let the coffee maker run its course before pouring my own cup.

As soon as I was done, Kelly was grabbing her second and looking far more alive.

"So, serious question: how awesome is it having a dragon libido? I mean, the way you make those two squeal. I have to imagine it's pretty awesome. And I've imagined quite a bit." She sipped her coffee, not making eye contact with me, but a smirk spread on her face.

I nearly spit out my fresh cup of coffee. But she was trying to get me riled up, and I was not going to take the bait.

"Yeah, it's pretty awesome. No complaints here, or out of them."

She laughed and bumped my hip, giving me a suggestive wink. "I'd imagine. Based on their moans, they're quite happy. But if you ever need more to be satiated, you know where to find me."

I wasn't dense. I knew she was straight up propositioning me, but I just didn't want to go there with her. Morgana was my focus, and I wasn't about to get distracted.

"I do, Kelly." Looking down at her hopeful eyes, I felt bad for wanting to slow things down between us.

She saw the look on my face and looked defeated. "Look, I'm really trying here. This is new for me. I haven't wanted somebody the way I want you before. To make things worse, I'm somehow supposed to be a god-damn alpha, but I'm here pining after you."

"I know." Giving her a side hug, I put my mug down and refilled it with one hand. "But things are already complicated with Morgana. And it has my head all messed up. I need to sort that out before I'm going to be ready to even think about anything or anybody else."

I waited, anticipating she wouldn't take that well, but it was the truth.

She sipped her coffee in silence, staring off into the distance, but she didn't pull away from me.

Jadelyn's home was terribly silent as the coffee machine made small little drips.

I waited, the moment stretching out before she finally spoke. "Okay. I can wait a while longer."

She eyed the coffee machine, which was slowing down in its production of coffee. She moved over, starting to refill it.

"And I came for more than just to hang out with you, so don't be so cocky." She sent a big smile my way. "I figured that if anywhere would have information on my pack's fertility issues, it would be here. I have appointments setup with the three fertility clinics in the city."

I kicked myself, feeling a little silly for thinking she'd just come because of me.

"Great, if you need any help with that, let me know." I knew it was partly my fault for changing up pack dynamics by making a female the alpha.

"Well…" Kelly trailed off. "It would be nice to not go to a fertility clinic by myself."

I paused, realizing what she was asking. "Sure. I'm happy to be supportive."

Jadelyn came out into the kitchen in her messy nightgown. "What are you two talking about?"

"Zach was just agreeing to go to the fertility clinic with me." Kelly smiled and raised her mug of coffee in a toast.

Jadelyn blinked several times, seeming to wake up. "That's nice." She finally settled on a non-answer. "I think I'm going to make breakfast. Want anything?"

"Bacon?" Kelly was looking over her shoulder into the fridge.

"Just make enough eggs for three people for me, and sprinkle some meat in there if you have it," I responded.

Jadelyn nodded, still looking a little sleepy as she started pulling ingredients out of the fridge and laying them on the counter to make a nice breakfast.

"So, do I need to know anything about your fertility, Zach?" she asked but still looked half asleep.

I facepalmed, but at least it let me clear the air.

***

"You sure you want to go in alone?" Scarlett asked for the dozenth time as we pulled up outside Grendal's Grog. It was the bar I was supposed to meet T's daughter at, in a rather neutral neighborhood that was just on the up-and-coming edge of what seemed to be a younger area of the city.

At least that's what all the young mothers pushing strollers on the sidewalk told me. It seemed harmless.

It wasn't fancy, but it looked well kept. Even at half an hour before noon, the place was filling up. I still had half an hour before I expected T's daughter, but I was already anxiously trying to spot her.

"I'll go alone. Hopefully, she saw the fliers. I'll sit at the bar and wait. With all four of us, she may not approach." I let my eyes roam up and down the street, looking for something out of place that would tell me why she had picked this bar.

Jadelyn gave me a pleading look. But it wasn't going to work. I would not let my mate anywhere near danger.

"If anything goes wrong, I have an open line with Scar. You can all run in to save me."

Scarlett had given me one of her men's earpieces, but I'd put it in my jacket pocket where it would be a little less inconspicuous.

"Damn right. We'll be in there, guns blazing, if something happens. Do. Not. Shift," she reminded me firmly. But her tails were beating against my chest as they happily absorbed the mana I was putting off.

I nodded, ready to go. I hopped out of the car.

It was an odd feeling to be having a secret meet up. Kind of like a blind date, only I was more anxious than I would have been on a blind date, especially not knowing what I was about to face here.

But I didn't have many options. I'd sit and wait and hope she found me.

"Just you?" the rabbit-eared hostess asked, her eyes roving me hungrily as I entered.

"Yeah, can I get a seat at the bar?"

"Sure thing. Seat yourself." She looked over her shoulder to double-check that there were seats.

"Thanks." I gave her a nod and slipped past, feeling her eyes move to my backside.

I was still getting used to the increased appreciation from women as my body had become more built from my transformation.

Sliding onto a barstool, the bartender took note of me but waited to finish with her current customer.

I took the chance to look around and take in the room. There was no glaring neon sign, nor a spooky, dark corner that said, 'secret meetings here.'

Darn, I'd just have to wing it.

"What can I get you, sunshine?" The forest elf had a sort of whimsical air around her as she worked. The wreath of flowers in her hair and the loose dress screamed flower child.

I wondered if elves liked the seventies? That time period seemed very elven.

"Just water to start. I'm waiting for someone," I replied.

"Can do." She pulled out a beverage dispenser and pushed the button for water, talking while it filled. "Got a name? Maybe I could help point out the regulars."

I shook my head. "Blind date. Don't even know what she looks like."

"If she's ugly, just give me the sign and I'll break it up to tell you there's a call in the back for you." She giggled and plopped the water down in front of me.

"Much appreciated."

Her light attitude was infectious, and I was already feeling more relaxed.

The door chimed, and I turned, maybe a little too quickly. There was a broad-shouldered paranormal that had almost a cloak of slimy tentacles coming off their shoulders.

"Tell me that's not her." The bartender was still giggling to herself.

"That's a he, isn't it?" I sincerely hoped it was.

"Nope. That's a girl, but I'm pretty sure not yours. They aren't known for being very friendly."

I turned back to my water, using it as a distraction from searching for T's daughter. The bartender floated off and circled the bar, attending to each customer in turn.

Keeping myself to my human range of vision, I didn't notice anybody sitting alone. But I was early. I told myself just to relax, taking some deeper breaths. She'd show up if I just stuck to the plan.

But I couldn't help myself from instantly turning the second anybody came through that door.

Patron after patron entered, but none that fit. T's daughter would be elven and... I wasn't sure, but I felt like I'd know a crazy alchemist's daughter when I saw it.

Soon my water was empty, and the bartender was refilling it again. "She isn't showing?"

"I don't know," I replied honestly, starting to think she must not have seen the flier. She was in hiding, after all. It would make sense if she wasn't out and about all the time.

"Here, this is on the house." She poured me a beer. "It's a crowd favorite."

I took a sip. It was a nice, heavy stout. It went down cold, but still warmed me up. "Thanks. I'll hang out a little bit longer. Just in case."

This stout had quite the kick to it.

Another door chime and I turned. It was finally a lone woman, but she wasn't an elf. She quickly made eye contact with another group, and they both shouted at each other as she joined a table.

Apparently, she wasn't alone.

The beer went quickly as I waited, and the bartender focused back on me.

"So, who was the unlucky lady who missed out on you?"

"Friend's daughter. It honestly isn't as much a date as a meetup," I said, my tongue feeling a little looser from the beer, and the bartender seemed friendly enough.

She nodded along with me. "Still, you have to know something about her."

"Just that she's an elf and probably a little scary if she's anything like her father." I kept to vague truths, deciding there was no harm in it.

Keeping busy, she rinsed and started cleaning glasses. "Why would you want to meet up with a girl whose father scares you?"

"I want to meet her because she can help me find another lady friend."

The bartender's eyebrows bounced at that. "Greedy, huh?" She laughed and poured me another beer. "Careful with this. The dwarven stuff is pretty potent; take this one a little slower."

I felt clear in the head, and my draconic nature should have handled the beer well. But I did have to admit that I was feeling oddly comfortable with the bartender. She'd probably perfected that charm over the years talking to strangers.

Taking another sip, I let my beast rise up a little and tried to see if it was detecting anything. But it just wanted to go find Yev and go take a certain kind of bite out of her.

I rolled my eyes at it, shoving it back down. But I paused my drinking.

The bartender noticed and gave me a questioning look. "Don't like it?"

"Feeling it." I waved off her concern.

She nodded, putting down her towel and walking over, leaning forward in front of me as her eyes became very serious. "Who gave you the way to meet up with me?"

Shock rippled through me as I realized that she was, in fact, T's daughter. But the bigger shock was when I instantly replied.

"T did. I needed to find Morgana after she ran off." I slapped a hand over my mouth. I had not planned on saying that; there definitely was something in my drink.

"Do you mean me or her any harm? Does anyone else know you are here?"

"No, I mean neither of you harm. Yes, my mates know I'm here." I cursed, glaring at the drink. "What did you do to me?"

She glared at me. "What are you?"

I clamped down my jaw, pulled my beast up as far as I could risk it to stave off whatever she had given me.

For once, the beast came to my aid, and rather than talk, I growled as my hand crackled on the edge of a shift and the wooden bar top splintered. I grabbed her by the collar and pulled her close.

I used no words, just my growl, to communicate that we were done talking.

She fidgeted with a vial in her hand before putting it back in her dress. "Let me go. I'll take you to Morgy, but your friends stay behind."

It would seem that I had passed the test.

I couldn't help it. I snorted at her nickname for Morgana. "Morgy. Oh, I'm going to use that one."

"Come on." She pushed off the bar, and I noticed the room was a little quiet as people watched us carefully.

T's daughter waved to the crowd, and that seemed to mollify them. They went back to their conversations, content that there wasn't an issue with their bartender.

"T could have told me what you did. Would have made this easier," I grumbled. "Got a name?"

She shrugged. "Since you call my dad T, call me H. But he didn't know about my job. All the meets are one time uses. I change up how I operate in them all the time."

"Oh, got it. But is the bar okay? You kinda just walked out on the job," I asked as I followed her back through the kitchen.

"I don't actually work here," she said flippantly as her hips swayed in front of me as she went out the back and through a few alleys before she came back out in a normal-looking street. Then she opened the first in a set of row homes.

The house was normal, plain. It was just the place no one would expect two very wanted people to be living.

My blood pressure spiked as I heard her say, "Morgy, you have a friend." H called it out into the house as we stepped in, hanging a set of keys on a hook by the door.

"I don't have friends. Who have you dragged back—" Morgana came around the corner, her normal outfit missing, but I would know her anywhere.

Standing in front of me was a beautiful drow nun. The baggy frock she was wearing couldn't hide her sinuous curves.

"Fuck." Her red eyes went wide as I barreled down the hall at her.

Lifting her up, I smashed her into the wall.

H was screaming something at me, but my focus was on Morgana, who was curling in on herself in pain.

"Come on, I've hit you a lot harder than that when we spar. Don't think you can pull one over on me by faking it." I clenched harder on her clothes and pushed her up the wall.

Her frock snagged on the wall, tearing across her chest, revealing her bra and bandages that were falling off nasty red blisters all over her skin.

"You said you meant her no harm!" H was there, about to use whatever was in that little glass bottle against me.

I glanced at H before focusing back on Morgana. "What the fuck happened to you?"

"Now I have to patch her back up. Put her down now," H yelled at me again.

I wanted answers, but Morgana was clearly in actual pain. Loosening my grip, I carefully set Morgana back on the ground.

Quick as a whip, she tried to catch me with a right hook, but it was laughably weak for Morgana. I grew even more concerned as I easily blocked it, stepping back as H pushed her way between us.

"Probably best to listen to her. Never know what is in any of the vials around here. Could melt your face off, could cure cancer. Never know with her." Morgana clutched at the exposed skin where the bandages were loose.

H rolled her eyes. "Hold still."

She pulled the bandages tight and made Morgana wince. But a small smile still sat on Morgana's face.

"I assume you're not going to go away no matter what I do?" she asked me.

I simply growled in response, and she nodded her head, wincing a bit.

"Okay. Where do you want me to start?" Morgana lay there while H worked on her bandages.

"From the beginning. I need to know everything if I'm going to get my partner back," I growled, pulling a chair over and sitting down to watch her.

"Fair enough." Morgana pushed her head back into the wall, letting out a puff of air as she started into her story.

CHAPTER 6

Morgana pulled back her frock so that H could work at the wound better. "It started back in the seventeenth century, when my clan and others, including her, were pushed out of the alps."

She frowned as H cleaned the wound. "Elven magic and our longevity are tied to our root trees, so when we were pushed out, we all moved or hid our trees. The only reason I was spared from battle and wasn't slaughtered like the rest of my tribe was because I was moving our root tree. An army of templars augmented with cherubs decimated my tribe."

I held up a hand for her to pause. "Cherubs? Like cupid?"

"No." H frowned, staring at me for a moment before looking up at Morgana. "Is he stupid?"

"He's a lost one," Morgana explained, laughing lightly. "He was my ward."

H's mouth made a big 'O'. I had a feeling that the pieces of the puzzle were starting to fall into place for her.

She looked back at me, this time looking more patient. "Cherubs are the rank and file from the celestial plane. They are pretty much human but with two little dinky wings on their backs." She flapped her hands for emphasis.

"They are still far stronger than a human and have a tiny bit of celestial magic. Think of them more like the strength of a werewolf." Morgana was less amused. "The Church had a stronghold in Western Europe and pushed east. They tore through Switzerland, pushing everyone east. I fled with my clan's tree. We all did what we had to do..." She looked at H with sympathy.

"What my father did was his own doing, but yes, thanks to him, I survived, and so did many others. Not that they rewarded him for it." H looked like she wanted nothing to do with whatever T had done to anger everybody.

Whatever it was would have to remain a mystery for now as Morgana continued her story.

Morgana focused back on me. "The Church didn't go unopposed. Southeastern Europe was still very wild and had been a hotbed for some of the larger groups of paranormals, mainly werewolves and vampires. Cherubs coming en masse was exactly what they needed to unite all the fractured, warring groups together around a common enemy."

"That's what happened to you?" I asked, knowing she was turned around that time in history.

"Vampires didn't really ask if you wanted to help. They just turned everyone they could find. Their army also benefited. The vampire that turned a person could control them to an extent." Morgana's lips twitched and a ghost of a smile flitted across her face. "The vapid bitch that turned me is no longer alive."

"What happened to your tree?" I asked.

She hung her head slightly, exhaustion showing on her face. "At the time, I hid it in Austria before I ran into the vampires. So I got vamped, thrown in with their rank and file, and told humans were the enemy. Then I was a part of the war itself. Most of it was a big slaughter, focused between Vienna, Budapest, and Zagreb."

"Your tree was behind enemy lines, wasn't it?" I realized that, if that's where the battle was, most of Austria would have been in the hands of the Church.

"Precisely. The war continued on, and my spatial magic came to life. Getting vamped fucks up a lot of things, apparently; people think that's what changed my magic." She winked, and I realized it wasn't exactly true. "But with my newfound magic, fueled quite literally by the blood of my enemies, I became a larger part of the war. I began taking on missions that brought me deeper and deeper into enemy lines.

"It was brutal; I killed tens of thousands. With how I could move in and out of battle quickly and without notice, I was often given assassinations or gruesome tasks by my sire, like burning down a fort with people trapped inside."

I could see the guilt play out on Morgana's face as she spoke.

"One day, I was technically following orders, but once I'd completed the task, she'd forgotten to order me to return immediately. So I went to check on my root tree." She paused, shaking her head in disbelief. "At the base of the Austrian Alps, the templars had set up a rear operating base where they were running a large project. They were connecting to the celestial plane to bring through cherubs, and they hoped, higher-level celestials."

I checked to see if H was surprised at all, but by the bored look on her face, she must have already heard all of this.

"Your root tree was in the middle of that, wasn't it?" I asked.

"Yep. There it was, soaking in holy water fresh from the celestial plane. And they had no idea. It has a millennia's worth of enchantments on it. But our root trees shape our magic, so mine being part of this project of theirs connecting to the celestial plane had changed my magic."

"So your magic has nothing to do with your change to a vampire?"

Morgana shrugged but then regretted it as she winced, earning an angry look from H, who was rebandaging her.

"I don't actually know," she admitted. "But the spatial magic I have is very certainly an aspect of celestial magic. Not a whole lot is known about the higher angels, since they rarely are able to come to earth. But in my brief stint in the celestial plane, I witnessed them use magic similar to my own."

Leaning back, I let what I knew catch up with what she'd told me so far. Morgana's tree was soaking up holy water and connected to the celestial place, changing her magic and her elven nature. It was almost like she'd become some sort of celestial elf.

But she hid it, pretending it was all because she'd been turned into a vampire. Nobody challenged it because there weren't any other examples.

I realized the story wasn't finished. Knowing Morgana, I knew exactly what was going to come next. I ran my hand over my face. "You stormed into heaven, didn't you?"

She grinned wide enough to show her fangs. "You bet I did. Drank lots and lots of angel blood. It was great while I was up there, snacking on them for days. I was burning through my magic as fast as I could recover, but I was surviving celestial magic that they were throwing at me even though that killed most vampires on contact. I even took out a big player and stopped their operation. All in all, it was pretty successful."

I knew there was going to be a 'but' to this story.

Sure enough, she continued. "The trouble started when I escaped back to earth. I'd been poisoned by celestial magic. And that became a problem when I didn't have the constant infusion of angel blood." She pointed at the blisters that H was wrapping. "Best thing I could do was hold back my magic and..." Morgana paused, biting her lip and debating if she should tell me the next bit.

"Whatever it is, it isn't going to change my mind about you," I pushed her.

Morgana hung her head slightly. "Cherubs aren't that uncommon now. I hunt them, and H here helps me make champagne from their blood. The low-grade angel blood helps keep this at bay."

But as I stared at the blisters covering her body, it was clear something was wrong.

"Are you out?" I stood, ready to go find some cherubs, but H motioned for me to sit back down, giggling.

"We have barrels of the stuff," H stated. "But it isn't helping."

Morgana sighed. "I think I pushed myself too far with Nat'alet."

"Okay, so that's not working. What's plan B?" I was here to help her however I could. She'd helped me when I had needed it, and I cared for her. My feelings for her had only grown in the several days apart.

And while I still wanted to wring her neck for running out on me, I needed her to be healthy first. Soon I'd wrestle her to the ground and pin her into a bed.

"Before you so rudely tore my robes, I was planning to see if I couldn't get to my root tree. It's the right time of year to give to it and have it give back to me. The ceremony can have great healing properties."

H nodded. "Tredelas has been known to heal the blind, restore limbs, and even correct brain damage."

I patted my knees as I stood up again. "Then what are we waiting for? Jade, Scar, and Kelly are here with me. We'll wrangle something up and get you to your tree."

"It's in the middle of a templar headquarters," Morgana reminded me.

"We'll get you to the middle of the damn Church itself if we have to," I growled back.

She pointed to herself. "I'm not exactly going to be much help. It's best if I do this one quietly on my own."

I crouched down and put my face right in front of hers. "You'll go nowhere without me. I'm your partner." I glared at her.

But weak as she might be, Morgana wasn't one to cower. She just raised an eyebrow at me, daring me to try to take her down.

H giggled uncontrollably. "I like him. No one else would dare speak to the famed Morgana like that."

"Yeah, he's something special," Morgana said dryly, but there was a twinkle in her eye as she looked at me. "But that doesn't mean you can take on the templars like that. You are already going to have enough trouble."

"Not your call, Morgy."

Her face when I used the nickname was priceless, so I decided to add to it. Leaning down, I kissed her forehead, her face becoming fully stupefied.

"Regardless of if I'm there or not, them coming after you means I'm at war with them. So I might as well back you up," I said.

Morgana's face went through several expressions as she thought through what to do next. I could see her playing out all her options, but she knew how stubborn I could be. And while we hadn't discussed it, she had to know that I cared for her.

"There's confidence and then there's stupidity," H scoffed.

"He's young, but he's tough," Morgana corrected H. "You haven't seen him fight a god. With a few decades of training, he could be a major player in the global game. He's also married into the Scalewrights."

H gave me a new, appraising look. "Doesn't mean he can do much right now."

I stood to give H a taste of what I could do, but Morgana jumped in.

"Fine." She spat it out like it was admitting she'd lost a sparring session. "We need to get transportation, and I run this mission. You do as I say. The templars aren't all like Jared; he's practically just an honorary templar because of his sister."

I raised a brow at that.

"Nephilim." Morgana grimaced. "Another one of the ways that they are trying to bring celestials down to earth."

"Doesn't that mean Jared is—"

"Half-sister," Morgana corrected herself.

"Give me the robe while you go," H said. "I'll fix it up and get the blood out of it."

Morgana kissed H's hand. "Thanks. Don't know what I'd do without you."

"Most likely? Die." H's tone was like a blunt hammer to the face.

"What happened to the cheery barmaid?" I teased her.

H stood, wiping her blood covered hands on her gown and gathered up some of the scattered supplies.

Morgana propped herself up, working herself to a standing position. Then she slipped the gown off right in front of me.

She stood there in just her bra and panties. Normally, I would have been checking her out, but I could only focus on the wounds and bandages scattered across her body. The beast in me desperately wanted to destroy what was hurting her, but it was more complicated than that.

She fished out a pair of leather pants and a dark leather jacket to wear.

"No corset?" I joked.

"Rubs the bandages," she said seriously, pulling her hair back and pushing me out the door.

I pulled the earpiece from my pocket and put it in my ear. "Did you get all of that, Scar? Come pick us up. Apparently, we need a ride to Austria."

Morgana yanked the earpiece out of my ear, placing it in hers. "No, you need to get me to 493 Gaxlix Drive. We'll pick up a car there."

I thought it would be a moment, but apparently, Scarlett had tracked us as we'd moved because her car quickly whipped around the corner.

Her tires screeched to a stop in front of us and the back door popped open with Jadelyn waiting.

"Get in." She seemed excited to be part of the action.

I grabbed Morgana and picked her up, bringing her into the car.

"I'm not made of glass, you know." She crossed her arms, but she also didn't try to escape my arms. We both knew she'd just get injured if she flailed about.

"You ran from me once. Fat chance I'm letting you do that again."

"Blue bitch." Kelly popped over the back of my seat by way of greeting.

"Fur Ball." Morgana glared back. "What are you doing here?"

Kelly stuck her nose up. "Didn't you hear? I beat you to his harem."

"She's just trying to rile you up." Jadelyn played peace maker, putting her arm on Morgana and pushing Kelly back into the back seat. "I'm so sorry to hear what you've been going through. But you should have stayed, not run."

To my surprise, Morgana didn't fight Jadelyn on that, she just stayed quiet, listening. Her lips were pursed, but she was just taking it. I realized she was letting them clear the air.

Scarlett spoke from up front, "Never run from a dragon, Morgana. it only makes things worse."

"Well, if it makes you feel better, I'm not in much shape to run now. And it made a lot more sense for me to try and break into a templar base on my own. It still does, and I stand by that," Morgana argued.

"Dressed as a nun," I supplied for the rest of the group.

Kelly covered her mouth, but it did little to smother the snort.

"Well, we'll just have to figure this one out as a group now. So where are we headed?" Jadelyn asked.

Morgana pointed down the street. "That auto body shop. He's the guy who outfits all of my custom cars."

"Like the van?" I asked, thinking back to the armor-plated minivan that was more akin to a tank. Morgana had once said it was the most expensive car in her garage. It drove like a sports car and had deflected more than its fair share of bullets.

"Yeah, Marco is the best in the business. But he's also flighty, so let me go in alone." Morgana sat up from my arms and opened the door to the SUV.

I hopped out right after her.

She almost argued, but instead just sighed. "Don't get used to getting your way. I may not be able to fight you now, but I will sure as shit remind you who's the better fighter later."

I just smiled and followed her, satisfied that she wasn't leaving my sight.

The sound of drills and clinking of wrenches filled the shop. Half a dozen goblins were moving around, working on three cars up on lifts. But the lifts only needed to be up a few feet.

In general, it seemed like any ordinary car repair shop.

One of the goblins noticed us and went and nudged another that was head-deep under a car.

A green grinning face popped out, covered in grease streaks.

"Morgana!" he shouted with a flare. "My favorite customer, What are you doing in town? Back to your old street racing days? I have a new one in the works. You'll love it."

He was already grabbing a set of keys from the back wall.

"Marco, I'm not here for that."

"Street racing?" I asked, suddenly feeling like her driving was making much more sense.

But the moment I spoke, Marco froze like a deer in headlights and narrowed his eyes as he lowered his shoulders and stepped back.

"Who is this?" He took a few more steps backwards, getting closer to the other goblins.

"My partner," Morgana said, quickly showing her palms in a sign of non-aggression.

The other five goblins had stopped what they were doing, moving alongside him. They congregated like a pack with their hackles up.

"I don't like the looks of him," Marco said, stepping to the side and starting to circle me.

Crossing my arms over my chest, I stared right back. "You have a problem with me being here?"

Morgana snapped her fingers in Marco's face. "Snap out of it. I want a car."

"This is all I've got, and it's pricey." He dangled the keys out for her, still keeping his eyes locked on me.

"Fine." Morgana took the keys, pressing the button. Lights flashed under a blue tarp as the car chirped.

She tore off the tarp, revealing a car that had a custom paint job. Dark black paint bled into a streak of neon green flames by the back of it. It looked like it had come right off the set of a car racing movie. It was even complete with a little back fin and neon undercarriage lights.

"It's got a V14 engine in there—built it myself. Thing only takes ultra-premium gas though. It'll go from zero to sixty in one and a half seconds. I even rigged it with something a little special." Marco gave a little chef's kiss as he walked up and opened the driver's side door.

Talking about the car, he'd come to life and ignored me once again.

"Fully enchanted exterior. Cops won't get a radar on you, and the paint will never chip." He slid his hands along the door-frame, as if he was about to make love to it.

"All leather interior, and this... this is the real prize." He pointed to a clear canister full of blue liquid just under the radio. "Mana charged. It's only got one go though, maybe two if you're careful."

I started to ask what that did, but Morgana put a finger to her lips.

I nodded. Best not to spook him again. He seemed to have forgotten about me in his love for that car.

"I need something with a little more durability to it, Marco," Morgana said, though her eyes lingered on the canister.

"It's all I've got, toots. Business isn't what it used to be. I don't sit on a half dozen ready cars anymore." Marco shrugged casually, but he was still a salesman. "It'll block small arms fire with that enchantment to prevent paint chipping."

I had to wonder if Scarlett had something better. She had more mainstream equipment, and probably more legal enchantments, but they might still do better than the racing car.

I looked around. Something about Marco's shop made me feel like it wasn't all entirely legal.

"Fine. Bill me." Morgana snatched the keys from him and slid into the car.

I had to run around to the side as the engine revved. I did not trust her not to drive off and leave me in the dust.

The second my door was closed, she gunned it. The wheels spun out as she turned ninety degrees, barely clearing the shop door.

Marco was grinning ear to ear as she tore out of his shop, as if it was exactly what the car was meant for.

"Where to?" Morgana asked.

"Jadelyn's place. We can get some gear there." I knew Morgana would want to go in armed to the teeth.

"Good. Give me directions." She punched the gas, and the car lurched forward.

I looked back, seeing Scar's SUV sliding into place behind us. I was glad she'd know where we were going, because Morgana was hard to keep up with. Eventually, they fell behind, and we beat them to Jadelyn's place.

While we drove, I inspected the little canister. It seemed to have a little line that ran up to a big red button behind the turn signal.

"Don't touch that. Not in the city, or even outside of it. Why the hell Marco would put that in this car, I'll never know." Morgana stopped the car just shy of Jadelyn's place.

I noticed the guards were more alert than before, not quite sure what to do with us. I waved out the side with a smile, hoping they remembered me.

The first frowned, but the second nudged him and whispered something. They both relaxed and opened the gate to Jadelyn's mansion, the big SUV pulling up behind us as the gates fully opened.

CHAPTER 7

"What do you mean you don't have a grenade launcher? That's basic equipment. I thought you were professionals." Morgana stared at the table, which now had an assortment of handguns and a few semi-automatic rifles.

"We operate a guard service, not a fucking military armory." Scarlett was getting angry at Morgana's assessment of her weapons. These girls and their guns.

Morgana grudgingly decided on the two largest rifles and a few loaded magazines. "This will just have to do. I can't believe we are going after fucking templars with these pea shooters."

Scarlett cocked her hips and crossed her arms.

Best we got out of here. I knew that look.

I picked up a single handgun and checked it over before sliding it and a spare magazine into my pants.

"You had a nun outfit. I assume that wasn't for theatrics?" I asked. It was time we started talking about a plan rather than just vague ideas of sneaking to her tree. "You also need offerings for your tree."

"Have those." She patted her chest. "I've kept a close eye on the place for a very long time. Right now, it fronts itself as a charity drive organization. There are a few ways we could get inside. It could be as court ordered community service, a customer, or a volunteer."

"Okay, but how do we get past the fact that you're blue?" I poked one of her pointy ears sticking out of her silver hair.

She slapped my hand away. "I do occasionally have to go out during the day."

Pulling a pendant out of her bra, she clasped it around her neck. As she did it, her skin tone changed down to a pale but human color, her eyes turned dark chocolate brown, and her hair was a dry blonde.

"See?" Her ears still poked out of her hair, but she could cover those with the nun outfit or any winter hat. "It's a wonderful enchantment. Only has a tiny pulse of magic every minute or so to keep it up. It's very hard to detect, even if you are looking for it. Although, I lose a bit of my extra flare."

I stared at her, still caught off guard by the sudden change of her appearance. Scarlett had to nudge me back to attention.

I quickly jumped back into the conversation. "Okay, so we volunteer there. I'm going to guess a tree soaking in celestial holy water isn't exactly out in the open?"

Pale Morgana grinning back at me was a little disconcerting. "Yep, so we sneak around. Or, we use our plan B." She patted the bag of guns. Morgana took off the pendant, returning to her normal blue self while in Sentarshaden.

I looked back at the rest of my crew. "All of us?"

Jadelyn wasn't really a fighter, and she was famous enough that she could get recognized.

"No, we'll have to sit back and let you go undercover," Scarlett said grumpily. "Jadelyn can't go in there, and I have to stay with her."

"I'm sure you'll be able to find something to do in Sentarshaden," I said, rolling my eyes.

Jadelyn looked a little hurt as she crossed her arms, and I realized that it was in fact our honeymoon. I had been so caught up with Morgana, I'd missed giving her the attention she may need as a new bride.

I tried to backtrack. "Either way, once this is done, I expect to see the city with you and really celebrate with all of you." Grabbing Jadelyn's hand, I ran my rough thumb over the back of her hand.

"Don't worry." She smiled. "We can always go on another trip later. I just want you back safe."

Morgana slung the bag onto her back. It clattered as its lethal cargo flopped around. She nearly toppled over as the weight settled on her shoulder.

"Fuck." I jumped forward, grabbing her and the bag before she hit the floor. "Let me carry things, and I'm driving."

She frowned but let me take the bag. The other girls watched as I half carried her out of Jadelyn's home.

We'd make this a short trip. We'd get in, get Morgana to do her tree magic, and hopefully get out with a much healthier Morgana.

And once we were back, we could explore Sentarshaden like actual tourists.

Morgana managed to throw herself into the car while I threw the bag of guns in the back. I moved quickly, sliding into the driver's seat before she could get impatient. I resisted the temptation to push the big red button. Even though it was almost mocking me to press it.

Morgana situated herself into the seat next to me, and we rolled out of Jadelyn's place.

I had to be careful as I drove. The slightest tap on the gas really kicked the car into gear. I found I couldn't even apply steady pressure in the city traffic.

"So, how do we get out of the city to Austria?" I realized that we'd gotten to the city via the train.

"We'll still train out. I'll just zap the car into a spatial pocket when we take the train."

"That'll tax you, and you are barely holding it together," I realized.

Morgana was unamused. "Some things need to be done."

We pulled up to the train station, and true to her word, she managed to stash it away in a spatial pocket. But doing so had her falling over, and I had to pick Morgana up, carrying her onto the train.

She was like a helpless blue kitten in my arms.

"Don't look at me like that." Morgana was unamused by my sympathy.

"Then don't let yourself get this bad again. I care for you Morgana," I pressed.

"I know." She refused to meet my gaze. The hardened fighter of paranormal legend was blushing. "I care for you, too."

***

We drove along the highway through the Alps, having already crossed into Austria.

Morgana was resting in the passenger seat, having been worn out from storing and removing the car with her spatial magic. She'd been asleep for most of the ride with how much it had taken out of her.

I wish there had been more time to talk on the way, but she wasn't well. That would have to wait until she was better. She was looking pale in a way that made my heart ache for her. I needed to help her recover if it was the last thing I did.

The car did not blend in as we raced across Switzerland, taking the most terrifying road I had ever driven on.

But the conditions weren't making it any better. I was combating winter weather and a mountainous road filled with switchbacks, all while driving a car that had no business on anything other than freshly cleaned asphalt.

I breathed a sigh of relief when we made it, barely, to the small town of Galtz just as the Alps settled down to slow rolling hills.

"Let's hide the car. It doesn't exactly sell our new cover," I said, driving through the town. I looked around, realizing there wasn't going to be a great place to hide it. It wasn't as if Galtz had a parking garage we could stuff it in.

"There. That barn looks abandoned." Morgana pointed to the side where a lone barn sat unattended next to a dilapidated farmhouse.

Cringing, I drove the car through snow. I swore it was about to get stuck every few feet.

We managed to make it halfway to the barn before its wheels spun out.

"Get out and keep watch; tell me if you see anyone." I pulled the keys and hopped out of the car, leaving it in neutral. Looking both ways and trusting my dragon instincts, I was fairly certain nobody was watching.

Grabbing the bumper, I let my body fill with draconic strength as I lifted the car's front and hauled it the rest of the way to the barn. There was a chain lock on it, but that did little to stop me as I snapped it with a quick jerk.

Inside the barn, there was some equipment sitting idle for the winter, but plenty of space for me to drag the car inside.

Once the car was in place, I opened the trunk, grabbing out our two big hiking backpacks. We could have used the spatial artifact, but for our cover, it would be odd if we didn't have luggage.

"Coast is still clear; this is a sleepy little town." Morgana waited outside as I closed the barn doors. I used the same chain to relock it, bending the broken ends together until they'd hold.

"That's fine. That makes it a perfect place for a backpacking couple." I bumped her hip. "Put on your backpack."

The packs had miscellaneous items, but mine was largely loaded up with guns, and Morgana's stuffed with blown up plastic bags. Morgana didn't travel with less than a small army's arsenal, and she couldn't carry much right now.

I looked over as she put on the backpack, once again finding myself doing a double take. She was already ready, wearing her pendant to look human and decked out in winter gear, a fluffy hat hiding her ears.

We'd changed our cover to a couple back-packing through Europe so that I had a clearer role to play. Her being a nun didn't leave me with many options. We'd tell the charity that we were willing to work for food as we passed through.

Heading out on foot, we continued into town with nothing but two bulky backpacks on our back.

The town was filled with tiny one-story homes nestled up close together for warmth. But there was also a massive build-ing that stood out with a sign that read 'Angelic Service'. And beyond it were more buildings that together had more space than the rest of town.

It was a small campus. I wondered why nobody questioned that it was an odd place to put such an extensive business.

I got a few odd looks as we walked through town, but no one seemed overly concerned to see two backpackers walking into town.

When we got to the Angelic Service store-front, I pulled open the door and rubbed my hands together as we walked in.

"Hello, we were wondering if you needed two helpful hands?" I caught the first person who gave off a supervisor vibe.

"No, we are fully staffed," Greg, at least according to his nametag, said before looking up and seeing the two of us. "Oh, visitors."

Rubbing his chin, he glanced back and forth in the store. "You know, we might be able to put you two to work hauling boxes in from the delivery truck. I normally unload them, but they are heavy." His English was rough, but understandable.

"That would be great; we're happy to work for food," I offered.

"I figured you might," he said. "The truck will be here in about ten minutes. We just need to unload it along the back of the building."

"We shouldn't bring it in?"

"Nope, they aren't for us. They'll go back to the campus; those guys will bring out trucks and grab it. The security back there is insane. They won't let the delivery trucks back there, so we unload here." He went back to work, seeming to not think the extreme security was anything of concern.

But it had probably been that way for so long that nobody questioned it anymore.

I jerked my head, and Morgana followed me out back, where we dropped our oversized backpacks.

"So, are we going to unload these boxes?" Morgana asked, wrinkling her nose at the idea.

I kept my head up to make sure no one else was out here listening to us. I scanned around. There was a fence topped with angled barbed wire nearby, separating us from the rest of campus. I could probably jump it if needed.

"Now it is the time to make the plan. What do you think of their security?" I shifted my eyes to look for enchantments. Thankfully, there was only magic that I could sense on some of the personnel and deeper in the campus.

"The tree is in there." She pointed towards the campus. "But the security here on the perimeter is false."

"What do you mean?" I looked at the fence and the security post, trying to decipher what she was saying.

She nudged me and pointed, making touristy gestures at the whole complex.

I caught what she wanted me to see. Past the basic security, there were so many cameras that every angle must have been covered twice.

People walking the campus seemed like they were going about their day, but paying closer attention, it was the same dozen or so people. They were constantly flitting between buildings, and I started noticing bulges under their shirts where they had concealed weapons.

I sighed. I should have known they'd try to keep things somewhat undercover and less noticeable.

Morgana gave me another nudge, and I followed where she wanted me to look after giving it a moment. Up in several of the buildings that looked like old office buildings, there were men stationed behind tinted glass. I didn't want to know what kind of firepower they held.

"Shit," I spat. "This place is a fortress."

The squeal of a big rig's brakes pulled my attention away from the compound. A semi came rolling up to the store.

"That must be our job." Morgana watched as it passed us and came to a stop, blocking our view of the compound beyond.

"Let me handle the heavy stuff." I stepped away from the wall and waved at the driver, who hopped out.

"I got forty-eight pallet crates." He looked around for something. "Usually there's more of you."

Shrugging, I played it off. "Guess just the two of us today."

"A few of these are heavy as shit, but you should be able to manage the others. Let me get the ramp down." He fiddled with a metal ramp that folded out the back. Then he threw the truck door open.

Square wooden crates about three feet wide were stacked up in the back, with big inflatable cushions keeping them in place.

Clambering up the ramp, I grabbed the first one. It wasn't too heavy, and whatever was inside rode very well as I picked it up. It must have been well packed.

"Strong," the driver whistled. "Lady, help me with some of these so I can get on my way."

It wasn't too hard moving the crates out and stacking them up until we got to the back. The last four crates felt like they were full of lead.

As discreetly as I could, I drew on my draconic strength to help. I tried to look strained as I dragged them out, huffing and puffing for effect.

"Alright, if you'd sign here." The driver pulled out a sheet.

I hesitated, not wanting to sign anything, but Morgana saved me. "The boss inside will sign."

"Suit yourselves." He went into the Angelic Service store.

"These are weapons," Morgana said as soon as he was out of earshot. "The heavy ones are ammo. Crack that one; I want to see what's in it. But don't break it. We can hammer it back down."

I got my fingers in the lip and strained, pulling the nail out of the crate and lifting the corner enough for Morgana to peek in.

She let out a soft whistle. "Hammer it back down."

Using my fist, I smashed the lid back on. "What are we dealing with?"

"RPGs in that one." Morgana eyed the stack of crates and bit her lip. No doubt it was a tempting load to steal. "Looks like these are shipped quietly through some independent trucking service. Surprised they don't have more rigor around this."

"Maybe that just keeps it quieter?" I suggested, also finding it odd. But delivering weapons through a charity drive wasn't a bad cover.

They were moving the weapons right under everyone's noses. Either they kept it all casual to keep the secret or they'd grown too confident.

"Either way, this place seems more actively militant than I expected. The last time I was here, it was always more of a research and development arm." Morgana nipped at her lip and showed off her fangs unintentionally.

"Keep your mouth closed." I tapped my own canines.

She paused before realizing what I was saying and covering them again. "Idle habits," she replied, lost in thought. "We'll have to see if there's some way to sneak in."

I looked down at the heavy crates that she assumed were ammo. I tilted my head, looking between them and our bodies. They were just big enough it might work.

"This is going to sound stupid, but how about we hide ourselves in the crates? The truck is blocking the view. Do you have enough left to use your spatial magic to get rid of the contents?"

Her eyes darted back and forth until she cursed, nodding. "These two. Crack the lids. And put a few boxes on top of mine once I'm in." She flicked her finger, and our backpacks disappeared. Morgana visibly sagged at the effort and had to hold on to a crate while I went to work.

I ripped open the two crates she'd pointed to, and she vanished their contents before she sagged and grabbed the edge of a crate to steady herself.

I was worried about her, but we didn't have time to stall. She'd done her part, and now I could help. I deposited her in the straw-lined crate and knocked the wooden lid back closed.

Stacking two boxes on top of her, I readied myself to get in the other.

I jumped inside, but figured out the gap in my plan the second I was settled. I didn't have a great way to get the lid closed again. Partially shifting my hand, I worked my claws into the wooden lid, trying to pull it down as tightly as I could. It wasn't perfect, but it would have to do.

"Alright, thanks for the helpers." The truck driver's voice was muffled through the box.

The truck's diesel engine rumbled and the air brakes puffed as he continued on his way.

"Huh, where'd they go?" The supervisor's voice wandered around the boxes. "Must have been too much for them. Didn't even try to get their food before they bailed."

He sounded tired. Clearly, we weren't the first workers to leave partway through.

I sat there in silence, realizing the part of my plan I hadn't thought about. Waiting. I was going to have to sit here without anything to do. I was tense. It felt like at any second someone was going to pop the lid on my crate, or I'd hear Morgana cry out as she was discovered.

My beast was riding just under the surface of my skin, ready to shift and tear the templars apart. Waiting was eating at me, my anxiety building.

So, when another rumbling engine pulled up, I was almost relieved.

Several thuds announced what sounded like a number of men jumping out of the back of a jeep.

"Check the manifest," someone barked.

Near my crate, I could just make out the rustling of paper. "Two, four, six, eight... All here, boss."

"Grab them. The armory will inventory when we get them there," the first voice said.

Grunts started near me as the men started moving the boxes. I suddenly realized that I was far lighter than a crate of ammunition should be.

As quickly as I could, I added more mass to my body. But I only had so far I could expand within the box.

Thinking quickly, I took out the spatial artifact and started pulling out water bottles I had packed in the event of an emergency. Morgana would have to figure out her own solution.

This was definitely not the emergency I had been thinking of when I had packed them, but it might just work. They were the densest items I could think of that I had in bulk.

Hopefully, it would be enough to fool these men because I was out of time.

"Alright, this one'll be heavy," a voice came right beside me.

I froze, trying to keep my weight as still as a crate full of ammunition.

"On three, two, one. Lift."

Two voices grunted, and I felt myself lift up as I was finally dumped onto the bed of some truck.

I was braced, ready to act if we were discovered, but everything stayed quiet. Morgana must have figured something out.

"Three more and we're heading back. Make sure to tie them down," the boss reminded his men.

I nodded, glad I wouldn't be spilling onto the road after all that work.

CHAPTER 8

S itting in the crate, we rumbled through the templar's security and moved deeper into the campus. I had time to let my thoughts wander. Naturally, I started wondering what was happening back in Sentarshaden.

I hoped Kelly would get the answers she needed to help the pack with their fertility issues. Even though she pretended that it didn't bother her, I knew that, by making her an alpha, I'd given her an extra burden. Wolves were pack animals. They were all still in college, but many of them would soon crave having children.

I trusted that Jadelyn and Scarlett would be fine on their own. If there was any trouble, they seemed to have an ally in Tyrande. Although Tyrande was probably busy with her own issues trying to keep Yev safe.

I still couldn't believe there was another dragon. And she hated my dragon's guts, even if she didn't know it.

The way my instincts seemed to take over, I knew it was only a matter of time before I didn't hold them down and she realized it. I'd have to own up to my mistake when we were back before it got worse.

I ran my hand over my face. That was a conversation I was not looking forward to.

But if I pulled it off, and she didn't hate me, there was a chance she might help me. She seemed to have a better grasp of her dragon form; she even had wings. Maybe she could help me realize more of my dragon potential. It would be nice to have someone else going through the same shit.

My thoughts continued to wander until the truck halted suddenly, and my face smacked into the side of the box.

I froze, waiting for somebody to react, but nothing came. I listened as the tarps were thrown off the cargo, and they started unloading.

When it was my turn, I braced.

They picked my crate up, tossing it off the bed of the truck unceremoniously.

Biting my tongue with the sudden drop and thump on the ground, I held back a surprised yelp and squeezed my eyes closed, trying to hold everything in. They must have been pretty sure there weren't explosives in my crate, or they just didn't care.

"Boys, leave them here. The armory will unpack them. We have a job to get ready for. These RPGs will be great for taking out a dragon. A chromatic deserves nothing but being put down."

A sudden fear that they knew I was here clenched in my gut, even though I had a feeling it wasn't me they were talking about.

"I can't wait to see the look on her face when she's shot down." One of the men made a noise that sounded like he was miming firing and an explosion. "We haven't had a dragon hunt in ages."

"You're a terrible shot. I doubt you'll be the one to take her down," another laughed.

"You all need to hurry up or you'll miss the last deployment for the mission," a gruff voice barked.

"Wouldn't miss it for the world." There was more banter about their excitement at hunting a dragon as the voices drifted off away from me.

They had referred to the dragon as a female, confirming my suspicion. They were talking about Yev.

This was the dark side of what it meant to be a dragon. Some wanted to protect you, and some wanted to hunt you. It sounded like the templars were more than eager to go hunt Yev. Even with the Highaen family behind her, the templars were willing to go after her.

Sitting there in silence, I waited, wondering if it was time to break out of the crate or not. Deciding to at least prep, I scooped up all the water bottles and stuffed them back into my spatial artifact.

I waited a few moments longer, listening for any noise. When none came, I decided it was as safe as it was going to get.

Bracing myself in the box, I pushed at the top. I applied steady force against it, but the nails didn't seem to budge. Leaning away and pressing in a bit more forcefully, I traded off stealth versus progress.

A few hits later, the nails finally gave, and I was able to get some progress pushing the nails out of the top. While I pushed, I realized there was something on top of the lid, so I did my best to keep my balance and lift the box up evenly as I poked my head out.

Surrounding me were more crates. It seemed they'd stacked them up just outside a pair of bay doors. Thankfully, we were on a part of the compound that didn't seem to have any foot traffic.

Not seeing or hearing anybody, I decided to go for speed. I moved up, letting the box on top drop off to the side, and moved quickly over around the nearby boxes.

"Morgana," I hissed as I walked around the crates. "Which one are you in?"

"Here," a crate spoke, and I beelined over to it, popping off the lid and pulling out my partner.

The crate tipped as she came out, making a bit more noise, but I didn't much care at that point. We needed to get moving, anyway.

Morgana looked pale, and not just because she had normal skin still. Trying to help her stand, I realized she could hardly hold herself up.

"Come on. Point me in the direction of your tree." I kept scanning the nearby area, waiting for somebody to come investigate the noises.

My body jolted as the bay door next to us began humming. It slowly lifted up, exposing two pairs of feet and voices. I pulled Morgana down behind a stack of crates as the doors continued to rise.

"Fuck's sake. Those boys made a mess of it," a woman's voice spoke.

"What do you expect?" the second spoke.

I knew our time was short. At this point, they would have seen the tipped over crate. And when they realized it was empty, all hell would likely break loose. And based on Morgana's current limpness, she wasn't going to be much help in a fight.

My best chance was to use surprise to my advantage and take them down before they could cause a commotion. As they approached the empty crate, I braced Morgana, leaning her against the nearby crate instead of my body.

I leapt out of my hiding spot, moving directly for one woman.

"Holy—" The woman's voice cut off as I tackled her, my hands stretching out and grabbing the other templar and pulling both women to the ground.

It was a quick tussle as they tried to toss me off, but I was already shifting slightly, adding on another hundred pounds and using all of my strength to pin them.

I had my knee on one's chest and my hand around the other's throat.

"I don't know who you think you are, but you just signed your death warrant," the older of the two wheezed from under my knee.

"Your base is in an inconvenient location for me," I grumbled as I lifted my weight, slightly before slamming it back down on her chest and knocking the wind out of her.

As they continued to fight me, I struggled, the heat of the battle lessening. I didn't want to kill them, but I also needed to keep them from alerting others. Morgana needed all the time she could get.

My heart clenched with my fist as I broke the neck of the younger woman.

I breathed deep, knowing it was what would give Morgana the best shot.

The lady under me saw it, and the horror of her own death reflected in her eyes as I turned my attention to her and quickly broke her neck as well.

"Morgana, think you can fit into their uniform?"

I hadn't noticed the uniforms before, too busy killing them. But they both were wearing the same thing, so it seemed like a good way to blend in.

Morgana practically crawled around the boxes, using them for support to get over to me. "Fuck, yeah. Give me a minute."

She dropped her pants right there and started to undress the older lady.

I checked the younger one before stuffing her into my old crate.

Morgana finished undressing the older lady, and I stuffed her in Morgana's crate, sealing them both up and adding them to the stack.

"That should buy us some time," I said. "Now, where's your root tree?"

She looked up, tilting her head around, but not looking directly at anything. It seemed like she was almost listening as she tried to find it. "That direction."

I started moving, but her hand grabbed my arm.

"Wait." She looked back through the bay doors, her voice wary.

I turned, ready to take on whatever threat there was. Following her eyes, I noticed for the first time what was just inside those bay doors.

It was a warehouse full of munitions—everything needed to outfit a small army was inside, ready to go.

"We don't have time," I told her, thinking she wanted to pick up a few new toys.

"No, not that. Although, yes, I'm sure there would be a few fun new toys we could pick up." She smiled at the thought, but then focused back on what she was saying. "I was thinking that it would make a very nice distraction if the place went up in a fire."

Catching her idea, I grinned. "We'll add these crates."

While we worked, I asked her, "Were you able to pick up on their conversation from inside the crate? It sounds like they were hoping to go after Yev."

"Yev?" Morgana asked.

"The green dragon that just revealed herself in Sentarshaden." I realized she might not have seen the news.

"Idiot," she spat, and I felt my cheeks burn. It was my fault that she'd ended up showing her secret to the masses. "We'll talk about that later. We need to move."

Grabbing the crates, I was no longer concerned with hiding my strength. I tossed them through the door, thinking the wood would be the perfect fire starter. Once they were inside, I just barely breathed a small plume of fire over them.

I could have sent the whole thing up in flames, but I wanted it to burn slowly. Hopefully, the alarm would go off in a few minutes once we were clear.

Grabbing Morgana, I helped her stay standing, practically dragging her in the direction she'd indicated.

When we rounded the armory's corner, the campus came alive. Many more people were moving about. Most were uniformed, but enough weren't that I didn't stand out.

"Which one?" I asked.

She pointed to a low, squat building. It was about three stories tall, and its architecture looked far more ancient than the rest. It had a Roman fort look to it, like it was something I'd see on the history channel, while the others were bland but modern construction.

Although, it was a Roman fort with intense security.

"Was that there before?" I asked.

"Nope. But it's been four hundred years since I've been here. The portal to the celestial plane was right next to my tree. Makes sense they'd build something on top of it. I'm surprised my tree didn't get uprooted in the construction."

Making our way across the busy street, I tried to take our time, hoping the armory would soon explode and give us the distraction it was supposed to be.

But with every step, it became clear we wouldn't get that lucky.

We made it all the way to the building before the man at the door stopped us.

"You can't go in here." His brow pressed down as he looked us over more thoroughly, not recognizing either of us.

Before he could say anything else, my fist connected with his gut. I stepped closer and jabbed hard enough into his gut to crack concrete.

He tried to block it, but I was a dragon. His arms did little but snap under my strength.

The guard wheezed and feebly tried to paw at me, but I'd just broken his wrist and several of his ribs. I'd likely crushed a few internal organs as well based on the way all of his strength left him after just a few moments.

I used my body to try to hide the attack from the pedestrians behind us, and Morgana grabbed his shoulders before he crumpled to the ground, making it look like some sort of hug.

It was all quick and casual, just as Morgana had taught me.

If we kept it subtle enough, people may not notice. Large, quick movements drew attention.

Boom.

An explosion sounded behind us and shook the ground. The armory had officially become a distraction. I rolled my eyes. It was about time.

Sirens went off on the campus and people scrambled. Nobody was looking our way, as people were screaming orders and pushing towards the explosion.

Pretending to be in the same hurry, I grabbed the guard and tried the door, but it barely moved. There seemed to be magnetic locks keeping it closed. He probably had a badge, but going through his clothes would take longer.

"Hold him." I handed him off to a weak Morgana, but I needed both hands for what I was about to do.

Digging my feet into the ground, I pulled on the door with my might. It wasn't so much a test of my strength as a test of my ability to keep my feet planted as I applied so much force to the door.

The door crinkled, the aluminum warping as the lock tried to hold. I smiled, pulling harder until the magnetic brick of the lock tore off the door frame.

Luckily, the noise wasn't very noticeable with all the chaos happening outside. It was a madhouse as the armory's fire was pouring out the doors and the leadership was trying to put purpose to the chaos that came from the sirens.

We slipped inside with the guard. So far, we hadn't been detected, but the door frame would catch the eye of some passer-by.

Another enormous boom rocked the compound, setting off a second wave of yells and screams outside.

We started moving forward, but two large, square-jawed men quickly blocked our path. Their expressions as they took in me and Morgana said they thought they had the advantage.

"Bad idea trying to sneak in here." The first man cracked his knuckles.

I waited for him to make the first move, ready to show him how wrong he was if he thought he could take me.

He threw a fist, and I couldn't keep the grin off my face as I matched him, waiting to hear his fingers snap. Unfortunately, that didn't happen. Our fists met, but he was not only remarkably strong, he was also far more durable than a human.

"Cherubs," Morgana spat, throwing down the human guard and baring her fangs. "Think of them like shock troopers for the celestial army."

"Put those fangs away or you are going to regret it, vampire." The second cherub squared up to Morgana.

But Morgana was no ordinary vampire. She rushed him and failed to dodge his fist, getting hit with a punch she should have been able to dodge. She stumbled, then blurred onto his back an instant later, her fangs sinking into his neck as she shook her head, widening the wound and slurping like a fat kid at a juice box.

Morgana desperately clung to him. That moment of speed had used all her strength.

Yet drinking from the cherub also seemed to give her a small amount of strength back.

"I guess that makes you mine." I threw another fist at the first cherub, packing a little more strength behind it.

He blocked and shifted backward, picking up a buckler and a gladius from just inside a door.

He put them on like he'd done it a million times before. In one fluid motion, he was armed as he raised his shield and blocked my next punch. My fist only left a small dent on the silver shield.

That was no ordinary metal.

"You're strong—must be a shifter." He swept the gladius in arcs in front of his body, warding me off and trying to get closer to his ally.

Morgana was stuck on the second cherub's back. She was like a tick, still sucking even as he threw himself into the wall, trying to dislodge her.

But she didn't care. Celestial blood was the best thing to stave off her current condition, and she seemed more than willing to take advantage of the opportunity.

I wrapped my arm in golden scales underneath my jacket and surprised my opponent, blocking his sword as it slashed down. I used the moment of shock to my advantage. Shifting my hand, I grabbed the gladius and pulled back, bringing him in closer.

My jaw clicked open, and I washed his face with dragon fire.

He might be a cherub, but dragon fire was potent. I braced in case a second attack was needed, but it wasn't. He went limp and fell to the ground, his head a half-consumed lump of char.

Satisfied, I turned to see how Morgana was faring.

She was still stuck to her opponent, who seemed to be losing his strength as he flailed helplessly on the ground. His eyes had taken on a glazed sheen that I assumed was from the narcotic in her saliva.

I waited, watching her back for any new-comers who might show up.

Soon she pulled her fangs off his neck and looked up.

I picked up the gladius and stepped over, removing his head for good measure.

"Feel better?" I asked.

"Much, actually. But them being ready for us isn't a good sign. They've likely put this building on lockdown."

I shrugged. We expected we'd be exposed at some point. For now, we just needed to get to the tree. And our chances had gone up now that she was a bit stronger.

"Let's get moving," I said.

Morgana tilted her head once more, working to locate the tree, and then we were off. She led us to the left, down a hall that appeared to arch in one big circle around the building.

As we walked, we came upon a pair of glass sliding doors that were far too modern for the rest of the Roman decor. Stepping up, the doors opened automatically, and we saw what was behind them.

Bodies of paranormals were strapped to autopsy tables, men standing above them, cutting into their bodies under bright light and documenting their findings. The room was modern, covered in sterile surfaces and white linoleum.

I had to hold back my revulsion and keep my focus, but it was hard when looking at the scene in front of us. Three white lab coats were working, ignoring the alarms as we burst in. They were as unperturbed by our entrance as the alarms.

"We don't need to evacuate." A lady turned her nose up at Morgana, thinking she was another one of the templars.

I didn't think twice as the gladius in my hand planted itself firmly in her throat. The way they were openly dissecting paranormals made me disgusted. The beast inside me roared with vengeance for the paranormals as I killed her.

As her body slacked to the floor, the other two finally became alarmed and alert.

"Get out. This place will be crawling with angels in just a minute," one of them warned us, trying to put on a braver face than his body language suggested.

"Kill the other," I told Morgana. I stepped up to the one that had spoken. "Speak quickly. What is this place?"

Taking a step closer, I pressed him into a corner. As he staggered backward, he stumbled, spilling a tray of scalpels.

"The most beautiful science ever. We have direct access to angels and all sorts of paranormals." He turned to the side, and I realized one wall was a large viewing window into the center of the building.

And that center appeared to be a beautiful courtyard.

In the middle sat a beautiful white willow standing nearly three stories tall—the biggest willow I'd ever seen. It felt unique and ancient, as if untouched by the modern world. Morgana's tree was beautifully wrapped in subtle magic.

But what captured my attention next was what was butting up against it.

A glowing portal stood next to it, a flowing anomaly in the very fabric of the world. The tree's trunk and one of its branches made up half of the arch, the other half of the arch were white bones.

"Beautiful, isn't it? The holy tree. We don't know what is different about it, but it radiates magic. And it has served as an anchor to the celestial plane for as long as we've studied it. We've managed to reinforce it and widen the portal with fresh dragon bones." The scientist puffed up his chest, clearly proud of the achievement. "If we feed that portal paranormals, we can balance the mana enough to allow through celestials. There has to be balance, but we've been working to bring through the army we need."

I felt my rage increasing as he spoke of fresh dragon bones and paranormals like a resource rather than living beings, but he didn't seem to notice. He was either confident or just that in love with his work.

I turned to Morgana, who was licking the blood of his fellow scientist off her hand. "Is that your tree?"

But I didn't need to ask the question as I took in the way that she was staring at it, mesmerized.

"Yes," she replied, stepping forward towards it.

"Your tree?" the scientist scoffed. "That's been ours for—"

My gladius got stuck in his throat, and I let him and it fall to the ground.

"From what he said, it sounds like your tree is now part of their connection to the celestial realm." I worried about what that would mean for the rest of the world.

But it seemed Morgana knew where my mind was going. "Don't stress too much. The celestial and hellish realms are different from the fae. Things can't pass freely from one to the other. There has to be an exchange. When they had tried to bring an archangel through, it had required the death of several dragons."

"Like a sacrifice?" I asked.

"Close enough. They need to displace the space they take up on earth. Like, when you pour out a bottle of water and air bubbles in. Otherwise, the bottle would collapse in on itself. They need to keep mana in the celestial plane; it's what keeps the plane's structure. Otherwise, the celestial plane would be like a deflating balloon."

"So can we just smash it?" I asked, leaning on my go-to solution.

Her face shuttered in an instant. "If you touch my tree, I'll kill you."

I held up my hands in a surrender gesture, knowing better than to come between her and her tree. It would seem that we were at an impasse with solving the larger issue. For now, we'd have to be satisfied with healing Morgana.

Looking around, Morgana grabbed a nearby tray and smashed it against the viewing window, trying to break it. Unfortunately, it just bounced right back.

She let out a frustrated grunt and raised the tray up, about to try again.

I grabbed it mid-air, stopping her and looking down at her when she glared up.

"Let me," I gently stated.

She frowned but nodded, dropping the tray.

I stepped over, ripping a desk off the floor. The drawers fell off as I hoisted it up and used it like a battering ram.

This time, the window shattered, and I threw the desk on the grass, marring the otherwise serene scene.

We stepped through it, careful of the broken glass, and entered the courtyard. Luckily, the other walls of the courtyard were stone. Only the lab's viewing pane and a door down the hall seemed to access the area.

I turned to Morgana. "Do what you need to do. I'll make sure no one bothers you."

But even as I said that, more square-jawed goons were picking their way through the lab we had just left behind.

CHAPTER 9

M organa didn't look back, trusting I'd take care of the approaching goons.

She started pulling items out of her cleavage and laying them at the base of the tree. I smiled to myself, now understanding how she managed to store so much in there.

It was strangely hard to focus on her when she was next to the tree. My eyes, even though I knew she was there, kept losing focus and sliding off of her.

As she was placing the items, a swaying hymn rose up out of her throat. She was so focused, meticulously arranging her offerings. I wanted to stand and watch her at that moment, caring so deeply for her tree, but she needed me to have her back.

I looked up around the central area, trying to spot cameras, but I didn't see any. I knew it would be hard to keep information from spreading, but without video documentation, I hoped it might slow the templars down. Their mutual desire to not have video evidence of that area might work to my benefit.

Turning back to the window, the four new cherubs were picking their way through the broken window. They were focused, squaring up against me with short swords in their hands, their little baby wings fluttering on their backs in excitement.

Thankfully, none of them seemed to be paying Morgana any attention.

Not feeling any need to hold back, my throat crackled as I let fire spill out and blast toward them.

They threw themselves to the side, splitting right down the middle. Only the center two cherubs had been singed.

But I had gotten what I'd needed and split their force, at least for a moment. Focusing on the right group, I made my move before they could all recover. My arms became golden-clawed gauntlets. I packed on mass and let my scales coat my body.

Towering two feet taller than the cherubs, I attacked with reckless abandon. I had a limited window to even out the odds. I knew they were tougher than many opponents I'd gone against, and they also had a skill and grace that didn't fit their stocky frames.

I was able to get in a few swings before the other two cherubs recovered, moving in and causing me to back up. I didn't dare give my back to either group.

"A dragon," the first spat, touching his chest where my claws had grazed him.

"A gold. Didn't realize there were any left. What do you boys say? We go back to the good old days and go dragon hunting?" another mocked me.

I had no idea how old these cherubs were, but they fought with just as much skill as Morgana. The only difference was they fought as a group, and they were clearly skilled at it.

Circling me, they probed with snappy jabs of their short swords. I batted the hits away, staying on my toes, ready for them to fully commit to an attack. They did a few more mock hits before they made their move.

I blocked one of the hits, pushing into the attacking cherub to try to break the encirclement.

Pain laced along my side, and I flinched away as a glowing sword cut right through my scales. Something about the sword reminded me of Morgana's attacks when she used her magic.

I pushed through the pain. My claws tore through his shoulder and hips as I did as much damage as I could before twisting and flinging him back into his allies.

He went down in a tumble. The other two moved in, trying to press me against the wall.

I was far stronger than any of them alone, but combined, they were a difficult opponent. Swords glanced off my forearms, and I realized their ability to use whatever magic penetrated my scales was limited, or they would use it repeatedly.

Yet, at the same time, continuing to fight with claws was going to be a problem. When they did use that magic, I was going to start losing limbs.

Letting loose a wash of my fire breath, I made space for myself. It was just enough to pull the templar's sword out of my spatial artifact.

The sword lit up with soft, white flames in my grasp once again. It was longer, and my strength outmatched them as I leaned into my overwhelming strength to fight back. At least in that, I had the advantage.

Morgana had given me basic weapons training, but I was outmatched by their skill. Strength was my ally in that moment. And I noticed that my dragon brain seemed to be a sponge, picking up small lessons even in the brief fight.

A low sweep of my sword forced a cherub to block, but I dug into the swing, stepping forward and lifting him off the ground. His own gladius pressed into his gut as I tossed him a dozen feet into the air, only to land in a heap.

I swung around, preparing for the next attack.

The cherub with a crushed shoulder and hip was still on the ground, groaning in pain. But the third able-bodied cherub was back on his feet, pressing me.

I blocked both of them with quick flicks of my wrist that would have shattered a human's wrist. I turned our fight, making sure I didn't expose myself to any of the moving cherubs.

The one I had sent flying was back on his feet, but I was satisfied to see him clutching at his abdomen as crimson blood leaked between his fingers.

Letting loose another wash of fire, I tried not to torch Morgana's tree as I hit that cherub. He went up like a summer bonfire, and I rushed the two still standing, plowing through them with sheer strength and breaking both their guards with heavy blows.

At that point, I had the advantage. They were all weakened and unable to regroup into their orderly formation.

It didn't take long to finish off the last of them, but once I did, I found myself breathing heavily. Reaching down to my side where I'd been cut, my hand came back dripping blood. I winced, trying to apply pressure to it as I checked in on Morgana.

Morgana seemed oblivious to the whole encounter, continuing her ritual at the tree. Through my dragon eyes, I could see mana linking her and the tree. Though, my attention kept being pushed away.

But most importantly, I could see that mana was being passed back and forth both ways. Her body was recovering.

My beast butted its head against my chest and growled.

I realized my mouth was full of saliva, as if somebody had rung a dinner bell. I tried to remember the last time I'd really filled up my dragon reserves, and I realized it was in fact dinner time.

Looking around, I took in the four cherubs and shrugged, figuring they were as good as anything. Cherubs had to be better than swamp trolls.

I shifted fully, falling to all four legs, and picked up the cherubs. I tossed them into the air and chomped them down in just a few quick bites.

They were tasty and filled my belly with warmth.

I was about to shift back to protect Morgana when another smell caught my attention, my dragon perking up. I followed the smell, finding myself right next to the portal, my nose pressed into the dragon bones.

They smelled... good. Great even.

I leaned in, giving one a lick. But I became distracted as the portal wavered slightly.

A female cherub popped through the portal, freezing as we took each other in. My jaws snapped forward just as she tried to duck backwards through the portal. I managed to catch her, my teeth sinking into her arm.

The cherub screamed on the other side of the portal, and it was like listening to someone under water. "Dragon at the gate!"

Before she could say more, I pulled her back by her arm and my maw opened wide yet again, chowing down on the surprised cherub.

I moved back towards the bones, still feeling them call to me. They radiated warm, familiar magic. I wondered if I could shut down the portal before more trouble came through. Or at least weaken it.

My teeth scratched the bones as I tugged, but they were locked tight around the portal. I decided my best bet was just breaking off pieces of it, so I started gnawing on them.

There was a strange desperation as the beast clawed at my chest for a taste of the dragon bones.

The portal rippled again as a handsome, blond-haired man stepped through the portal, ducking my snout that was gnawing on the dragon bones. He was thin and athletic, with sharp features that made him seem a little sinister despite the white wings and glowing halo over his head.

"Ah. The bones of an ancient dragon seem to have attracted a hungry whelp." He flourished a thin saber as a pair of white angel wings flared out to his side. "Too bad you won't get to enjoy them. But maybe you can join them."

He stabbed forward, and I nearly roasted him. But I quickly realized I'd also roast Morgana and her tree, so I paused.

Instead, I used one of my front claws to drive him backward.

Unfortunately, he had real wings and took to the air, soaring over my claws as he rushed my face again.

I rolled to the side, crashing into the wall and showering myself with debris. I needed to be more mobile, so I shifted back into my smaller dragon knight form.

"Ah. Yes, that would be much better to fight in," the angel said, flourishing his sword and waiting for me.

Apparently, he had some sort of code he followed.

If he was going to give me a moment, I figured I might as well also arm myself. I moved, snagging the templar sword from the ground.

I found the man tilting his head, studying me.

"How curious. A dragon wielding a celestial sword. But I suppose they did say that metallic dragons were always creatures of justice and order," the angel commented to himself. "Too bad you are more valuable dead."

Waiting for him to make a move, I was happy to buy Morgana a bit more time. I hoped that she might be fully healed soon and be able to fight by my side.

The idea of Morgana in her full glory excited me. I knew she'd been holding back with me in practice. I couldn't wait to see what she could do.

"You seem confident. You have yet to see what I can do," I said.

"Ah, but I've seen enough. You are limited in experience. Even if by some miracle you defeat me, the humans we've trained will descend on this place in numbers you cannot take. Your body is ours. But we will put it to a worthy cause, I can assure you."

As he said that, I saw a slight blur in the portal, and I realized it was a form. A great man with six wings fanned out behind him stood just on the other side, and something about him set alarms off in my draconic instincts.

He was truly dangerous.

"Ah, don't mind him. He's just pouting that he can't come and fight you." The angel smiled, his sword leveling back at me.

I countered his stance, readying myself.

He burst forward, his wings giving him a small lift at the end, making his sword change course from what I'd anticipated. It slipped up and over my guard, forcing me to roll backward. I barely avoided getting a new hole to breathe through in my throat.

Not wanting to be caught on my back, I got back to my feet quickly, but he hadn't pressed his advantage. He was playing with me.

Letting him come again, I chose not to block at all. Instead, I let loose a jet of flame as soon as he got too close to dodge.

Unfortunately, as the flames spilled out, he seemed to slip off to the side in an unnatural way, like there was a pair of invisible strings that had tugged him sharply to the side.

I realized that it felt like fighting Morgana when she used her magic.

I charged him, coming in strong with my sword, leaning into my advantage in strength. But he parried my powerful blows and called my feints, blocking them and pushing me back.

We continued on, and I finally saw my opportunity for a hard strike. I took the moment, but he threw his hand up, and I found myself blinded by a white light while I was thrown backward.

It was like a wall of light had just smacked me in the face.

"You aren't even using magic. Just how little do dragons know now? I'm surprised such mighty creatures have fallen so far down." The angel sighed. "Although, I am ashamed that I had to use my magic against somebody so untrained. I was trained by Azrael himself."

His eyes flickered to the powerful archangel waiting on the other side of the portal.

I glanced in my peripheral vision to check on Morgana, who so far the angel had ignored. Whatever magic kept pushing my focus away must be hiding her from others.

She was bent over with her head pressed to the base of the tree as blood flowed out of her mouth. I sincerely hoped that was part of the ritual, but I couldn't go check on her to make sure.

"Too bad you are just a whelp. Your body will only support a few angels like me coming through. But at least that's something."

I didn't like the thought of being used to bring more of these assholes to earth, but I also didn't plan on letting him take my bones.

The angel came again, and this time, he seemed to be ready to finish it. He pressed me hard, his saber flickering with light as he used his magic. It bent to his will, his thrusts trying to curve around my sword.

I stepped back countless times in a circle around the portal. I was starting to run out of ideas on how to take him down. He was a superior swordsman, and with his magic and wings, he'd managed to avoid all of my fire and strikes.

I needed an opening. A chance to turn this around. But I wasn't giving up. Scarlett and Jadelyn would never let me if they were here.

The idea of Jadelyn's reaction if I died ripped through me. Her potential anguish flooded me, making rage bubble up inside of me.

The beast went rampant in my chest.

The aura of fear washed out of me, and I could see the moment it hit the angel. Horror struck his face, and I took the opening. Lashing out with all the speed and power I could muster, I struck.

Unfortunately, he recovered quickly. He whirled, throwing his wings forward in a last-ditch effort to stall my blade.

Making contact, my silver celestial sword cut right through his wing and his right arm. Celestial blood spilled on the ground and whet my appetite.

I surged forward again, my sword leaving behind white streaks from the fire that still burned along it.

The angel had lost his sword with his right arm and was sending up small flares of magic with his left in an attempt to block my sword.

I knew that was taking a lot of his focus, so I sent out another pulse of fear.

This one stuck a moment longer as I shifted, rising up and snapping my jaws around his remaining wing. He flailed, but it didn't matter. I had him caught right where I had wanted him.

My front claws raked his body, turning the small angel into minced meat before I tossed him slightly and swallowed. I stopped to eat his other wing and arm, licking my lips at the taste of celestials.

Turning back to the portal, I took in the archangel, who was glaring angrily. His face promised death.

I paused, fearful he'd push himself through in a fit of rage, but it became clear that he was trapped on the other side. At least for the moment. Based on what Morgana had said, he must have been concerned that his entry into our world might collapse his part of the celestial plane.

Sure enough, he gave up. Finally, he turned his back and disappeared from view.

Feeling more comfortable, I moved back to the portal, once again drawn to the dragon bones. I lay down, starting to gnaw on them once more. I chomped on them a few times before Morgana spoke.

"What are you doing?"

I rumbled an answer, always forgetting that I couldn't talk as a dragon yet.

"Let me." She sighed, and a flick of dark, silvery magic arced from her finger, slicing off the largest bone from the portal frame.

I smiled, leaning forward and swallowing it whole. The beast was giddy inside of me, bouncing around like a kid at its first Christmas.

I looked up at Morgana, waiting for her to slice off another piece, when a pain in my gut suddenly caused me to double over.

"Please tell me that didn't just cause you indigestion," she said dryly.

I looked up to glare at her, but when I realized I was looking at a healthy Morgana, I couldn't bring myself to hold the glare.

She was standing tall, no signs of red blisters peeking out from the uniform she was wearing. And I swore she had a little more blue to her now. Morgana was an odd mix of elven grace and seductive vampire darkness. Those crimson eyes of hers often held disdain for the world, but I didn't miss the slight sparkle in them when she watched me looking at her.

"We need to get going if you are done ogling me."

I nodded, moving, but the pain in my gut redoubled.

Between the pain, I also felt mana flare inside of me. My body seemed to absorb the mana from the dragon bone. It seemed to feed my dragon like nothing I'd experienced before, including the celestials.

My back itched, like I had a swarm of mosquitoes going to town on me. I rolled over, trying to rub my back on the ground before something crackled and pain in my back had me back on my feet again.

But as the noise continued, I felt my mass shift, increasing on my back.

Moving side to side, I realized two large wings had emerged on my back. I angled my body, trying to get a good look.

"Oh. That's progress," Morgana said as more men came charging through the lab.

There were a number of cherubs among the mix. I turned my butt to them, wiggling the wings so they could see them. These were real wings.

But I couldn't be smug for long. We were in trouble, and we needed to get out safely. Taking a deep breath, I washed the lab with fire, pouring everything I had into it. I melted the steel, even setting fire to the bricks.

"We need to go," Morgana repeated.

I looked around the mess in the courtyard, trying to find my jeans and my sword.

Morgana realized what I was doing and grabbed what looked like most of a pair of jeans and used them to wrap around the sword's hilt before picking it up.

"No more stalling. We go. Now." She jumped onto my back.

I grunted in agreement as the cherubs pushed their way through the ashes and flickering fires, making their way back towards us. Letting loose another blast of my fear aura, I jumped, sinking my claws into the wall and pulling myself up and over the edge of the building.

Morgana was clinging to the horns on my head as I threw myself over and stretched out my wings for the first time. It was odd seeing the world from above, but I couldn't focus on that. I needed to fly.

The beast was riding at the front of my consciousness, sort of like a translator between my mind and my body. Thankfully, the bundle of instincts knew how to fly. I caught air, flapping my wings furiously, trying to gain altitude.

Feeling a strange shimmer under my wings, I realized they were coursing with magic. It made sense. Despite my wings being large, my body was massive. The magic must help power my flight.

I beat my wings, pulling us higher, but we were still within range of what I knew was about to be many guns pointed up at us from below.

"Zach..." Morgana's voice was worried. "You need to get higher."

I was trying, but I could only tilt up, not fly directly up. Getting higher was going to take time. My grumble to her said that much, only in fewer words.

"Then I need you to roll right when I say so." She pulled out a semi-automatic rifle and clung tightly to the horns on my head. "Roll."

I did as she said, feeling clumsy as I did my first barrel roll.

Morgana fired at something below us, and then the air shuddered with two explosions.

I couldn't help but tuck my head and look down behind me to see what had happened. But when I did, Morgana nearly fell off of me, barely hanging onto my horns with one hand.

"Fuck's sake, just fly. They are bringing out more surface-to-air missiles."

The idea of those helped spur me forward. I lifted my head back up towards the clouds and pumped my new baby dragon wings for all they were worth.

"Shit," Morgana cursed, and I felt my body tense, knowing that didn't bode well for whatever was coming at us next.

CHAPTER 10

The sound of propellers beating the air below me made it clear what had caused Morgana to curse.

"Zach, we have two helicopters inbound. If you can get up to the clouds, we can ditch them."

I grumbled back a response, continuing to beat my wings as hard as I could. I thought I was doing pretty damn well for a guy who had never tried to fly before. Thankfully, my beast was helping me pull through—the bundle of instincts was really paying off its rent right now. But the wings were new, and I wasn't sure just how far I could push them.

The sound of the beating propellers was growing closer, though, so my wings would just have to hold up a bit longer.

I worked on trying to go higher versus further ahead, trading off, letting them close in on us in an effort to get some cloud cover.

Bullets whizzed past us as a spray of gun-fire just barely skimmed past. A few of the bullets pinged off my body, showing me just how close that had been.

And it also drove a new realization. The webbing of my wings didn't look nearly as sturdy as my scales. I knew they wouldn't hold up to gunfire.

But the clouds were getting closer.

I strained my wings to lift me just a little higher. It worked, and I poked my head through the cloud and broke out on the other side. It felt almost like I'd stepped into a new world.

"Good job. Now stay high. Most heli-copters can't get this high," Morgana advised me.

Unfortunately, more bullets popped through the clouds in little puffs as the helicopter's blades rose up behind me.

"Okay, never mind," she spat.

My pride dimmed quickly, replacing itself with anger over the pesky contraptions. With two hard flaps, I rose up and turned.

Morgana braced against my horns as I took in a deep breath and dove. I let the fire build up in my chest as I closed in on them.

The helicopters scrambled, trying to turn as gunmen on the side brought their guns up as they hung out the side of the cabin.

My dragon fire roared out of me at the first helicopter even as the guns flashed.

The bullets got caught in my fire, melting and losing their trajectory. The side of the first helicopter warped and crumpled, and I lifted my body just over the melting propellers, feeling the wind off them as I rushed over.

I blew past both of them as the first helicopter became nothing more than a melted tin can and stalled midair before plummeting.

A roar tore itself from my chest. I felt on top of the world.

"Settle down. Normal people are going to hear that. Besides, you still have one helicopter to deal with, champ," Morgana reminded me.

The other helicopter had apparently managed to turn, because another distant spray of bullets pinged harmlessly off my scales.

Now that I was getting more comfortable flying, it felt more like I was swimming through the air. I dipped my wings, swooping down to gain speed as I banked to the right to get a view of my last opponent.

The helicopter tilted forward and was going full steam once again, working to keep up with my speed.

But I noticed the man in the side door had wings as he clung to the handles. I rumbled at Morgana, keeping my eyes on him.

"I see him too. But you just got your wings. Might I suggest not trying aerial combat with a seasoned angel?" she said sarcastically.

While I understood her point, the first helicopter had gone down pretty quickly. Maybe I could take this one the same way.

I circled back to let loose another blast of fire.

This time, though, they were ready. A screen of light blocked my fire from torching the second helicopter. And as soon as my breath was out, a flash of white wings shot out of the helicopter as the angel beelined for me.

This angel was quick, but I had a feeling my top speed would out wing him any day of the week. My wings were far larger than his.

As we approached each other, he ducked his wings and dove under me. I felt a sharp pain lance across my stomach as the angel pulled out of a dive on the other side of me, his sword wet with my blood.

"You worry about the helicopter," Morgana shouted over the wind, and I felt her balancing on my head and walking down my neck. I tried to keep my neck steady as I turned my head to watch the helicopter.

The angel was circling, rising higher into the air above me, no doubt to take another diving attack at me.

But I trusted Morgana to have my back. I could feel her squaring up her stance between my wings.

As I watched, the helicopter banked away. It would seem that the helicopter had done their job as they turned and tried to outrun me. Apparently, dropping off the angel had been their job.

Like shit I was going to let it end there, so I headed after them.

"Zach," Morgana warned me, but I didn't need it. I knew the angel would be about to attack once more.

I decided to try picking up my speed. I tucked my wings close to my body, Morgana pressed herself close to me so as to not get thrown off my back.

Then I hurtled myself down, aiming for the helicopter that was descending as it tried to seek refuge back at the templar base and within range of the weapons on the ground.

My body streaked downwards, my weight turning me into a giant golden missile hurtling through the air. I felt like I was going a million miles an hour. My tail twitched behind me trying to guide my descent.

In just seconds, I caught up to the helicopter. My claws came out, grabbing the tail even as the propeller blades cut into my arm.

I ignored the pain, riding the high that came with my success.

The helicopter crumpled under my claws, and I crushed the cabin as I tore the tail of the helicopter from the body. The blades bent out of shape as I forcefully stopped them, receiving a few more cuts along my arms.

Satisfied that the helicopter was done, for I pushed off of it just as steel rang on my back. Morgana had blocked the angel.

The angel flew over my head, and I snapped my wings open trying to slow my fall. My webbing strained in a sensation I'd never felt before. The closest thing I could equate it to was like stretching your legs past where they were comfortable going and then having someone force it further.

Metal clanging continued out on my back in quick succession as Morgana tried to protect my wings. The angel was repeatedly diving at me, trying to cut my wings and send me falling to my death.

I heard Morgana curse as pain laced through my wings further out. More clanging sounded as Morgana caught up to his moves, parrying his blows.

There was little I could do at the moment, so I focused on not slamming into the ground. In an ideal world, I didn't go splat. That had my sole focus.

I careened over the compound, spotting the barn where we'd stored the car in the distance. I aimed towards it, but I knew I was still going too fast.

The beast inside of me was screaming to pull up.

Another burst of pain from my wing surged through my body, and I could tell that I'd just lost quite a bit of functionality on my right wing as it struggled to maintain the same lift as the left.

Throwing my claws forward, I braced for impact as I cratered into the ground, sliding for dozens of yards. Everything hurt as my bones were jarred from the impact.

The angel floated nearby, a smug smile on his face.

Morgana leapt off my back and blurred forward. "Fucker, fight me on the ground!"

She made it happen, too. She jumped, taking him by surprise as she grabbed him and threw her body backward, slamming him down into the ground.

He tried to blast her with celestial magic. It flung her off, but I could tell he was surprised that it hadn't done the damage he'd expected.

Not about to give him the chance to get into the air again, Morgana darted forward with supernatural speed, carving his wing off. She finished the combo with a round-house kick straight to his jaw.

Stunned on the ground, he made a perfect target. I gathered my strength and jumped on him, my maw open wide for another angelic snack.

His bones crunched as my mouth closed in around him. I licked my lips as I looked over at Morgana, my body slumping slightly. Feeling the weariness of my first flight and the damage I'd sustained creeping back up on me, I shifted back to human.

"Can you still get the car out?" Morgana asked.

"I think so." Gathering my strength, I made one more push, picking up the car and placing it back on the road.

I could hear noise in the distance. The town was coming alive. I had a feeling there would be more than a few additional helicopters about to be searching for us.

"I'll drive." Morgana pushed me into the passenger seat, throwing my torn pants and the templar sword in the back. "It's the least I can do after all you've done to help me."

"I'd go to the ends of the earth." Now that Morgana was healed, it was time to have a different conversation. And I wasn't about to dance around it. "You are mine, Morgana."

She did a double take before she put the car into gear and slammed the gas. "Is this really the time to be having this conversation?"

"Not much conversation needed. I knew you wouldn't want to do this while you were still weak, but now you are healed. And I'm not letting you avoid this anymore. Morgana, you love me."

I settled into the passenger seat, buckling my seatbelt. With Morgana driving, I'd likely need it.

"Yeah? Well I don't know if I deserve to love," Morgana brooded as she floored the car and tore out of the town.

I looked out the back window. Our car wasn't exactly stealthy with its neon green flames. I knew it was only a matter of time before one of the helicopters came to investigate us.

"Lucky for you, I think you do. You are one of my mates."

She snorted and shook her head. "Ridiculous. You can't just—"

"It's done, Morgana. You'll either have to accept it or take me down. Because my dragon counts you as a mate, and it won't let you go far." There was no arguing. I knew from fighting Morgana that, if you gave her any room, she would take the opportunity. I was holding my ground.

"Fine. We'll talk about it later."

My jaw crackled as it shifted slightly. Realizing what was happening, I leaned over, letting the magic gather in my jaws. I smiled to myself, not giving her a chance to sense my next move.

I bit down hard on Morgana's shoulder, imprinting whatever magic had created Jadelyn's mark into the bite.

"What the fuck?!" Morgana screamed, barely staying on the road.

"There. Now no more discussion is needed. You're claimed."

For a brief moment, Morgana's face flickered with vulnerability.

"You have no idea what you just got yourself into." She swallowed, clearly feeling conflicting emotions. "We need to get out of here, but then we really should talk."

I leaned back in my seat, feeling comfortable for the first time. My dragon was satisfied. "Let's just get back to Sentarshaden."

Morgana wove around a car that was stopped at a stop sign. I nearly put my feet up. I felt so relaxed at that moment.

"You say that like we don't have three more helicopters after us. Zach, the templars will put everything they can into stopping us."

"I have faith in you," I replied.

Morgana leaned over the wheel and reached into her bra before awkwardly pulling out an assault rifle. "Lay down some cover fire for me then, sweety?"

The way she said it made the hairs on the back of my neck stand on end.

"Of course, babe." I threw a pet name back at her, but it didn't seem to have any effect on her.

I rolled down my window, exposing myself to the freezing Austrian air. Taking aim, I fired it at the inbound helicopters.

Sparks pinged off the frame, and a big crack went through the front windshield. But they were too far off for me to get a clean shot.

"Don't worry, I just want them to think twice about getting too close." Morgana pushed the car to its limit, outpacing the helicopters.

I watched the helicopters, aware that soon we would approach the switchbacks. While we might outrun them at a straight shot, they'd overtake us quickly as we wound around the Alps.

"Think you can shift again for me? We aren't going to outrun them for long." Morgana had clearly been following the same line of thinking.

"What are you thinking? Not sure I have the wings for flight right now."

"I'm feeling like a little dragon off roading through the mountains?" Morgana smiled.

I laughed, realizing what she was asking. "Let's do it."

Morgana did a hard turn off the road into a snowy forest. The car only made it about a dozen yards before it got stuck. When it did, we threw ourselves out of the car and Morgana stuffed it away in her spatial pocket.

I was already shifting, but this time, I was silver in the frigid mountain.

Morgana hopped on my back as I tore through the woods, keeping my head low and letting out a massive bank of icy fog to hide us amid the alpine forest.

"Fuck, that's cold. We need to talk about this whole multiple colors thing." Morgana rubbed her shoulders, riding on the back of my neck.

"I tried to read your books." For once, I spoke coherently. I could speak!

"Good luck. Half of those are in dead languages. But congratulations on learning to talk."

I could practically hear the smug smile on her face.

"Minor victories. Wings and talking," I said, happy about the progress.

The helicopters were circling overhead, but between the dense trees and the icy fog I had created, they hadn't pinpointed us yet.

I kept the fog rolling as I ran through the forest. In the cold air, the fog hung in the forest and even expanded outwards, rolling down the mountain, creating a massive bank of fog.

We kept at this for the better part of an hour until I thought that my dragon throat was going to give out on me.

"Think we can duck out, shift back, and find some place to hole up for the night?" I suggested.

"Yeah. Might be our best chance." Morgana peered out of the fog.

Up above, I could hear three distinct helicopters. All this time, they hadn't given up, and there were likely far more than three out there searching for us.

Running through the woods a while longer, I spewed several miles' worth of chilling fog. Once it spanned between two small towns, I shifted back.

"Here." She handed me the templar sword, once again using my pants to not touch it directly. She seemed scared of what it would mean if she did.

I pulled the spatial artifact out of the pocket and tucked away the sword before pulling out a spare pair of clothes.

Morgana waited there, hand on her hips as she stared at the bra pad. "Missed me that much?"

"I found it when I was looking for clues about where you'd gone."

"So you decided to keep the padding to my bra?"

"It's a bag of holding."

"It's bra padding," she said, the corner of her lips twitching.

If I let her, she was going to remind me about this for the next decade. I waved her away. "Let's get going."

She put on her amulet, with a smirk still lingering on her face, and her skin tone turned human again. She tucked her ears under a big woolen hat as she hid her corset and leather pants under more normal winter attire.

The helicopters were searching overhead, casting a large net. But that meant they couldn't figure out where we were. I'd created miles' worth of fog; they couldn't cover all the ground.

We slipped away into the nearby town, both of us appearing like visitors.

Jackbooted thugs and square-jawed cherubs were making themselves known, roaming the town as we ducked inside a motel.

"Crazy out there," the lady at the desk said, looking up from her book. "That fog came out of nowhere, but good for business."

"Nuts on the highway. Thought it would be better to spend the night and start again in the morning." I put on my best smile.

"Uh huh." She looked Morgana over distractedly, a flicker of heat in her eyes. I didn't blame her. Morgana was gorgeous.

"Room for the night?" I pressed her.

"I have to warn you, the thugs going around town are going to come knocking, and there's not much I can do to stop them from rummaging through your stuff or messing up your room."

I respected her candor.

"Thanks," Morgana said with a smile and patted her on the hand before grabbing my hand and pulling me away.

"What's that for?" I asked, confused.

"Permission to break into one of the rooms. If we aren't on her books, then she won't have to report us to the thugs."

"Somehow, that isn't the message I got." I squinted at Morgana, but she just strolled around the corner and slipped a finger into the keypad before it beeped angrily several times and clicked green.

She pushed open the door and did a quick sweep of the room. "We have no car out front, and they have no reason to check this room. It should be safe for now, but we can't be too careful." She braced a chair up against the door.

We didn't even turn on the light as we moved to the back of the room, crouching low in the shadows.

We sat in the quiet for a moment before she spoke, "Zach, I need you to do me a favor."

"Anything."

"Survive. If I'm going to open my heart for the first time in a long while, I need it not to be short," she said slowly as if even talking about it was opening old wounds.

I realized that, given her past and the troubles that surrounded her, she wasn't closed off for no reason.

"Of course. I'll be here and by your side, no matter what comes our way. The templars aren't going to be the thing that takes us down. Neither is your situation with the elves."

"And the vampires," she reminded me. "I feel like I've cursed you."

Grabbing her hand, I pulled her close even as a commotion happened outside the motel. I could hear men yelling and someone screaming a few doors down as a door banged.

"They are checking the rooms," Morgana said calmly.

But there were more doors banging than people shouting. I realized they were going to check all of them.

"Move the chair. I think we can hide in the ceiling." Looking up, they were cheap drop ceiling tiles.

Despite them being thorough, they wouldn't be that thorough.

Morgana was quick, moving the chair back into place as I lifted one of the ceiling tiles and hoisted her up before climbing in myself. The little aluminum braces gave slightly under my weight. I froze, trying not to shift my body weight.

I breathed a sigh of relief as they managed to hold.

The door to our room slammed open, and I could hear boots thumping their way around the room. The clack of straps against guns felt like bombs in the otherwise silent room.

"All clear."

"I told you, the two I mentioned turned back." The lady from the front desk sounded tired.

"We still need to check every room," a gruff voice replied.

The door closed behind them, and I cracked a ceiling tile. The coast was clear.

I jumped down, and Morgana followed me shortly after. We quickly put the chair back in place against the door handle. I turned to check out the window, confirming they were moving on.

"Things should calm down, at least for a while. They'll look elsewhere," she commented from behind me.

When I turned around, she was prowling up to me, her hips swaying. As she stepped up to me, her nails traced down my jawline in a way that covered me with goose bumps.

"You don't know what you signed up for." She kissed my neck softly, leaving a soft wet spot behind. She slowly blew on it, causing a soft chill to run along my neck, but I quickly realized it was combined with the venom in her saliva taking effect.

It wasn't as strong as her bite, but it gave me a light high that made me feel like I was floating back up above the clouds.

CHAPTER 11

Feeling a pleasant buzz from Morgana's kiss, I let her lead me over to the edge of the bed. She sat me down on the bed and put one leg on either side of me, climbing up and straddling me.

She was beautiful, sexy, and dangerous. Morgana's blue skin caught the faint moonlight coming through the motel's barely curtained window. So did her every curve, accented with leather pants and corset, even if that jacket hid some of her frame. Her silver hair was free of any bindings as it spilled over her shoulders.

She was breathtakingly beautiful. Fangs, red eyes, blue skin and all.

"Riding on a dragon was pretty fun," she whispered into my ear. The blue-skinned bomb shell in my lap made me think of other ways she could ride me.

I didn't realize it from my last experience, but whatever was in her saliva made every touch electrifying. She ground her hips against mine, and I felt myself come to attention quickly.

Her lips trailed down my neck. I could feel her lips stretch into a smile before two little pricks dragged down my collar.

I'd never been into vampires, but something about the moment of it was both dangerous and incredibly sexy. I waited, anticipation coursing through me as she teased me, planting little kisses along my neck and making my head buzz delightfully.

Her leather pants creaked as she rocked herself in my lap as she ran her mouth along my exposed flesh.

My hands wandered down her curves, finding her deliciously tight rear and giving it a squeeze.

"Harder. I'm not a delicate thing," she teased, her voice smooth and throaty.

I smacked her rear and bounced her on my lap. I needed more and she damn well knew it by the smirk on her face. Growling, I picked her up by her ass and pressed her against the wall, crushing her lips to mine.

Morgana moaned as she parted her luscious blue lips, her nails digging slightly into my scalp before trailing them down my neck to my back. I was fairly certain she'd left red lines all the way down my back.

"Whoa." I took a breath after the kiss, feeling almost disoriented.

"Oh no, you don't get to rev me up and then pull back." Morgana smirked as her hands slid under my shirt and hoisted it up and over my head.

With my shirt off, her hands traced my chest carefully for the first time. She took a slow breath as those ruby red eyes studied every plane of my stomach.

"What?" I was busy studying the best way to get her corset top off her.

"I can't believe you are the one, after all these years, that's managed to get me to this point." She dragged a nail along the soft skin of my neck, making me look up into her eyes.

"Believe it," I growled.

"Sit back down." She pushed off the wall and knocked me back onto the bed before rolling off and swiftly unbuttoning my pants, pulling them and my boxers off in one motion.

"You have me at an unfair advantage," I grumbled, taking in her delicious but fully clothed body.

She smirked, pulling her jacket off one shoulder slowly, then the other. Pulling it open, she struck a pose that made her legs seem impossibly long in her leather pants. "I thought you might enjoy this part."

Morgana whipped off her coat with a flourish, leaving her in her leather pants and corset.

Her fingers plucked down the laces that kept her bountiful chest constrained all day long, slowly but surely loosening them, until the corset was loose enough that she wiggled out of it.

"You do not need that thing for those," I said. Her breasts were defying gravity by the way they sat perkily on her chest.

Morgana smirked with a twinkle in her eyes. "I like it because it keeps them out of the way, not because I need the lift."

She stuck her thumbs into the waistline of her leather pants and started sliding them down her hips, her hip bones just starting to become visible. But then she turned around, putting her back to me. As she looked over her shoulder, she slowly inched them lower, peeling them away from her rear.

I started to move towards her but she tisked, starting to pull them back up.

I growled, but I stayed put.

Smiling, she returned and slid them slowly back down, continuing this time as she slid them down her legs and onto the floor. There was something immensely satisfying watching her butt pop out of them.

By the time she turned back around and stalked towards me on the bed, I was more than ready.

Grabbing her shoulders, I pulled her down on top of me.

I grabbed the back of her head, pulling her in for a kiss and enjoying her lips. I let my hands wander over her soft skin as I found her breasts, rubbing my thumbs over her nipples until her skin pebbled at the edges.

"My third mate," I growled.

The beast butt his head against my chest in agreement.

"We'll see if you can handle this." She pushed my hands away and dipped low, covering my cock in wet kisses. The tingling that she left behind should have been jarred and sold instead of whatever sexual jellies they currently sold in the stores.

Morgana worked her way slowly up my chest, her hands climbing up me as she positioned herself over me.

The only warning I had was a sultry smile before she lifted her hips and impaled herself on me with a hiss.

"There's no rush," I said, laying back on the bed to let her adjust to the speed she could handle. Being inside of her felt amazing.

"Monster cock," she gasped. "Thank mana I heal quickly. How do the other two manage this?"

I shrugged, pleased to be able to fill her completely.

Morgana eased herself up and down on me, bracing against my chest as she made small wet slaps. She bottomed out on me with each stroke, her grunts turning more pleasurable as she sped up.

But as she sped up, I realized she wasn't stopping. She started stroking me far faster than I was used to as she rocked and bounced on my cock.

I tensed up and looked at her in shock. I hadn't considered a vampire's speed when it came to sex.

Morgana was jack hammering herself onto me, and it felt amazing.

"God. Please don't stop." Her tight pussy rode me to the peak in a hurry.

"So big, so delicious." She threw her head back, continuing to slam herself down on top of me. Her nails dug into my thighs as she continued to ride me. "Yes!"

I held onto her hips for dear life, as I released inside her. "I'm coming."

I barely managed to get the words out before I pumped my seed inside of her tight, blue pussy.

Morgana smirked. "I'm not even done yet."

She wiped a finger down at our union, pulling a glob of my white spunk and tasting it. "You know, they say this stuff will keep a girl looking young."

"Take all of it that you want," I joked.

But she took it seriously and lifted off of me just to spin around and put that tight, blue bubble butt in my face as she rode me reverse cowgirl.

"Don't mind if I do." She started up again.

Luckily, my dragon stamina didn't fail me. It wasn't long before I was ready for her again.

She twerked on my cock, jiggling her globes as she once again used her vampiric speed to ride me. "Yes, give me another one."

Her hand was between her hips, and I could feel her touching herself while she rode me.

Grabbing her long, silver hair, I pulled her head back, but she didn't slow down one bit, even as her head tilted back at a dangerous angle.

I realized I'd snapped her neck once, only for her to get back up. I wondered what it would take to surprise her.

Getting an idea. I licked my fingers and timed it right, stabbing my pointer finger into her ass.

"Oooh," Morgana let out a tight moan. "Careful, you are playing a dangerous game."

"Maybe I like danger." I wiggled my finger in deeper, prodding her fleshy insides even as she bounced on me rapidly.

I must have hit the spot because she came hard, soaking my balls and letting out a cry that was sure to wake the neighbors. But Morgana continued wailing into the night.

I chuckled, enjoying the moment as a warning bell went off in the back of my mind. I tried to push it away and enjoy the beautiful woman above me, but the idea stayed, wanting my attention.

Taking a moment to pause, I worked to figure out what my instincts were trying to tell me when it hit me quickly.

We were supposed to be in hiding. And we were anything but quiet.

I cursed.

"Morgana, we have to go." I tried to sit up with her on top of me.

"Huh?" Morgana looked up at me, her face a bit dazed from her orgasm.

She took in my concerned face, and a moment of vulnerability flashed on her face as she tried to figure out what she'd done wrong.

I was about to squash her concern and explain when her face cleared, and she realized what had me concerned.

"Shit." She hopped off of me and wiggled back into her pants and corset, donning the amulet again to hide her blue skin. "We'll hit the highway. Hopefully, their forces are spread out searching for us, and we can race out of here."

I was only seconds behind her, getting my pants on and double checking to make sure I still had my spatial artifact.

"You're too goddamn loud," I grumbled, getting my clothes on.

"Well, if you weren't so big, maybe I wouldn't be so loud."

I could only smile. Despite the situation, I couldn't really regret making her scream. "Let's get going, and if we live through this, maybe I'll make you scream again."

Morgana was already headed out the door. As we stepped out, she dropped the car out of her spatial storage.

As we hopped in, the motel owner came out the door, clutching her coat and shaking her head.

"Get the fuck out of here," she yelled. She looked around, clearly concerned we'd bring more trouble to her business. As she looked at the car, she paused, confusion spreading across her face.

I was glad she'd come out after Morgana had produced it.

I hopped in the driver's seat before Morgana could. "You're the better shot." I explained, hitting it into gear and peeling out of the snowy motel parking lot.

We needed to get moving.

It was about five minutes before two big, heavy military trucks showed up in my rearview. We were already maxed out on how quickly I could get the car to go. It wasn't built for winter roads.

"Think you can do something about those?" I asked.

Morgana rubbed her hands together and blew a puff of warm breath into them. "It's been a while since I've felt this good. Maybe it's time to have a little old school fun."

I cocked an eyebrow, wondering what she meant by that, but she was already cracking her window and throwing half her body out as she pulled out an axe as long as my forearm from her cleavage.

With two hands, she hurled the axe with all of her supernatural speed. The weapon spun like a buzz saw and went straight through the first truck's driver side window.

When the shattering glass cleared, I saw the driver impaled to his seat.

The passenger was stretched over the middle console, trying to keep the truck steady as it swerved off the road and rolled into the ditch.

"Guess those windshields aren't vampire-thrown axe rated," I joked as she pulled herself back into her seat with a smug smile.

"Guns are good for a lot of things, but if I'm honest, not many people are ready for an actual blade."

"Not when you throw like that." I wondered if I needed to start keeping a few in my own spatial artifact. I was curious to see just how hard I could throw a blade like that.

I checked the rearview. The second truck was pulling off to help the first rather than pursue us. But I couldn't help but notice them yelling into their radios as they did so.

More trouble was going to come our way.

I went through a few switchbacks with no issue, waiting for when we'd turn and find company. It was the last stretch where the

Austrian border came up when it finally happened. Military vehicles blockaded the road, and I could see several cherubs and angels among them.

"So, that's a problem," I said dryly. If we could see them, they certainly could see our black and neon green racing car. I slowed the car, waiting to hear how she wanted to handle it.

Morgana was already pulling her signature two blades out and strapping them to her thighs. "Get out of the car."

I did so in a hurry, and it disappeared once again.

I was glad her spatial abilities were back at full strength, and I found myself wishing Scarlett had had some larger arsenal items for the force we were about to go up against.

The beast rose up in my gut from seeing those arrayed out before me. They had become a challenge for it to stomp.

"Push right on through?" I suggested.

"As messily as possible," Morgana confirmed, twirled her blades menacingly.

Ducking my head down, I charged forward, wrapping myself in golden scales and packing on mass. I waited until we got closer to finish my shift, taking my spatial artifact and clutching it tightly in one hand, lest I lose it.

Suddenly, I was a several-ton dragon charging the blockade.

If there was ever a question on what would win between a car and a dragon, I made it pretty clear that a dragon wins.

I impaled the first car with my horns and used it as a shield as I rammed my way through the blockade. I only lifted my head to wash the surroundings in dragon fire.

The night lit up with my flames. Men and cherubs screamed as they were set on fire.

The two angels lifted off the ground, saving themselves from the fire, but not from the angry drow vampire that launched herself off my back.

She took the first one by surprise, riding the angel to the ground with two swords in his chest. Then she rolled under me as a painful lance of celestial magic hit my back.

I scooped her up and continued charging through, using the car still stuck on my horns like a football helmet.

Despite my best attempts, the wings tucked into my side had still accrued enough damage that I wasn't sure if flying was in my best interest, especially if there was an angel pursuing me.

"Morgana, we need a better exit plan," I said, before tossing her on my back.

"Working on it." She rode my back like a surfboard for a moment before leaping back into action against the remaining angel.

It was messy, but we were breaking through the blockade. I kept pushing through, unable to see what was coming next, but focusing on using pure brute force to make a mess of the blockade.

Suddenly, my neck jarred as I hit a barrier. I twisted and slammed my shoulders into the glowing barrier that took up the rest of the road.

Four men wearing familiar looking tabards and silver swords stood before me. They were all chanting with crystal rosaries in their hands.

Shaking the stars out of my vision and tossing the car off my horns, I squared up against the templars that had finally shown themselves.

"Pleasure to meet you, Monsieur Dragon." The first templar had a thick French accent that frankly made him sound like a pompous ass.

It was also possible he was one. The smug smile and waxed mustache weren't helping.

"The order of the templars insists you remain in Austria. A gold dragon should be an implement of justice, used and ridden by those who serve justice." He lifted his sword as it gave off a faint white glow.

Ridden? Excuse me, no man rode this dragon. Hot drow vampires? Yeah, they could ride me all day.

I took in his sword, deciding to fight fire with fire. I shifted back into my eight-foot-tall dragon knight form and pulled out my own silver sword from the spatial artifact.

Instead of the soft white glow theirs gave off, mine roared to life with a white flame.

"It seems that you are mistaken about who is in the right here." A smug grin plastered itself across my face at their reactions.

"Impossible," another spat, lifting his rosary and forming a barrier behind me.

"Calm down. It must be a trick. No monster stands in the right," another calmed them all down.

They leveled their swords at me with a renewed purpose. They were all zealots lost in their cause, and that single-minded focus only made them more dangerous.

Attacking, they came at me with strength and speed that no human should have.

I sent out a burst of fire, pushing all but one back as our swords clashed. I was able to overpower him, pushing him back.

Crushing his own sword to his chest, I cut him deeply. I was satisfied until I saw magic seep out of the tabard. His wound healed before my eyes.

Morgana came up behind me. "Careful. Templars are trained from a young age and are given enchanted items to hunt monsters. Unlike angels, their actions are far less restricted, not to mention that they fight like maniacs."

"Morgana. Interesting to see you here." The Frenchman recognized her. "I thought we had a truce."

"Sorry, I left something behind on the celestial plane. I had to go retrieve it," she mocked him.

"Interesting friends you have now. Since you broke the truce with The Church first, I must apologize, but we'll stop you here." The Frenchman pointed his sword at her.

One templar stepped back, and they raised their rosary. I instantly sensed the magic barriers that became erected around us, containing us with them. These were weaker, but they had needed to stop a charging dragon then. Now they just needed to contain me.

The Frenchman charged at Morgana. Their blades sparked while the two remaining templars focused on me.

I was pleased that they considered me more of a threat than Morgana, although I wasn't positive a gold dragon was more terrifying than the vampire that had once invaded heaven.

The two templars came at me from both sides, and I was forced to use my fire breath to push back one while I used my sword on the other.

But they fought recklessly, trained to kill and maim, not survive. The one that I had burned ran straight through the flames, even as his face burned with red bubbling welts.

I cringed. It was a level of blind commitment I hoped I never felt.

Pulling my sword away from counteracting the other templar, I kicked backward, catching the burning templar in the knee. His knee buckled and bent the wrong way, even as his sword cut along my back. He smiled like it was a win, even as his knee crackled with healing energies.

I rolled into the templar I was fighting to lessen the blow, but I still ended up with a solid gash on my back.

Morgana had described them as maniacs, and she was spot on.

The templar I had rolled into let go of his sword with one hand and socked me in the face.

I once again went back to my tried-and-true way of combating multiple enemies, letting fire spread out from my mouth, cooking his arm up to the shoulder in response.

Even after his broken knee, the other templar still managed to limp towards me, skin starting to peel away from his face where he'd had the unfortunate encounter with my flames.

I rolled off the other templar and shifted into my dragon form, using my bulk to catch both of them off guard and knock them back. That second was all I needed to lock my jaws around the templar on the ground and tear him in two.

Cooked-Face still cut me along my side, his magical sword doing far more damage than I expected, but I could now focus on him. I whipped my tail around, growling as it got caught in the barrier and lost its momentum.

Another heavy blow hit my side.

I moved again, once again hitting the barrier. I swore it hadn't been there a second ago.

Looking over, I realized that the remaining templar was erecting additional barriers against my dragon form, making my already unwieldy body difficult to maneuver.

Bullets pinged off my scales as the blockage we had cleared regrouped to fight.

Frustration bubbled up inside of my gut, and I slammed my horns forward, shattering the next barrier and unleashing a gout of flame. I caught the templar making barriers, making him stop to put out the fire.

I swung around, finally able to move, using my tail to crush the spine of Cooked-Face.

"Morgana, finish up," I growled.

She was locked in a high-speed battle with the Frenchman. I could tell that he was on another level from the three I was fighting.

My mouth opened wide, and I finished the barrier maker before I ground

Cooked-Face into the ground with my back foot.

We needed to get moving, and with his skill, we didn't have the time to take down the Frenchmen before the rest of the cavalry could back him.

Barreling forward into the Frenchmen, Morgana got the message, and the two of them separated for a moment as I passed. Morgana caught my extended right wing and swung herself onto my back before I launched myself off the side of the road and beat my wings with everything I could manage.

Thankfully, they caught enough wind that I didn't go crashing down into the snow. I lifted up into the snowy night sky. I could fly, and thankfully, no angels were rising off the road to greet me, because my battered wings didn't look up to evasive maneuvers.

"They won't stop there," Morgana reminded me.

As if to confirm, helicopter blades sounded behind us.

"Shit." Even before my wings were banged up, I was only slightly faster than them.

We needed a faster way out of here and I could only think of one other thing. "Morgana, just how fast can that car go?"

"One eighty, maybe two hundred. It would be a long way to out race those helicopters. Not to mention the switchbacks will get us."

"But what about the button?"

"Oh, hell no." Morgana shook her head.

But from where I was flying, I could see a long straight away on the highway. We didn't have to make it all the way back to Sentarshaden, just escape the helicopters.

Already, I was angling back down towards the road. Thankfully, the Church's blockade had cleared the road.

We landed, and Morgana whipped the car out of her spatial pocket.

I was shifting and getting into the front seat, still buck naked. I turned the keys, and the car came to life. There was no time to waste.

The engine roared as I slammed the pedal down to the floor and the back swerved before the tires caught and ripped me forward.

Morgana looked scared and was buckling her own seatbelt. "This thing is going to punch when you press that."

That only made me want to push it more. My seatbelt clicked, and I slammed my fist down on the big red button.

It felt like a giant had cupped my back and was picking me up. The street blurred and my face pulled back as my jowls were pressed back by the force of us shooting forward.

Fire lit up the night behind us that brought a whole new meaning to burning rubber.

"Mooorrrgaaannnaaa." The word stretched out as I tried to talk. "What the fuck is happening?"

"Hold on," she said, short and clipped.

It felt like I was dough being extruded out into spaghetti. My whole body felt like it was being warped and stretched before I finally snapped back together.

We had not only tore straight through that straight away, but somehow just made over an hour's progress on the highway.

"Why the fuck would anyone put that in a street racing car?" I screamed. It would have plowed straight through a dozen blocks.

"It's magic. It works on intention." Morgana pinched her cheeks. "Now, let's get the fuck out of here."

CHAPTER 12

M y wings rippled in the air as I continued to soar above the clouds, ducking into them anytime a plane came into
sight. The last thing I needed was to be spotted and have a thousand pictures circling
the internet.

We had needed to ditch the car after it had
puttered out fifteen minutes after using the
magical nitro. By puttered out, I mean the
actual engine block tore itself apart. However, we had been far enough ahead, so I
had shifted and flown into the night, hiding
among the clouds.

I was fairly sure we had ditched the
Church's forces.

Morgana rode on my back as I headed for
Lucerne so that we could take the train into
Sentarshaden. I only got lost once and had
to land to use our phones to get us back on
track. GPS didn't work so well miles up in
the sky.

"Damn templars did work on you," Morgana said as she finished stapling my side.

She hung from my claws, which I kept steady as I beat my wings. She'd been working on patching me up while we traveled in case I needed my strength for another fight. I was healing quickly, but those staples would speed things along for the two large cuts the templars had landed on me.

I was surprised at how little a cut several feet long bothered me as a dragon. But I guess it wasn't so bad, given my sheer size.

"Those swords go right through my scales," I growled.

"Yeah, the celestials arm the humans well. I suppose it lets them have humans do a lot of their dirty work without having to come down here themselves," Morgana agreed. "So, any chance you have a plan for when we get to Sentarshaden?"

"A rough one? I need to warn the Highaen Family. Jadelyn is friendly enough with the daughter, Tyrande, so I'm hoping she can give them the warning." I paused. That was about as far as I'd gotten.

Morgana finished patching me up, so I hoisted her up to my back again.

She made herself at home behind my horns, using them as a windbreak. "If they know she's part of the Highaen family, then they are going to come prepared. Even if she's well protected, a full-grown dragon will help their cause too much for them to ignore it. They could bring through many angels."

I snorted at the sound of me being worth less than another dragon. The beast agreed.

"Calm down. No one knows what you really are, including us. Like I said before, I think you are some sort of dragon king. The fact that you can change colors is unique, and nothing I've ever heard before," Morgana mused. "And it was pretty impressive that you were able to grow your wings from just a few dragon bones."

I almost nodded, then remembered I had a passenger. "They called to my beast. I don't know. Is one dragon eating another common?"

"Who knows? Most of dragon culture is lost or hidden. You'd have to meet the Bronze King and ask him."

I sighed internally. "I have a feeling that'll happen sooner rather than later."

The way things were going, I was going to be outed soon. I kept having to use my abilities more and more publicly.

Morgana stroked the top of my head. "The templars will keep your nature a secret, at least for now. It gives them the advantage of getting to you before any of the groups that would want to protect you get involved. But knowing you travel with me, it's only a matter of time before they put things together and know your life story."

I wrinkled my nose in distaste. I was sure everything about me was for sale somewhere on the internet. "Well, at least I don't have any family they can go after. I'll just have to stay safe. When we are back in Philly, the Scalewrights will become a nice shield."

"Yes, Rupert will be so happy to learn that you're a gold dragon," Morgana laughed.

I smiled, basking in the sound of her laugh. We might be in a bit of a mess, but having her back and healthy was well worth it.

"Let's focus on the near term. How do I get into Sentarshaden without showing everyone I'm a dragon?"

"I suggest we take the train in. If you land outside the city, you can shift back and get dressed. We'll take a cab to a train stop first thing in the morning."

I almost asked why take the cab when we had a car, but I realized the red sporty car did not blend in. We needed something that would gather no attention.

Tilting my wings, I continued to glide over Switzerland through the clouds, heading towards Lucerne.

***

I back-winged a landing behind a barn outside the city. Snow went flying everywhere, like a small snowstorm around me.

My landing startled more than a few goats, and a dog at the farmhouse started barking up a storm.

"Quick." I shifted back and held out my hand for my spatial artifact.

Morgana smirked, handing it back to me. "Still funny that you are carrying around the padding for my bra. Do I need to lock up my panties?"

I ignored her, quickly trying to get my clothes on in the snowy field. Meanwhile, Morgana was putting on her amulet to look more human.

A light went on in the farmhouse. The dog's bark had alerted the family. That was our signal to get the heck out of here.

Putting my coat on, I pushed Morgana forward. She took the hint, leading the way through the snow and out onto the street before anyone noticed us.

We hoofed it for several miles before a taxi pulled up.

"Morgana?" the man asked, peering out his window.

Him knowing her name surprised me, but then I realized she must have used an app to call the ride.

"Yes, we'd like a ride into the city."

"May I ask what you are doing out here without a ride?" The driver looked at the two of us skeptically as we waited, not answering his question. But finally he shook his head. "Get in. You'll freeze to death out there."

"Thank you," I said, opening the door for my newest mate and piling in behind her.

We both did our best to pretend to be cold as he drove us back to the Lucerne train station, but neither of us were really affected by the cold.

Riding all the way to the train station in silence, Morgana paid the taxi driver handsomely for his help, and we hopped through the false wall in the train station just as the sun rose into the sky for a new day.

"Finally, I can take this off." Morgana slid the amulet off her neck and back into her bra, showing off her blue skin once again.

I let my dragon eyes out, enjoying the release of not having to hide them. I looked around, feeling a little anxious being out in the open while we waited on the platform.

"How will the templars get their people to the city if they are going after Yev?" I asked, wondering if there were other routes besides the train.

"Not all at once," Morgana answered. "I'd imagine that, if one of these trains filled up with cherubs or templars, it would go somewhere and never be seen again. You don't fuck with the Highaen."

"How'd they survive the seventeenth century?" I wondered.

"They held their ground after gathering every high elf in Europe. And it didn't hurt that T kept the Church pretty distracted in Switzerland." Morgana went quiet, picking at a nail.

I nudged her. "Not going to spill the secret on T?"

"Not mine to tell. But everyone was scared of him. No one will touch him as long as he stays under wraps, and he's minded his own business. After all of it, he left Europe quickly and never came back," Morgana explained. "It would be like poking a sleeping bear to mess with T now."

Understanding that she wasn't going to tell me what he had done, I dropped it and waited patiently on the platform. My dragon eyes scanned the platform, but I didn't see any sign of the Church.

Then again, I'd have to wait until after we warned Tyrande to do anything, lest I had a run in with whatever served as the local law enforcement. It would be a pain to get arrested trying to protect Yev, which was why we'd need to bring them in on what we knew, and likely my secret too.

"So…" Morgana hesitated. "What do we tell your other mates when we get back?"

"That I did what I went after you to do," I said casually. The idea of having multiple women was just part of my life, and they each knew that. I was growing to accept it as well.

Morgana scratched the back of her neck, for once looking quite nervous.

Thankfully, the train pulled up a moment later, saving Morgana from having to talk about it more.

She might have been comfortable killing people and teasing me, but apparently the idea of joining a dragon's harem was harder for her to handle.

I was glad nobody identified Morgana, letting us make our way quietly onto the train. I even noticed another drow waiting on the platform, taking in the similarities with Morgana's skin and build.

I was starting to understand why all the noise from being a celebrity got to Jadelyn. It was nice to travel without all the hubbub.

We jumped on the train and made our way to Sentarshaden.

***

As we stepped off the train, back in Sentarshaden, having lost our ride we had to snag a taxi.

The security guards eyed us clearly wary of the taxi, but once they saw me, they waved us in after talking into their mics.

Scarlett and Jadelyn were already coming out the door as we came up into the circle drive.

"How did it go?" Jadelyn asked anxiously as we got out.

"Well, Morgana seems to be in wonderful health now," I spoke for the both of us.

Jadelyn grabbed Morgana in a big hug that left the feisty woman at a loss for what to do. After a few moments, Morgana wrapped her arms around Jadelyn, returning the hug.

"Thank you," Morgana said.

"You're welcome. Anything for a... sister wife?" Jadelyn struggled with what to call Morgana.

"That sounds so... like the same sort of people that would marry their cousins." Scarlett made a face. "Is there a dragon term for this?"

I raised my hands in surrender. "How am I supposed to know?"

"I'm sure he'll collect us and forget about us like his hoard, won't he?" Jadelyn hit a dramatic pose.

"Never." I scooped up my siren mate, carrying her inside. "You can all be dragon wives or mates. Does that sound better?"

"Dragon wives," Jadelyn spoke the words, trying them out for herself. "I like it. It makes me sound fierce."

"You are as fierce as a newborn kitten," Scarlett commented, following along behind us.

"Hey! Remember that magic duel I did not too long ago?"

Morgana coughed into her hand. "The one where there was an attempt on your life, and your entire guard group nearly shit themselves? That one?"

Jadelyn puffed out her cheeks, still stubbornly clinging to it as a counterpoint to her lack of ferocity. I carried her into the kitchen and planted her on a bar stool before kissing her.

"I like you just the way you are. But we can't stay here for too long. We learned some things while we were out adventuring through the templar headquarters." I started into the story.

Several times, I had to stop and clarify a few points for the girls, but when I got to the point of Morgana's tree, her nails dug into my arm.

I paused, looking down into her anxious eyes. I knew she was protective of it, but we had to keep things open in our family. We couldn't keep secrets from each other.

"Morgana, they will keep your secret."

"But root trees are—"

Jadelyn interrupted her. "Can we pick it up and have it planted in one of my homes? Or we can just buy out whatever this town is, and I can have my family build a fortress around it."

Of course she'd jump to solving it that way.

"The templars won't sell that site for all the money in the world," I told her. "Somehow, Morgana's root tree is serving as an anchor for a portal to the celestial plane."

"Oh." Jadelyn's mouth made a large circle. "Yeah, they won't sell that. It also makes quite the pickle, doesn't it?"

"We ended up leaving the portal. I guess technically I took one of the dragon bones attached to it, but I don't think that did much."

I trailed off, wondering how to add the next bit. "The other thing you two should know is that the portal is what we believe gives Morgana her unique magic."

Jadelyn and Scarlett nodded along as if that made complete sense.

"So, then, how did you guys get out?" Scarlett asked.

I went through the rest of the story. Jadelyn winced several times when I talked about the fights. When I got to where we had to run out of the motel, Scarlett held up her hand and stopped me again.

"Why did they know you were there?" she asked, the grin on her face saying she had a strong leading theory. "I mean, you were just hiding in a motel room, right? Certainly nothing happened?"

I didn't think her grin could grow any wider at that point.

"Shut it," Morgana snapped.

I rolled my eyes, knowing what I said was about to lead to more teasing. "We may have gotten carried away."

"Ha!" Scarlett grinned. "Who was on top?"

"Me, of course," Morgana said proudly.

"Damn it, Zach," Scarlett grumbled as she rummaged in her pockets.

Jadelyn held out her hand in the universal sign of 'pay me'. "I knew she'd ride the dragon her first time."

"It's so big though!" Scarlett shook her head.

Morgana leaned forward conspiratorially. "Massive. Hurt so much at first."

"You get used to it. Sort of," Scarlett agreed.

"Enough," I said, feeling awkward at that moment that was quickly descending into talk of my dick.

I went back into the story of our escape, covering off on the rest of the time in Austria and our trip back to Sentarshaden.

"So we have two big issues. One, the templars are coming for Yev, and that's my fault. Two, the templars will probably come for Morgana and me sooner or later."

"Well, Tyrande will come over again tonight. She and Yev have been spending the evenings here after the Tredelas ceremonies," Jadelyn said simply. "We'll tell them about what you've found."

"Jade, will it be that simple?" I wondered if they'd even believe the story.

"You are my mate," Jadelyn said proudly. "Trust me. Your words will carry a new weight."

I nodded, knowing she was probably right. The Scalewrights were an enormous power in the paranormal world. My words would at least be considered.

"Okay, then tonight we'll tell Tyrande and Yev. I also want no backlash on Morgana," I said, worried for my newest mate to meet the high elves knowing there was tension between the two.

"Won't be a problem," Morgana said. "I'm hated, not hunted."

"That and she'd never do something like that in my house," Jadelyn confirmed.

Scarlett seemed less than pleased with Jadelyn's comfort. "If the templars are coming for him and Yev, then we'll need to run through the safety drills again tonight. Now that Morgana's part of the team, she can help too."

"What am I getting roped into?" Morgana asked as she was starting to get more comfortable in Jadelyn's home. She walked around, opening cabinets and looking around inside.

"Safety drills. Anything I can help you find?" Jadelyn asked, eager to help.

"Do you happen to have any blood?" Morgana asked. "I've been drinking the same kind for far too long, and I'd like a little something different."

"Um, I think we have some in the cooler downstairs." Jadelyn hopped off her barstool and ran to grab some.

I'd expected her to be thrown off by that request, but I should have guessed that blood was a standard drink for some paranormals their family would entertain.

Jadelyn popped back up a minute later with a dark red wine bottle. The bottom of the bottle had a blood drop sticker on it. I tucked that away in my mind in order to not make a mistake later.

"Oh, that's quite a nice one. Virginal women 1863," Morgana said, taking the bottle.

"Wait, really?" I said, leaning over to get a look at the label.

The rest of the room laughed at me.

"No, idiot. Virgins taste terrible," Morgana said. "This is an Italian vampire company, 1976. Probably decent."

"Ah." How was I supposed to know how blood wine vintages worked? "Got a favorite year or place?"

"Nope," Morgana said swiftly. "I've been drinking champagned cherub for over two hundred years to keep everything at bay. I'll still drink it, but damn, is it nice to have something else for a change."

She pulled the cork out deftly with a knife and drank straight from the bottle. When she paused, she let out a drawn-out sigh. "That hits the spot."

"I'll make sure to have more of it on hand." Jadelyn smiled. "You should send me some of the cherub wine, too. I'll keep it stocked here and in Philly."

Morgana almost seemed uncomfortable with how quickly Jadelyn was assimilating into her life. I'd felt the same, which made it even more amusing to watch happen to Morgana.

"Where's the fur ball?" Morgana asked, looking around as if she were half expecting Kelly to pop out any second.

"Um, not here right now." Scarlett looked uncomfortable, catching my attention.

"What's up?" I asked.

"I'm not quite sure. She seemed mad when you weren't here today and stormed out. Said something about an appointment?" Scarlett winced.

I put it together pretty quickly. I'd said I'd be there to support her at the fertility clinics. I'd been so lost in all the chaos that I had forgot this would be the day of her appointment.

Pulling out my phone, I started to text Kelly and stopped.

Instead, I started calling the only three fertility clinics in the city, asking as a dumb husband when my appointments were.

The first told me in an apologetic tone that I'd missed my appointment and that my wife hadn't looked too happy. The second told me that the appointment was in just a few minutes and my wife was already there.

"I'll have one of my men drive you." Scarlett was already putting down her phone, no doubt texting them.

"Thanks. I told her I'd help her with the fertility clinic visits."

"Just be back for dinner," Jadelyn said. "Tyrande and Yev should be here when you get back."

I kissed my three mates in turn. The beast was extremely satisfied. It even paused at Scarlett, considering if she should be marked too.

Something for later, beasty, we need to hurry.

After the goodbyes, I headed off to find Kelly. I was the one that had put her in this position, and I wanted to help her get through it.

CHAPTER 13

I pulled up to North Root Healthcare and darted inside, finding suite 202.

As I opened the door, I found Kelly grumpily sitting in a chair. She looked pissed, arms crossed, her legs tight together and a cute little frown on her face.

"Kelly?" an attendant asked from the other side of the room before I could get her attention.

When she got up to follow the attendant, I strode quickly across the room and caught the door, following behind her.

She looked over her shoulder and then did a double take, blinking several times. "Zach?"

"Sorry I missed the first one. I just got back. I'd like to be here now if you still want me here."

The smile that spread across her face was priceless. "Yes! Thanks."

"Oh, you must be the man," the attendant greeted me. "Here, both of you wait in room five here. The doctor will be in shortly."

She closed the door behind us. It felt all rather familiar, the same as any doctor I would have seen before I had become part of the paranormal world.

"I didn't think you'd make it," Kelly said, sitting down in one of the two chairs that weren't the awkward patient seat. Neither of us really wanted to sit there.

"I told you I would. Morgana and I just got held up a bit. So, what are we doing?" I let her take the lead.

"You'll need this." She pulled a sample cup out of her bag.

I was about to correct her when I realized it had already been filled. "That's disgusting. Did you just hand me a cup of semen?"

"Grow up. Just do me a favor and pretend it's yours. It's from a beta back home."

At least the cup was clean.

There was a knock on the door. That thankfully pulled my attention away from the cup as I set it on the counter.

"Come in!" Kelly said, seeming happy that I didn't have any more time to rethink the cup of semen.

A tiny lady about two feet tall floated in on pixy wings and landed on the counter beside us, washing her hands as she spoke. "What can I do for you two today?"

I did my best to keep my jaw from dropping. It was all so casual; it took me by surprise seeing the little pixie doctor.

"We are interested in options. There's a problem in our pack, and I was wondering if it would be possible to get a beta to be fertile." Kelly gave the doctor her best smile.

"Interesting." The pixy noticed the sample cup next to me and opened a drawer, pulling out a brown paper bag. "Put that in there. I'll have someone take a look at it. We don't get requests from werewolves; their pack normally takes care of everything."

I stuffed the cup in the bag, glad to be rid of it.

"It's a unique situation," Kelly hedged. "Generally speaking, what kind of options are we looking at?"

"Why don't we get this started, and then we'll have some more definitive answers after I run through some of the scenarios?" The pixy picked up the brown paper bag and fluttered out of the room for a minute before returning.

"Now, scenarios. I'm not sure there's much, or really any, literature on the nature of beta male reproduction. But there's likely either little or no viable sperm in the betas. Which means your options come down to the problem itself. We'll need to determine why the sperm isn't viable. If there's no motility, then we can fix that with some medical intervention. If there is some deficiency in them, we can fix that. The biggest struggle will be if there aren't any sperm at all."

"Then what was that?" I gestured toward the door and the jar she had taken away.

"Semen is more than just sperm. That could just be a mixture of other parts of the secretions. If there's no sperm at all, we'll have to figure out another solution. There are drugs we'd have to test on werewolves for the right dosages that could help," the Pixy doctor explained.

Kelly let out a heavy sigh. "With our metabolisms, that's going to be a rough process, isn't it?"

Thinking about how much she had to drink to even hold on to a buzz, I suddenly understood why that might be a problem. They would have to take an unholy amount of any drug to correct the problem.

"We have a lot of options to explore here. I am optimistic we can figure this out." The doc came over and patted Kelly on the shoulder.

Kelly sagged a bit. I knew it was weighing on her that her pack may not be able to have children. They would likely do everything they could to remove her as alpha if that were the case.

A knock at the door made the pixie flutter across the room. When she opened it, an orc in scrubs handed the doc a sheet of paper.

"That was quick! Let's see..." She trailed off, hiding herself behind the piece of paper as she read it. Then she turned to us. "I'm afraid I have hard news."

"What's the damage, doc?" I asked.

"I'm afraid to say that there are zero sperm in your semen." She gave me a pitying look that would have withered my balls if it were really my problem.

I felt for the beta men. That was rough.

"So, meds are our best approach," Kelly said. "Do you know of any para meds that might help?"

But the pixy shook her head. "No, sadly, this sort of deficiency in humans is because of a structural issue or severe hormone imbalance. It's a symptom of a larger problem. We can try to fix it as if it is a hormone imbalance, but we'll need to schedule some blood work."

She finally sat down at the computer and started typing by banging her fists into the standard sized keyboard. Apparently, there weren't pixie-sized keyboards, or the clinic didn't splurge on them.

"I'll just be a few minutes typing this up. You can schedule a blood work up with the front desk," she commented before going back to hurriedly pounding the keys.

Grabbing Kelly's hand, I led her out of the office. "Was that about the same as the first one?"

"Yeah. The second one too. I was kind of hoping all three of the guys wouldn't be complete duds."

I frowned. I hadn't realized she'd had three different betas checked out. The pattern was hard to ignore. "Then we'll keep trying. Maybe go see a wizard about a fertility spell? Something must exist."

She considered it. "They probably use an alchemist of some sort."

I paused, turning to Kelly as she sparked an idea. "Kelly, we happen to know the craziest alchemist and his daughter." I was nearly brimming with excitement for her. Surely T or H could help us.

"Wait, you want to use Morgana's friend to try and solve this?"

"Why not?" I pressed her. If the answer was an alchemist, we knew some of the best in the world.

Kelly sighed. "Sure, but I'm not sure what sort of crazy concoction they'll brew up."

When we exited the office after most definitely not signing up for blood work, Jadelyn's driver was still waiting in the parking lot. I walked up and waved before getting in the back.

"Could you go to this address?" I held my phone up and dropped a pin in the street behind Grendal's Grog. It was about where H had taken me.

"Sure, buckle up. That's not far." The driver pulled out.

"Are you sure she'll help?" Kelly asked skeptically. I understood her hesitation, but I knew H would at least hear us out.

And if she didn't agree, I'd see if Morgana could get her to help us. Morgana may not be besties with Kelly, but I was fairly sure she'd help keep the entire pack from falling apart.

Deciding to get ahead of any problems with H, I pulled out my phone and gave Morgana a call. "Hey, Morgy. I'm going to visit H. Is there a safe word I need or a favor she owes you that I can call in to get her to help Kelly?"

"What does Kelly need from her?" Morgana asked, sounding a little annoyed at my use of 'Morgy'.

I looked at Kelly, but she shook her head. "Sorry, you'll have to talk to Kelly about that one."

Morgana sighed, but answered me. "Just don't startle her. Tell her I sent you," Morgana said. "Oh, and don't drink anything in her house, ever."

"Roger." I didn't have any intention of drinking anything she served me after she had managed to slip that truth serum into my drink at the bar.

Morgana hung up on me, and I put my phone in my pocket as the driver came to a stop.

"This the place?"

Looked right. "Yep, thank you."

We both got out of the car.

"I'll be around the corner. Come over when you want to head back."

I almost argued, but I knew he was operating off of Scarlett's rules. There was no sense in trying to break them.

Checking the door again, I was trying to remember if it was the right place. I hadn't been paying as much attention, my mind had been focused on what I'd say when I saw Morgana again last time I'd been here.

Finally deciding it seemed right, I stepped forward and knocked on the door.

But nobody answered.

"H, open up. Morgy needs a favor," I said, knocking again.

The lock clicked and H peeked out the door at me. "What does she need?"

"Can we come in?"

"No."

"Please, it's important." I pressed up against the door and pushed.

H offered little resistance and grudgingly let me in. "Fine, just come in, I guess. Morgy told me not to mess with you."

"Of course, she's my mate." I smiled back.

H nearly choked. "Mate?"

"Yeah, we resolved some things on our trip."

She grumbled something before speaking up, "I can't even imagine Morgana letting a guy touch her. But she was surprisingly amenable to you last time." She looked me up and down. "She's better? What does she need?"

"Yeah, we got to her tree and got her all healed up. Thanks for all you did to protect her up until then." I gave her a nod of thanks. A hug seemed like far too much for H.

"And in terms of the need, it's more of a favor for a friend. This is Kelly." I pulled her through the doorway; she'd been hesitating outside.

"I mean you no harm." Kelly held her hands up. "Alchemists are terrifying."

H smiled, seeming to like Kelly more after that. "So, what do you need?" she clarified.

"My friend here, and likely future mate, is the world's first female alpha of a wolf shifter pack." I said it with a heaping of pride as I pushed her forward and clapped my hands on her shoulders. "But that causes a gigantic problem with her pack's fertility. If all the males are betas, none of them can have kids. We went to a fertility clinic with some samples, and they all turned up a big fat zero for sperm count."

H gave a sympathetic hiss. "So her pack is doomed to be barren."

"Yeah, unless we can find something to get her betas locked and loaded. And that's where you come in, or I can ask your father when I go back to the states."

"My father won't help anyone," H said with certainty.

"He gave me your location. I think I get along with T pretty well." I did my best to keep a friendly smile on my face. Sure, it might cost me a few nail clippings or locks of hair, but T would do it.

"Right. First Morgana, and now you're telling me you won over that crotchety old fossil?" H snorted, but she made her way back to the kitchen where it looked like several herb bundles were freshly hung to dry. Cabinets were left open, letting the hanging herbs dry in the open air.

There were so many scents in the air that it was overwhelming, making my eyes water.

"He likes me, but that's another story." I pushed forward with the issue at hand. "What do you think about the werewolf beta issue?"

"There are a few problems." H picked up a handful of fresh herbs off the table and wrapped them in twine before moving to hang them. "First, you'll need something to kick up the libido and boost the swimmers. That's pretty easy. Old wizards have been using it for ages."

"Great," I encouraged her, only for her to give me a sad smile.

"But." She emphasized the word. "There's not a recipe for werewolves, and they are notoriously hard to drug with their regeneration."

"So we give them a shit ton," Kelly said, re-joining the conversation with a little edge of desperation in her voice. "Trust me, these guys will chug a gallon of anything that you tell them makes them an alpha in the bed-room."

H paused, blinking several times. "First, eww. Second, it isn't that simple. It needs to be more potent, not more quantity."

She fumbled around in her kitchen for more herbs, gathering them in bundles. "And I know what you're going to ask next, but making it more potent is also going to make it much more expensive. The options to make it potent are pricey. Most alchemi-cal recipes can be upgraded through higher quality material substitutes."

"Okay, so what do we need?" I was getting impatient.

"I mean, the recipe is simple. You use the semen of another creature for reference, some dryad leaves for life, crushed oyster shells, some fugu, maybe a few other in-gredients for an extra kick. Crushed Viagra works well."

A laugh escaped me, and I earned an un-amused look.

"Modern medicine goes great in alchemy, too. The problem is that there aren't many upgraded agents for what I described. We should be able to get some really old dryad leaves, but on their own, it won't do much. I don't know of any paranormal upgrade agent for fugu or Viagra. That really just leaves the semen."

H shook her head in disbelief at what she was about to say. "To really get the potency you need, you'd need the strongest kick out there: dragon semen. Which means you're screwed. That stuff is worth several times its weight in gold. There are less than ten living dragon males in the world. Fuck, they even suspect that the stuff extends lifespan."

She started getting lost in thought. "People have been watching the Bronze King's wives, and a lot of them aren't aging. Which has started a bunch of gossip and has made what little stuff there is on the market go way up in price. I mean, to extend life! Do you have any idea how amazing it is... the alchemical properties required for such a feat..."

H started speaking faster as she got lost in her work, describing the suspected alchemical properties of dragon semen.

I traded an awkward look with Kelly as we both came to the same conclusion. I tried to jump in, but H just continued talking.

Finally, I had an opening. "Look, I know it's expensive, but if we could get you dragon semen, would you be able to do it?" I asked.

She stopped and stared at me like I was an idiot. "It would be a real waste to use it to let some beta wolves have kids. You'd be paying out the wazoo for the entire pack."

"I'm married to the Scalewrights. Money isn't the issue," I lied. "How much do you need?"

H snapped her jaw shut and stared at me. "Enough for the pack?"

I could see the gears turning in her head as she tried to think through how much she'd need and how much she wanted.

"A liter. That would get you nearly a barrel of the potion. Is that enough for the wolves? They'd only need a few drops." She licked her lips, and I knew she was already calculating what else she could do with a bit of the dragon semen that would likely not make its way into the barrel.

"How much would be left over for your personal use?" I asked.

"Only a little. There'd be no need for payment either." Her eyes were lighting up now. She was at least excited about the prospect.

"Deal. We'll get it to you... soon." I didn't like the idea of being milked for this, but it was for a good cause, and I owed Kelly. I had made her the leader because I believed in her, and I needed to help her keep that position.

And I was sure my women could help make the process of getting it enjoyable.

H held out her hand. "Gimme your phone and I'll put my number in."

I handed it to her, and she quickly put her number in, texting herself for my number.

"I can see how you won over my father if you are willing to go to such extremes," she said, handing my phone back.

Shrugging, I took it back. "My mates and my friends mean the world to me. There's little I wouldn't do for them."

"Tell Morgy she should come by soon."

"You could always come over. We are staying in the city for a little longer," I offered.

She looked uncertain. I had a feeling she enjoyed staying in her safe houses as much as she could. "I'll think about it."

I nodded, not wanting to push too much. "Well, if you do, we are at the Scalewright home here in the city." I texted her the address.

Kelly came up to H and grabbed her hands. "Thank you so much for helping my pack. I thought I had failed them by becoming their alpha."

"Don't thank me yet. You are going to be hard pressed to get that much dragon semen. Even if you can afford it." H dropped Kelly's hands.

Kelly nodded, doing a poor job at a poker face to hide her confidence and excitement. "Don't worry. Zach will get it done. He has a way with things."

I felt a blush on my face at how sincerely she had said those words before I pulled Kelly away and out the door.

We walked a few doors down before Kelly spoke. "Well, it seems you are going to have to get to work. After all, you caused this whole mess."

"You don't need to push me. I'm happy to help, but I'll need a hand for a whole liter."

"I'd suck you off until my jaw cracks. Maybe even keep going after."

Giving her a side glance, I smirked. "Is that a promise?"

Kelly did a double take. "Excuse me?"

"A pack's alpha needs to provide for her pack, right? This is the least you could do," I teased her.

She stopped in the middle of the sidewalk. "Stop fucking with me."

She frowned, but I could see the vulnerability in her eyes.

"I told you that once I figured out Morgana, there would be capacity for me to think about other things, including us," I said clearly. "Morgana is figured out, for the most part, and I'm not blind."

Kelly paused, looking at me for a moment, before a small smile spread across her face and a flicker of hope lit in her eyes.

"I mean, you are still my alpha." She stepped up, running a hand along my chest, waiting to see what I did.

Stepping forward, I pushed into her touch. "I'm not your alpha," I growled.

"If you say so. Then what do we call you? Master?" She toyed with my shirt, looking up at me seductively.

A sigh slipped out of my lips.

Kelly was a werewolf, creatures that drew very specific lines in their relationships. They were either dominant or submissive. Even within the pack, there was an established pecking order.

Despite how aggressive she was to her pack, she considered me her alpha.

"Fine, you can call me alpha, but just in private. You have an image to keep. I'd hate to take away your thunder as the world's first female alpha."

"A girl needs a break from being the boss every now and then," she said as we turned the corner.

The driver was outside his black SUV, leaning against the door. As soon as he spotted us, he stood up straight and did a small sweep of the car before letting us in. I had to admit, having a personal driver didn't suck.

"Where to?"

"Back home for the day," I said, finding it strange to call one of Jadelyn's houses my home. But in reality, anywhere my women were would be home to me. And it was time to face what I'd done to Yev.

CHAPTER 14

As we walked up to Jadelyn's front door, Kelly let go of my arm, but she still walked with a bit of a bounce. I wasn't sure if it was the good news on her pack's fertility, our moment, or a little bit of both.

"Zach, welcome back," Jadelyn greeted me as soon as I turned the corner into the kitchen area.

Tyrande and Yev were there along with Morgana, Scarlett, and Jadelyn. All of them except Jadelyn were lounging in the area just off the kitchen.

Meanwhile, Jadelyn was pulling dishes out of the oven. "Just in time for some of the food. How did your trip go?"

"Everything turned out well." Kelly beat me to the punch. "The problems are all fixable, and we have what we need to help."

"Did... my friend... come through?" Morgana stuttered as she realized we had guests, and her friend was in hiding.

"Don't be like that," Tyrande said, leaning back on the couch. "It isn't like we don't know Hestia is in the city. We're leaving her alone if she leaves us alone. Her father has been quiet in the States; no one wants to do anything to rile him up or give him reason to come back."

There was an air of tension between Morgana and Tyrande. I realized they didn't play well together.

"Hestia was able to help with the problem. We just need to gather some ingredients for her." I used H's name now that I finally knew it.

I laughed to myself. Hestia. What a perfect name for a crazed elven alchemist.

"Your husband has an interesting group of friends," Tyrande addressed Jadelyn.

"Mates," I clarified.

That made the high elf pause. "Mates? You're sharing him?" she asked Jadelyn.

"Yes. It's made my life quite lively; I wouldn't trade it for the world. Now, Zach, can you help me get some plates out for our guests?" Jadelyn continued to host as if there was no problem, but the tension in the room was growing thicker with Tyrande's judgment.

"Is there going to be an issue between you and Morgana?" I asked her.

"No. But it is kind of like eating with the boogeyman," she said, eyeing Morgana.

"I'm not a monster. We came here for Tredelas like every other elf. I just happen to have a second aspect to me." Morgana crossed her arms and got up to help herself to more blood. "Besides, your family owes much of your survival to T and myself."

Tyrande clenched her jaw. "We do."

Her admission surprised everyone, and the room went silent.

"But that's why we don't do anything to Hestia, nor will we do anything to you. Both out of respect for your strength and because some of the Highaen family do realize what you've done," Tyrande admitted, even though it looked like she was pulling her own teeth.

"Well! That went better than expected." Kelly said, breaking the tension.

"Yes, now that we got that over with," Scarlett pushed the conversation forward. "Do we want to talk about what you found at the templar base?"

"Templar base?" Yev perked up.

I put the plates down and started gathering silverware to put with them. "We went on a little exploration into Austria. I went into a templar base and poked the nest a little bit."

Both of the Highaen girls were looking at me as if I had two heads. "Why would you do that?"

"My own business." I made it about me rather than Morgana. "I run a small mercenary business and there was a job."

I looked up at them. "But I did get additional intel I think you'll be interested in. They are planning their raid to get Yev now that they know she's a dragon." I dropped the news like a bomb.

Tyrande leaned back and laughed. "Good fucking luck. No one is touching Yev in Sentarshaden."

"Sister, this is serious," Yev tried to reason with Tyrande.

"You can't actually be worried, can you? Here, under Sentarshaden's shade, no harm is going to come to you. No one would dare pick a fight with the Highaen here." She turned to her sister, her voice full of sincere confidence.

She really thought that they were untouchable here in the city.

Yev looked around, seeming to want to pull her sister to the side. But then she looked up at me. "You said you run a mercenary company, and that you were able to go into and out of a templar base? Did you fight any?"

"Four templars, three angels, a shit ton of cherubs." I ticked off my fingers, shrugging like it was a normal day. "Oh, and I took down two helicopters."

I got an angry glare from Jadelyn. "You shouldn't put yourself in so much danger," she said.

Yev turned back to Tyrande. "I love our family, but I don't think you fully respect the risk their zealotry poses. They wouldn't care about angering the Highaen family."

"She's right," Morgana agreed. "As someone who's fought them plenty, they are like rabid dogs. The threat of your family isn't enough to keep Yev safe. Dragons are rare now, and they need them for their plans."

Tyrande glanced around for someone to support her, but all she found were more concerned faces. "Then what do you suggest, given you've fought them so much?" she asked Morgana.

"You could hunker down, but then they'll always be out there, looming over you. It'll eat at you. Baiting them and being ready for it is a much better approach," Morgana suggested.

"I will not use my sister as bait." Tyrande's voice rose in challenge.

Yev put a hand on her shoulder. "I'm interested in this bait strategy. Not only for the templars but for others that would come after me now that it is known that I'm a dragon."

Tyrande slumped back onto the couch.

"Well, it is pretty self-explanatory. The trick is doing it in such a way that they bite. Groups like this look for patterns in your schedule to plan and set up an attack. So, you need to limit your schedule to one or two repeating tasks so that you can control what they will choose. The trap then gets laid around those two tasks."

"Like coming over here every night for the last few nights?" Yev asked.

"Yes, like that, but I'd rather we didn't make Jadelyn's home the trap." I wasn't about to let my mate's home become a dangerous place for her.

"We won't," Yev was quick to agree. "But that sounds like a plan. You and Morgana are a mercenary company? What are your rates?"

Morgana rubbed her hands together, a vampiric grin spreading across her face, but I interrupted her.

"We'll do it as a favor."

"Excuse me?" Morgana turned, her eyebrows high on her face.

"If you'd like, I'll pay you." I rolled my eyes. She had plenty of money, and we could use some additional allies.

And Yev didn't realize it yet, but we had the same enemies and threat. I was happy to get a chance to weaken their forces.

"No. I'm not going to take your money." Morgana rolled her eyes. "Your precious pile of gold is safe from me."

"A favor for the Highaen family is worth quite a bit," Jadelyn reminded Morgana, not that it did much good.

"Why would you do this?" Tyrande asked me.

"Because I don't like the templars or what they stand for," I told her. "We'll do this for an opportunity to take a shot at the templars. It's not like I'm on their favorite people list at the moment, anyway."

I switched into tactical mode. "We'll need you two to plan out Yev's next two weeks. Pick one or two places that you'll repeatedly go that are low security, like a favorite coffee shop."

"I don't like coffee," Yev said.

I paused. Who didn't like coffee, or at least the caffeine boost? "That's fine. It doesn't have to be a coffee shop, just something like that."

"We could go to the magic range every other day," Tyrande suggested.

I wanted desperately to ask what that was, but I decided to save that question for later. I had a close enough guess. It sounded like a shooting range, but for magic.

"Would be an easy place for them to come in armed too," Morgana agreed with the idea. "We'll be there at the same time, and I'd suggest quietly stationing Highaen men in the surrounding buildings. The other key is to make sure you do not let them have another option as to where they would attack when we aren't ready."

When Yev didn't say anything, Morgana reemphasized the point. "This all falls apart if they try to nab you outside the trap. No deviations."

"Got it. We'll make up a plan for the next two weeks. What do we do about common places like my home?" Yev asked.

"Does it already have its own security?" Morgana asked.

"Full Highaen security; we both live there," Tyrande clarified.

I nodded, thinking about Jadelyn's level of security. If a full templar and angel contingent came, I wasn't sure their security would be able to do much. But they would at least be able to stall them. And I trusted that Scarlett had plans in place that made that level of protection work for Jadelyn.

"Scar, would you do us a favor and double check their security teams?" I knew she'd spot any flaws.

She wrinkled her nose at the idea, but she nodded. "I can do that. But I doubt they'll love the idea of showing me all their protocols."

"We'll make sure it happens." Yev was starting to seem agitated with all the talk of an impending attack.

"Don't worry, we're on the job. Waiting will suck, but you are in good hands with me and Morgana."

Yev stopped fidgeting, growling back at me. "I'm not some helpless girl. I'm a dragon. Fighting them head on is what I want to do, not hide."

"What's it like being a dragon?" I asked suddenly.

She shrugged. "It's like secretly being enormous and aggressive, but having to hide yourself in polite society all the time."

I nodded. I understood what she was saying. It was nice to know I wasn't the only one with an inner beast.

My mates did a good job of helping me release a lot of the emotions I kept bottled up inside. I realized that might be one of the big reasons for dragons to have harems. They helped tame all of our energy.

"Let's move onto happier topics." Jadelyn inserted herself into the conversation. "Dinner is going to get cold if we talk much longer about this. Come on, everybody, get your food!"

There was a grudging agreement to drop the dark topic of Yev being hunted, even though many of us had entered a work mindset.

"These meatballs are amazing," Kelly said, happily popping one into her mouth straight from the serving dish.

"Thank you." Jadelyn's eyes pressed into thin lines with her broad smile.

I walked over and squeezed her into my side, giving her a kiss on the forehead before I jumped in to grab some food.

As we all sat around the table, we settled into lighter topics, ignoring the templar challenges for the moment.

***

After the sisters left, we found ourselves with a new problem. We had to divide up the bedrooms.

"I'm not sleeping in the same bed as her." Kelly pointed a wild finger at Morgana.

"Bite me." Morgana crossed her arms. "Have you even formally become a mate?"

"My bites hurt, blue bitch. Careful what you wish for," Kelly bit back, but she softened as she turned to me, wanting my input.

I wanted nothing to do with this argument, but I knew I'd play this role with the multiple women in my life. They'd need me as a mediator. "We share a bed. It's not too late to back out if that's a problem."

Kelly looked like I'd slapped her, and I wished I'd softened it a bit.

But then she just smiled and nodded. "Got it, alpha."

She headed off to get ready for bed.

"What about me?" Morgana joked.

I grabbed her, pulling her head to the side, and bit her neck possessively. "Mine," I growled.

Her skin pebbled with goosebumps under my fingers.

I knew it would take Morgana a bit to get used to a serious relationship, but I wasn't about to let her put up any walls. She'd spent years pushing people away, and I was determined to tie her down and make sure she understood that there wasn't any running from this dragon.

"Are we starting already?" Jadelyn asked with a smile as she leaned on the door frame in a sheer silk negligee.

I took her in hungrily, and the look on my face seemed to spur Morgana to go get ready for bed.

Scarlett was off somewhere in the house. After refreshing Jadelyn on her drills, she had disappeared to talk to the rest of the staff. Given the impending attack, we were on high alert.

That left just Jadelyn and me as I scooped her up and closed the bedroom door behind us.

She wrapped her arms around my neck and clung to me as she stared into my eyes.

"How's my big, strong dragon? Everyone is worried about a dozen other things, but someone needs to look after you." She kissed my cheek.

My heart melted. Jadelyn was soft in a way that I desperately needed. She could politically maneuver and negotiate like I'd never seen, but her heart was what had truly endeared her to me.

"Scared," I said honestly. "Scared of the change I know is coming. My secret is going to be out. And I wasn't entirely sure what that would look like before, but now, seeing Yev go through it, I do. I'm not sure I want that."

"No one likes change. Though we aren't human, we have that in common with humanity." She patted the bed next to her, and I realized I'd started pacing.

"Come here," she said. "Lie down and let me take care of you."

I walked over and lay down with my head in her lap, and she immediately started running her hands through my hair.

"It'll all be okay." Jadelyn sang a note that made my head light, as if it almost scattered the worries. Her hand softly traced my temples.

I groaned, pressing the back of my head into her thighs. "I thought you were going to take care of me another way," I mumbled, still lost in the relaxation.

Jadelyn kissed the tip of my nose. "We might later, but you are too stressed. I can see it. I'm in tune with you, my dragon. What else is on your mind?"

"You, Scar, Morgana, and now even Kelly. I'm changing all of your lives. Putting you all in danger."

"A gold dragon is significant," Jadelyn reminded me. "We all know that global winds will shift around what you do. That we are all here means we have accepted it. What else can I say to help you understand that?"

Jadelyn kissed my forehead, leaving a small cool spot. Then she let her fingers trail down the side of my neck. They pressed into my collar, finding two spots that, when massaged, did amazing things for the tension in my shoulders.

"It's my fault that Yev is being targeted," I said, turning to putty under Jadelyn's touches.

"You offered to protect her for free. It sounds to me like you are doing everything you can to make it up to her. And maybe it wasn't you? She thought it was some old dragon. If her senses are right, that doesn't sound like you." Jadelyn quickly put yet another one of my worries to bed as her fingers kneaded my shoulders and down my arms.

The beast wanted to rise up and nuzzle Jadelyn to death. It was so content. I hadn't realized how much I had needed this.

"Shh," Jadelyn shushed me. "Don't think too much. We'll work through all of this as a family. You know, I've never met the Bronze King before. I'm kind of excited to go on that adventure with you once you're outed. Plus, I desperately want to be able to brag to everybody that my husband is a gold dragon."

I chuckled. "And silver. Who knows, maybe there's more I can be."

"The Pendragon." Morgana stepped back into the room, wearing nothing but a leather corset that impossibly cupped her breasts. "The king of the dragon tribe. We will explore that together."

"What did you say?" Kelly came in after her.

There was something about their posture. They stood too far apart and almost leaned away from each other. I sighed, the stress starting to return at the idea of them bickering.

But Jadelyn spoke softly, a not-so-subtle threat was clear in her tone, "You two cut it out. I don't care if you bicker, but for both of you to be part of this family, you need to work together. Most importantly"—she paused to look between the two of them—"you do not bring more stress upon our dragon."

"I—" Kelly started.

Morgana was smart enough to stay silent.

"No." Jadelyn's tone was cold. "You'll end up somewhere dead in a ditch if you keep fighting. Both of you. I'll have no one who causes ripples in our family. Is that understood?"

I paused for a moment. I'd never seen Jadelyn be so terrifying.

Even Morgana was pausing to consider her. "Understood. There needs to be rules and order if this is supposed to work. Zach isn't the kind to grind us all under the heel of his boot into happy, submissive wives. We need to police ourselves."

"Kind of like a pack among his wives," Kelly interpreted it herself.

"If that's how you best see it then, yes." Jadelyn had stopped massaging me. "Now come to bed. I think our dragon needs rest more than he does excitement."

"I could use—" But one look from Jadelyn told me not to fight her.

Scarlett strolled in and took one look at Jadelyn, pausing. "Who pissed her off? That's a royally bad idea."

"Hush, you, get in bed," I told Scarlett.

"Yes, sir." She snapped a salute and practically bailed out of her clothes as she bound across the room and dove into what was becoming a pile of women around me.

CHAPTER 15

I was the last to wake up the next morning. I reached over, finding cold sheets next to me.

Apparently, Jadelyn had been right; I had needed the sleep.

Rolling out of bed, I got dressed. As I was rustling around, getting my clothes on, Jadelyn bumped the door open with her hip, holding a breakfast tray.

"Good. I was wondering when you were going to wake up." She smiled brightly at me. "Eat in here or out in the kitchen?"

"I'd like to join all of you for breakfast," I replied, and she turned back around.

Once I had finished getting dressed, I followed after her.

The girls were lounging around, enjoying their own form of breakfast. Morgana and Scarlett were bonding while cleaning knives and guns, while Kelly manned the waffle maker.

Jadelyn was whipping about the room, preparing everything else needed for a lovely breakfast. She had put the tray for me on the counter.

Walking in and seeing Morgana and Scarlett spending time together, even if it was over ammunition, warmed my heart. When I'd met Morgana, she had had employees, but she hadn't had real friends. I knew it was hard for her to get close to people, and I was proud of her for trying.

"Morning, sleepy head," Kelly said, checking the waffle iron.

"It is sort of odd seeing you all act so domestic," I replied.

She rolled her eyes. "I'm still a girl. And for the most part, I live a normal life. Or at least, I did before I started trying to woo a dragon." Kelly winked at me. "Although I guess this is far more domestic than that." She pointed a fork at the two cleaning guns.

Morgana looked up from her current project. "This is very domestic if you work as a mercenary."

"Or security guard," Scarlett piped up.

"What about me?" Jadelyn asked.

I smiled, grabbing her and pulling her over. "You are the glue that holds all of us together. You're essential."

Seeing her satisfied smile, I kissed her forehead and wandered over to the counter. My stomach had woken up with all the amazing smells. A dragon had to eat.

I started in on my breakfast. The plate was filled with strawberry waffles with bananas and some chocolate chips on the side to mix in. And I smothered it in enough syrup to fill the little cups of the waffle grid, as life intended. I ran my fork along the top, distributing the sugary goodness across the waffle before grabbing my first bite.

As the first bite melted in my mouth, I moaned, going to take another before I had even swallowed.

I worked to make sure each bite had just the right amount of syrup. I realized just how much my life had become about balance. There was the need to balance the amount of time and love and intimacy I had with each of my women. I was sure I'd get it wrong sometimes, but I was dedicated to making this life with them work.

"Thank you for the waffles; this is fantastic," I said, after devouring a few bites.

Kelly perked up at that. "Thank you."

"You two want to bring your projects over here?" I wanted us to all sit together, like one family.

Jadelyn snapped to attention, moving to grab some hand towels. She got them down on the counter before the other two could lay their oily weapons all over her white marble countertop.

After I got up, I kissed Morgana and Scarlett on the lips. I got a little buzz as I kissed Morgana, which only made the feeling of

Scarlett's fluffy tails even more enjoyable. I found myself a bit distracted as Kelly jumped in.

"So, what's the plan for today?" she asked, amusement in her voice.

"Tyrande already sent over a schedule for the week." Jadelyn laid her phone down on the counter for us all to see. "I've forwarded it to all of you, but today will be their first day at the magic range."

"They must be eager to get the trap set." I speared a banana on top of my next piece. "We'll go and mess around at the range ourselves?"

"That's the plan," Morgana agreed. "It's a good time to play with magic, too. I'm hoping we might be able to have you harness your own."

"I'm more worried about learning to fight in the air," I said. "Angels are going to be in play when they come."

My mates paused.

Scarlett gave me a concerned gaze. "But that would mean you intend to shift into a dragon at some point. Expose your secret?"

Letting out a heavy sigh, I nodded. I'd been slowly accepting that the time was coming. It wouldn't be long before I was pushed to show more people my secret as attacks kept coming. I'd do anything to keep my women safe. And I still owed Yev an explanation. I hoped she'd keep my secret, but who knew what she would do in the heat of the moment.

The world was soon going to know that there was a gold dragon in town.

"Hush. There's something about the Bronze King." Kelly pointed to the TV, which had been running in the background.

A hauntingly beautiful woman in what looked like a belly dancer outfit stood before a podium loaded up with microphones. She looked mostly human, but a snake tail wound around the side of the podium, telling me that there was more to her.

Her eyes were covered with a thin white cloth as she spoke into the microphone. "The Bronze King will hold a press conference next week in response to the new dragon in Sentarshaden. It is his intent to protect all dragon kind, and it saddened him to see the world's response as this new dragon has become known to the world. He is planning several announcements."

She lifted herself away from the microphones, even as camera flashes bombarded her. I wasn't surprised when she slithered away on a snake tail rather than walked.

"What was that?" I asked.

"Gorgon," Morgana said quickly. "She's one of the Bronze King's women." She went back to cleaning her weapons, not interested. "I love it. The cocky bastard sends someone to tell the world he's going to open his fat trap a week in advance."

I turned, surprised at her apparent distaste for the Bronze King. "Not a fan?"

"He's old, cocky, and suddenly a concern for me." Her eyes roved up and down my body. "You are an anomaly. I'm not sure how he'll react."

"Anomaly?" Kelly asked.

I realized she didn't know all of my secrets.

"I'm not just a gold dragon. If I want to, I can shift into a silver dragon, too."

"Oh. That's... odd," Kelly stumbled over what to say. It didn't sound like it concerned her, though.

"When we get back, I'll look through my library with you," Morgana promised. "But the Bronze King is a problem for another day. Today, we focus on saving the green hussy and setting a trap for the templars. And to do that, I agree that you should get training and experience fighting in your dragon form."

"How? It isn't like he can just dragon up somewhere and fly around." Kelly poked at the next waffle to see if it was done. "He'd need a massive space that was protected from onlookers."

"Up in the Highaen tree is about the only place he could practice without being seen, but that means we'd have to let Tyrande in on the secret," Jadelyn pondered.

I remembered that, when we had arrived, I had seen sparks of something large and magical flying up in the boughs of the massive tree. Morgana could make spaces, and she had made the Atrium and expanded the space in her bar, but I thought making a space big enough for me to fly would be out of her ability.

"Maybe Yev has a place she can fly?" I suggested. Once again, I knew we'd need to tell them the truth to use it, but I'd planned on apologizing at some point, anyway.

"We'll figure out something for you, even if I have to go buy a small country for you to play in." Jadelyn patted my hand reassuringly, but the idea of her buying a small country did not put me at ease.

"Maybe we'll hold off on the small country. Save that as a backup," I joked.

When my secret came out, it would be nice to not spend so much time trying to remain hidden. Heck, I could even fly us back to Philly.

Thinking about Philly, I changed the subject. "How are we going to manage living arrangements when we get back to Philly? Do I need to get a bigger place?"

The girls all looked at me, then at each other as silent questions flitted between them.

"Jadelyn has some obvious advantages," Kelly said slowly. "But I'm not sure you should live with her parents given the...

noise level... you can bring out in each of us."

Morgana snorted. "I think his apartment next to mine in the Atrium has obvious advantages."

"Too small," Scarlett voiced her opinion. "We can't bring him into the sorority house, and I don't see us all waiting a year."

Morgana set down a reassembled gun. "I can make his space larger and connect it anywhere we want. I'm back at full strength. That means there's little I can't or won't do to make all of this more comfortable for him."

The idea of upgrading my place in Morgana's magically constructed space was certainly appealing.

"Just how big could you make it? Could I fly around?" I asked hopefully but knew it was unlikely.

The whole group paused and turned to Morgana.

"I haven't tried something that big. But that was when I was conserving myself. At the very least, it would take me weeks to make." She tapped at her lips. "I think it is unlikely to be enough space to practice much more than flying in circles."

Figured. I'd been hopeful that we had a quick fix. But at least we had options for our home in Philly.

"I like the idea of connecting that space to Scar and Jade's sorority room, and another connection to Kelly's choice of home, either the bunker or her dorm room."

"You put it in the bunker and a bunch of bitches are going to be wandering into your bedroom at night," Kelly warned me. "Which reminds me." She looked at the other girls. "Hestia can make a potion for my betas to get fertile and frisky with their bitches, but she needs dragon semen to make it."

Scarlett burst out in laughter. "We have buckets of it on demand."

"I am not some fire hose," I grumbled.

"Big enough," Morgana said, and they all agreed while Kelly stared at me wide-eyed.

"Holy shit, you're that big?"

I held my hands up in surrender. "No, they are exaggerating." She'd seen me naked, but I didn't think she'd seen me at full staff.

"Only slightly," Jadelyn sighed. "You should have seen how worn-out Scar was getting when she was trying to satisfy him alone."

All this talk was making my cheeks burn, so I focused on the news for a break. The word 'templar' caught my attention on the ticker as it just scrolled past, and I grabbed the remote to turn up the volume.

"The long-standing truce of the Knights Templar was formally broken today, as iron-clad evidence of them capturing shifters in Germany has surfaced."

"Well, Tracey, it's a sad day for the paranormal world. We all often worry about being hunted, and to see the Knights Templar returning to medieval scare tactics is a disappointment," the other anchor threw in his opinion.

Given what I'd seen in Austria, I thought it was unlikely that they had stopped hunting paranormals. But it seemed like they were becoming less concerned about hiding it.

Things were heating up, and I was concerned about bringing women I loved into the fire. But as I scanned the room, I knew that none of my women were weak-hearted.

Jadelyn might be the weakest in a direct confrontation, but she had her own strengths and a heavy hand to play should someone come after her or any of us.

Morgana was a legendary fighter, centuries old, with more experience than anyone I knew in combat.

Scarlett ran what was likely the world's finest security services.

And Kelly was the first female alpha werewolf. She still had room to grow, but having seen her father, I knew she'd be a force to be reckoned with.

I shouldn't question if these girls were going to get hurt, but who would get hurt trying to take them out.

"Seems like the templars were already on the move before we poked the hornet's nest," Morgana said, pointing at the TV. "There's no way that wasn't planned a week ago."

I nodded, thinking about what she's said. "Do you think they knew about Yev before she transformed?"

It was odd they'd be able to assemble and move so quickly. Getting the gear and the people ready to hunt a dragon was likely a several week operation, and they were already prepped to go when we'd entered their base the day after her reveal. Something seemed off.

"Either way, it doesn't change our next steps. Gear up, and let's head over to this magic range." I finished my waffle, only for Kelly to put another on my plate.

"You are a growing dragon from everything I understand. You need to eat." Kelly smirked.

Folding it over, I bit viciously into the side of the waffle as I stood up. "I'll eat on the way."

I was stubborn like that.

***

When they had said magic range, I'd expected some secret, out-of-the-way building in the corner of the city.

But I was dead wrong.

Right off a busy street, the massive building stood with big, red storefront letters.

"Ace's Range for wands and magic," I read it aloud as we walked up.

"You can shoot guns too. Magic and wands have a higher rating for the building, though," Scarlett said, pushing open the door for our group.

Jadelyn went in ahead of me once Scarlett had stepped inside and checked it first. Scarlett had argued against her coming, but Jadelyn had been firm that being with me and Morgana was one of the safest places she could be.

Scarlett had eventually bent under her relentless pressure.

Jadelyn bounced through the door and up to the counter. "We'd like…" Her eyes scanned the board behind the counter. "A private blasting room for seven."

"'Fraid I'm all out," the lady said with a tired shrug.

"Maybe Tyrande beat us to it," I added. "We're here to shoot with Tyrande."

"Sure you are," the clerk chuckled. "Let me check here. Yep, they're not here."

She did not, in fact, check anything.

Jadelyn held up a finger for everyone to wait and put the phone to her ear. "Tyrande, we're here. Can we join you in your room? Uh, huh. Come out, they don't believe my mate."

The lady at the counter raised a skeptical eyebrow, but we waited for about thirty seconds before Tyrande herself came out. At that, the clerk raised her hands in surrender and let us through without issue. She knew when she was beat—Jadelyn had that effect on people

"Glad you guys could make it today. Yev has some steam to burn off." Tyrande gave a nervous chuckle. "Hope you guys aren't skittish."

She led us down the narrow hall and opened door number two.

As soon as she did, an explosion went off in the room and air rushed out to greet us like a punch in the face.

Tyrande wasn't worried though; she just smiled a crooked smile.

Yev was standing inside, a sheen of sweat clinging to her as she stood there, arm outstretched, palm facing down range.

"Oh. You guys made it," she said, turning around to greet us.

I looked around. The range was split into two areas. There was a lounging area, complete with some drinks sitting in a bucket of ice and a few untouched appetizers. Then right next to the lounging area was a platform, standing over what looked like a blasting chamber.

Beyond the platform was a ten-foot-deep bowl and a thirty-yard range. Magical constructs were being reconstructed before our eyes as a display in the lounging area read out some numbers from Yev's latest blast.

"This is pretty cool," I said, stepping over to see the numbers. It calculated both her penetration and her overall power in numbers. "What's the measurement?"

"In grams of TNT. Or rather, the explosive equivalent," Tyrande explained.

"So she just put out a blast equal to twenty thousand grams of TNT?" That was a solid blast.

"That would be like a stack of TNT the size of your torso." Morgana helped me visualize what level of bomb she was packing.

Surprisingly, my plastic explosives experience had been limited despite working as a mercenary. Morgana often went in guns blazing. But I could imagine the damage of an explosive that size.

"Want to give it a try?" Tyrande asked our group.

"Sure." Jadelyn stepped up, eager to show off. On the platform, she tapped on the screen. When she finished, a large werewolf appeared down in the blast chamber.

"Hey! Why are we shooting werewolves?" Kelly disagreed with the target, crossing her arms in protest.

Jadelyn gave her a sheepish smile. "Sorry, it's the default."

Kelly grumbled something about being the 'default' paranormal.

But Jadelyn continued on, walking up to the edge of the platform. As she walked, she sang, her voice picking up and carrying itself into the air.

It was a harsh, lilting tune before she bent sharply at the waist and screamed. Ripples filled the air in front of her as the scream had an almost visible quality to it as it launched at the target.

As her scream rang out, I found myself on edge but also immensely curious to see what she could do.

I watched as the werewolf down below took the brunt of her siren ability. The magical construct exploded as if it had been hit by a truck going eighty.

Jadelyn turned with a smile on her face and a few beads of sweat running down the side of her cheek. "How'd I do?"

I looked at the data. "Four thousand grams of TNT. Good job, babe."

She still frowned. It wasn't nearly what Yev had done, but she was trying to compare herself with the raw fire power of a dragon.

"That's amazing for a siren's scream," Tyrande said, clapping. "We can't all compare to Yev here. She blows me out of the water too."

"Let's see it," I encouraged her, hoping she'd be more comparable to Jadelyn and make her feel better.

Tyrande took the challenge, jumping up on the platform.

"Highaen are masters of frost magic. It's based on the environment around their tree," Morgana said as I watched Tyrande.

Her sharp elven features were a mask of concentration as she stood on the platform, staring down at the target below her. She held up one hand. Her magical eyes seemed to swirl with power as mana gathered into a small, blue sphere in her hand.

"Oh, wordless magic," Jadelyn said. "Hard stuff to pull off."

Tyrande shot the little blue ball out into the center of the blasting area, and it exploded into crystalline shards. The shards pierced through the werewolf target.

"How'd she do?" Jadelyn was eager to measure herself.

"Six thousand," Kelly said before I could think of a way to soften the results.

But Jadelyn didn't seem to mind, knowing her limits already.

"That's incredible, Tyrande. Frost magic isn't known for its sheer force," Jadelyn encouraged her friend.

"Thanks. Who else is up?"

Scarlett raised her hands in surrender. "I only have illusion magic. Kelly might be an alpha, but pack magic doesn't do much like this."

"Alpha?" Tyrande looked heavily confused.

"Yep." Kelly perked up. "First female alpha. I've got a lot of shit to figure out, but it's working so far."

"That's freaking awesome!" Yev held her hand up for a high five. "You go, girl."

I was suddenly feeling like I was surrounded by maybe a little too much girl power.

"I'll give it a shot." Morgana stepped up, and we all paid attention.

Morgana was always a bit of a mystery in her abilities. I was just as curious as the others about what she'd show us. She tapped on the screen several times, and not just one target showed up. A dozen heavily armored rhino men popped up.

"It isn't always about raw power," she said.

She swished her hand in the air several times, each of her fingers seeming to catch the fabric of reality. In response, a shower of slashes that made the air blur around them descended on the rhino men.

The dozen rhino men slid as they were each cut at different angles. Their bodies toppled to the floor before the constructs vanished. The read out barely registered any explosive power, but yet the results were plain to see. She was lethal.

"Zach, why don't you give it a try? I want to see what Jadelyn's husband can do." Tyrande turned her attention to me.

The other girls looked over at me too, curious about what I would do.

CHAPTER 16

I glanced around between the women, not quite sure what to do. Technically, I had magic, but besides the innate forms of my dragon breath, shifting, and flight, I hadn't used any real magic.

Scarlett saw my indecision and came to my aid. "He was a lost one until recently. He's never used his magic this way," she reminded them of my recent lost one status.

"What?" Tyrande shouted. "That's a crime! We need to get him to use his first spell then today."

Scarlett was going to jump in again, but I started walking forward onto the platform. I was in a place built for testing magic, with some amazing magic users. I wasn't going to get a better shot to learn. And it might become needed as we went up against the templars.

"Okay, tell me how this all works," I said to the group.

"It's mostly about intent," Morgana started quickly, shifting into her instruction mode. "Words are powerful channels for intent, but you can move beyond words eventually. For now, let's start with the simple 'Envokus' to throw raw elements. The stronger the emotion you channel into the intent, the more powerful the spell."

"The type of emotion makes a difference, too. If you are angry while healing, it will hurt like a bitch." Jadelyn winced from some memory.

"I want to see someone else first." I stepped back.

"Fine, I'll go again." Yev stepped up to the platform and tapped in a code that put a large tank at the bottom of the blasting pit. "Don't worry about mimicking what I say. Dragons have different voice boxes."

Everyone's eyes were on her, and I shifted my eyes to get a better view.

Her throat lit up with magic as she shifted just that part of her to allow her to use dragon magic. She said 'Envokus' but there was a guttural hum below the words that made the hairs on the back of my neck tingle.

From Yev's hand launched a massive, green fireball that hit the tank. It exploded in a deafening boom. The room filled with a green haze that she banished with a deep breath.

"Way to intimidate him." Tyrande rolled her eyes at her sister.

I looked at the readout of the blast, and I realized that she was holding back. It wasn't near as big a blast as the one when we had entered. This one had only registered twelve thousand, nearly half of the first blast.

"Go on. I want to see this." Kelly sat back, popping chips into her mouth as she lounged in the table area.

"Just do your best," Jadelyn encouraged, her smile so wide that it pressed her eyes partially closed. She was ready to brag about me.

I took a moment to process what I had seen Yev do and what I needed to mimic. All in, it seemed simple enough. I was glad I'd been able to talk in my dragon form. Otherwise, copying her would have been impossible. I would have just growled my words.

But I had to admit that I was nervous to try it for the first time in front of all of them. I didn't want to embarrass myself.

I stepped up to the tablet and keyed in a repeat of the last order. The tank appeared again, and I stepped up to the platform. But before I made a move, a hand fell on my shoulder.

I looked over, and Morgana was standing beside me. She gave me the same look she had when we were in her training space, and it brought me back to those moments.

This was simply an exercise, and I could do it. I raised my hand, pointing it at the tank, shifting just my throat.

"Envokus." It came out like a proper dragon.

A bright light formed on my hand and fizzled out.

"You have to put some emotion behind it," Jadelyn encouraged me.

I cursed but prepared to try again, falling deeper into the exercise. I dug around for emotions, and I realized one of my deepest fears was something happening to my mates.

Protectiveness rose up in me and shifted, turning into the cold rage I would feel if anybody ever tried to harm them. I turned those feelings towards the tank, picturing it posing a threat to my women. My instincts homed in on it, focused on destroying the tank.

My emotions blossomed in my chest, and I spoke again, "Envokus."

Blue and red light erupted from my hand. A swirling ball of frost and fire shot at the tank. It hit, and there was a momentary pause. It was like the entire world froze for a second as I waited to see what would happen.

The swirling sphere penetrated the tank, absorbing into its center. For the briefest moment, I thought I'd done something wrong, and the spell had dissipated.

But then the tank expanded. It vaporized from the inside out in an explosion that rocked the blasting chamber.

The explosion was too big, and I realized I was about to be thrown by the blast. Quickly, I braced myself by holding onto the input pad, barely keeping myself from flying off the platform.

I heard the girls' screams behind me, but I could tell they were yells of surprise, not pain.

When the blinding light cleared, I looked back to confirm that they were all unharmed. I noticed a faint shield glowing around their sitting area, along with the cracks in the concrete blasting chamber.

Most of the girls were looking at me in awe, but Yev looked pissed as hell.

She rose out of her seat and charged me, her skin turning an emerald green. She expanded, taking on her dragon form.

I did the only thing I could to react and counter. I shifted as well.

Her fat green ass hit me going full steam just as I finished shifting, and the two of us rolled into the blasting pit.

I wrapped myself around her and latched my jaws on her neck in a move of dominance. But Yev didn't give in, sinking her claws into my side, holding on tight as she twisted her head around to sink her teeth into the back of my neck in return.

We were in a twisty, knotty grid lock of dragons.

"What the fuck are you doing, Yev?" Tyrande rushed the platform.

She said something, but it came out garbled by my neck.

"Zach. Don't kill her," Jadelyn instructed.

"She'll be better off dead than what I'll do to her if she seriously harms Zach." Morgana had her swords out.

Tyrande looked at the drow vampire with more than a little concern. "Yev, cut it out. Talk to us."

I felt her brace for a moment before her jaw unlocked, releasing my neck. I was very aware, though, that her claws were still in my side.

She looked over at her sister. "He's a fucking dragon."

"Yes, Yev. That's pretty clear. Apparently, he's a gold dragon," Tyrande stated the obvious. "I'm fairly certain that means he's even rare among dragons."

I was trying to listen to the conversation, but my beast was raging inside of me. It wanted to take down the other dragon. And I could see that Yev was fighting the same struggle.

"Uh..." Kelly raised her hand. "Is this some sort of dragon mating ritual? Because you'd be cutting me in line."

Of all things, that was what diffused the situation.

"No." Yev practically threw herself off of me, and I rolled to my feet, growling as fire built up in my chest.

"Then what the fuck is wrong?" Tyrande threw an empty bottle that bounced comically off of Yev's snout.

Yev paused "I... I don't know. I just... lost it."

Shifting back into a naked human, I padded up the sloped wall of the blasting chamber. "Now that we are past that initial moment, I think we talk about this like rational people."

I got to the platform and found my shredded jeans. Sighing, I fished my spatial artifact out of my pocket.

"Is that—" Yev looked at the bra padding in my hand.

"My spatial artifact," I interrupted her and stuck my hand inside of it, pulling out a new pair of boxers and jeans. They'd already seen me naked, so I didn't worry about it as I got dressed on the platform.

"Are you going to shift back?" I asked Yev, who hadn't moved from when I had walked away.

"Yeah." She sounded confused, but she shifted back.

Morgana pulled out a loose hospital gown for Yev and tossed it down into the pit.

"Well, that was a surprise," Tyrande tried to clear the air. "Jadelyn, you nabbed yourself a gold dragon. Holy shit." She held her hand up for a high five from my mate.

Jadelyn blushed at the compliment but gave her the high five. "It was the other way around."

With a pair of jeans on, I scooped up Jadelyn and carried her back over to the couch. I put her down, placing myself between her and Yev. My dragon was still not sure if Yev was a threat.

"Touchy," Tyrande commented.

"When a dragon comes at you, it tends to do that." I was still feeling a little prickly. "You need to explain yourself." I turned on Yev, more than a little annoyed.

She crawled out of the blasting range in her hospital gown. "I realized what you were when you cast the spell with your throat shifted. Then I just... lost it."

"I get it was all quite sudden, but I'm afraid this is quite sensitive, so it would be helpful if you could provide more about why you attacked him," Jadelyn pressed.

Tyrande seemed to pick up on what Jadelyn was saying, nudging her sister as she whispered, "You attacked Jadelyn's husband for what he is."

"My husband, who had already agreed to protect you from others who wanted to hunt you for being a dragon," Jadelyn added salt to the wound.

Yev looked like she wanted to bury herself in the sand, but she also perked up at the last sentence, locking eyes with me. "I get now why you'd be willing to help me without knowing me."

"Yes, I want to protect dragons. But I also feel responsible for your predicament. For you shifting in the first place."

"What?" Yev looked confused. "Your dragon is nothing like what had made me shift at the parade."

I froze, processing what she had just said. "But my dragon was acting up. I thought…"

"No." Yev shook her head. "I might have just gotten territorial on you, but now that I am looking, I can sense what you are." Her eyes became slitted dragon eyes as she stared at me. "You are nothing like what hit me during the parade."

I frowned. I was glad that I hadn't been the one to out her, but if it wasn't me, that meant there was a third dragon in the city. And not only that, but it had forced Yev to shift.

Then I realized my dragon must have been responding to whatever it had done to Yev.

"Still feel like jumping me?" I asked.

"No. I'm fine now. Our brief scuffle seems to have put it at ease. That, and it seems to recognize you as an ally now."

"Great." Jadelyn clapped her hands. "So now that this is out in the open, how about you ask her about the other thing?"

I knew what Jadelyn was getting at.

"Other thing?" Tyrande pushed.

"He wants to practice fighting in the air. And get answers to about a million dragon questions. He hasn't met another dragon until now." Jadelyn practically pushed me at Yev.

Yev nodded in understanding. "Like what?"

I had almost too many questions. They jockeyed to come out first and smashed a gridlock in the front of my mind. As a result, the one that came out first might not have been my best first question.

"Do you know any other dragons?"

"Not anymore," she said. The wilted expression on her face told me that she'd lost someone close to her. I could only assume her mother or father.

"I'm sorry for your loss."

She waved it away. "It was years ago, and I'm happy with the Highaen family. My mother was a high elf and a friend of the family."

"We took her in after her parents died," Tyrande added. "Her father was hunted. That's part of why the current situation is so stressful for her."

"Understandable." Jadelyn scooted over me, giving Yev a hug.

Tyrande seemed relieved that Jadelyn had forgiven Yev.

She might not have the firepower of my other mates, but being able to intimidate the rulers of a city with her displeasure was Jadelyn's own superpower.

"We can help you fly. Up in Sentar-shaden, we have a preserve for several powerful creatures. There's a layer of the tree that you can fly freely within; Yev uses it," Tyrande offered.

"That would be nice." It had only been a day since I had last flown, but I was itching to spread my wings again.

"It sucks being grounded all the time, doesn't it?" Yev asked.

I nodded enthusiastically, glad someone understood. "Like an itch you can't scratch," I agreed.

There was another question I needed to ask. "I've been growing rapidly lately. And sometimes, I'm hungry for... uh... paranormals."

"That's normal." Yev's answer relieved me. "We need to eat a ton, and things that use mana are more nourishing. According to my dad, dragons used to fight and eat each other pretty often."

My face must have looked horrified. "Isn't that cannibalism?"

She shrugged. "Wild beasts don't mind eating an enemy. It's nature. Apparently, the best thing for us to grow are other dragons."

Even though I had eaten that one dead dragon bone, I couldn't imagine eating a freshly dead dragon. Even if the bone had progressed my power considerably.

For a moment, my more primal side surged forward and eyed Yev, realizing how much power I could likely get, but I quickly shoved it back down. That wasn't how I planned to get my power.

"That makes sense. Dragons are potent in their own right; it's part of why we are hunted. We can probably boost each other, too."

"It's part of why there are so few dragons," Yev said. "They kept their own numbers under control even back before humans took over everything. Otherwise, dragons would rule the world right now."

Some of the history of dragons that I had learned from the magi at the convention was making a little more sense now if the dragons of old were trying to eat each other.

They had taught humans magic to fight and weaken each other. Ate each other for power.

"So, did you want to eat him to grow stronger?" Jadelyn asked.

"Oh no. He's a whelp. I was surprised and territorial." Yev held her hands up in surrender. "I won't try that again."

I tried not to growl at being called a whelp. She clearly did not recognize the magnitude of that blast I had made.

"Good. I'd hate to have to go to war with the Highaen family." Morgana let that little threat linger out there in case there were any second thoughts.

I realized she was just then putting her knives away. She'd been seriously ready to carve up a dragon. It was her own way of showing love.

"Maybe we should call it a day. This was quite a bit of excitement, and we need to get moving to the next item on the schedule. We'll be back here in two days. We can let the two dragons practice their magic a little then," Tyrande suggested. Her eyes shifted to the damaged blasting chamber. "Maybe we also try not to go overboard. Control is part of magic."

"That blast was pretty intense. I wonder if we worried the front desk," Scarlett added.

While they were saying that, I glanced over at the display to see just how much power I had packed into that spell. Thirty thousand.

A smile crept over my face.

Whelp my ass.

"You girls leave first; we'll follow after." I figured it might help to shoot a few more fireballs. They nodded and headed out.

Jadelyn sagged on the couch after they had exited. "That was scary."

"I had it under control," I tried to reassure her.

"Watching her get her jaws around your neck, I thought my heart was going to give out." Jadelyn shook her head.

"We wouldn't have let that happen." Scarlett moved to her other side and put a hand on her shoulder.

Jadelyn nodded weakly, but she really did look tired, and I didn't like that one bit.

The frustration inside of me was boiling, so I stepped up to the platform to use it. I aimed my hand down range in the blasting chamber.

There weren't any targets setup, but I just wanted some rough practice. So I let the emotion flow out of me. The frustration I was feeling at seeing Jadelyn worried blossomed.

"Envokus. Envokus. Envokus." I shot three large, burning, red fireballs down range.

They each exploded. They were far less impressive than the dual elemental fire ball I'd thrown earlier, but they still packed a punch. I figured they could likely take out a tank.

I sagged after releasing them. Casting the spells had tapped that emotion and worn me out enough that the emotion had lost its edge.

"Careful." Kelly was at my side, grabbing me as I became wobbly on my feet. "You can't just pump out spells endlessly."

"Yeah, you're right. I just wanted to try."

Kelly helped me over to the couch, where after just a moment of sitting down, I was feeling better. Still, I had touched upon my limits.

"Mana is a core part of the spells we use, but drawing on them rapidly like that is both draining on your mana and body," Jadelyn informed me.

"That, and you basically just turned it up to eleven and started pumping out everything." Morgana watched me, knowing exactly what had riled me up. "You need to be careful of your emotions. They may fuel spells, but they can also cause you to wear yourself out when you need your strength. It takes control to master magic."

I nodded, cementing that advice. It was good to have my partner back.

"For now, let's get out of here." Jadelyn stood up and braced her shoulders in a show of strength.

We all got up and headed out, but Kelly stopped just short of the door. She pulled me to the side as the other three let the door close behind them.

"Zach, why am I here?"

"What do you mean?" I frowned at her sudden question. "You're here with us. You came to Sentarshaden to learn about fertility."

She shook out her brown hair. "No. I came to Sentarshaden to chase you. But..."

She looked at the door. The other three had just gone through.

"Look, I'm a badass chick, and I can hold my own against male werewolves. But your women, they are a whole different level. They can take on the Highaen family like it's just a casual day. Morgana does it by being terrifying and Jadelyn does it more subtly, but still. I'm nowhere near them. Scarlett is thankfully a bit more normal, but she was your first. She'll always hold your heart a little differently."

I started to tell her how wonderful she was, but she held up a hand to stop me.

"I'm not trying to have you build up my confidence. I'm great. But I'm also not looking to get attached to a man who is going to put me on the back burner to a bunch of other women. I want to be an equal in this family or nothing." Her voice cracked a little at the end of her statement.

"You're the world's only female alpha. You have heart and protectiveness in spades. You're a badass shifter, and you're mine." I growled the last bit.

I could see Kelly softening, but as she looked up at me, she said, "I'm still just a werewolf. I'm no dragon shifter, and this is the big leagues."

Then it hit me. I realized what had brought up the discussion, shaking my head as I grabbed her and pulled her into my chest. She was comparing herself to my women and then to Yev.

"Mine," was all I growled as I kissed the top of her head.

The beast made himself known long enough to demand we push her up against a wall and claim her, but I held it back. I needed her to believe in us without that.

"You need to stop doubting yourself. This is like a pack. Everyone is going to support each other to balance out everyone's strengths and weaknesses. It will take time to find your place among the rest of the girls, but you have a place."

Kelly chewed her lip. "Normally, the alpha just tells us what our roles are."

"You were the head bitch before you were the alpha. I thought you did a great job of covering for Chad and keeping him in line. Think you can do that for our family?"

"Keep you in line?"

I paused, not loving the idea of it immediately. But as I got stronger, I'd likely need it. Power tended to turn people into assholes.

Someone to help me keep perspective would be useful.

"Something like that. I trust you to be a strong second, keeping me balanced and helping me see all perspectives," I tried to encourage her.

"I can do that." She bobbed her head. "Thank you, alpha."

I still cringed a bit at the term, but it helped her create a structure she was comfortable in, so I just held her a moment longer before we headed out after the others.

CHAPTER 17

"You help Kelly with whatever was bothering her?" Morgana asked as soon as we were back at Jadelyn's place, and we had a moment alone.

"That obvious?" I pulled her aside into one of the unused bedrooms. I sat down in one of the overstuffed chairs.

Morgana made herself at home, draping herself over me. "She was fretting during the confrontation, unsure what to do. You've pulled her out of her pack structure."

"Exactly." I pulled my lovely blue vampire tighter to me, feeling where the hard leather of her corset ended and her soft bosom started as she pressed against me. "I tried to get her to think of this as a pack in terms of how she fit."

"Good. That'll help her." Morgana kissed the side of my neck, the venom in her saliva making me tingle.

I ran my hands down her waist and cupped her ass, pulling her firmly over my growing erection. It was hard not to appreciate her in my lap.

Morgana's ass had very little give. I loved squeezing it in my hands.

She let her fangs trail down my neck and soothed my skin with little succulent kisses. With each touch, she lingered just long enough to make me think she might do a little more than kiss the spot.

Nuzzling her head to the side, I nipped at her pointy ears in revenge for her teasing. Morgana moaned as I caught one ear and let my tongue trace all the way to the tip.

"I knew those would be sensitive," I whispered as I softly blew on the still wet ear.

She shivered in my lap, and her fangs pressed slightly into my skin. They didn't break the skin, but they were getting dangerously close.

The door to the room opened up.

"There you are! Oh." Jadelyn had wide eyes as she took in the two of us. "That's hot. I'll leave you two to it. Come find me when you are done, Zach. And Morgana, if you drain him enough that he needs medical attention... well, we'll just let your imagination take that one."

Jadelyn flashed us both a bright smile and closed the door behind her.

Morgana laughed. "Jadelyn really loves you."

"She does. This whole thing is complex." Having another of my women walk in on me had made me tense up. While they all knew about each other, I just assumed jealousy would come into play and make me get in trouble with them.

Jadelyn had taken me by surprise by being almost turned on.

"Are you okay to continue?" Morgana kissed my neck again, this time running her hands along the back of my neck and shoulders, working to relax me once more.

"Still getting used to this. Sorry I'm tense. I just braced for a negative reaction when she caught us."

Morgana stopped teasing my neck and looked me in the eye. As she leaned back, I found my eyes drawn to her soft chest, which was rising faster at the moment. But I caught myself and returned my eyes to hers.

"It isn't crazy. I definitely never thought I'd be in a dragon's harem, much less a serious relationship. But that's the direction our relationship took, and I'm not going to turn back. Besides, I don't think you'd let me."

"Damn right," I growled, looking at her shoulder where I had marked her. That mark made a smug smile cross my face. "I'd chase you down."

"And each of your women would chase you down too if you tried to run. I'd help them." She gave me a wicked smile.

Running my fingers through her hair, I pulled her in and savored a sweet kiss from her sanguine lips. Goosebumps ran over my skin as every sensation shifted to a deeper sense of bliss.

Her tongue, coated with her venom, invaded my mouth, twisting with my own in a heady bliss that had me crushing her to me, craving more.

"Oh god," I said, breaking the kiss as Morgana pulled off my shirt and trailed kisses down my chest.

My head buzzed pleasantly. I had enough of a mind to lance my fingers in her hair and rub at her ears.

The cool air touched my pelvis as Morgana jerked down my pants and my erection sprang free, pointing to the sky. I suddenly realized what was about to happen, and I wasn't sure I was ready for it.

Morgana hovered over my cock, a little spittle slipping down her lips as she gave me an incredibly wet kiss right on the tip.

Tingling pleasure started at her kiss and spread down my cock in a moment of pure ecstasy.

"That is incredible." I managed to mutter around the bliss coursing through my body. Unable to help myself, I pulled her head forward, wanting more.

Morgana smirked, her tongue coming out and catching my cock. She drew it past her lips, enveloping all of it in a tingling sensation that had me pressing my head into the back of the chair, nearly overwhelmed.

Every crease in her lips and every bump on her tongue came to life; it felt like my entire mind's sensory capacity was taken up by my cock.

The smooth flesh of the back of her throat came next, a slippery silken sheath as she plunged my cock deeper. And throughout all of it, she was running her tongue along the underside, stroking me.

Morgana knew exactly what she was doing as a hum rose from her throat. I had to grip the arms of the chair to keep from jerking too hard. It felt like I was going to blast off the seat with how much tension was building up in my balls.

The effect of her venom was spreading, and my balls tingled delightfully. Every brush of her body against them felt like a wash of pure pleasure.

Morgana sucked hard, drawing herself down on me until I could feel her fangs bump against my pelvis at the base of my cock. The head was wrapped tightly in her throat as she bobbed quickly, tucking her chin and twisting her face slightly, giving me a wonderful friction as I felt my cock twitch and my balls clench tight.

"Morgana, I'm going to cum," I groaned, gripping the chair and pressing myself back into it.

She pushed herself all the way down, and I felt two little pricks before euphoria flooded me, filling me with a high that only redoubled as I unloaded into her throat.

I determined in that moment that this had to be what heaven felt like. I basked in warm bliss while pleasure rode up and down my body. It was one of the most satisfying releases of my life.

Feeling Morgana slide her throat back, my cock twitched, begging to be back inside that warm, blissful sheath. Her tongue dragged along the underside as she moved, sending shivers through me as overstimulation threatened to rear its head.

When she popped off me, the cool air felt especially brisk after her warmth.

"Morgana, if you want to feed that way, you are welcome anytime," I said lazily, feeling boneless in the chair.

"Sweetie, I'll take that whenever I want. Lustful dragon is delicious. Though, I'm only taking a taste." She wiggled out of her leather pants and straddled my lap.

My cock was rising back to attention, pushing into the cleft of her ass.

I could barely move, feeling like jelly, but I managed to put my hands on her hips.

"Now, where were we when we were interrupted at the motel?" She raised her hips, and my cock sprang up just before she slid back down on top of me. "That's right, I was taking dragon riding lessons."

"Better not fall off," I growled. "You could probably use a little more practice."

I was just coming down from the high of her bite. My cock tingled delightfully in her sex as she worked her hips to take it fully.

Morgana let out a pained hiss but continued to stretch herself open on me. "I'll get used to this monster eventually."

Grabbing her hips, I wasn't gentle. I slammed her down onto me.

Her cry was a mix of pleasure and pain. I waited to give her a moment, but the way she wiggled her hips told me that she wanted more. Morgana braced against my shoulders as she worked herself along my rod, eyes closed as grunts picked up with her rhythm.

As much as I loved being ridden by my sexy blue mate, I wanted to be in control this time.

The venom was leaving my head, and my body was once again responding to my brain. Picking her up by her hips, I stayed speared into Morgana as I stood.

She didn't seem to mind as she continued to grind her sex against me, her chest bouncing as her soft breasts smacked my chest.

I pushed Morgana up against the wall, slamming myself to the hilt. As I bottomed out, I waited, holding still for a moment.

Her body froze for a minute before she cracked one eye open, giving me a look, telling me she was waiting for more. I smiled, slamming her back up against the wall more forcefully as I pulled myself in and out of her. She groaned in satisfaction.

Sliding my hands up her waist, I kneaded her chest and pinned her shoulders to the wall as my hips pulled back, sliding my sensitive cock slowly from her folds. Thrusting forward, I slammed into her again.

Her sex squished as it accepted my length eagerly again and again. The wall thumped as the nightstand next to us bounced.

I pounded Morgana against the wall, her lips quirking as she tilted her head back and let her moans follow the pace of my thrusting.

My body moved to a beat, hormones coursing through my body and driving pleasure in every thrust. The tempo picked up as I craved to hear her scream. I continued thrusting, desperate for my own release.

"Yes, harder, harder," she screamed, and I knew the entire house could count my thrusts as I crushed her hips to the wall with each one.

Morgana clung to my head, pressing my face into her chest. Her nails dug into my scalp as she shuddered in release and let out a wail of pleasure. "Don't stop!"

I wasn't planning on it. I savored her slick sex, plunging deeper and feeling my own pleasure slowly inching its way to a peak.

Moving faster, I felt almost dizzy but pushed through it towards the release my body so desperately craved. As I came, I slid Morgana down to the floor, my cock slipping out and dropping its last juice on her stomach.

"Bed," I said, picking her up and tossing her onto the bed.

There was something primevally satisfying about seeing my white seed spilling out of her sex as she lay there in bed.

Morgana knew I was watching and curled seductively on the bed, giving me a small pout and a come-hither curl of her finger. "We aren't done yet, my dragon."

"Not by a long shot." I towered over her and came in from the top, worshiping her lovely breasts as I settled in for our next round.

*****

Jadelyn was putting several decorations back on the shelves as Morgana and I emerged from the bedroom.

"Just tidying up a bit."

I felt a little heat dusting my cheeks as I realized we were the reason for the mess on the bookshelves. They'd been on the wall where I'd been pounding into Morgana.

"Sorry about that."

"New things for everyone." Jadelyn smiled. "I hope that if you ever find a more vigorous lover that my walls make it."

"That's a legitimate concern," Scarlett called out from the kitchen, where she was wearing an apron as she cooked. A little patch of flour clung to her nose, making her look absolutely adorable.

"Yes, well, I guess that's just life with a dragon for a husband." Jadelyn shrugged it off.

I still had a broad grin plastered on my face, and I didn't think it was coming off any time soon. "We learn new things about dragons every day it seems."

"Yes, like how they fight at the drop of a hat," Kelly said as she came back in. "I put the laundry room back together," she told Jadelyn.

"Thanks. Yes, your fighting with Yev was not ideal. But we did get your secret out there, and now you've been invited to fly up in the boughs of Sentarshaden. So all in all, I'd say it was rather productive." She pulled her phone off the counter and showed me a QR code. "Apparently, we just show this at the Highaen estate, and they'll let us take a teleporter up to a private space there."

"Won't they know what I am then?"

"I was told that the whole space has a variety of uses, and no one monitors things up there. Apparently, a few of the rarer species use it too; there are a few phoenixes in the city."

I thought it was an odd place for a phoenix, considering that the Alps were frigidly cold most of the year. But who was I to judge?

I sat down at the bar while Scarlett continued to cook. Kelly joined her, but mostly just stirred and chopped while Scarlett put everything together.

I smiled, happy that Kelly was finding her place.

"Something is bothering me," I told the group. "If I wasn't the one who startled Yev out into her true form, then what was it that I felt?"

"Maybe you were reacting to it as well? Your beast rising up against another male who was making himself known sounds very dragon-like," Kelly replied. "Wolves do something similar if another male howls."

I nodded. It made sense, but there were other questions that the other dragon raised. Like what the dragon was doing in the city in the first place, and why it had tried to out Yev.

I wondered if the dragon had gotten startled by the explosion? Though, it seemed odd that an old dragon would startle easily. But if it hadn't been startled, then the explosion could have been in tandem with why it had tried to claim Yev.

"What are you thinking?" Morgana joined me at the counter.

"I'm thinking that maybe someone meant to draw Yev out. It matches with the speed with which the templars are mobilizing." It felt like it was all too convenient.

Morgana tilted her head back and forth in thought. "I was thinking something similar, but how would they know that Yev was a dragon? Why not just go after her when no one knew?"

I nodded. That part didn't make sense. Unless... "What if they didn't know Yev was a dragon? Maybe they were just testing to see if there was a dragon in the city. A crowd like the parade would be a great spot for that dragon to just exert his pressure and see if they could get one to pop."

"So the templars work with this old dragon, testing to see if there's a dragon in Sentarshaden. And then plan to take the ousted dragon after," Morgana fleshed the plan out.

"But they bit off more than they could chew," Scarlett said. "It would be one thing if it was a random person in the city, but they are targeting one of the heirs to the Highaen family."

From what I saw, it might slow them, but it wouldn't deter them. "I don't think it matters to them, at least not meaningfully. The templars were already planning to show force in Sentarshaden. There is no way they weren't already planning contingencies to deal with the Highaen forces. The fact that she's directly protected will make things harder, but it won't stop them."

"They've been planning to confront the Highaen family the whole time." Scarlett frowned. "That seems ridiculous. Sentarshaden was a bastion through the whole war with the Church. If they could take on the city, they would have already."

I turned to Morgana, curious in her thoughts. She had the best information on what had happened before.

She thought for a moment before speaking. "The city was ignored because it would take more forces than they were willing to commit here. That was partly because of the forces in Southeastern Europe, and because T was making a mess of Spain."

"Wait, T was the one in Spain?" Scarlett whirled mid-chop.

Morgana made an uneasy smile, realizing she might have just spilled the beans. "Yeah."

"Care to fill me in?" I asked, wondering if I'd finally find out what T had done.

"So, besides the forces Morgana was a part of, the other big threat to the Church was an unnamed lich. He ran through Spain and parts of France, raising an army and flooding the Church with undead."

"He didn't seem that scary," I said, turning to Morgana for confirmation.

"T mellowed out. When all but his daughter were killed in the Church's initial push... he went to a dark place. Did some things that elves really don't approve of."

That seemed like a mild way to phrase it. A lich. That at least explained why everyone was so terrified of him, and why he was kept under tight surveillance.

They likely wanted to make sure that he wasn't raising an army of undead. He was a natural disaster waiting to happen. But if he was just living his life, it was probably better for them to leave him alone. After all, weren't liches supposed to be unkillable unless you found their phylactery?

That made something else clear. "He's tied to his tree. Does that mean Hestia is a lich?"

"No," Morgana was quick to clarify. "She's kept herself clear of that magic and focused entirely on alchemy. Says it makes her feel gross."

"Well, yeah. Undead are gross." Kelly wrinkled her nose. "Can we take a vote? No undead in the harem."

"I'm not sure that's how it works..." Jadelyn looked over at me for confirmation.

"Many would consider vampires undead," Morgana pointed out, crossing her arms.

Holding a hand up, I tried to keep the women on topic. "I think we are all new to this. The last thing I want is to add someone to the harem that will cause strife. No banning, but please speak to me if there's a prospective member that you have an issue with."

"Just wait until the world knows what you are," Scarlett said. "We'll have to look through stacks of applications taller than you are."

I cringed, once again reminded of the fame I'd have. I could practically feel my secret slipping out with each additional person that knew. And flying up in the boughs of Sentarshaden would add some level of risk.

Everything I did seemed to add to that risk.

I was coming to grips with the reality that my secret wasn't going to last much longer. I didn't love it, but I also couldn't change it without hiding as the new dangers came forward.

Yev would need my help, especially if an older dragon was involved. Why a dragon would work for the celestials was beyond me, though. They were a clear enemy of any paranormals.

But regardless, it was working with the templars, and the templars were coming for me and my family. So, when the time came, this dragon would have to die.

CHAPTER 18

Two days had passed since the magic range. And if I was honest, I was avoiding Yev and Tyrande.

When we went to the magic range because their schedule had them there, I opted for my own room and even spent some time at the coffee shop across the street.

Yev had seemed fine after we'd wrestled, but my dragon was feeling on edge. I wasn't sure if I needed to stretch my wings or if all this waiting had sent the beast into a spiral. But the last thing I wanted was to cause another big incident with Yev.

Eventually, I became jittery to the point that I caved. Now I found myself before a Highaen guard, holding out a QR code. The Highaen estate was right up against the base of the massive tree, and it seemed miniscule against the tree, yet thousands of the Highaen and their clan lived here.

Kelly was practically vibrating at my side.

"Alright, you are clear. Please step into the circle. Keep your hands, feet, and anything you want to keep inside the circle at all times," the guard repeated words he'd clearly said too many times.

"This is so exciting," Kelly said, clinging to me as the runes glowed brighter and brighter. Soon they were so bright that they washed out the rest of my vision.

When they cleared, we were in the same circle, or at least, one that looked exactly the same. But the scene beyond it had changed. We were not looking at a guard station; we were looking at a massive tree branch that extended out for miles.

We were up in the limbs of Sentarshaden itself.

"Hold this." I gave Kelly the spatial artifact.

She held it like it was precious as I got out of my clothes and stuffed them into the artifact.

"Damn." Her eyes roved over me, and she let out a soft howl.

"Enough. You said you were going to help me with my dragon." I let the shift come, growing larger as gold scales covered my body.

I grew and stretched my neck out, shaking like a wet dog before craning my neck and getting a look at my whole body. It felt good to stretch out.

"How long would you say I am?"

Kelly stepped back so that she could take me in. "I don't know. Maybe twenty, twenty-five feet from your snout to the tip of your tail. The main body is about the size of one of Scarlett's black SUVs."

I grunted. "More than twice the weight of one of those too."

Cars were actually pretty hollow; dragons were not. I'd put myself between four and five tons. Even in the last week, I had continued to grow at a rapid pace.

"Yev is bigger than you." Kelly said, prompting a growl. "Not by much, though!" She quickly raised her hands in her defense.

I huffed out a cloud of smoke in her face for that one. "Hop on. So, what are you thinking? I let my dragon out for a run?"

"Fly, let out a few roars. Mostly, I just came to ride a dragon." She gave me a big grin.

Nudging her up my back, I let out one last little shake that nearly threw her. I paused, letting her readjust herself at the base of my neck.

"Don't fall off." A smirk crossed my draconic face.

"I'm not going to—" Kelly cut off with a scream as I jumped off the massive branch. Her hands shifted, and she dug her nails under one of my scales as she tried to hold on.

It wasn't much more than a slight discomfort, and making her jump sent a little thrill through me. It was fun messing with her.

My wings were tucked into my sides as I let myself free fall down through the branches. The wind in my face felt amazing. It was freeing in a way that I could never have experienced before.

"Zach! We are going to die! Flap those wings." Kelly apparently wasn't as at home in the sky as I was.

Letting myself fall a moment longer, I snapped out my wings, but continued to fall. It was only slightly more controlled.

I let the beast guide me, tilting them slightly and slowly angling up. My speed caught the wind, and I leveled out, rocketing on a curved trajectory back up further into the branches.

Kelly whooped and pumped her fist. "That was better than any rollercoaster ride."

"I thought we were gonna die?" I teased her.

"You try riding on a dragon who has admitted that it's only his third flight. Let me tell you, that's a terrifying way to start." She stood up for herself.

"I wanted to generate some speed." Without even realizing it, I had done what I had wanted. My instincts from the beast had guided me.

Slowing down to a gentle glide as I continued upward, I beat my wings and rose back to our starting level amid the branches.

The tree was massive, and the branches made an almost orderly section of tiers among the branches. The space between them was wide open, certainly large enough for a dragon to play around with flying.

Here in the green shade from the tree, my gold scales were dim and reflecting green. It almost made me look like Yev's green scales.

"Do I look green to you?"

Kelly paid attention and barked a laugh. "Yes, but not in the color changing kind of way."

I knew that.

Banking hard to the right, I did a small dive, pulling out of it and swinging back left. It was supremely fun to build up a little speed and take those hard turns, yet I knew my agility in the air was nothing compared to an angel. I'd seen one stop mid-air and reverse.

As the thought crossed my mind, I felt a new challenge. A draconic smile spread across my face as I pulled my shoulders back and tried that kind of maneuver, quickly flapping forward with the shift of my shoulders.

"Warn a girl." Kelly clung onto my horns as I arrested my flight after several flaps.

My wings strained from the effort, and I had to beat my wings hard to hover. Even then, I was slowly sinking, just less as I struggled to remain in the same place. Treading air was not as easy as treading water.

Tucking my wings, I dove again before snapping them out and returning to a glide. "Just trying out a few things, learning my limits."

"You should let out a big roar. A howl always makes my wolf happy." Kelly brought us back to our trip's goal.

But somehow, just roaring didn't feel right. Like a wolf wanting to howl on a run, I needed momentum.

Diving to build up speed, I arched back up, and at the peak, pushed my beast forward as I roared into the leaves. The smaller branches quivered in fear of my mighty dragon. Or at least, that's how I liked to think of it.

"That's it," Kelly cheered. "Again, really belt it out."

I took a deep breath and let out a roar so forceful that a small jet of fire sprayed out and my vision spotted.

But it felt so damn good after.

"Good idea." I turned, ducking into another dive.

"What did you say?" Kelly cupped her ear. "My hearing is shot."

Chuckling, I hoped she was joking, but I knew she'd heal quickly if she wasn't.

A flicker above me caught my attention, followed by the feeling of something burning hitting my back.

Surprised, I lost the angle on my wings, and I tumbled into a branch.

"Haha," the phoenix laughed, perched on my side. "Got you, Yev— oh shit." A high-pitched yelp came from the phoenix before darting away.

I roared, this time in anger, and blasted fire at the phoenix.

"Shit, I'm sorry. I thought you—"

My claw tore up the branch as I launched myself at the stupid burning chicken.

She twisted mid-air gracefully in a flourish of flames and dove straight down between the branches. She was far smaller than me, but I'd just have to force my way through.

"Zach! I don't think she meant to attack you!" Kelly was tugging at my horns, not that it did anything.

I ripped my way through the small branches and hurtled down like a meteor after the phoenix. Even if I wanted to, I couldn't stop. Hitting me and running away had set my dragon instincts on fire. My entire brain was focused on catching her.

The phoenix might be more agile than me, but in a straight dive, I had far more mass to throw down.

She looked over her flaming wings, saw me catching up and spun, cutting into a layer of branches and leveling out her flight.

I smiled, up for the challenge.

Putting my trust in the beast, I twirled, flaring out my own wings. It hurt, but I tore forward, still chasing after the phoenix.

Seeing me keep pace, she spun onto her back while still flying. "It was an accident. My bad?"

Unfortunately, the only answer my beast could give in that moment of primal chase was a small burst of flame that didn't quite reach her.

I continued beating my wings, trying to catch the stupid bird. If only I could catch her... then... then... something.

I couldn't think straight as my instincts demanded I catch the running bird.

"Big sister! Big sister!" the bird screamed at the top of her lungs as she banked hard to the right.

I couldn't quite follow her turns, swinging out farther and losing ground, only to make it up in the straightaways.

I was so close that I could practically taste the phoenix before another piercing cry echoed through the branches, and a second phoenix more my size flew down between us.

There was no time for me to stop.

Throwing my claws forward, I grabbed the new phoenix, and the two of us went down in a tumble until she landed on a branch, my weight crushing her down.

"Oh good, we stopped. But you got the wrong bird, golden boy," Kelly mocked me. "Calmed down yet?"

I growled at her before focusing on my stunned prey beneath me.

The phoenix groggily opened its eyes and chirped at me before burning brightly and blasting me with fire.

After a moment, her fire went out, and I still stood over her, proud and unscathed. Her fire had no effect on my golden scales.

"Uh. Please let me go?" she squeaked.

That only made me wonder if phoenix tasted like chicken. She probably tasted like spicy chicken. My mouth was watering.

"What's going on?" a deep draconic voice roared as Yev swooped down to this level, the smaller phoenix hovering behind her. "Zach, get off of her."

Kelly jumped forward, standing on my snout and getting my attention as she grabbed the scales on my face. She put her-self as the primary thing in my vision.

"Hey, dragon boy, you need to focus on me."

I huffed a puff of smoke out my nose, and it floated over her. A deep grumble came from my throat, but my logical hu-man brain was starting to catch back up with my body and my instincts.

The branch shook as Yev landed, and my eyes were drawn to the smaller phoenix, who was cowering behind Yev.

"He's crazy!" it was yelling.

My instincts zeroed in on the squawking fire chicken when Kelly tugged at my face, drawing my attention back to her.

"I need you to calm down and get back in the driver's seat." She turned to Yev. "Tell the little bitch to shut up. The last thing we need is her setting him off again."

I beat my wings but didn't go anywhere. It was more of a statement.

"Look at me." Kelly bopped my snout again, forcing my attention back to her. "Don't you want some of this?"

She brushed her chest against my dragon face with a smirk as one of the scales caught her shirt and pulled it down, displaying her chest to me. She planted a few kisses along my face, and my beast became distracted. As it relaxed, interested in Kelly, I started being able to calm down.

I took several deep breaths, snorting out smoke as I regained control and stepped off of the other phoenix. It shot up and flapped away from me.

"There you go," Kelly cooed and corrected her shirt before crawling back up to hold my horns. "Well, folks, we've learned one way to get a dragon off a murderous rampage. I'm going to call that a success."

"Showing him your tits?" Yev laughed. "Not sure that would work on my dragon, and I have to admit it hadn't been my plan, but it was rather effective."

I didn't have to say anything.

Kelly pointed her hand over my head at the smaller phoenix. "That little brat tackled Zach while he was flying, then ran away. It set off his predator nature."

Yev whirled on the pair of phoenixes. "Is that what happened?"

"Maybe?" the smaller phoenix hedged. "I thought it was you."

Yev shook her big draconic head. "So you attacked a random dragon, and he chased you around the tree?"

"He was going to eat me!" The small phoenix flapped herself several feet higher as her wings sped up. "Then my big sister saved me," she chirped.

"Saved is a nice way to put it." The larger phoenix wasn't flying, still swaying on her feet. "I got in the way of a dragon barreling at my little sister. I'm an idiot."

Yev seemed satisfied with their answers and looked at me. "What's your excuse?"

The way she said it made me want to raise my hackles. "She attacked me and ran. I chased. It's not hard to understand," I growled.

Her head rose a couple feet above mine, and it was making me feel a little scrappy. My dragon wanted to prove I was superior.

My claws flexed, tearing up the branch under me. Yev's eyes dipped to the sound, and she took a single step back. My eyes zeroed in on her, waiting for her to run.

But she didn't.

"I see." She dragged out the word slowly.

"Don't run, please," Kelly said. "He's so wound up."

I tossed my head, not liking what Kelly said. "I am not."

"You are," Yev agreed with Kelly, taking another step back. "Wound up too tight. Ladies, I think it's best that you go home."

"I'm not some monster," I said. Her taking slow steps back and telling others to run was not necessary. "Kelly and I will go."

Jumping off the branch, I let my wings snap out and flew away from the situation.

The entire time we flew, my beast was up in arms, wanting me to go back and pick a fight with Yev for blocking me from the undoubtedly tasty, spicy chickens.

The beast was jumpy as hell. I had no idea why my instincts were rearing for a fight and ready to go on some murderous rampage.

Something was bothering my instincts; I just didn't know what it was.

Part of me wanted to blame the fact that we'd been sitting around waiting for an attack the previous few days. It had frayed some of my nerves; patience didn't seem to be one of my strengths.

But it had to be more than that.

Yev crept up in my peripheral vision, but she stayed far enough away that it wasn't a threat. I assumed she wanted to keep any of her other friends in the tree safe.

"Maybe you should talk," Kelly said, bonking me on top of the head.

"My dragon wants to fight. Why would your wolf itch to fight?" I asked her.

"Wolves want to fight all the time. Though mostly it's play, or practice."

I tossed my head slightly, making sure not to throw Kelly. "It isn't play."

"Then wolves fight because they feel threatened, or because they have something to gain," Kelly said.

Those two options sunk into my head, and I slowed down, landing on a branch and turning to Yev in an agreement to talk.

Did my beast want to kill and eat Yev? Or maybe establish dominance? No, the aggression wasn't pointed directly at Yev. She was just one of the available options at the moment.

Yev back-winged, slowing her flight and abruptly landing. "You've been avoiding me."

I respected the directness.

Kelly snickered, "Yes, he has."

"I can speak for myself," I rumbled, padding in a small circle on the branch before sitting my rear down with a thump. "Yes, I've been avoiding you."

"Is it because of the other day in the magic range?" The green dragon before me lowered its head apologetically.

"No." Even though I didn't quite know what was bothering me, I knew that wasn't it. "I'm finding myself irritable in Sentarshaden."

I hadn't felt this way before entering Sentarshaden.

"The city is bothering you?" she asked, her head rising and tilting in a way that reminded me of a cat. "Is it your women?"

Kelly's head came over the top of mine. "Are you not enjoying the blueberry?"

"No, damnit." I tossed Kelly back up over my head and stood, pacing on the branch. "I don't know what it is, but something is driving me up a wall, like a constant itch."

Yev watched me as I paced the branch several times before speaking again. "You could be reacting to something magical in the city. Maybe one of the Highaen wards is bothering you at a low level? There are some to try and drive normals away."

"Do I look human to you?" I stopped and stared back at the green dragon.

"No, but there are more wards than I know. There could be something."

I paused, sensing. I didn't feel like I was being pushed out. It was as if I wanted something; I wanted to fight something.

Lifting my head, I stared at Yev and tried to probe that feeling.

"You said there was another dragon in the city, another male. Do dragon males fight?" I asked Yev.

Her eyes opened wide and blinked. "Maybe. You are the only male I've ever met. There's less than ten male dragons in the world."

Chewing my lip, I prodded the beast and brought up the image of another big male dragon, trying to imagine one standing right here with me on the branch.

The beast went rabid, and I had to rein it in and shove it deep down before the aggression made me do something stupid.

I smiled, glad I at least knew what was getting under my skin.

"I think I'm somehow sensing this other dragon, and it's setting off my instincts." Letting out a breath, I managed to stay in control. "I just tried to imagine another male dragon here and nearly lost it."

"Need me to show you my tits again?" Kelly asked helpfully.

"Men," Yev scoffed. "But if you can sense him, is that something we can use?"

I didn't know, and I was getting tired of questions I couldn't answer. "Who knows? I'm flying blind. But I'll have to see what I can figure out."

But if I could sense this other dragon, we could go on the offensive and find the celestial ambush before they sprang it. It was worth trying.

"Thanks for talking me through this. We're going to head back," I told Yev, leaning off the branch and letting myself fall backwards. As we plummeted, I snapped my wings open and wandered back through the tree for our portal out of there.

CHAPTER 19

It was the next day, and I was feeling much better. Knowing what was bothering me took an enormous weight off of me, and I felt more in control of myself.

While I loaded up dishes from breakfast, I pitched my idea for the day. "I'd like to drive around the city and see if I can't use this instinct to find the other dragon."

"What do you need?" Jadelyn was quick to ask.

"A car. Actually, I could use someone to drive me around that knows the area. I might get distracted as I try to reach out and sense the dragon."

"I can drive around. You'll be here to protect Jadelyn?" Scarlett asked Morgana and Kelly. When they nodded, Scarlett turned, smiling at me.

We didn't have much else we could do for Yev. While the trap may be closing, nothing in her schedule for the day should give them an opportunity. So it was a day at home for Morgana and Kelly, too.

"Great." Scarlett snagged a pair of keys from a hook. "I'd like to get out of the house."

"Be safe, you two." Jadelyn waved to the two of us.

I was eager to get going, snatching Scarlett's hand and pulling her along to the garage and into one of the black SUVs.

"Where to?" she asked, turning the keys, the engine roaring to life.

"I'm not sure. I was thinking we circle the city and just see if I can pick anything up? And then we go from there?" I didn't have a concrete plan for this one. Beyond the fact that the dragon was likely still in the city, we had little to go on.

"One drive around the city coming up." She rolled out of the garage, and I tried to focus on my irritation, but nothing was coming as I tried to pick at the feeling.

"How are you, Scarlett?" I asked, taking a break from trying to force it. "I know you agreed to open up our relationship, but this has all moved quickly. From Jadelyn, to Morgana, and now Kelly, are you still okay?"

She was silent for a long moment.

"Thank you for asking. If I'm honest, I'm still getting used to the idea." Scarlett let out a long sigh, and her tails wiggled between her back and the seat.

Reaching a hand over, I grabbed one and pulled it into my lap, petting it. The action visibly calmed her down. "You are still my first mate."

"But you haven't marked me."

"Is that the problem?" My jaw crackled with a shift as my teeth sharpened. I leaned over her shoulder.

"No."

I started to pull away, but she grabbed my head and stayed looking at the road.

"Don't stop. Do it."

I trusted her to know what she wanted, so I leaned down. My teeth clamped down on her shoulder, and I pushed the beast forward. Magic channeled through my jaw as I felt myself imprint my mark on her.

I let my face shift back and sat back in my seat, still petting her tail. "Better?"

Scarlett stopped at a stop sign and pulled down the visor mirror to look at her shoulder. "It healed."

"It does that. It will leave a faint scar and a magical imprint," I told her, using a finger to trace it. Even if the scar was nearly invisible, I could feel exactly where it was.

She put the mirror back up as she started driving again. "Thank you."

"If that wasn't the issue, what is?" I pressed my lovely kitsune. With everything going on, we hadn't had a chance to reconnect since Jadelyn had joined the harem.

She looked straight ahead and let out a soft sigh, resigning herself to speaking her mind. "It's just a lot. I told you to go after Jadelyn, and she's like a sister to me. Then Morgana seemed like an obvious next step, and I get the thing you have with Kelly."

She paused. "It's just, it keeps growing. And I need to know that we will keep getting time together."

Petting her tail, I did my best to just listen. When she seemed like she was finally done, I spoke. "There's only one Scarlett. And my relationship with her is more important than any new women circling me. I have all the love I need right now."

"That's what you said when it was just you and me," she reminded me.

"It still stands true. But, if I'm honest, my nature is changing. You met mostly human me. I'm slowly becoming more like my dragon, and it seems to be greedy for a horde of women."

The beast slammed itself into my chest in response.

"Can you slow down?" she asked.

I wanted to say 'yes', but I wasn't sure I could promise that. "Once my secret is out, I'm likely going to have to meet the Bronze King. If I survive that, I suspect more than one female dragon is going to come knocking."

Scarlett let out a noise of pure frustration. "I'm not going to be left behind?"

"Never. Don't even let that thought enter your mind. You are my kitsune, my first mate. Though there will be others, you will always be first." I needed to make her status as first mate more of a thing, for her own sake.

"In fact, there's a request I have of you. When my secret comes out, I need your help in screening the dragon females that come." I knew putting her in charge of something like that would give her the control she sought.

Scarlett's training and life as a guard had made her used to planning. She always had contingencies in place, ready for all the possible outcomes.

"Really? What if they are stupid sexy?" Scarlett probed.

"Doesn't matter if they don't pass first mate muster," I confirmed, smiling as she seemed to relax slightly.

"Good," Scarlett finally declared after a moment of thought. "I'll take that up as your first mate. We can never be too careful. Once your secret is out, there will be plenty of gold diggers."

"My gold!" I shouted in play but also to hide the part of my dragon that clenched tight at the idea of some woman taking gold from my hoard.

Mostly, I was elated that she took to the idea so well.

Scarlett shook her head, and her playful little fox ears wobbled in such a way that I just had to reach out and caress one. Once I'd finished feeling it, I let my fingers trail down the back of her head and along her neck.

"I love you, Scarlett. If anything is bothering you, please find the time to tell me." I leaned over and kissed her shoulder.

As I sat back, I cupped her cheek, and she turned her face into my hand, nuzzling it affectionately.

"I will, my mate. I will. This is just taking some getting used to," she said.

I kissed the tail in my lap and continued to hold it against my chest as I stroked it. The tail softly wiggled against me.

We sat there in silence for a while as Scarlett drove around the city.

My sense for this other dragon was a low thrum in the back of my mind, but as we rounded the southern end of the city and followed one of the main roads towards the eastern side, I felt it pick up.

"Scar, it's growing stronger. We must be getting closer."

"Really? Shit." She made a turn. "Is it getting stronger still?"

Closing my eyes, I focused on the sensation that had been nagging me for the last few days, feeling it subtly growing stronger. "Yeah, it's still growing."

"We are going north now. Let's try to triangulate this thing. I'll find three spots and we can see which of them feels strongest."

Scarlett pulled off into a parking lot. "How about now? Give it a rating."

"Maybe a four?" I hazarded, thinking it was going to get much stronger.

"Okay, off to the next spot." She tapped on her phone and put it down.

I could see that she'd dropped a pin on the map.

Pulling out and driving several miles east, she stopped again. "Stronger or weaker?"

Closing my eyes, I really tried to get a sense of it. "Maybe a smidge stronger. Let's call it a four point five."

"Got it." She tapped another pin and note on the map, and I checked it, seeing where she was going to drive next.

Sure enough, she took a street headed north for the final of the three points.

"Six, maybe even a seven," I said, getting a sense for the variation.

"Alright." Scarlett tapped it into the phone and then did a little math. "We are going to guess it is mostly north of here, a little east at a four to one ratio." She drew a line on the map that went through several streets. "There, we'll go up that direction and see if we can't pinpoint it."

I nodded, on board with the idea and letting her drive.

We ended up driving until the sensation started to fade again and then used another three points to try to guess the direction. The resulting line went back southeast, and we drove to where the two lines intersected.

"Stop here." I grabbed the dashboard as a shift nearly overcame me. "He's here, somewhere close."

My breathing came out heavy, and I was practically salivating for a fight.

"Where?" Scarlett asked.

I looked around, trying to keep it together as I scanned everything nearby. There was a small outdoor shopping center just on the corner. A residential neighborhood wrapped around the back of the shopping area.

"The shopping center. Drive through it." I could feel it from that direction. Now that we were close, the pull was much more distinct.

Scarlett had her phone up against her ear as she made the turn. "Hey Jade, can you get Morgana and Kelly packed up? Zach thinks he found the dragon."

There was some chatter on the other end before Scarlett spoke again. "Yeah, just check my GPS. It's the Goblingrove Shopping Mall."

There were a few more words exchanged, and then they hung up. Scarlett put the phone down as she rolled into a parking spot.

"You holding yourself together?" she asked with a knowing quirk of her brow.

"Well enough," I growled.

"They'll be here in twenty. I'm not going to let you identify which building it is before they are here. You look like you are practically frothing at the mouth."

It wasn't that bad, but I felt like I was going to burst out of my clothes at any second.

Scarlett's seatbelt came off, and she slid over the center console into my lap. "Kelly said she found a good way to distract you that I wanted to try."

She kissed my chest and up the side of my neck as she pressed her chest into me and grabbed the back of my head.

I let her distract me, kissing her and using my tongue to pry open her pearly white teeth and tangle my tongue with hers. It was working. My restless energy found an outlet as I grabbed her hips and pressed her to my erection.

I knew it wasn't the time or place for sex, but some heavy petting would serve as a great distraction.

"Down boy," Scarlett teased, but she was completely soaking up all the attention I was giving her. Her lips were spread in a big smile as she twerked her hips over my erection.

"You are going to find yourself in trouble if you aren't careful," I growled, pressing her back into the dash and burying my face between her bountiful chest.

Scarlett continued to tease me until I was rock hard, and I was sure more than a few shoppers had given us dirty looks.

Someone knocked on the window.

Jadelyn stood outside the car waving with a smile.

Scarlett threw herself off of me and jumped out of the car. "Jade, what are you doing alone?"

"I have backup." She pointed to Morgana behind her and Kelly on watch further back.

"That's not the point." Scarlett tilted her head down, glaring at the siren, who continued to smile, completely unaffected by her bodyguard's glower.

"It's fine. We are just looking for the place," I replied, knowing that Jadelyn wouldn't allow herself to be bubble-wrapped at all times, but not liking the idea of her near danger either.

Standing in the parking lot, I had a very uncomfortable bulge in my pants. And now that Scarlett had stopped teasing me, the irritation was also making itself known.

I adjusted myself as I scanned the shops. It was a cluster of strip malls, all centered around two roundabouts.

My senses were pulling me further north, towards the second roundabout. "Come on. He's this way."

Like a hound dog with a scent, I let it pull me forward, crossing two streets before I found myself in front of an unnamed shop.

The front, like the rest, was all glass windows, but they were filled with for sale posters and then a big 'SOLD' across them No mention of who was moving into this spot, but my sense of the other dragon was telling me a dragon had moved in.

"Here?" Morgana confirmed, stepping forward with a hand over one of her swords. The other was ready to try the front door.

I looked around, trying to figure out how to approach it. It was a public space and just blowing the front of the store out was more likely to cause us problems.

But before Morgana could get to the door, it opened, and a woman stepped out. But as she stepped out, I realized it wasn't a woman. It was an angel. Two downy white wings were folded on her back.

Wearing a tight-fitting, white blouse over a dark pencil skirt, she was all business in how she dressed. But the way she moved, and the cut of her hair falling just below her jaw and jutting back at an angle, reminded me of a spartan warrior's helmet.

She had a terse expression as her head turned slowly, taking in Morgana. She clearly recognized her. The angel turned to the door, knocking twice on it.

"Morgana. What brings you to Sentarshaden? I didn't think you were welcome in these parts," the angel spoke, the haughty expression staying on her face.

"Devin Nashner," Morgana replied, her hands on her blades. "It's funny you say that. I could say the same for you."

"I'm a paranormal, aren't I?" Helena replied.

Morgana snorted. "Questionable, at best. We both know nephilim have a reputation of siding with other groups."

I realized Morgana was dropping hints to help me piece everything together. She'd only mentioned one nephilim to me: Jared's sister. And she'd said his sister would be far stronger than the angels we'd fought before.

As much as I was curious to see how I would do against her, my instincts alerted me that the dragon was moving further away. He was heading out the back.

Those two knocks of hers had been a signal, and she was the distraction.

I made a plan quickly. "Morgana, have fun with her. Scar, get Jadelyn back to the car. Kelly, with me."

Morgana's two blades slid free of their sheathes with a lethal hiss. At the same time, beads of white coalesced into a massive silver spear in Helena's hands.

"Okay, we're out, Jade." Scarlett wasn't playing games. She grabbed Jadelyn and dragged her, not holding back any of her strength. And as they moved, we branched into three pairs, all moving in different directions.

"Go. I've got you," Kelly called as she ran towards me.

I turned, moving into a full sprint as we rounded two shops to get to the back of the shop. Concrete cracked and chunks of sidewalk sprayed to my side as Morgana and Helena clashed.

I looked over my shoulder, catching the briefest of moments in the chaos. I tried not to be stunned. Helena was at a completely different level than the angels I'd handled before. Many of them had been skilled, but the raw power I'd just felt behind me was something else.

I would have had trouble leaving anybody but a fully healed Morgana to face her.

Kelly's legs were shifting as she moved, tearing through her jeans as she kept up with me. We rounded the corner, coming face to face with a group of cherubs pulling three trucks up to the back of the building.

There was another group of several cherubs and angels escorting a figure in hooded robes.

But what caught my eye were the forearms of the robes. They bulged oddly. And as it moved, I saw glimpses of a silver chain glowing brightly with magic.

As soon as I rounded the corner, the robed figure stopped, despite the angel pushing on him, and turned towards me.

I couldn't see past the shadows of the cowl at this distance, but something about its stare unsettled me. My dragon instincts were going off like a blazing alarm. They were screaming that the robed figure was the dragon.

"Get moving!" the angel screamed, slamming a hand into the dragon.

But it was like he had punched a mountain. The dragon didn't so much as twitch. Instead, the cowl fell down, and I felt sick when I saw his face.

It was weathered and worn, his head shaved bald, and his eyes gouged out. Every inch of his exposed skin was covered with rune-shaped scars.

Despite having no eyes, it still felt like he was staring right at me.

"Move." The angel pushed the dragon.

Several runes lit up, and the dragon took one step of its own volition, as if doing the minimum to comply with the command.

"We have company." One of the cherubs had spotted us and pulled out a handgun from the front of his pants.

"That's the gold dragon," the angel scowled before looking back at the scarred dragon. "Get it out of here."

I paused, all of a sudden not sure what I should do. The dragon wasn't my enemy; he was a prisoner and tool for my real enemy. Any anger I had rushed out of me, replaced with pity.

I hadn't been expecting this, and I hesitated.

One of the trucks pulled up to the dragon, and a cherub screamed for him to get in.

The scarred dragon continued to stare at me with his empty eye sockets, even as runes lit up on its neck and head. With the runes, I could see his muscles tense as if he was resisting, but more and more runes lit up as his tendons and muscles in his neck strained.

After just a few more moments, the runes won out, and the dragon threw himself sideways into the back of the truck. All three vehicles floored it, burning rubber as they peeled out.

"Are we just going to let him get away?" Kelly asked in confusion.

"I'm not sure." I had mixed feelings, and I wasn't sure what I should do about what I'd just seen. "But we have company, and I can't wait for you to show me what an alpha wolf can do."

The trucks left behind a small contingent of cherubs and two angels, and they were moving towards us.

"Happily, alpha." Kelly's clothes ripped as she shifted, and I got to see her transformation for the first time since she'd become an alpha.

CHAPTER 20

I'd seen Kelly's wolf at the hangar before she was alpha, but this was different. Seeing her draw on her pack and transform was something magical to watch with my dragon eyes.

Kelly swelled from a cute, petite cheerleader into a ten-foot-tall werewolf. I ignored the oncoming cherubs and angels, just amazed at how gorgeous and ferocious she was.

And her eyes had a soft orange glow as she drew on the web of power of her pack, which magically connected her all the way back to Philly. Orange mana from her pack flooded her body, and she became a powerhouse to rival any alpha wolf.

She wasn't as big as Chad or her father had been, but she was still larger than the other male wolves I'd seen in the past.

A lupine grin spread across her muzzle as she realized I was watching her. "Alpha, join me."

I wanted to join her, but despite being in a paranormal city, I wasn't quite ready to let my dragon out so publicly. We were already attracting a lot of attention. People were getting out of their cars and holding up cell phones to video whatever was going to occur.

So instead, I drew the silver sword from my spatial artifact and turned toward the oncoming group.

I also packed on mass as the seams on my shoulders split open.

The added muscle would do little to change my strength, but fighting with extra mass would give me a vital weight advantage. The damage a tackle from a three-hundred-pound man and a hundred-fifty-pound man could do were wildly different.

Kelly gave our opponents her attention again as they moved forward in a line, guns raised.

As soon as they started firing, Kelly was in front of me, her arms spread to block.

It was a strange sort of horror to watch them fill Kelly with lead, even though I knew those low caliber bullets wouldn't slow her.

As blood trickled from her wounds, the beast in me rose, ready to tear them apart. And this time, we were on the same page.

The moment the guns clicked empty, I was running around Kelly, sword swinging for the first cherub.

I caught him completely flat-footed. He'd been focused on Kelly, and I was ready to show him that I was his real problem.

Although, it didn't go quite as planned. Even with my strength, the sword didn't slice through him like butter. The movies lied. Hitting the cherub with my silver sword was more like hitting him with a baseball bat. Cherubs were durable, and I was still learning my sword skills.

The blade barely tore into him, but I did bash his side. With my sheer strength, eventually my sword tore through him more than sliced, spraying blood and viscera out on the other side.

I was already spinning the sword around for an overhead chop on the next cherub as Kelly barreled through the group.

And it was hard not to marvel. She was a tank.

Kelly dipped her shoulder and plowed through the cherubs, slashing claws and even taking one by surprise. She latched her jaw around his crown, bringing her hands down onto his shoulders and liberating his head from his body.

Seeing what she could do, the angels' wings flared. They shot into the air, well clear of Kelly's reach.

My alpha wolf had single-handedly sent the contingent of cherubs into chaos.

And I was right on her heels, my sword cleaving through its third cherub and ensuring that I would never be able to wear these jeans again as I soaked them in blood.

"Blessings of arms," one angel shouted, and glowing white weapons appeared in the hands of each cherub.

I grumbled, staring at the white weapons with skepticism. They were going to be a problem.

Kelly must have realized it, too. She tossed one last cherub into the mass and sprang back twenty feet, sliding to all fours before they could cut her.

My exit wasn't quite as dramatic, but equally effective.

"Not good," Kelly said, staring at the glowing blades in their hands.

"Any idea how long they can keep powering those weapons?" I asked, looking at the angel. From what I could see with my dragon eye, the angel was actively holding the spell to equip the cherubs.

Kelly's lupine face had a droll expression. "Why yes, I have extensive experience in angel fighting, after all." Her voice was dripping with sarcasm.

I rolled my eyes, taking the point. It wasn't like there had been much fighting between the Church and the paranormal in our lifetime.

But the cherubs were coming at us, and they outnumbered us. We had to do something.

I decided to buy some time.

Taking a deep breath, I let loose a jet of dragon fire that cooked the air and melted the concrete before me. Fire roared in the space between us and the celestials, at least buying me a few seconds.

Think, Zach, think.

Then, like a light bulb popping up over my head, I remembered that I had magic.

"Evokus," I yelled, shifting my throat and slamming a hand forward.

Following the wave of fire that had been my breath, a fireball shot into the cherubs. It hit their group center mass and exploded, launching a handful of them up and away from the fight.

That had been immensely satisfying. Almost like bowling, only with explosions and asshole celestials.

My move had done its job and given us a small reprieve. They had paused, clearly waiting to see if I would throw another fireball. Now that they expected it, I changed it up.

Thinking chilly thoughts, I tried to summon up my silver dragon rather than my gold. A faint ripple went through my throat, but it was so slight that I wasn't sure if it was real or not.

But there was one way to find out.

I took a deep breath and let my breath rip. A freezing fog spewed out much farther than my fire, coating the front cherubs and flowing out to the side in a dense white mist.

"So cool," Kelly whispered beside me.

My mouth was a little busy at the moment, but the edges of my lips curled up. I had to admit that it was pretty cool to switch the elements. I really needed to test the limits of it soon.

I let up on my frost breath and stepped back, pulling Kelly with me.

"Let them come to us," I said, continuing to walk backwards with her out of the fog.

It was slowly settling and spilling further out away from us. Inside the fog, there were shouts and screams. The two angels were staring down at me from above the fog, slight frowns on their faces.

After a few more moments, cherubs came rushing out of the fog. Ice hung from their faces and more than a few of them were looking a little blue lipped.

Kelly moved forward, socking the first cherub to come out of the fog in the face. The poor guy didn't even get his arms up to defend himself as her big, meaty werewolf fist crumpled his face and sent him flying back into the fog.

The others raised their glowing weapons, but their reaction times had severely slowed. The cherubs shivered as they tried to ready themselves for a fight. I almost felt bad for them; they looked pretty pathetic.

The second angel raised his arms, and bright white light washed down on the cherubs.

As soon as it disappeared, the cherubs were standing up a little straighter, and the ice on them was falling off in clumps. Whatever the angel had done was counteracting the cold.

"Envokus," I said once more, ready to keep at it.

A blue ball shot into the cherubs, exploding and spraying razor-sharp ice shards over the cherubs.

Kelly was there in the moment's distraction, lifting the nearest cherub and crushing him to the pavement.

Sirens blared somewhere close by, and cars flashing the green and gold colors of the Highaen family were roaring into the parking lot.

A large magical net came to life overhead as more trucks rolled in. And the next set of cars each had two or three elves riding in the back with glowing hands outstretched.

"Halt. Any further action will result in the use of force to apprehend you," an elf with a megaphone announced to the rest of us.

In the short time of this fight, it would seem the Highaen family had come and in force. There had to be at least fifty elven mages present.

I appreciated their support, but I wasn't about to drop my guard. These cherubs would gut me in an instant for the good of the celestial plane.

Helena flew over the building and hovered for a moment over the rest of her people, taking in the scene. It wasn't long before she decided to fight another day.

"We're leaving," she said.

The nephilim wasn't looking too bad. Her blouse was torn and her skirt was ripped up to her hips, but otherwise, she had fared well against Morgana. She wasn't even bleeding.

"Land and put down your weapons," the megaphoned elf yelled at Helena.

But she ignored him. She thrust her spear upwards, and the spear glowed so brightly that I had to look away.

Following her movement, a pulse of light shot up and shattered the glowing dome above us that held us in.

Magic spells shot into the air from dozens of Highaen elves in response to her move, but Helena rocketed to the ground, slamming the spear against the concrete.

The entire group of celestials became wrapped in bright white light before they shot off into the distance at an incredible speed that none of us could match.

Morgana flipped over the building. I quickly scanned her for injuries. Her corset was torn, and one of her breasts was on display. Additional cuts in her pants told me that she may have even been on the losing end of the fight.

"Bitch. Can't believe she ran," Morgana spat.

"You... uh... are showing." I gestured to my own chest.

Morgana looked down and, after a sigh, pulled out a shirt from her bra and threw it over her corset. It was odd seeing her in something other than leather, but she was still hot.

"Got another change of clothes?" Kelly's big lupine head hovered several feet over my shoulder.

"I got you." Morgana pulled out another set and handed it to Kelly as she shifted back.

Doing my best to block Kelly from view, I let her have some sort of privacy.

The Highaen family could see the de-escalation and closed ranks, moving towards us.

"Think we are in trouble?" I joked.

Neither of the girls thought it was funny.

"Yes. Fighting like that in the open will have consequences." Morgana eyed the freezing fog, which was slowly dissipating, leaving a few well-chilled corpses behind. "And we have bodies. Shit."

"Put your hands up and do not resist," the Highaen authorities announced.

I realized more than a few of them still had glowing hands, spells at the ready if we did anything stupid.

I put my hands on top of my head and crouched down, putting both knees on the ground. "We won't resist. But I ask that you notify Tyrande and Yev. We were here in defense of their safety."

Megaphone Elf let out a laugh, and I realized I'd asked him to go to one of their highest-ranking members. There was no way he was going to pass on the message. He might not even have a way to get them the message.

"I'm Morgana Silverwing," Morgana stated simply. "Please be advised in case you need to take extra precautions."

Megaphone Elf's face fell, and his mouth soured like he'd just eaten a toad. "Everyone, please monitor the suspects."

He stepped back and pulled out a phone to have a conversation that I couldn't hear.

But the smug smile on Morgana's face as her pointy ears twitched told me it had worked as expected.

"They have special rules should someone of my caliber be involved, involving escalation to higher ups," she said by way of explanation. "That also means someone knowing the full situation is more likely to hear this."

"Smart. Glad I have such a scary mate," I said, giving her a wink. "So, how was Helena Nashner?"

"Strong. Rumor is she's the daughter of Jared's father and the archangel of love. That spear is no ordinary weapon." Morgana's gaze shifted off in the direction the celestials had fled. "She's powerful. My swords didn't scratch her."

"Archangel of love? He must have been a lucky dude for at least one night." Kelly paused as we both turned to her. "What? She's gotta be amazing in bed with a title like that."

I shrugged, not concerned with how great sex with the archangel of love would be. I was more concerned with our current situation and the two strong opponents that had just appeared before us.

We weren't just dealing with some cherubs and a few angels. They had two heavy hitters in the mix. As much as this small army of elves around me showed some of the strength of the Highaen family, I wasn't sure if it would be enough.

That dragon had felt terrifyingly powerful.

I expected my beast to roar up in protest, but it seemed to agree. That dragon had been much stronger than we were at the moment. Not to mention, Morgana hadn't been able to cut Helena with her blades. What kind of insane defenses did she have?

Megaphone Elf put down the phone and stepped back over to the three of us. "Alright, let them up. They aren't a problem, but I'm supposed to ask you to wait here."

"What for?" I asked.

"For the Highaen," he said with a tone of reverence that told me it wasn't some general reference to their people, but to the actual Highaen royal family.

"We can do that, can't we, Morgy?" I tried to lighten the air with the nickname.

The glower I got in return was priceless.

"We can. Get up," Morgana said then spoke to Megaphone Elf. "We have two more with us that are back in a car, I believe. May we get them?"

"Yes, but please return quickly. I'd rather not have to explain why you aren't here waiting when they arrive." Megaphone Elf looked more concerned with his own hide than ours at that.

I hopped to my feet and walked with a purpose around the side to the parking lot where we'd left Scarlett's SUV. Though she was trying to protect Jadelyn, I suspected she wouldn't leave until there was a more direct threat.

Sure enough, Scarlett was idling in the parking lot, ready to swoop one of us up or get Jadelyn out of there.

Seeing me, she turned the keys and her car quieted down.

Jadelyn shot out of the car and rushed across the parking lot into my arms. "I'm glad you're okay!"

I picked up my siren, her voice already calming my nerves from the battle. "Same. I don't know what I'd do if something happened to you. Thank you for letting Scarlett protect you."

The feeling I'd had back on the platform to Sentarshaden reared up again, but I pushed it down. The last thing I needed to do right now was cause a panic by releasing an aura of fear.

Instead, I lifted my head to my kitsune. "Thank you for doing what needed to be done to keep you both safe."

"It is quite literally my job." Scarlett smirked. "But I'll take it."

Holding Jadelyn wasn't enough, so I grabbed Scarlett too and crushed the two of them to my body.

"Come on. It sounds like we are about to have important guests show up here," I told the two of them. "I need backup if I'm going to have a conversation with either of Tyrande's parents."

Looking down at Jadelyn, I quirked a brow, asking for her help.

"They aren't too bad. I've got this." Jadelyn straightened her shirt and gave me one last peck on the cheek before slipping out of my arms.

After nuzzling into my cheek, she took on an air of importance as she strode towards the frenzy of officials. It was kind of cute watching her go from my lovely siren to slightly scary heiress of the largest shipping conglomerate in the world. Also likely, the Highaen's only great way to get things shipped into a secret paranormal city.

"Don't worry, this is her element," Scarlett commented to me as we trailed behind Jadelyn. "You almost look nervous to meet them."

"We are causing a huge stir in their city. It would only be natural for them to come into this with a bone to pick. That, and I feel particularly vulnerable since I can't shift without making my life a whole lot worse right now," I told Scar.

She nodded, her fox ears flopping against her head. "Yeah. I get it. If I was told no illusion magic, I'd feel like I was handcuffed going into a fight."

We rounded the strip mall again, and now that the fog had cleared, she could see the almost two dozen frozen cherub corpses.

"Yeah, totally handcuffed. Must really suck to only have enough power to kill two dozen cherubs by yourself," she scoffed, suddenly not so sympathetic to my plight.

"Hey, I helped. He just froze a bunch," Kelly, now in a flannel shirt that was a few sizes too big and a pair of sweatpants, called out.

I laughed as I scanned her outfit. The petite cheerleader and Morgana had about a foot in height difference.

Kelly swatted away my laugh as she worked to adjust the shirt by tying it up around her waist, squeezing her chest, and then rolled up the top of the pants so that they hugged her hips tight. Her showing more skin had the beast drooling.

Thankfully, I had more tact.

While she was becoming more presentable, a forest green SUV pulled into the parking lot, and I knew the Highaen had arrived before the door opened.

The doors popped open, and two slim legs exited first.

Tyrande's mother was tall and lanky, like many of the elves I'd seen. She had a sharp face, and her hair was pulled back into a tight bun. It made her look a little stuffy as she walked with her head tilted slightly up, even though she was just a hair shorter than me. Like all high elves, she had the same magical blue and purple eyes.

Tyrande and Yev exited the SUV behind her.

Both of them were shorter than their mother by a few inches, and somewhere in the gene pools, both of them had gotten chests. Although, Yev was adopted, so it made sense there wouldn't be many similarities. But really, the two of them could pass for sisters.

"Greetings. I was with my daughters today when the head of my police force gave me an interesting call." Her eyes landed squarely on Morgana. Her nose wrinkled with a bit of distaste, but then it was gone in an instant, a slightly polite mask sliding back over face.

"My daughters were kind enough to inform me of what you had been hired to do, but I want answers. Now," she demanded.

I just looked at her. I had always wondered which came first, power and authority or this intense self-importance. They both often seemed to go hand in hand.

Not feeling like dealing with her, and partially because my dragon didn't enjoy having things demanded of it, I turned and spoke to Yev and Tyrande.

"I tracked the dragon in the city to this shop here." I pointed behind me. "Upon arrival, I was discovered by Helena Nashner, a nephilim believed to be the daughter of the archangel of love. She quickly ordered the dragon taken away and left men behind to prevent us from chasing them down."

As I said it, I realized that the irritation hadn't gone away. The other dragon was still possibly within reach. I looked off in the direction they'd left, momentarily distracted as the clearing of a throat brought me back.

Their mother was less than amused as her face pressed into a bitchy frown.

Before I could tell her what I thought, Yev jumped in. "There's a dragon working with the celestials? But that means…" She trailed off into her own thoughts.

I was already thinking the same thing. The dragon that had forced her out in public was all part of the Church's plan from the beginning.

"The dragon is enslaved. It is all the Church's doing," I added.

Yev paused, taking that in. "Why me?" she finally said.

"We aren't sure. But it would seem that this whole ordeal has been caused by the Church in an attempt to get you." I glanced at Morgana, wondering how much to say. "There's a chance they want to use a dragon to bring through more angels into this world to arm themselves further."

The thought of the lab where they were dissecting paranormals came to mind and made me shudder. There were a host of reasons they could want a dragon. We were just taking a stab in the dark.

"Either way, we are closing in on them."

"You should have notified the Highaen and allowed us to bring our forces to bear. Your rash actions just wasted a ripe opportunity." Tyrande's mother stepped forward, anger on her face.

I wanted to be angry, but she wasn't entirely wrong. I hadn't known that I'd find the dragon, and in the excitement, I hadn't considered them escaping. And I definitely hadn't expected an enslaved dragon and a small army of celestials ready to protect it.

But I wasn't about to let her walk all over us. "I can search for him again and find him. I'd be happy to coordinate the next approach with the Highaen family now that we know the size of their forces."

Her anger cooled slightly, but only a little. Turning, she motioned to the elves to load back up, and we did the same, heading to Scarlett's car.

CHAPTER 21

"Fuck. We are chasing our tails." Scarlett slapped the steering wheel as we came up empty again.

Now that they knew I could track the dragon, he was being moved constantly. They were either keeping him in a car and driving around the city non-stop, or they were only staying in one place for fifteen minutes at a time.

Every time I tried to track him by triangulating my senses again, he was gone by the time we got there. And that was when we were lucky. Sometimes my second attempt to locate him indicated an area in an entirely different direction than the first.

"It's okay." Yev sat in the back of the car, ready to call in the Highaen support if we needed it.

The longer we went without tracking him, the more Yev's mother's words sank in. I might have missed our best shot by not calling in reinforcements.

I ground my teeth in frustration.

"It's not okay. You didn't see the other dragon," I said.

"What was wrong?" Yev asked.

I realized I hadn't gone into many details about the other dragon when I had been annoyed at her mother.

Getting quieter, I tried to tell Yev about what I'd seen. "He has been enslaved by them. They've cut his eyes out, and his body is covered in magically carved scars that seem to make him have to obey commands. Across his wrists, he has a pair of manacles that also seem magically powered. He tried to fight back against their orders, but whatever they've done to him seems to make him bend to their command."

Yev shuddered in the back seat. "I can't imagine that."

"Yeah." I let out a sad sigh, just remembering him. The loss of freedom was painful enough, but I just couldn't imagine the horror he'd experienced. "Seeing it for the first time made me pause, and that hesitation let them get away. I could tell he tried to resist. He even looked at me, despite not being able to see me. I felt... a sense of hope from him at my presence."

"Dangerous?" she asked.

"Incredibly. I don't have any dragons to compare him to, but if we compare ourselves, we are like little candles before the sun."

That dragon had been old, ancient even. I could only wonder at how much power was behind those hollow eyes.

"Maybe we shouldn't be hunting down this incredibly powerful dragon, then?" Yev hedged, being uncharacteristically skittish for a dragon. Then again, she was being hunted.

Scarlett was already piloting us back to Jadelyn's anyway. "We are going home for the day. It's getting late, and a worn-out dragon isn't going to be of much use tomorrow if I let him search all night. We need our sleep in case they spring their ambush tomorrow. They may even move it up given today's events."

"You think it'll happen?" Yev asked.

I nodded. Morgana had been discussing it with us earlier before we had separated into two cars. Now that they knew they were discovered, they would want to make a move before we had more time to regroup.

I looked back at her. "Their timetables have sped up, but by how much, we have yet to see. I don't imagine they'll want to keep moving the dragon, so I'd guess one of the next two trips to the magic range, we will see an attack."

"Makes sense." Yev nodded to herself. "We'll just have to be ready. Can you swing by the Highaen complex and drop me off?"

"Sure. We are five minutes out," Scarlett said, already changing directions. "Stay safe, Yev. I'd hate for my mate to lose his first dragon friend. It is kind of cute that he has someone he can relate to."

"Yeah, it's nice to know another dragon," Yev agreed. "Sorry for being so aggro with you at first."

Shrugging, I turned to face her before I spoke. "I think it comes with being a dragon. No harm, no foul. Just be prepared one day for me to be bigger than you and return the favor."

"My dragon won't go down easy." The challenging smirk on her face made me smile.

I had a real friend, one that understood what it meant to be a dragon.

"So, what are your hobbies, Yev?" Scarlett asked.

At first I thought it was just idle conversation, but there was an unusual aggression in her tone.

"Magic. You've seen me at the blasting range, but I do some constructive magic as well. Mostly art sort of stuff with it." Yev went along with her.

"Uh huh." Scarlett sounded unimpressed. "What about your home? We haven't been there, but is it tidy?"

Okay, that was going into an oddly personal angle.

"I guess..." Yev squirmed in the backseat, but for some reason, kept answering Scarlett. "Clean enough that I can tidy up before a guest comes over, no problem."

"You don't clean regularly?" Scarlett pressed.

"No?" It came out of Yev like a question as she sat confused.

That's when I realized what Scarlett was doing. It took everything I had not to facepalm right then and there.

She was interviewing Yev, as my first mate.

I thought there might be a little something between us, but maybe that was just me dreaming, having met my first other dragon ever. Yeah, I was probably just clinging onto it a little because she was the first I'd met.

Soon Yev would know other dragons, though. The Bronze King would give his announcement, and I expected she'd be invited off to Dubai. Once I became known, the same thing would happen.

I wasn't sure what would await us in Dubai, but I had a feeling the Bronze King was interested in making sure dragonkind continued. And that meant there would be some matchmaking involved.

"What kind of guys have you dated before? Do you have a type?" Scarlett asked, and Yev blushed a deep red.

"Taller than me, and I like them strong. There's something comforting about a guy who could pick you up and carry you if need be." Yev surprised me by answering.

Scarlett continued, "Probably hard to find someone stronger than a dragon."

At this point, I tuned them out, letting Scarlett do her thing until she dropped Yev off at the Highaen estate.

"Scarlett, you are imagining things. We are just friends," I reassured her.

"Uh, huh." She didn't sound convinced but dropped it, staring out the window at the Highaen estate that was all green and gold.

Seeing the Highaen colors again, paired everywhere in their decor, made me wonder what the Highaen family would do if they knew I was a gold dragon. It was odd. Their colors were green and gold, and that was Yev and my dragon's colors.

Once Yev was gone, I addressed Scarlett, "You didn't have to probe. I told you I'd slow down after Kelly."

"First Mate duties. I wasn't probing her. I was testing her." Scarlett kept her eyes on the road. "You *are* going to have a dragon wife, or maybe even multiple, before this is all done. I'm going to push and test every female dragon you meet to see which one is right."

I nodded, realizing I had asked her to form an opinion. It made sense she'd have her own way of feeling them out.

"Then how did she do?" I asked.

"So-so." Scarlett wobbled her hand. "She's got a good background. Highaen counts for something, but she's not really romantically available, as I can see it. Though, that might be because she's more focused on being hunted right now. That and I'm not convinced she isn't messy. But you seem to be her type." She tapped her lips in thought before shrugging it off.

Being hunted did seem like a good reason to not get too romantically involved. As for everything else, I would not concern myself with it. Romance came first.

"Well, for now, we are just friends. If it becomes more, there's time."

"Hah. Maybe. I have a feeling that, once the Bronze King gets involved, it's going to get a bit more complicated," she chuckled.

I grunted in response. I hated the unknown of what the Bronze King would do. "We'll take those problems on as they come. We can't worry too much about him or we'll paralyze ourselves with inaction. Right now, I want to deal with the other dragon. I have a feeling he's a critical part of their plan."

"How so?" Scarlett asked.

"He's big, Scar. Crazy big and powerful. I can feel it. You don't bring an indispensable weapon like that into the city unless you are going to use it."

My words made both of us go quiet in thought for the rest of the drive until her tires finally came to a halt. Looking up, I realized we were back. I'd been so deep in my thoughts that I hadn't noticed.

"Come on. Let's see if we can perk you back up." Scarlett bounded out of the car and came around to my side, hooking her arm in mine as I exited and made my way into the home.

As we entered, Jadelyn was already walking up to us, opening her arms as she wrapped me in a hug.

When we separated, she grabbed my arm and pulled me into the kitchen where she'd started dinner. The oven was still going, but it smelled amazing.

"No luck?" Morgana asked, looking up from her spot on a couch, surrounded by her weapons.

"They keep moving him."

She nodded as if it was what she had expected. "They are professionals. After we found them once, they are going to overreact and be paranoid. We got too close."

Giving Scarlett a kiss, I pulled her down on the couch to cuddle as we all talked. "So that means it is going to happen soon."

"I'd bet on it." Morgana grabbed the glass of blood on the side table and took a sip. "The question is, what did we learn today?"

I laughed to myself as her voice took on her teacher's tone.

"They have a dragon, a very powerful one, enslaved," I stated the obvious. "Are they just using it to out other dragons?"

Kelly joined the conversation, pulling an ottoman up and sitting in front of me, grabbing one of my legs and kneading my tired calves. "That might be one use, but if that were the case, it would be put back away wherever they keep it."

"The celestial plane," Morgana said quickly. "What you described makes me think that he's been subjected to archangels. If he's as strong as you say, then that's who would have had to hold him down and enchant him like that. They'd need several for a dragon like that. I doubt there are multiple of them out of the celestial plane at one time."

I paused, trying to think through what she'd said. "If he's so powerful, why don't they just use him to allow an archangel through to our world?"

"I bet they have in the past, and will continue to use him to help anchor the celestial plane." Morgana paused before continuing.

"Think about Helena. The archangel of love had to come to our plane, consummate with the old Nashner, and bear a child in our world. I'd bet they had been using the dragon for years to allow an archangel to play in our world, which brings another question. If he's worth enough to keep an archangel from joining this battle, what is it they have planned for him that makes them keep him here?" Morgana laid her thoughts out.

The more I thought about it, the more I realized she was right. "He's part of their plan to kidnap Yev."

Kelly was distracting me, working magic on my legs.

"Where did you learn to do that?" I asked.

"Something like this is a great way to warm up a superior wolf. I learned it from watching others as a kid. But that's not the point. What is this old dragon for?" She pulled me back on topic.

"We don't know what color he is," Jadelyn tried to help from the kitchen. "That would make a big difference."

"Two things come to mind," I said. "One, you bring a dragon this big to snatch a smaller dragon, overpower them, and pull them away. Two, you bring him as a distraction and a giant meat wall."

"Why not both?" Scarlett said. "You send a team in and try to separate Yev from a crowd, and then you have a massive dragon to pin her and extract her."

"Hell, if they get her alive, they could do what they did to him to her," Kelly stated.

I'd considered it before, but not with the celestial plane angle. They could chain her up in heaven and carve her up until she was obedient, maybe even fatten her up so she could help anchor the celestial plane for another archangel to come down.

I cringed, suddenly antsy. I stood up, pacing the room.

"We can't let that happen," I declared "Under no circumstances do the angels get to do anything like that to another dragon. So help me, I'll tear every last one of them apart piece by piece if I see that happen to another one."

My stomach churned at the thought. They presented themselves as holy and pure, but there was nothing pure in their actions. Anything that could stomach what they had done to that dragon was nothing less than a vile being that should be wiped from the face of the earth.

A hand pressed into my chest, pulling me from my anger.

"Calm down," Scarlett said, getting in my face.

I took a deep breath, but it wasn't very deep. I tried again, gritting my teeth. "Sorry. It just makes me so angry seeing what they did to that dragon."

"Almost happy I didn't see it." Jadelyn bumped the oven closed with her hip as she carried a casserole dish with two oven mitts over to the table. "But let us forget that for now. It's time for family dinner."

She walked the casserole over to the table where there was already a tossed salad waiting and several bottles of wine ready for us.

I prowled into the kitchen, catching Jadelyn as soon as she put the hot dish down and grabbed her, kissing her neck. "Thank you."

"You are very welcome. But if you don't let me go, we're going to have to serve it using our hands." She batted me away with a smile.

Feeling like I needed to love on my women before the potential chaos from battle, I pulled out the chair next to mine. "Kelly, come sit here."

When she sat, I pushed the chair in, leaning over her and kissing the side of her face. "You did wonderful today, my wolf."

"Thank you, alpha." She blushed, turning to me and stealing a kiss.

Morgana sat down next to Kelly with a big smirk, immediately claiming one of the bottles on the table and placing it directly in front of her.

I pulled out the chair on my other side for Scarlett. "A special thanks today to Scarlett, who helped me dial in my instincts and track down the other dragon. Cheers."

I poured everyone a glass, and we raised it in a small toast before taking sips.

"It was a good day. Felt like we made progress instead of just waiting." Jadelyn sat opposite of me. "That feels good."

"Indeed. Cheers to that." I took another sip of wine. "Now, what do we have here?"

Kelly grabbed the hot lid with her bare hands and lifted it off, only to flood the room with a lovely aroma of chicken and cheese.

"Baked cheddar-stuffed chicken. It isn't fancy, but it is very tasty," Jadelyn explained.

It looked like the chicken breasts were soaking in some cream-based sauce.

"It looks amazing," I said.

"I'm making muffins after, for dessert," Scarlett said happily.

Remembering how much the little minx loved muffins, I was surprised I hadn't been eating them every day. Then again, she had a love/hate relationship with them and what they did to her waist.

"I look forward to more of your muffins. You need to make them more often." Then I turned to Kelly. "What is your favorite?"

"Bacon," she blurted. "Anything bacon. The wolf in me loves it."

Jadelyn had a slight frown on her face, looking at her dish. I knew she was thinking that she could have added bacon. I rubbed my foot along her leg, breaking her from her thoughts.

Her eyes connected with mine, and her face lit up in a small smile.

"Not just a wolf thing. Everybody loves bacon," I said, leaning forward to spear two chicken breasts and placing them on my plate before digging in.

The dinner table quieted down as we ate, with an occasional mumbled thank you to Jadelyn as we stuffed ourselves with her food.

"I'd like to talk about what we are going to do as a family once my secret is out." I pushed away from the table as Scarlett was starting to make muffins. "With the new dragon and everything happening... I... I think I'm going to let myself stop hiding," I declared.

The girls were quiet for a moment, soaking in what I had just said.

We had all known it would be a problem, but one for the vague future. I'd now put the issue of my secret getting out into the very real, very near future in a way that made us all face it.

"Well, the first thing I'm going to do is rub my dad's face in it," Jadelyn tried to lighten the mood. "Ah, we should let my mother in on it. She'll want to see my father's reaction."

"Not sure if there will be that much control over how quickly it spreads." I scratched the back of my head. "My plan was to hold it in until we fought with the templars. But I know some camera is going to get me shifting, and then it is just a matter of time."

"Don't forget the pack of furballs that know the truth. Your secret might already be out." Morgana gave Kelly a languid stare.

Kelly was up in arms. "Hey! My pack can hold a secret. I think..."

We all knew that, with two hundred wolves knowing, it was only a matter of time. But we might beat them to it.

"It doesn't matter. I can't hold on to this secret and protect Yev. So, I wanted to make sure you were all ready for it; it affects you too." I looked around.

Jadelyn rolled her eyes. "I get to brag now. There aren't any downsides for me."

"You aren't worried about what it'll do for your security?" I frowned. She seemed completely okay with it. I thought the increased attention and possibly a need for more security would bother Jadelyn.

She gave me a flat stare. "Those are already huge concerns for me. At least now everyone will know that if they fuck with me, they get a big, angry dragon coming for them." She turned to Scarlett. "Actually, can I get lighter security once it is known?"

"No." Scarlett didn't even look up from the mixing bowl. "But it won't matter; your guard will be the same as always. But we may extend guards and training to him as well."

"Yay!" Jadelyn clapped. "You can join me for evacuation drills. They are the best." Her voice dripped with sarcasm.

"But a necessity," Scarlett butted in, pointing her dough-covered spoon at Jadelyn with a frown before she went back to mixing. "At least having a dragon around should scare away plenty of people."

Morgana cleared her throat. "Not to mention having other mates that might have reputations."

"I completely agree. Having the world's first female alpha will be a great boon." Kelly and Morgana locked eyes, and tension spiked between the two of them.

"Maybe one day," Morgana threw back.

Holding a hand up to forestall any conflict between the two of them, I quickly put it to rest. "Both of you will add a wonderful threat to anyone who tries to touch one of my mates."

"Or you," Kelly added. "Someone touches any of you, and my entire pack is on the hunt."

"With that, we can agree," Morgana said. "I'll be right there, with every connection I can pull, standing with you if someone touches any of our family."

Jadelyn gestured wildly at the two of them while looking at Scarlett. "See, who is going to hassle me now?"

"People are idiots, even if they are soon to be dead idiots," Scarlett replied, clearly not willing to budge.

Jadelyn sighed, going quiet.

I watched them all, smiling to myself. My women all supported my decision, and they were ready for what was to come. I'd need them in the coming days, and I'd do everything in my power to protect them.

CHAPTER 22

I walked into the magic range, the girls
following in after me.

The lady at the counter recognized us this
time, and we didn't have any trouble being
guided to the proper room once she saw
Jadelyn.

"Hey, you made it this time." Yev turned
away from the blasting chamber before she
cast her spell.

I waved awkwardly. Having gotten over
some of my own issues, I was more comfortable coming into the magic range today. "Sorry we weren't able to locate them
again."

"Don't mind my mother; she gets into
people's heads like that. It's how she gets
what she wants. I get it. You were investi-
gating and suddenly came up with a much
larger lead than you expected." Tyrande
shrugged it off, and I was pleasantly surprised. I'd thought that she might take after

her mother, but she was clearly more understanding.

Time and time again, the high elf heiress
surprised me with just how down to earth
she could be.

"Besides, we are just waiting for the trap to
close," Yev agreed. "We have three hundred
Highaen mages on standby within a block
of this location."

Kelly let out a soft whistle. "Damn."

It was an impressive display of force, yet
I knew the Church was preparing for the
Highaen response.

I hoped it would be enough, but only time
would tell. With Scarlett with us, I was confident that we could whisk Yev from immediate danger if it was needed.

"Good, we should be prepared today. And
it's probably best if we don't wear ourselves
down from shooting at fake targets." I eyed
the setup that Yev had input down range.

"Oh, that's a good point. I'm just so damn
nervous. It felt good to take it out on the
dummies." Yev rubbed at her tired eyes.

"She didn't sleep much last night,"
Tyrande pointed out, earning herself a
growl from the green dragon.

"You try sleeping with an impending
kidnapping attempt. And then add what
they did to that other dragon. Sleeping
would only mean nightmares, anyway." Yev
stomped her way over to the lounging area
and plopped down on the couch.

Jadelyn sat down next to her and put a comforting arm around the dragon. "It's okay to be scared."

"I'm a tree-damned dragon." Yev crossed her arms, but she seemed to relax with Jadelyn next to her.

I smiled at Jadelyn, once again noting how important she was for our group. Finding my seat, I was instantly surrounded by Morgana and Kelly. Scarlett looked at my empty lap but ended up sitting next to Jadelyn.

Tyrande must have been equally nervous because she didn't sit down. Instead, she just paced back and forth, constantly looking at her phone. She must have been getting updates from her people outside the building.

I didn't enjoy waiting any more than them, but I felt ready for the fight to come. I'd left my spatial artifact back at Jadelyn's place; Morgana was carrying a few spare changes of clothes and the silver sword for me.

I tried to reassure Tyrande and fill the silence. "We are here and ready, and your teams are in place. We've done all we can to prepare, now we just need to wa—"

Boom.

An explosion sounded in the distance, and dust fell from the ceiling.

I tried to sense the distance, but in the fortified room, it was hard to know for sure.

Tyrande's phone chirped, and she read aloud. "Explosion on the east side of the building, they think—"

The back wall of the blasting chamber blew inward with another controlled explosion.

"—that they are breaching into our room," Tyrande finished, ending with a heavy sigh at the late information.

Men in black with face masks poured into the room, leveling guns at our group. Beyond them, the busy street outside was chaotic. Screams and sirens began to sound from the explosion and clear intruders.

Yev leapt to her feet with an angry growl, green scales dotting her skin.

I grabbed Yev before she could shift. "I believe the plan is to extract you; it's best if you stay back."

Even if Yev was strong in her own right, as the target of their attack, she still needed to get out of here.

Scarlett was quick to grab Yev, Tyrande, and Jadelyn. "Out this way, with me."

This fight was for me, Morgana, and Kelly while the sisters and Jadelyn were evacuated out.

"Good luck, love!" Jadelyn shouted back at me as she followed Scarlett out the door into the hallway of the magic range.

As they exited, Morgana, Kelly, and I turned toward the intruders. I hoped that the three hundred Highaen mages weren't too far away because we were massively outnumbered.

But I'd made my decision the night before with the blessing of my women, so charging forward, I didn't hesitate as I let my body shift.

All we had to do was stall them so that the Highaen forces could overwhelm them from behind. I knew the Highaen forces would have some trouble with the dragon and Helena, but I was hoping that, between the three of us, we could take on that challenge.

As I shifted, bullets pinged harmlessly off my scales. I twisted and turned as I charged forward, trying to sense the other dragon, but I didn't feel him among the group.

Hell, I barely even sensed much mana from them. Only a few of them had more than a bare flicker. I let loose a jet of fire that cooked the front line of gunmen, but it wasn't even satisfying.

"Something is wrong," I told Morgana even as bullets continued to pelt my side. "This group doesn't have near enough firepower to go after a dragon."

Morgana paused, striking down a few of the men while looking around, sensing the same thing.

I realized that we didn't have a good way to tell the Highaen mages it was a diversion as frozen barriers slammed down around the mass of men.

The Highaen mages were spilling into the streets behind them. And it was complete overkill. The gunmen were encased in a sphere of ice at least twenty feet thick and had no mana. They weren't going anywhere.

"Kelly, text Scarlett. These aren't the Church's main forces."

I knew immediately that these were scapegoats meant to spring our trap. I felt a little sorry for the men. They'd been sent to their slaughter.

"This way." Morgana was running out the door, chasing after the girls, and I had to shift back, running naked after her as Kelly brought up the rear.

Kelly was nearly smashing the screen of her phone as she got the word to Scarlett. Werewolf fingers weren't the best for texting.

As we made it out front, Scarlett was hopping into a black SUV. Jadelyn's face was pressed against the back window. Spotting us, I saw her start shouting. Scarlett's head dipped down, likely to check her phone. Seeing whatever Kelly typed, she looked up and quickly scanned the area.

And that was the moment when a dozen angels landed next to the SUV and grabbed hold of the bumper, lifting the car straight up into the air.

I expected my dragon to panic, but it was as if the entire world went out of focus, and the only thing I could see was my mates being lifted away.

Golden claws dug into the concrete below me as I lifted my head, roaring in anger as I shifted right there on the front steps of the magic range. The beast was right there with me, and the two of us were on the same page. All of those angels needed to die.

As I went to take off, though, the doors of the SUV flew open.

Scarlett, Jadelyn, and Tyrande jumped out of the car, falling roughly a dozen feet to the ground.

Scarlett dissipated the impact of her fall with a roll, quickly on her feet once more. The other two were less graceful, but they stood, a bit wobbly but not too injured.

I looked around, wondering why Yev hadn't jumped with them.

But a second later, the black SUV crumpled as it expanded. Safety glass shattered and rained down onto the street as a green dragon burst out of the side of the car. Yev took a bite of an angel before the car split into several pieces. As it did, she let herself fall to the ground, using a few flaps of her wings to soften her fall.

Yev belched green flames, causing the car to sizzle and dissolve before our very eyes, and three of the angels caught in her caustic breath, screaming and falling to the ground before they died.

"Fuckers," Yev screamed, taking to the air after the remainder of the angels.

I wanted to chase the enemies as well, but I was more drawn to protect Jadelyn. I crouched over her, daring anybody to attack.

"I'm fine." She pushed my muzzle away. "Help Yev."

I paused, sniffing her for injury, before making sure Scarlett was nearby and able to protect her. Feeling satisfied, I threw my head back up and launched myself from the ground with a few flaps of my wings.

The angels turned to me in shock, surprised at my sudden appearance behind them.

The stunned moment was all I needed to close my jaws around the first and grab two other angels with my front claws. I felt the satisfying crunch of the angel between my teeth as I held the other two up to my jaw. Once I'd swallowed the first, I released a powerful breath of fire over the two in my grasps.

Flames licked over my claws, doing me no harm, but the two poor angels were nothing but ash by the time my breath was done. I smiled, satisfied at the brutality of my direct fire blasts.

I went to move on the others as bullets fired up around us. The remaining four angels put up barriers to protect themselves from the spray of bullets.

The Highaen forces had turned their attention to the second threat. Although, I had a feeling Scarlett would have some opinions on the speed at which they'd managed to reach us.

Something hit me hard in the side, and I tumbled out of the air as I heard shouts rise up below. As I tumbled, I saw cherubs racing into the area, attacking the Highaen forces.

Determining my mates weren't in any immediate danger, I turned back to find the source of the blast that had knocked me out of the air.

Helena floated just off to my side, her spear pointed at me and gathering light for what I assumed would be another blast.

I shifted down to my dragon knight form just in time to avoid another beam of light from her spear.

She followed up by diving at me, and I decided to meet her halfway. I kept my dragon wings while still otherwise wearing my typical dragon knight form. Rising to meet her charge, I let loose a wash of fire to break her momentum and create a screen for what I was about to do next. Two powerful flaps of my wings later, I was above her as she darted around my fire, only to find the space empty.

I dropped down on Helena, grabbing her shoulder and one of her arms. My weight was a surprise, her wings unable to hold us both. As a result, we fell into a nearby alley, landing in a tumble. I made sure to land on top of her.

"Get off of me, vile monster." Helena struggled, her spear swinging dangerously close to my face.

I thought I'd be able to simply overpower her physically, but it seemed I had underestimated the nephilim. She got her feet out from under me and kicked off the ground, crashing me through the building's wall.

The hit was enough for me to lose my grip on her. The second I landed on the ground, I lunged to the side, anticipating the next hit. Sure enough, her spear slashed the space I'd just been in.

I scrambled to my feet. We were in some basic office space, our entrance knocking over a few empty cubicles. I grabbed a printer next to me and threw it at Helena to make some space for myself.

She cut it in half before it could reach her, but it had thankfully stopped her in her tracks.

"I'm the monster? Have you seen what you have done to that other dragon? You don't stand for anything just," I growled.

"Shut up. I won't listen to your lies," she screamed, a hint of fear in her eyes.

I understood, in that moment, that she knew she was wrong. And on some level, it bothered her. Pointing it out had been like irritating a splinter.

Helena charged forward a bit more frantically, and this time, I grabbed a cubicle divider and swung it like a blunt weapon. I waited until I was partway through the swing to release my actual attack, spraying a jet of fire right into her face.

Helena stopped trying to block the divider wall and instead threw up a glowing white shield to block my fire. The divider caught her in the side, tossing her into another bank of cubicles as it broke in my hands.

Dropping the divider, I threw myself on top of her before she had a chance to get up. I got my hands on the spear and pressed the shaft to her chest to hold her down.

Knowing her strength, I packed on another several hundred pounds as I pinned her to the floor. My claws dug into her skin, but they barely did more than scratch her. She was far tougher than she looked.

She glanced down where the spear squished her rather bountiful cleavage and her gaze came back up, full of fury. "Get off me!"

A shockwave of magic slammed into me with her words, and it pushed me up and off of her, smashing through the ceiling.

It was the ceiling of the next floor that halted me. I bounced off, landing as I let some of my mass fade away, restoring myself to my normal dragon knight form.

This floor seemed fancier, but it was still mostly office space, like the one below. I straightened up as a pissed off nephilim shot through the hole I'd made, thrusting her spear and aiming to kill.

I rolled to the side, forcing her spear to hit the bookshelf, utterly destroying it and all of its contents as a blast of white light vaporized them all.

Her spear twirled, and she chopped down at my new location.

Morgana had taught me how to fight a spear, and the right move from her training was to catch the shaft of the spear in my hand. But the glowing weapon had me hesitating. I had no idea what it would do if I tried to hold it.

So instead, I flapped my wings once, launching myself back and away from her strike as it caved in another section of the flooring.

The office we were in was ruined at that point, and the floor dipped dangerously under my feet. I stomped hard, giving the floor the last push it needed to cave in as I jumped through the door behind me and out into the hallway.

Helena's footing disappeared, and she fell down out of my view for only a moment before she rode back up on her fluffy white wings. The wings were a stark contrast to the utter rage on her face.

She went wild, her spear destroying the office in a flurry of attacks that had me dodging back, trying to stay out of her superior range.

I let her work herself up, watching for an opening.

We darted around the room as I waited and waited, but then I saw it. She'd left herself open.

I barreled forward, catching her by the waist and lifting her up. Not giving her a chance to maneuver, I pulled her body back down, slamming it into the floor.

As her momentum hit, the floor gave out underneath us and we fell. I rode her torso like a surfboard, landing straight on top of her and letting myself fall forward.

I landed with one hand on her shoulder and one on a squishy globe.

Not interested in being blasted again, I rolled off, knowing I couldn't pin her effectively. Sure enough, the world went white as she sent out another shockwave and a scream of rage.

Then she swung hard, collapsing multiple walls on the first floor. The building groaned; wood creaked and crackled before a heavy snap told me I needed to get the hell out of the building.

Shifting into my dragon form, I crashed through the walls of the crumbling building, escaping before it came down on top of me. I barely made it out before, one by one, the floors collapsed. The ground shook as debris pelted my side.

Morgana was there, angel blood on her blades, looking tired, but relieved to see me again.

I scanned around, taking in pure chaos and war.

Hundreds of cherubs and angels fought as the Highaen forces flooded the area with reinforcements.

"What happened to you?" Morgana asked.

The collapsed building shuddered, and concrete and scraps of wood went flying as Helena screamed, throwing herself out of the mess. Her hair was scattered, her blouse was torn, and her pencil skirt was ripped clear up to her hip. Yet she didn't have a scratch on her pale skin.

"That." I pointed at the raging nephilim who was now wreathed in holy white fire.

Helena looked around, a frown crossing her face as she saw that her forces were being overpowered and pushed back.

"Clear the area!" someone shouted, their voice enhanced by magic as it cut through the sounds of battle.

I paused, curious as to why the Highaen forces would hold back, when a soft blue light washed the area.

Looking up towards the light, I watched as the tree above produced a massive ball of glowing magic. I realized they were about to do the magical equivalent of an artillery strike.

Highaen forces found cover as the ball of magic pulsed ominously with frosty magic.

Taking it in, I quickly ducked behind cover and shifted to silver, assuming that blue and the Highaen specialty of frost magic meant that I could use my silver form to weather this.

Helena stopped focusing on me, her eyes zeroing in on the blue light.

She raised her voice and yelled at the top of her lungs, "Release the Silver Slave!"

I paused, trying to figure out what they were talking about, when it finally clicked. I still didn't know what color dragon they had, but at that moment, I was willing to bet he was silver.

And that also made him the perfect weapon against the Highaen forces, which used almost entirely frost magic. If that ancient dragon was really a silver, then the Highaen magic would be nearly useless against it.

Buildings a row over bowed outward, crashing down as a massive silver form rose from them.

I kept thinking it would stop growing, but it just kept getting larger.

Its eyes were gouged out, and each of its scales was carved with runes. The Silver Slave let out a hoarse, but no less deafening, roar as it finished transforming. What

struck me as odd were the massive manacles that had enlarged with its shift.

It was big enough that a football stadium
would look like a dog bed to it.

The sheer size of the Silver Slave boggled
my mind, making me wonder just how big
dragons could grow. This one was easily
over a hundred yards long, and its head
rose above an eight-story building.

Up in the boughs of Sentarshaden, the
blue ball of magic shrank, flickering for just
a moment before a massive, frosty blue
beam shot down.

The Silver Slave hopped, catching the
beam on its side, and protecting all the
Church's forces below.

Blinding blue light filled the air on impact, and the world seemed to pause as
we all held our breath, wondering what we
would see when the blinding light cleared.

As my vision returned, the dragon had
easily survived the blast, with only some
frost on its side to show for the massive
magic attack. It shook like a dog, sloughing
off the frost as its tail whipped back and
forth, smashing buildings and raining debris down on the Highaen forces.

"That's... a dragon." Morgana said from
my side, in awe.

We were all frozen, watching the massive
beast destroy the area. I had been hoping
that the tree would have been able to take

down the dragon, but this dragon was be-yond what I could have imagined.

And I wasn't the only one. Everybody around was stunned, the noise of the battle pausing in everybody's disbelief.

When I finally came to my senses and looked for Helena, she'd darted among the Highaen forces, snatching Tyrande and holding her as a captive in the middle of a standoff.

I paused, trying to figure out what to do next.

CHAPTER 23

Helena threw back her head, laughing. "Clear out," she told her troops.

Tyrande smashed a blast of icy magic into the nephilim, struggling in her grip.

Ice plastered itself to Helena, doing no damage. She glared down at her captive before a swift blow to the head stunned her.

Tyrande looked like a grumpy kitten hanging from Helena's hand after that.

The Silver Slave raged, smashing buildings and sending freezing fog down the street.

I wanted to chase after Helena as she flew away with Tyrande, but I also knew that was part of why she had been taken. She was bait to snag a new dragon.

Two more blasts from the tree were blocked by the Silver Slave as it protected the angel's retreat. Cherubs were disengaging on the ground and escaping through pre-planned routes.

Dozens of angels took to the air, and even the Silver Slave flapped its wings several times, lifting its massive body up into the air at the cost of more buildings.

They had successfully smashed into Sentarshaden, proving that they could attack the high elves even in their fortified city. We'd kept them from their target, but we'd lost the Highaen heiress.

"What's the play here, Morgana?" I asked, hoping her experience would lead to a simple plan.

"I don't know. We came to a knife fight, and they pulled out a gun. No, they pulled out a goddamn grenade launcher," Morgana spat on the ground, staring at the retreating forces.

A few yells sounded from nearby, and as I turned, Yev burst from a cluster of Highaen forces. She had shifted, and I could tell that she had homed in on the enemy. I knew that look. She was single-mindedly chasing her sister.

I cursed, flying to try to catch and stop her.

Morgana threw herself onto my back, and I was glad for her support. If we ended up in that mess of angels, I would need her.

"Yev! Get down, you can't do anything," I shouted, my voice a low draconic rumble.

My wings were churning the air as I raced after Yev.

Beams of frost magic shot from Sentar-shaden, but the Silver Slave dove in and out, covering their retreat.

They were moving quickly, and I was struggling to keep up. My dragon screamed inside of me, wanting to catch the enemy. I felt it almost stretching in me, calling on me to go faster.

I followed the instincts, taking all the emotion I was feeling and shoving it towards my wings, urging them to go faster.

Pouring my urgency into the innate magic of my wings, I felt it bolster them. My speed began to pick up, and I was able to catch up to Yev just as we left the city.

The illusion of a mountain snapped into place behind me, and I realized we were potentially in full view of any humans nearby. I looked around, knowing a few mountain climbers might spot us, but otherwise, the area looked relatively uninhabited.

"Yev, stop. You are only going to get yourself in more danger if you chase. They want to lure you away from your family's forces." I was only moments away from trying to tackle her out of the sky, though that could end poorly for both of us.

"They have my sister!" Yev's eyes were bloodshot, and she looked frayed. "It's my fault. I need to get her back."

Yev had lost it. I wasn't sure if it was the lack of sleep or her dragon instincts, but she was becoming more manic by the second from watching the angels fly away with her sister.

Not sure what to do to shake her out of it, I got close and bit her tail.

Yev let out a very undragonlike squeak. "What the fuck?"

"Get your head out of your ass. Look where we are. You need to head back to the city."

For the first time since I'd been chasing after her, there was a hint of clarity in her eyes as she looked around and then behind her. It finally clicked in her brain that she'd left the safety of Sentarshaden.

But the angels had also figured it out by the time I'd gotten her attention, and several angels had carved off from the fleeing troops and were coming towards us.

"We have company," Morgana hissed, seeing the same thing.

I nodded, preparing. We could handle a few angels.

But then the Silver Slave slowed, and my stomach dropped. Sure enough, he turned and started heading towards us, his expression telling me it wasn't what he wanted to do.

"Oh fuck. We need to get back to the city." I banked hard, intending to turn around and fly right back into the mountain.

"You can't. At least not like you're thinking. There are only a few spots where you can permeate the illusion," Yev called out.

"We are locked out?" Now I was panicking. The Silver Slave looked like it was just floating through the air, but that was a perspective thing. As big as it was, it was devouring up the space between us.

"No, we can get in. We just need to circle around the mountain." Yev led the way.

Morgana tapped the side of my neck and spoke quietly enough so that Yev wouldn't hear. "Do we really want to lead that thing back into the city and show it and the angels where the city is vulnerable?"

My immediate answer was no, but that meant I had to deal with the giant fucker outside of it. How I'd do that and survive, I wasn't sure.

I grit my teeth, hating what I was about to say. "Yev, let's lead it deeper into the mountain range."

"What?" Her head turned, filled with shock.

"That thing could smash your city. We were lucky that they fled."

Yev stared at me for a long moment, processing what I had said. "So then what are we doing? Sacrificing ourselves?"

"I don't know. Our best bet is to take down the angels with it. Maybe that will free it? Or keep it from getting more orders?" It was only a guess, and not a great one. But it was the best plan I could come up with at the moment.

"There's always a chance," Morgana encouraged me. "You came out on top against an alpha wolf before you knew how to shift. And while you were still understanding your shifting, you took out a god. Do not underestimate yourself, Pendragon."

I nodded, appreciating the pep talk. She was right; I had overcome odds in the past, but this felt like a huge leap. But we were about to find out if we'd survive because the dragon was almost on top of us.

As we passed by the illusionary mountain that hid Sentarshaden, the Silver Slave was closing fast.

I looked for the angels, realizing they were currently riding on its head in comfort. I could nearly make out their faces that I was sure were smug smiles.

The Silver Slave's runes lit up as it tossed its head. I could tell it was fighting the commands like it had behind the storefront.

A roar shook the mountains, and I watched in horror as dozens of avalanches started around us. If there were any mountain climbers on those mountains, they were now in some deep trouble.

And so were we.

"Dive," Morgana screamed.

I didn't question her, tucking my wings into a dive as a frosty blue beam tore through the air above me.

It was already cold, but the surrounding air dropped dozens of degrees with the blast.

The air boomed as the Silver Slave flew over us.

"Zach, what do we do?" Yev asked, looking up at the massive dragon, terrified.

And I didn't have an answer.

"Capture them," an angel screamed above the wind.

There was only a momentary pause before the Silver Slave dove.

I watched it coming, trying to puzzle out some sort of plan. It was faster and larger than us; outrunning wasn't an option. And even if I did manage to avoid the dive, Yev would become the target.

The dragon descended closer as I prepared my throat, deciding my fire was my best bet.

Just as I was prepared to blast it, a piercing cry broke the air, followed by another. Dozens of paranormals streamed out of the mountain that contained Sentarshaden.

Flickers of fire at the front announced the phoenixes, but they were far from alone. Dozens of paranormals turned into hundreds as a massive flock of flying paranormals broke free of the mountain, diving for the Silver Slave.

"Yev, to the right," I said, dipping down and to the right, hoping to escape the massive dragon's clutches for another minute in the distraction.

I knew we weren't safe yet. The paranormals streaming out of the mountain weren't some military unit or hired by the Highaen. They were the citizens of Sentarshaden, standing up for themselves and protecting their city.

During the assault by the angels, they had left it to the authorities, but seeing the Silver Slave come back, the citizens had finally stood up. They had understood the threat it posed to their secret paranormal city, and they weren't going to take it.

We just needed to stall for another minute while they got here.

"Zach." Yev's voice was full of worry. I knew she hated to see her citizens at risk.

We pivoted once more, but I realized that we were flying straight down into one of the avalanches created by the Silver Slave's roar. I nodded towards it, hoping we could hide in the avalanche and evade the dragon's grasp a moment longer.

"Morgana, come here." I opened my claw next to her, not wanting to risk losing her in the avalanche.

She didn't hesitate, jumping into my grasp as I closed my claws around her, bracing for the oncoming wave of snow. It made my heart warm that she didn't question me, or even pause. She jumped into my hand as

I dove into a natural disaster without hesitation.

As we descended into the avalanche, I flared my wings, once again trying to channel my emotions into them as I flapped two powerful beats of my wings to slow my descent.

I hit the snow, sending a spray of white into the air. Yev was right behind me, hitting the side of the mountain as the avalanche caught up to both of us.

Despite my size, I was swept up. I held Morgana close and curled around her to protect her.

The avalanche took control of my body, spinning and twirling me among the snowy wave. I wondered if that was what it felt like to be in the laundry during the tumble cycle.

I put out my senses, my stomach dropping as I knew that the Silver Slave had landed on the mountain.

Knowing that we were relatively safe for the moment, I tried to use the claws that weren't holding Morgana to get a grip on the side of the mountain.

My claws couldn't get a good grip for a few tries, but soon they caught, and I pulled myself free of the snow, bracing myself against a large rock as my vision stabilized itself.

The world continued to shift and swirl around me as my head swam.

"Zach," Morgana groaned from my claw, and I lifted her clear of the snow, opening my claw even as snow continued to pour around us, the rock at my back holding me steady.

"Here." I tried to give her a view while I tried to make sense of what I was seeing in my own brain.

Streams of smaller paranormals swarmed the Silver Slave. It was clinging to the side of the mountain, its massive maw snapping at the paranormals harassing it as they dove and shot away, spraying fire, lightning, and all manner of attacks at the massive dragon.

"Looks like the backup is working." I felt a big grin grace my draconic face.

"They need to kill the angels." Morgana pointed at the angels, still sitting on the head of the massive dragon.

Raising my head, I poured mana into my throat and relayed her message at the top of my lungs. "Kill the angels."

It felt somewhat futile given the distance and the chaos, but slowly it seemed to have an effect.

The swarm's attacks shifted. They started throwing more and more of their attacks at the angels, who were forced to block with white barriers or dodge along the back of the Silver Slave.

Yev's head popped out of the snow, looking dazed and wobbly. She tried to fly sideways out of the snow and ended up going back under the avalanche.

I snorted, but the avalanche was thinning, and I could see her green scales even as she tumbled further down the mountain.

Launching myself up over the rock, I glided down after her, grabbing her back and pulling her out of the snow and over to a safe ledge.

"Is it my birthday?" Yev asked.

I stared at her, wondering if she hit her head. "No, but some of your people came to save us."

I nudged her and made her look up at the fight happening further up the mountain.

Hundreds of flying paranormals were continuing their barrage on the Silver Slave and the angels on his back. But I knew it wouldn't last very long, and we needed to use the opportunity.

"Come on. We need to end this," I growled, taking flight once again.

"How exactly are we ending this?" Morgana asked from my back.

I wanted to answer her, but I hadn't figured that part out yet. Despite the help from the city, the many flying paranormals were like flies trying to take down a horse.

As we flew back up the mountain where the battle raged, the last of the angels tried to command the Silver Slave. His eyes flashed dangerously as he took note of us.

"Capture those two and return them to the celestial plane." He gave his last commands to the silver dragon before throwing himself at a pterodactyl-like paranormal, taking it out with him as the two of them fell down the mountain, lifeless.

The Silver Slave whipped its head. Somehow, it still managed to find me despite its hollow eyes. Its neck strained as more of those runes lit up along its body.

"Please, free me from this misery," it pleaded.

"How?" I shouted.

"Kill me." Its voice was hoarse.

I could only imagine what it had gone through. Even now, it suffered countless small scratches along its back, but it didn't even flinch.

Squeezing my eyes shut, I wanted there to be another way. But I knew there wasn't.

The silver dragon snapped its wings back out, flapping them twice and launching itself high into the air. I could think of only one way to kill something of its size.

"Yev, it's last order was to capture us. Follow me." I turned in the air and started circling, trying to gain as much altitude as I could.

Even if she didn't know what I was planning, Yev followed.

Enhancing my voice yet again, I shouted to the mass of paranormals from the city. "Stand down. We've got this under control."

At first only a few, but then more broke from the fight, landing on the nearby mountains to watch.

I knew that, in a straight shot, the dragon may be able to outpace us, but climbing up higher into the sky would be difficult with its weight.

Up and up, we circled, until I broke through the clouds, riding on thin air.

"What's the plan?" Yev puffed clouds out of her way.

"As soon as he's up above the clouds, go for his wings," I told her my plan.

"Wait, what? You want to drop him out of the sky?" Yev said frantically. "What if he crushes one of these mountains?"

"He isn't that big," I laughed. "But Switzerland will probably get a reading on the Richter scale."

Morgana was climbing up my neck to hold on to my horns. "Your plan is insane. But it might work. Get me on his back and I'll see what I can do to help."

At that moment, the massive silver dragon's head breached the clouds. It was like some leviathan coming out of the deep ocean as it rose through the clouds inch by inch.

Those haunting, hollow eyes stared right at me.

Yev was already diving, her green, caustic fire splashing onto his back and scattering onto his wings. I was happy that she managed to melt tiny holes in his wing. It wasn't invincible, just so large that even her attack was nothing more than a paper cut to it.

The Silver Slave sprayed frost after her, but she swooped down and around the massive dragon for cover.

I was up next. Making a pass just over his back, I felt Morgana leap off of me. Wanting to distract him from my mate, I washed his left wing with fire.

He roared in pain, and his massive jaws tried to snap at me as I flew over his wings. But something told me he wasn't giving it his best.

Everything I could see of the enormous dragon told me that he was tired and ready to die. The only thing keeping him alive were the damned runes carved into him.

Flapping higher into the sky, getting ready for another pass, I watched as Morgana scampered over his back like an ant, her blades and magic leaving what the dragon would barely consider as scratches where its wing joined its back.

But she was damaging it where I most needed it. The least I could do was help continue distracting the dragon.

Swooping down, I did another pass. This time, I focused on his other wing, trying to burn out the webbing.

Yev joined me as the silver dragon sprayed blasts of frigid air that went wide.

By now, I was sure it was missing on purpose.

Then it let out a scream, and I saw the wing Morgana was working on losing its rigidity. The wing flopped uselessly on his side and for a moment he stalled in the air. She must have nicked a vital ligament.

He dipped that direction, still flying, but that only lasted a moment before the silver dragon tumbled down into the clouds.

I went to celebrate, but froze and dove after him. Morgana was still riding on top of him. While I knew she had serious recovery abilities, I wasn't sure if she could come back from being splattered along the mountainside.

I broke through the clouds, watching as she jumped off the back of the dragon. She spread her arms, trying to slow her fall.

I dove deeper, spreading my wings and managing to catch her. Back-winging to slow our descent, I caught air and managed to pull us out of the dive just in time to watch the Silver Slave hit the mountain below.

Its body hit hard, sliding down the side of the mountain, completely limp.

The earth rumbled, and the boom no doubt could be heard by even the neighboring countries.

Snow rushed down from the peaks, his body setting off another chain of avalanches through the entire mountain range.

Flying paranormals flocked into the air, all getting clear of the falling dragon and coming in closer to watch. We all wanted to confirm he was dead.

"Careful, Zach. We don't know if it survived," Morgana warned me.

I nodded, watching carefully. It wasn't moving. And even as the snow settled, the massive silver dragon lay amid the mountains, motionless.

I swooped down through the other gawking, flying paranormals as Yev joined me on the ground near the silver dragon's head.

It twitched, and the nostrils on the massive creature snorted, "Thank you."

Now that we were closer, I could see its stomach. It was ripped open and bleeding all over the snow, its legs bent in every direction.

The silver dragon was messed up and dying, but it still had moments of life, and I wanted answers.

"Yev, get all of these paranormals back to the city."

"But—" she tried to argue.

One look from me made her snap her snout shut. She turned and followed my command.

I waited until they all started flying away before turning my attention back to the silver. "I'm sorry."

"No, you saved me from committing more atrocities. Their original plan was to use me to capture a female dragon."

"Why a female—" Morgana started before her face shifted to one of disgust. "They wanted to breed you?"

"Yes, and I wouldn't have fought them. As the last silver, I wish for my kind to flourish once again. Maybe with new generations, there will be hope one day."

My heart ached with his words and the passion behind them. "Thank you for taking it easy on us."

The massive silver laughed and then curled in on itself, wheezing. "In you, I see an opportunity to atone. To give you my strength so that you can face what is to come, my king."

"King?" I wondered if he'd hit his head on his way down.

"Yes, Pendragon." The silver let out a heavy sigh. "From you, there might yet be another silver. Please, promise me that you will bring another silver into the world."

I didn't know what to do other than to accept and promise the dying dragon his wish. "Yes, if I can figure it out, I'll bring back the silver dragons."

Never before had I given thought to what my ability to shift between colors meant. But it seemed the Silver Slave recognized something in me and believed with that ability came the ability to restore the silver dragons.

He gave a dopey smile. "I believe you." And his body relaxed.

I had thought we lost him, but then he spoke again. "Then take my strength. Let that be one last thing I do to help my kind after all the problems I have wrought."

When he'd finished, he relaxed, and his head sank into the snow with a finality.

CHAPTER 24

"What do you think he meant by 'take his strength'? I don't feel any different." I stared down at my hands, like somehow some magic would all of a sudden show.

Morgana stood next to me, hesitating before she stated, "I think... I think he wanted you to eat him." She looked at the massive corpse before me.

I froze, turning my gaze from my hands to his body. My stomach turned a bit at the idea. His body had been used against him for years by the celestials. Breaking up his body to eat him seemed too much.

"I don't know if I can do that," I replied, unable to tear my eyes away from his body.

"I know, Zach. But it isn't like you're taking. He's giving," Morgana tried to console me. "And, Zach, remember what that bone did for you? He can make you stronger, and I think he's right. I think you're going to need it."

There was nothing I could say to that.

What she said was true. My chances against the team that had taken Tyrande at my current strength weren't looking great. Being stronger could turn the tide.

I looked back at the silver dragon, sitting down on my back legs next to his body.

I sat there for a little bit, needing a moment. Morgana stood quietly, understanding and giving me a little space.

When I was ready, I took a deep breath and leaned forward to where his stomach was ripped open and took a bite.

I hated it instantly, not because it was terrible, but because it tasted so good. I hated to admit it, but he tasted amazing. As dragon meat melted in my mouth, it warmed my insides and trickled out towards my skin, making it tingle and itch.

It reminded me of how human bodies were made to process sugar and fat as fuel sources. It tasted good to us because it was perfect fuel. Dragon bodies seemed to have mana-rich meat that satisfied dragon bodies in much the same way.

Already, from just that one bite, I could feel myself growing.

"Morgana," I mumbled around a piece of scale that was crunching like candy glass between my teeth. "Keep an eye out for me. This is going to take a while."

"You got it. Just do what you have to."

I wrinkled my snout and pushed forward, eating the massive silver dragon. I loved every bite, which almost made it harder.

***

Time flew by as I ate away at the massive dragon.

It wasn't until Jadelyn's voice roused me from my task that I finally looked up and swiveled my head, looking for my mate.

"Jadelyn?" I realized it was growing dark and my eyes were well adjusted to the darkness, but I couldn't find her.

"Down here, love."

I looked down, trying to figure out how Jadelyn had shrunk so much.

"What time is it?" I asked, lifting one of my bloodied claws to get a measure of how big I was compared to her.

"It is almost nine." Her arms were wrapped around herself, wearing a heavy coat. I realized she was likely freezing.

I scooped her up and pressed her to my warm chest. "I'm sorry, I have to do this."

"That's why I'm out here, to be with you." She huddled up against my chest.

Looking around, I realized the rest of my wives were there as well. They'd let Jadelyn break my focus and bring my attention back.

The Silver Slave was now silver scraps. I had been devouring his corpse for the better part of the day, and as I'd grown, it had gone faster. There was still some left, but for the most part, I was done.

"You've gotten pretty big." Scarlett stepped up next to Jadelyn against my flank.

She was right. Compared to the Silver Slave, I was still small, but I had more than doubled in size. From snout to tail, I could probably cover half a football field. My torso was the size of two stacked school buses, and I didn't even want to try to guess my weight.

A throat cleared beyond my mates, and I realized we weren't alone.

Yev stood behind her mother, who was the one who had cleared her throat. An elven man stood next to her. I assumed he must be Yev and Tyrande's father.

"Yes?" I said slowly, wondering what had brought them out beyond the protection of Sentarshaden.

"You have caused more trouble today. Do you have any idea how hard it has been to quell the videos popping up all over the internet? It is hard to explain a massive dragon falling out of the sky." Her mother walked up to me angrily, jutting out a finger at me accusingly.

I was tempted to bite that hand right off. I raised an eyebrow. "You're welcome for saving your city, and stopping your daughter from charging off and making you lose both of them." I leveled a hard look at her. "Now, it's been a long day. Go away."

I felt Jadelyn's soft touch on one of my legs, but I was still annoyed.

Yev's mother was not picking a great time to push a very testy, large dragon.

Something about my words, or maybe my blood-stained snout, made her pause.

"You have to get my daughter back. They hired you to protect my daughter," she demanded, her voice betraying the slightest bit of weakness.

I covered her face with a smoke-filled snort.

"We were hired to protect Yev, and we did. The fact that they changed the play and went after Tyrande isn't on me." I was being stubborn as their mother blamed me. That and chasing after them now would do little.

I was exhausted, and my body desperately needed to rest and recover from my rapid growth. Not to mention that going in without a plan was suicide.

"Zach," Yev's voice was pleading. "We have to get Tyrande. You don't understand."

"Then explain it to me." I softened as I turned to Yev. She'd been through too much today.

She looked at her mother and father, who nodded in agreement, seeming to authorize whatever she was about to say next.

"Tyrande is the heir to Sentarshaden. She's keyed to the tree. With her in their hands..." She paused, struggling to say the next words. "They would have access to the tree."

Morgana's eyes were the ones that went wide in understanding first. "Shit. They could move it, use it on the city itself. The Church could steal your family tree."

The Highaen matriarch refused to meet any of my family's eyes.

I realized the implications. Tyrande's capture meant possible destruction for an entire city of paranormals.

I groaned, my choice clear. "How long do we have?"

"What they did to the dragon would have taken years, but something simpler could be done to an elf. She'd have to go to the celestial plane for the archangels to work on her," Morgana thought out loud. "It will take time, we don't have to rush."

"Austria," I said in understanding. "They are headed to Austria to bring her to the celestial plane. Once there, how long would it take to make her obedient?"

Morgana shrugged. "I have no idea. It's not exactly something I practice. It won't happen in a day or even a week though."

For that, I was thankful.

Glancing back at the rest of the silver dragon, I sighed. "I have to finish this, then rest. Tomorrow I will work with you to plan how to rescue your daughter."

"Thank you." Yev hugged one of my legs. "For protecting me today, and for helping get my sister back."

I grumbled and turned back to the remaining scraps of the silver. A part of me had thought to give them to Yev, but I was being selfish. It was becoming more and more apparent that I needed every ounce of strength I could get. Giving up a portion of it to Yev might just endanger my life down the line.

"Eat up, then we'll go home," Jadelyn encouraged me.

***

I glided over the city, spotting Jadelyn's home from above.

I wasn't worried about being spotted. According to my mates, my secret was out. There were already videos of me running naked out of the magic range and shifting on the front steps.

Unlike all the coverups we performed on the normals, there was no one taking down those videos and changing the narrative. The paranormal world was already up in a tither about the gold dragon appearing in Sentarshaden.

So as I flew low over Jadelyn's home, I was unsurprised to see camera flashes from pedestrians on the street trying to get a picture of me.

"Think we should video chat with your parents and see if we can beat the news?" I asked as I landed amid several very nervous looking security guards.

Jadelyn's home security watched with wide eyes as my mates all slid off my back, and I shifted back into myself, naked in the middle of the circle drive.

"We might need bigger circle drives if you plan on getting any larger." Jadelyn said, not worried in the least about the other ramifications. "But yes, we should call my dad before he learns it from other sources. It'll be front page news even in the Philly para community tomorrow. Sooner if he's keeping tabs on this city since I am here."

"If my dad hasn't already figured it out," Scarlett added, grabbing a blanket from inside the door and throwing it over my shoulders as if that solved my modesty issues.

I let the blanket hang over my shoulders, comfortable with my body around my mates.

"Let's get it over with," I told the two of them. Detective Fox's investigation wall likely only needed a few more pieces to realize what I was.

As I walked into the kitchen, and lounging area, the news was still running. Either one of the guards had been watching it, or it had been left on when the girls had left this morning.

The elven news anchor was trying to make constant conversation, spewing out all kinds of thoughts about the gold dragon. It seemed I was the hot topic and the green dragon had become yesterday's news story.

"Gold dragons and silver dragons, both thought extinct, have reappeared today. The entire world is wondering who the young gold dragon is."

A blurry picture of me was cropped and hanging over his shoulder. I knew it was me on the steps of the magic range, and if it wasn't cropped, my junk would be out for the entire news audience to see.

"Anyone with details on the gold dragon should call our tip hotline. The world would love to meet him," the anchor continued.

The co-host cut in, "But I'm sure the Bronze King will address this in his announcement tonight. If you are out there, gold dragon, the city of Sentarshaden thanks you for your actions today."

She stared directly at the camera in a way that sent a chill down my spine. Being directly talked to by news anchors was creepy.

"When is the Bronze King's announcement?" I asked.

Kelly already had her phone out. "Forty minutes."

"We can put off the call to my father?" Jadelyn suggested.

"No, let's get that done with. Then we'll see what sort of bomb the Bronze King is going to drop." I had a feeling that a doozy was coming.

Jadelyn nodded, grabbing a tablet from her room and arranging some books on the coffee table in front of the couch to prop it up.

"Dad says they'll be ready in just a minute," Scarlett announced, looking up from her phone. "Ready?" she asked me, sounding concerned.

"Nope. This is going to be harder than fighting a colossal silver dragon," I said, honest with myself.

Fighting the Silver Slave had been an exercise in heroics, and that somehow didn't extend to coming out to her father.

Jadelyn's tablet rang, and an image of Detective Fox sitting next to Jadelyn's Father popped up on the screen.

Scarlett's father, Detective Fox, looked just like usual. His permanent five-o'clock shadow gave him a slightly messy appearance. It made him unassuming, but I knew better.

Rupert, on the other hand, looked like a marble bust of Poseidon come to life. The old siren had managed to remain impressively fit, even as his hair turned white. The white hair was a stark contrast to Detective Fox's orange.

As I looked them over, I had a thought. "You should text your mothers to join them."

"Already done. They'll be there shortly," Scarlett informed me, before swiping accept.

I guess this was it. I took a breath, bracing for the moment I knew would eventually come.

"Jadelyn." Rupert ran right over anything I was going to say in greeting. "We are already arranging a way out of Sentarshaden for you."

"Yes, after we saw the reports today of the Church attacking the city, we are pulling every string we have to pull all of you out of the city quietly and safely." Detective Fox was quick to follow up.

I held up a hand to forestall anything further. "Thank you for your work on that, but it won't be necessary. I —"

"As much as I appreciate your bravado, there are angels and even dragons in play around the city. Those aren't things you can stand up to." Detective Fox glared at me from across the globe.

Despite the distance, I could still feel the heat of an angry father trying to protect his daughter.

"You are a lost one, and you might not understand just how terrifying dragons can be. You all need to get out of the city."

Rupert looked to the side. "What's so funny?"

"Nothing." Jadelyn's mother came around into the camera's view. "Just coming to see my daughter." A small twitch of her lips betrayed her.

"We are working on getting them out of the city and back home. Dragons are coming out of the woodworks. Angels are fighting in the streets. It's mayhem." Rupert shook his head. "That is no place for my daughter."

"Dragons." Jadelyn's mom stared right at the camera, staring at me while she spoke to her husband. "I heard there was a gold dragon that showed up and dealt with the problems."

Detective Fox turned. A slight pinch to his eyes told me he read something off in her statement.

But Rupert continued to blunder forward. "Yes, well, it isn't as if we have the kind of firepower over there to deal with a dragon. Now, we have a friend in the area—"

"Dear." His wife laid a hand on her shoulder. "I think you should give your daughter a moment to speak."

We had all given up on trying to interject into the conversation as the two over-protective fathers steamrolled the conversation.

"Fine." The muscular siren crossed his arms, agreeing to let us talk. His face twitched, at odds with his agreement to let us speak.

"Well, we had news to tell you." Jadelyn smiled and looked at me to continue.

Scarlett's mom had entered and stayed behind the two men. She chose that moment to position her hands as jaws in front of her mouth and clamp them open and shut as she pretended to fly behind them.

I tried to keep it together as the two men watched me, oblivious to the woman behind them.

"You're pregnant?" Rupert blurted out. "Then we definitely need to get you out! You have a baby to protect! That's even more reason that you hurry and leave the city."

Her mother laughed hysterically in the background. "She's not pregnant, at least I don't think. Are you, honey?"

"I'm not pregnant." Jadelyn's face was bright red. "Anyway, Zach had something to come clean about."

She practically shoved me into the jaws of her parents.

Scarlett was on my other side, eagerly awaiting my announcement as well.

"Well... you see..." I scratched the back of my head, trying to figure out the best way to say it. And maybe also hesitating a bit. This was a big step.

"Get on with it, boy. We have other things to talk about," Rupert grumped and earned a small smack from his wife.

I nodded, going for a rip the Band-Aid off plan. "I'm a dragon."

"Alright, now back to the extraction pla — Wait, what?" Rupert did a double take.

"Dragon, Father. My husband is a dragon." Jadelyn bounced on the seat next to me, looking at me like I was the best and greatest thing in the entire world.

Her mother cleared her throat. "Yes, and what color of dragon, dear?" She tried prompting more out of me.

"Gold, ma'am." I said, politely addressing her.

The two fathers on the screen didn't move for several seconds.

"Is the call frozen?" I whispered to Scarlett.

"No, just our fathers," she said with a barely contained laugh on the edge of her lips.

"Gold dragon," Detective Fox said slowly. "I think we'll need some proof."

His wife tugged at the fox ear on top of his head. "We already have verified. And I would think your daughters would know a gold dragon when they saw one."

Rupert began laughing, but it cracked, bordering between hysteria and elation.

"You're a gold dragon. You're... a gold dragon." He broke into more hysterical laughter before his face cleared with excitement. "Golfing! You need to come golfing with my buddies and me. Oh, they won't' believe this. I can't wait to shove this in Tony's face. He's always bragging about his son-in-law the unicorn."

Then another thought crossed his face, and he leaned forward. "You aren't pregnant with a dragonling, are you, daughter?"

His eyes were wide with excitement.

"No, I'm not pregnant. For the last time, none of us are pregnant," Jadelyn laughed. "I thought the dragon husband was big enough news."

Rupert coughed into his hands, and I realized Detective Fox was scanning between the four women around me.

"Ah. Some of this is starting to make sense," Detective Fox said. "I assume you approve, love?" He looked behind him to Ruby, who answered with a single sharp nod.

Claire leaned over her husband. "I saw the articles already coming out. You fought the angels and the silver dragon?"

But then a frown came over both men. "You are part of the conflict in Sentar-shaden."

They clearly didn't like their daughters being even closer to the conflict.

I ignored their comment, focusing on the mother's. "Yes. But it isn't as impressive as you think. The silver dragon wanted to die, to be free of the Church's influence. So we took his life. And as for the angels, we were just trying to protect the Highaen family from having their daughter kidnapped. And unfortunately were only partially successful. The other has been taken," I quickly explained.

"Scarlett, you are doing everything you can to keep Jadelyn safe?" Detective Fox asked.

"Yes, father. It also helps to have a gold dragon with her most of the time," she answered with a roll of her eyes.

Both men nodded slowly at that.

"Indeed, that would change how you react to many dangers. The answer is simply get her to the gold dragon if he isn't part of the conflict." Detective Fox was already rolling through the new protocols in his head. "A gold dragon is probably the safest place to be."

"Then do you need help getting out of the city?" Rupert asked.

"No, we are fine. Worst-case scenario, I just take them and fly us home," I replied.

The idea of flying over the Atlantic was terrifying, but I thought I just might be able to do it. With my current size, I was pretty sure I could make it in a day. I was still far slower than a plane, but it was doable.

"Yes, of course." Rupert nodded, seemingly fine with me taking care of his daughter all of a sudden. "Do you need anything from us for the conflict in Sentarshaden?"

"No, daddy, it's fine. We just wanted to be sure you learned the news from us. After today's events, Zach is worried his secret will be out." She paused. "And we learned more about dragons on this trip. We need to start stocking mana-rich foods for him. He eats a lot."

Her mother giggled. "Eight courses last time he was here," she bragged.

"Of course! He's a dragon." Rupert agreed. "Twenty courses of the finest food we have, and no less."

I was somewhat uncomfortable with the change in tone from their fathers now that they knew I was a dragon. But I had the feeling it was the first of a lot of changes as the world found out.

CHAPTER 25

"That wasn't so bad," Scarlett said as we ended the call with their fathers. She tilted the tablet down, putting the camera against the table for good measure.

"I think they took it quite well," Jadelyn agreed.

Kelly burst out laughing. "Pretty sure they are going to cling to your husband more than you."

"They were... eager to meet you again." Morgana's lips twitched with mirth. "And they will push harder for grandchildren."

I leaned back into the couch. "I'm not a show pony."

My women nervously looked at each other.

"People are going to have extreme reactions to you, either positive or negative," Morgana responded.

"Great," I sighed then grabbed the remote and turned the TV on. "Let's see what other surprises your dragon is in for."

The Bronze King was due to speak soon. But at the moment, we were only looking at an empty lectern with microphones mounted all over the front.

A man stepped up to it. If he was the Bronze King, he wasn't exactly what I had pictured in my mind. He was actually kind of short.

He was Caucasian, with skin so sun kissed that he could easily be confused for middle eastern, but his blue eyes and light brown hair indicated otherwise. Dressed in a simple but immaculately tailored black suit, he paused, waiting for the camera flashes to stop.

"Hello," his voice rumbled, much larger than made sense for his human body.

All the camera flashes stopped at his voice, and even through the TV, it commanded a certain kind of respect.

"Today, I had had a speech planned to invite young dragons from around the world to celebrate our heritage and welcome the newest green dragon."

He paused, his gaze hardening.

"But today, for the first time in a long while, I was surprised. Two lineages of dragons thought lost appeared today in Switzerland. One will be celebrated, the other mourned. A tragedy occurred, one that tells me the world has long forgotten the destruction of a dragon's wrath."

The lectern crackled, and the corner that his hand held splintered underneath it.

"So today, instead of a heritage celebration, I am calling a conclave of all living dragons. There must be a response to the atrocities seen here today. There will be repercussions, and our enemies will learn the consequences of awakening a dragon's displeasure." The Bronze King's face flickered with anger, then relaxed as if purposely giving the world a brief glimpse of what was to come.

I couldn't help myself. I swallowed. He was pissed. And the Silver Slave had shown me just how large a dragon could become. I could only guess how powerful and impactful the Bronze King could be.

Cameras flashed again, and reporters started shouting questions as the shot panned out from where it had been focused solely on the lectern.

"Is this a declaration of war?" a particularly loud reporter shouted.

The Bronze King leaned over the microphones again.

"You should expect change. For the first time in centuries, a gold dragon has appeared. With the absence of the gold and silver clans, I have led dragonkind. But the appearance of this gold will change many things." He gave a non-answer that sounded suspiciously like he was going to hand over his role to me.

Jadelyn looked at me. "Wait, is he implying that you'd lead dragons going forward?"

I held my hands up, baffled at the concept. "Don't look at me. I know less than you all do."

"That is what it sounded like," Morgana commented as we all watched the broadcast closely. "I didn't know their hierarchy was that strict."

"No one knows that much about them," Scarlett reminded everyone. "Dragons have pretty much secluded themselves from the world for hundreds of years, and before then, they were still fairly secretive. Their history goes so far back that no one but them has it well documented."

I was feeling a headache brewing, the weight of potential responsibility already hitting me. I wasn't sure I wanted all of it.

There was one person who might understand that I could call, but she was struggling with her own issues. I didn't want to burden Yev further.

"That is a matter for dragons," the Bronze King answered another question that I hadn't caught. "Thank you all for your questions, but I am not in the mood today. To all those dragons out there, be safe and look out for my messengers."

The broadcast suddenly cut back to the two news anchors. The male anchor sat with a stunned look for a moment before snapping out of it and speaking.

"That was... news. It seems the Bronze King is upset at the actions of the Church today."

"And rightly so," his co-host threw in to soften his language. "The footage that's been made available showed enslavement of a dragon. I don't imagine the Bronze King will stand for that."

They paused, letting the weight of that settle before the female co-host perked up. "And we have new information on the gold dragon that's even caught the interest of the Bronze King."

Poorly taken pictures of me flying into Jadelyn's home in Sentarshaden filled the side of the screen as it zoomed in on the attractive co-host.

"Tonight, the gold dragon was seen flying into the Scalewright home here in Sentarshaden. Our sources say the home has been active recently, housing the heir to the Scalewright shipping empire, Jadelyn Scalewright. She and guests have been in the city for the last few days. We can only wonder what dealings this new gold dragon has with the Scalewright family."

I covered my face with my hands. "Fuck. Everyone is going to know by the end of the night, aren't they?"

Jadelyn's phone chirped once, a new text popping up.

Then again.

And again.

We all sat there waiting for it to stop, but for the next five minutes, her phone continued to ding with new texts.

"Are you going to answer those?" I asked.

She looked over at the phone as if it might bite her. "I think, maybe, I should just let them sit for a while."

She turned the volume off. The phone sat there vibrating, nearly falling off the table.

Then her tablet started ringing, and Scarlett turned it over to see that their fathers were calling again.

"Hello?" Scarlett answered. "Forget something?"

"We are tripling the guard around the Sentarshaden home. Please work with the men to include them. Also, we've been contacted by the Bronze King's people... do we tell him who Zach is?"

Scarlett looked to me for an answer.

I was honored they would refuse the Bronze King if I wanted a bit more time under the radar. But it would come out soon, and I needed to stop hiding in the shadows.

"Yes, you can tell him. We plan to stay in Sentarshaden a little longer to help retrieve Tyrande, but then we'll be coming back to Philly," I told the fathers.

"Alright. Good luck, son." Rupert smiled broadly as he said son. "We just watched the announcement too, exciting stuff."

"Thanks, bye, dad," Scarlett hurried them off the call. "Sorry, I know this is all a lot."

"Are you okay?" Jadelyn asked me.

"No? But I'm not sure I have the option of freaking out." I looked to my women. "Today has been a lot. I knew we'd likely be fighting the Church, and I knew my secret would come out, but it's still a lot to process. As a result, one of the most powerful paranormals in the world is hinting at war, and also me taking a position leading a group of paranormals when I didn't even know I was a dragon until recently."

I let out a frustrated sigh. We knew this had been coming, and I thought I was prepared. But it was a hard change to prepare for. Apparently, I would either sink or swim.

I had expected the media attention, but the Bronze King's deferral to me and suggestion of war was additional weight dropped on my back. The ramifications of that made my head spin.

"Zach." Kelly got my attention, and she had a tight jaw. She didn't often have such a serious look on her face, so I paid attention. "You have responsibilities now. They might have been placed on you, but you can't change what you are. Buck up, alpha. Because it sounds like you were just promoted to alpha of the dragons."

"That doesn't make this better," I groaned. "I don't want that level of responsibility." I gestured towards the TV. "I'm not exactly excited at the prospect of deciding if I drag everybody into the next paranormal world war."

Kelly grabbed my hand and forced me to look her in the eye. "Suck it up, alpha. I know you can do it. We all do. Remember, you aren't even just a gold, you are this whole Pendragon thing. Whatever that means. There's no running from this responsibility. Besides, I'm sure the Bronze King isn't going to just walk away and leave you on your own."

I nodded, realizing what I was feeling was probably similar to what she'd felt when I'd made her an alpha of the pack. It might have been on a different scale, but she'd never thought it would be possible and definitely hadn't prepared for it.

I looked back at her, this time seeing a bit more of her. She nodded, giving me a soft smile. She knew what I was going through. She'd done it, and I could too.

The idea of leading a bunch of dragons should have been thrilling, and a part of me relished the idea of the power. But the weight of that role wasn't lost on me, and I needed to process it.

I could cause the deaths of millions of people based on my actions. All of those lives were now resting in the back of my mind for every decision to come.

"This doesn't change anything." Jadelyn patted my hand. "We are still here for you.

Your short-term decisions don't need to factor this in. We have time to figure it out."

"Yes, we need to refocus. This distraction could cost us saving Tyrande," Morgana agreed. "You promised to talk with the Highaen tomorrow."

Grinding my palms into my brow, I pushed aside all the possible outcomes of meeting with the Bronze King.

It actually felt good to focus on a problem I could solve in the short term.

Tyrande had been taken. It was a change of plans from the templar's original goal of capturing a dragon, but it still gave them a huge opportunity. Through her, all of Sentarshaden was at risk.

"We can't let them use Tyrande. Not just because it is wrong, but because she's a friend," I firmly told the girls.

There was no way that I'd sit around while they did to Tyrande what they had done to the Silver Slave.

As I called him that in my head, I realized that I didn't even know his name. I made a mental note to ask the Bronze King and make sure I did something in the dragon's memory.

"How do you intend to save her?" Scarlett asked as all of my mates sat, waiting to hear my answer.

And I paused. I hadn't decided on a course of action yet.

"You can ask for help figuring that out. Just because you are a leader doesn't mean you can't ask for help; part of being a leader is gathering a knowledgeable group you trust." Kelly prodded me.

I nodded. Her reminder was just what I needed.

"What do you think, Morgana? In all of this, both dealing with the Church and this kind of mission, you have the most experience." I leaned on my mate for ideas.

"Your main options are to try to negotiate, run a stealth operation, or ram in their front door," Morgana narrowed my options down for me.

"I doubt negotiation is going to work." We all knew that wasn't the answer. "Ramming in their front door is very appealing, but that might be a better backup plan."

The Church also had the ultimate bottleneck if they decided to retreat through the portal to the celestial plane.

The girls all nodded, knowing which one that would leave.

"To confirm, you, a giant ass dragon, are going on a stealth mission." Scarlett's face was amused, her tails swinging behind her.

"Not exactly," I said, a plan starting to form in my mind. It could even be called two plans.

"Morgana, what do you think of this?" I started laying it out.

***

The girls were helpful in ironing out the plan, yet it was still rough. It was getting late. We still had more details to hash out, but sleep was calling for me. It had been a stressful day, and I knew I'd feel loads better after a good night's sleep.

The plan wasn't entirely ironed out, but it all hinged on the Highaen agreeing to half of it anyway. And we were only willing to tell them half of it.

Scarlett had pointed out that the angels had been ready and waiting to snatch the SUV, which meant that the Highaen evacuation plans had been compromised. We didn't know where their leak was, so we couldn't risk them knowing too much.

"Alpha." Kelly grabbed my shoulders from behind and kneaded them. "You need to relieve some of this stress. When the alpha is stressed, so is the whole pack."

"I think these stress knots just settled in for life," I muttered as I leaned back into her. I groaned as she found one particular knot, her thumb wriggling into it. It hurt so good.

Kelly kissed the side of my neck. "Now, if only dragons had women ready and waiting to help them relieve stress in the most natural way possible." She kissed the other side of my neck. "Wouldn't that be wonderful?"

I nuzzled her head as she brushed up against my neck. "Kelly, I don't know if that's what you want for your first time."

"Helping my alpha relieve some stress is exactly what I want. You do so much for us, even if you don't realize it. I'm more than happy to do what I can for you." She kissed my cheek this time.

I turned my head to claim her lips, my mind already pushing aside all of the worries and stress from the day. My body followed suit, starting to dream up more pleasurable ways to spend my time.

I pulled back, checking Kelly out. Her shirt was tied up, putting her toned abs and firm chest on full display. And the short cheerleading shorts she wore fit her toned thighs like gloves. She smiled, turning and grabbing my hand, pulling me up as she led the way down the hall with her butt swinging back and forth.

"That's it." Kelly turned into one of the guest bedrooms. "Though, I'd like it to be just me and my alpha for the start."

"Of course. You don't all have to share." I knew that might be awkward for them.

"I don't know. It sounds a little fun." She gave me a coy smile that sparked my imagination. She laughed as she took in my expression.

I had to admit, the idea of two of them at once was making me excited.

Kelly tugged me further into the room, looking back towards me with a grin that promised a good time. "Maybe later. Come on, alpha."

I grabbed her ass and lifted her up, suddenly thinking entirely about what I would do with my favourite werewolf.

"I have a lot of stress." But my warning fell on deaf ears.

"Werewolf, remember? I'm tougher than you might think. Now, show me what all that noise on the plane was about." She bit down hard on my shoulder, and I tossed her into the bed.

She bounced, and I was on her before she settled.

I trusted what she'd said and took what I needed. Soft and loving wasn't what I needed at this moment. I needed hard. I needed mind-blowing pleasure that made me lose all my other thoughts.

Claiming Kelly's lips, I pushing her into the bed and twisting her about as my hands grabbed and claimed every inch of her.

Kelly came up for a breath as I kissed down her neck, pulling a breast out of her shirt and sucking on it vigorously enough that her nipples peaked in an instant.

"Yes! Use my body." Kelly cupped the back of my head and pulled me over to her other breast to repeat the action.

Smiling down, I was more than happy to help. I slurped up her nipple, curling it between my lips, playing with it.

My hands weren't idle as they dove into her tight shorts. I expected to find fabric, but my hands slid along smooth skin.

She wasn't wearing any underwear.

"All ready for you." She kissed me when I lifted my head off her chest.

Our kiss was fierce and feral. She bit my lip, tugging it out just enough to give a twinge of pain.

Encouraged, I played a little rougher.

My fingers found her folds, slipping in and feeling the wet warmth of her desire. I probed her folds, stroking them while I pulled beads of her juices out. I nipped at her chest, loving how her skin gave to me, only to bounce back.

Her fingers ran through my hair as I played in her incredibly perky chest. My lips and tongue covering them with my saliva.

She was wonderful, and all mine.

The beast butted his head inside my chest, claiming her too.

"Roll over." I slipped my fingers from her folds. They were soaked, and I knew she was ready.

Kelly rolled over, putting her bubble butt up in the air. She wiggled it a bit, smiling over her shoulder at me. "Whenever you're ready, alpha."

Jerking down her tight shorts, I left them at her knees. I liked keeping her legs bound together.

Sitting up behind her, I let a possessive hand trail over the curve of her ass and down her back before grabbing her hips with both hands and leaning over her.

I sank myself into her ready and waiting sex. "You feel incredible," I moaned.

She was slick and she expanded easily, taking my girth.

My body pulsed with satisfaction, tension beginning to leave me as I stroked into her. I savored the slick friction as her tight pussy wrapped itself around my cock.

"Alpha, I can handle harder. Stop being delicate with me."

I swayed my hips, driving myself deeper with the next thrust and deeper still, until I bottomed out in her.

Her legs held together, making her so deliciously tight as I started pumping harder and harder into her. Our flesh slapped as I started pushing and pulling her hips opposite of my own driving. I plowed faster and faster into her.

But I craved more.

Picking her up by her hips, I started to slam her down onto me as I pumped into her, chasing my release.

Kelly moaned, only encouraging me as I went harder.

All of the tension and the stress of the day built up in me and threatened to boil over.

I had one hand on her hips while the other braced her chest, my forearm neatly between her breasts. I used that grip to pull her off the bed, hammering into her with intense need.

Her sex clenched down on my cock, tighter than anything I'd felt before. It only took two more strokes before I emptied myself into her.

I felt like I was a fire hose inside of her, my own seed spilling out onto my thighs. When my release finished, I kept twitching inside of her.

"There you go, alpha. Now do it again. I want to suck you dry of all that stress." Kelly wiggled her ass up against me and started twerking on my cock.

My brain was foggy, but I realized she might have interest in my seed. "Should we get something to collect this?"

"Later. The others will join us in a bit, and we'll see if we can't fulfill Hestia's order." She continued to ride me, looking back over her shoulder. "Or do you not have enough stamina for that?" she egged me on.

The challenge was just what I needed. I pushed her face into the pillows and shook the bed with round two.

Chapter 26

"Just deliver it to this address." Kelly eagerly showed one of Scarlett's men Hestia's address.

I still felt a little boneless, but I knew I'd have to rouse myself soon to go meet with the Highaen family. They had told Jadelyn they'd be ready at ten, which apparently meant 'be there at ten'.

"Uh... what is it?" The guard in a black suit looked at the mason jars filled with... well... dragon semen.

"Precious alchemical ingredients," Kelly answered, avoiding telling him exactly what it was. Though, they all knew I was a dragon.

He nodded, but glanced at me with a look of pure terror. I suddenly felt that new, more exaggerated rumors of dragon sexual stamina were going to circle the Scalewright home.

As our eyes met, I knew he had a good idea what was in the jars, but the quantity was clearly boggling his mind.

"Got it," he said, shaking it off and taking the jars. He tucked them into a box before hurrying out.

"They all know," Scarlett said as soon as he left the room. "And the crowd at the front seems to have put it together as well."

I winced and pulled the tablet off the table. Scarlett had shown me the security cameras earlier this morning.

I cringed, seeing that the crowd had gotten even worse.

A crowd of several hundred, maybe even spanning to a thousand, was gathered outside Jadelyn's home. Many had signs of some sort in their hands.

The guard we had just sent out was in a black SUV and had to have a mob of other men part the crowd just so he could get out. And even then, people threw themselves at the SUV to see if I was inside.

Picketers jostled signs of 'Free the Dragon' outside the house.

"You'd think you'd chained me up in the basement," I said, putting the tablet down. I really didn't want to deal with the crazies at that moment.

"How are we getting out of here?" Kelly asked, a bounce in her step and a stupid grin on her face. I knew she was excited that the cure for her pack was within reach.

"Fly," I said simply. I figured the backyard should provide enough room for me to shift.

"Oh. I get to ride a dragon to a formal meeting?" Jadelyn grinned. "Sounds like a dream."

Scarlett raised her hand to get my attention. "Do we have straps or seats for her?"

"Uh... no?" I hadn't thought about a saddle, and the idea of strapping something like that to me made me want to throw a fit. "Not planning to wear a saddle, either. You all did fine last night."

"Bareback it is." Jadelyn nodded in agreement. "Those horns of his work pretty well."

"There's a little flat spot where his neck meets his shoulders that I'd recommend," Kelly suggested. "It has a pretty good wind break, too."

I glanced at the clock. We needed to get going, or we'd be late. "Okay, let's move; who's holding my spatial artifact?"

I got off the couch and started stripping, putting my clothes in the little bra pad.

"Morgana, you should really make him something that works a little better than this." Jadelyn plucked the spatial artifact out of my hand once I was done with it.

"What about those manacles that the silver was wearing?" Kelly asked.

"You want me to wear manacles?" I growled, suddenly upset at the thought.

Kelly waved her hands in front of her in an attempt to stop my anger from rising further. "No, but they resized with him when he shifted."

"What happened to them?" I realized they had disappeared while I'd been eating him.

"Blueberry took them," Kelly whispered.

Morgana bit her lip in thought as she followed me out the back door. "It might be doable. I'd have to look at them more closely. But we might be able to make a bracelet, ring, or something simple for him."

"You figure out what'll work, and I'll make sure you have everything you need for it." Jadelyn flopped the little bra pad in her hand. "It would go a long way for our beloved to not have to keep track of this thing."

I agreed. I wanted something that stayed with me when I shifted, but was small enough to keep out of the way. That would be fantastic, and I loved my mates more for thinking of it.

"Please do that. But for now, it's time to take the dragon express, ladies." Stepping clear of the house, I let my dragon rise within me and shifted.

Bones crackled, and I expanded rapidly, golden scales popping out of my skin. My vision began to change as well, as did my other senses.

I smiled as I looked down, enjoying my new size.

Dipping my head, I let the girls clamber on before launching myself from Jadelyn's backyard. In just moments, I was soaring over the crowd that had gathered around her home.

They were all shouting and looking up. Phones and professional cameras alike were snapping upwards. There was a cacophony of sounds as devices clicked to take photo after photo.

In a very real way, I felt violated. The utter lack of privacy was disconcerting. But I also acknowledged that I couldn't go back. I could only move forward.

And as a dragon, I could move forward very quickly.

It didn't take long before the crowd was far behind us. I soared over the city, toward the base of the tree and the Highaen estate.

As we got closer, I spotted the home and circled high above, trying to figure out the best place to land.

But I got a guide pretty quickly. A green dragon rose from the Highaen courtyard. Yev circled below me and landed back down in a large garden below.

Taking her signal, I tucked my wings, gliding down to as smooth of a landing as I could manage with my mates all piled on my back.

I thought I did pretty well, coming to a solid, but small thump when I landed.

Yev was waiting there. She'd shifted and put on a gold and green dress that had been laid over a planter.

"I'll lead you in..." She paused. "A word of warning: my mother is not in a good mood."

Shifting back, I accepted the spatial artifact from Jadelyn and pulled out my clothes, getting dressed in jeans and a shirt.

I didn't feel the need to dress up when I was doing them a favor.

"She has every right to be in a bad mood with her daughter gone. But I'm not about to be a punching bag for her," I warned Yev.

The grimace on her face said she couldn't promise anything. She turned and led us inside the Highaen estate.

As I'd expected, everything was gold and green, focusing heavily on nature in the decor. Even though quite a bit was painted gold, it didn't seem like they'd overdone anything with real gold.

Most of it was brass or painted to look gold. My dragon senses would have told me otherwise. Overall, besides the intense color scheme, their house was relatively simple.

"Nice home," I commented.

"Too big if you ask me." Yev turned down a hallway. "But there are a lot of elves in the clan. Only about twenty percent of them live here; many live throughout the city."

She pushed through an ornate set of double doors, and we entered a large, vaulted room. It felt like someone had converted an audience chamber into an office space.

Looking around, I realized that might be exactly what had happened.

Cubicles lined the lower level of the large space. And three steps separated them from the private offices, where I could see one very familiar and unhappy mother elf.

Her head snapped up as the doors opened and she stood, gesturing for us to follow her. Not even waiting to see if we followed, she strode into one of the side meeting rooms.

"Anything I should know before I dive into the belly of the beast?" I asked Yev.

"Nothing in particular, but I hope you have a plan for my sister."

We all piled in after her mother, who was already seated. Her laptop was closed on the table, her arms crossed over it.

Another elven man joined us, taking the seat on her right. He was different from their father, who I'd seen before.

"This is Marco. He's our chief of security and able to offer our more militant resources," she said by way of explanation before once again folding her hands and staring me down, clearly wanting me to speak.

"You have a beautiful home." I was no Jadelyn, but I tried to start with something pleasant.

As Jadelyn giggled to my side, I determined that I hadn't been very successful. And based on the hard, stony stare from Yev's mother, it hadn't charmed her very well either.

Morgana cleared her throat. "We know where one of their bases is located, and it makes the most sense for them to bring her there given some of the details we know about it. Do you have a map?"

"Yes, one second." Marco put a tablet on the table and opened up the map. "Here, mark it on this."

Morgana swiped on the tablet, dropping a pin in the town of Galtz. "Here. It's a large compound masquerading as a community drive organization. Angelic Service."

He took the tablet back, looking over the general area. "That's where they took Tyrande? Are you sure?"

"Positive," I said. "That was where we ran an operation recently and where they had planned the attack on Sentarshaden out of. Your daughter is there."

"Why not go after them last night if you knew where they were going?" Her mother glowered at me.

"We weren't going to catch up to that wing of angels. I'd much rather we regroup and make a concerted push for her. This isn't going to be some cake walk."

There was a slow nod, and she surprised me. "Then how many dragons are you sending?"

"Um..." I was confused. As far as I was aware, I had two dragons max that were possible, myself and Yev.

"I saw the broadcast with the Bronze King. He basically handed you the authority over dragons. So, how many dragons can we expect?" The look of impatience on her face made me want to forcefully remove it.

"None," I growled. "There are no reinforcements from the dragons."

She slammed her hands on the table. "Then why have I been—"

"We're done," I interrupted her and stood.

It was obvious that she wasn't going to listen to me. She had been waiting this whole time, expecting me to come in this morning and tell her I was calling in the Bronze King and a dozen ancient dragons to get her daughter back.

And I'd just shot that down. In her eyes, I had wasted her time.

Tyrande's mother jerked her head back like she'd been slapped. "Excuse me?" She motioned slightly towards Marco.

I had an inkling that she was ready to use force, so I reminded her. "It would be a poor decision for this to devolve further. I will take my leave, and I don't recommend putting anything in my path. There's no reason for me to take out your defenses that could be put to better use protecting you or going after your daughter."

"You were hired to protect my daughters!" she sputtered, a brief flicker of panic showing on her face.

I turned, exiting without looking back.

As we strode off the premises, Jadelyn gave me a worried look. "So, it worked?"

"Perfectly," Morgana whispered, quiet enough that the elves nearby wouldn't hear. "They have the location. We can almost guarantee that the Highaen will send an army at them."

"Plan 1 is in motion, then. Now we just have to do our part." I looked between them. "I hadn't expected it to be so easy to have that discussion devolve."

The plan had been for me to storm out, but I hadn't expected Yev's mother to give me such clear attitude. I couldn't believe she'd thought I'd raise a dragon army the second I'd heard the Bronze King's announcement.

Kelly bounced along beside me. "Yeah, she was a queen bitch."

Jadelyn gave her a droll expression. "Maybe wait until we aren't in a Highaen territory to say that."

I looked around, noting all the elves in the nearby area.

As we left, Yev caught up to us, breathing hard from running. "Zach. I'm so sorry about my mother." She grabbed my arm. "But please help. They have my sister."

I wanted to tell her everything would be okay. But this plan hinged on the leak in the Highaen team thinking we wouldn't be there.

"Yev, I'm sorry. There is too much weight on my shoulders for me to go into a battle with the Church right now."

The hurt and betrayal on her face stung.

The beast thumped inside of me, demanding I comfort the female dragon. But I was not a slave to my instincts. I was helping her with the moves I was making; I just couldn't make that clear to her at the moment.

"I hate you," Yev declared. "When we need you most, you run away. You aren't worth your scales, you coward."

Jadelyn whirled on Yev. "Take that back or you've crossed the Scalewrights. You have no idea what he's doing and going through right now."

Yev's face remained hard. A stubborn clench of her jaw indicated that the threat of upsetting the Scalewrights wouldn't overpower her love and devotion to her sister.

I thought her loyalty was endearing, and I hoped that, when all was said and done, she could forgive me.

Turning, we left the way we came, but my mood was quickly going down. Upsetting

Yev, lying to her mother. I didn't like it at all. But it had to be done.

"Hear me out." Kelly got my attention as we stepped into the garden. "Maybe we don't help."

I shook my head. "It's what is right. And even if I didn't want to help save her, the ramifications of the Church stealing the tree from Sentarshaden would be catastrophic. Maybe even a problem for me and the dragons down the line."

Turning to Morgana, I posed a question. "How many archangels could the tree help them bring through?"

"At least three," she said, looking up at the tree as big as a mountain. "Maybe all seven."

"If the dragons do really go to war with the Church, that's not something we can allow," I said. "Either way, we continue. Hop on."

I took off my clothes and handed them to Jadelyn before I shifted and flew off with my mates in tow. This time, we didn't head back to Jadelyn's home. Instead, I flew us directly for the train to get us back to Lucerne.

I was aware of the eyes on us the whole way. I would normally use the clouds as cover, but I knew we wouldn't be in the air for long. So instead, I just ignored all the shouts from below.

As we landed, I quickly shifted and moved to get on the train with my wives.

Reporters lined the outside of our train car, but it was more a nuisance than anything. My identity was out at that point. There was no reason to hide.

"How does it feel?" Jadelyn asked, and I could hear the concern in her voice.

"Heavy," I replied, not sure what else to say.

"That's a good way to describe it," Jadelyn agreed. "It gets easier."

***

"Eh." The pilot hesitated. "I'm not sure how I feel about this." He looked at Jadelyn. "What you're proposing is only an emergency procedure."

"This is an emergency," Jadelyn stated, daring him to question her.

We were on the tarmac in Lucerne, talking to the pilot at the bottom of the steps to her private jet.

He looked back at the rest of us, his eyes rested on me with a hint of awe.

I ignored the look, pretending we didn't both know that he knew.

"I guess. We can do it. Have you taken care of the mid-flight charter reroute?"

Scarlett nodded. "My father is taking care of it. Two hours into the flight, your charter will update in all the systems. You can then turn around and land in Vienna. And you need to be ready at any time to return immediately. Delays could be deadly."

She made eye contact, making sure he understood what she was saying.

"We'll keep the engines warm," the pilot promised, before sighing. "This seems overly complex. But so be it. I'm just the pilot."

He knew something was up, but luckily, he didn't ask too many questions. He seemed to figure not knowing was probably better for him.

"Thank you." Jadelyn grabbed his hand. "This is very important."

"You pay me enough. I'll just keep flying the jet where you tell me." He seemed to have made peace with the plan and shrugged it off. "Let's get going."

We all went up the gangway and piled into the plane.

"What was that about?" the copilot asked as the pilot joined him in the cockpit.

"Doesn't matter. We have a gold dragon on board; we fly where we are told to." He settled into his seat, and the door closed behind us as my mates and I entered the main cabin.

"This is exciting." Jadelyn smiled, clapping her hands. "It's all coming together."

"I can't believe you are agreeing for her to come with us," I told Scarlett.

"The safest place is with the gold dragon," Jadelyn mimed Detective Fox.

I wasn't sure that was true in this case, but I had a feeling that line was going to get used a lot as Jadelyn tried to escape out from under the thumb of her security.

"I have to come with you all for this plan to work. Better we keep her close than have her ride this plane alone to Vienna. Without one of us, she's at risk. And without me, you can't do your plan and stay safe. This is what's best for our family." Scarlett eyed Jadelyn while Jadelyn gave her most angelic face.

The jet's engines whirled up, and we all got to a seat for takeoff.

Jadelyn bobbed her head eagerly in agreement. "See! I get to go on the mission."

I squinted at her, but she gave me a pleading look that melted right through my resistances. "Fine. But you stay on my back until Scarlett has her part, then you stay hidden with her."

"Do you think the Highaen force is going to react this quickly, though?" I asked Morgana.

"Absolutely," Morgana was quick to answer, holding up her phone. She had texts from Hestia, who had kept watch on the city. Highaen was moving out in force. Semi-trucks full of troops had clogged the road less than five minutes after we had left.

"They really are going to war," Kelly said, looking at the texts.

"If it puts their tree at risk, then they have a damn good reason," Scarlett replied. "If the celestial plane gets ahold of Sentarshaden, the Highaen clan will be lost, along with millions of paranormals. And it has meaning beyond just the city. This was a stronghold against the celestial forces. Watching it fall could seriously demoralize any resistance. This isn't just a fight for a rich daughter—this is a fight for millions of lives and potentially the spark that starts another war."

The plane climbed high into the sky, circling as it gained more altitude before cruising.

"By the way, when we aren't flying into battle, I'd like to join the mile high club," Kelly said with a smile. "Blueberry can join too."

Morgana was texting with Hestia, but paused to look up and roll her eyes. "Do not call me that, furball."

I jumped in, "I think that will have to wait for later."

Best that the two of them didn't start going at it. I gave Kelly a look that told her she needed to focus.

"Let's go over the plan one more time." As the plane settled in at the higher altitude, I unbuckled my seat belt and pulled out our resources, once again talking through the details of the plan.

CHAPTER 27

T he pilot came into the back cabin hours later. As part of our plan to make it more convincing that we were not going after Tyrande, we'd gone all the way to Spain before circling back towards Austria.

It also served the purpose of buying the Highaen time to move their forces.

"Let me clip in." The pilot went to the emergency exit and put on a harness, belting himself tightly inside the cabin so that he wouldn't fly out when he opened the door. "Everyone ready for this?"

My mates had changed out their clothes, covering their skin as best as they could. They stood to the side, holding onto the seatbelts nearby.

"I'll go first," I stated. Handing my spatial artifact to Jadelyn, I stood naked before the exit door.

Even knowing that I could fly, jumping out of a plane still filled me with nerves.

The pilot must not have sensed my apprehension, though, because he moved forward, tugging open the emergency exit.

Powerful wind filled the cabin, and I squinted, trying to peer through it and take in the clouds below us. It all seemed so peaceful, but the harsh wind rushing into the cabin was a sharp reminder that we were going to have anything but a peaceful trip.

"Let's go," I shouted over the wind, unsure if anyone had been able to hear me. But not wanting to waste time, I jumped out of the plane.

As I cleared the plane, I shifted, packing on well over a dozen tons of mass. Gold scales covered me as my wings spread wide, working to control my fall.

My mates jumped out of the plane in such quick succession after me that I had to wonder if one of them had pushed the others out. All four of them tumbled into the air, and I swooped back towards them, angling myself to cruise right under them.

Jadelyn shouted excitedly as she fell, whooping into the air.

I snatched her out of the air first; of all of them, I was worried about her ability to catch onto my back.

Two thumps announced that Morgana and Scarlett had landed, catching my back and planting themselves on me. Kelly missed me on the first try, her fingers not finding purchase on my wings as she slid off the side.

I waited to make sure the others had found good grips on me before I angled and dove, working to beat Kelly to the ground.

Jadelyn clutched to me, but she cheered as we flew. I wondered if she'd ever ridden a roller coaster, or if theme parks were too hard when you were famous.

Dipping down just a bit lower, I was able to snag Kelly out of the air.

Taking a deep breath now that my mates were safely with me, I growled, trying to project over the wind. "Scarlett, you are up."

"On it!"

Magic gathered around me, and an illusion to make me blend in with the cloudy sky wrapped around me.

"Done. It's taking both my tails, but I can hold this for a while."

"Stealth bomber dragon is a go!" Kelly laughed from my clutches.

Lifting Kelly up to my neck, I let the others help her get situated on my back.

I flew in the compound's direction, seeing it become visible in the distance. It was hard to make out too much, but there was definitely some sort of force approaching and surrounding it.

I leveled out my flight, changing to a slow cruise in the air. I didn't want to make any noticeable noise that would draw attention to us. As we got closer, I slowly descended upon the compound.

Highaen forces were already pouring out of their trucks, forming a massive wall of elven mages. Meanwhile, the templars still appeared to be scrambling to get their defenses together. There had to be ten thousand among the Highaen.

Meanwhile, the templars only seemed to have half of that, and that was being generous. But they had the advantage. This was their stronghold. They'd have weapons and defenses to stop the attack that was coming.

And while the Highaen were likely skilled fighters, the celestials had some powerful fighters among them as well. I hoped that at least some of the Highaen could fight on Morgana's level.

"It's starting," I told my mates.

Bright flashes of magic rained out of the Highaen forces, smashing into the buildings around the edge of the compound. Simultaneously, muzzle flashes came from the Church's forces as they defended.

Knowing that the ground forces were now busy and less likely to spot me, especially within the illusion, I sped up my descent.

While I wanted to smash forward, brute force wasn't really an option. We couldn't risk harming Morgana's tree, and if the portal came down, we would have no way to get to Tyrande if they'd taken her through it already.

But the Highaen forces provided the perfect distraction, allowing us more cover on our stealth mission.

We were hoping to swoop in and extract Tyrande before the fight came to the point of possibly damaging the tree or portal. And while great for the distraction, the enormity of their forces meant that we had less time than we'd originally anticipated.

They would breach and destroy as they went. We needed to finish our mission quickly.

"Morgana, is your tree still in the same building?" I rumbled, looking down at the buildings below and spotting the short circular building.

"Yep, that's the one. Dead ahead."

I nodded, but I didn't dive. Instead, I angled my glide lower, circling down quickly to the building with Morgana's tree.

"Kelly, Morgana, ready?" We were only about twenty feet above the building. I felt them moving along my spine, getting into the right position behind my wings.

"Ready," they said in unison. Kelly was once again serious, staring at the targeted building.

I swooped down as close to the building as I dared, seeing Morgana's tree now that I was closer. The white willow swayed in the breeze, peaceful and protected amid the attack.

Kelly and Morgana jumped from my back, landing neatly on the building as I swept up and away. Before I could land, I needed to wait for the rest of the templar forces to commit to the fight with the High-aen forces.

Up in the sky, Scarlett's illusions were able to hide us, but I knew on the ground she'd have more trouble. There were too many new textures and patterns to alter, and I was a rather large dragon.

I looped lazily around the compound, watching as Morgana and Kelly went in through the roof. I started getting antsy from having them out of my line of sight.

"You know, I could have joined them," Jadelyn said.

"Sirens don't heal if you land wrong from a fall," I grumbled.

Morgana and Kelly were far more durable. While I'd swooped down, there had still been a good bit to fall.

I pivoted back to take in the fight at the perimeter.

The templar continued upping its forces in the fight. I waited as another wave of soldiers moved from the central building out towards the battle before I swooped down, deciding it was time to land.

"Remove your illusion and hide yourselves," I said as my weight settled.

Ever since I'd marked Morgana or the other women, I could sense where they were, my instincts driving me towards them.

But I fought those instincts, moving slowly down the hall on the opposite side of the building. I needed them both out of the way for what I was about to do, and the plan was for Kelly to stick with Morgana.

Taking a deep breath, I let loose a jet of flame. It was the first one I'd tried since I'd grown significantly.

As I'd hoped, the brick building turned red hot. The mortar gave, and stones started to fall while wood went up in flames instantly. I reduced much of the newer construction material to ashes from my breath.

I smiled, successfully opening up the building. I reached forward with my massive claws, ripping a hole in the building for myself to enter. As I strode into the courtyard, Helena stood in front of the portal. I'd had a feeling she'd stay behind to guard their most important treasure.

She was alone. But it made sense; they'd be less concerned about an army breaching into the celestial plane. There were seven archangels within, and it was the perfect bottleneck. They could easily defend from the other side.

"You seem bigger." She eyed me. "I assume the silver died?"

"Set free from your horrors," I growled, angry she would even mention the dragon.

Helena twirled her spear and leveled it at my face.

I moved to the side, shifting her attention the furthest I could from Morgana and Kelly, who were waiting for me to distract her so that they could do their part. I waited for Helena to make the first move.

After studying me for a moment, she charged forward, using her spear like a beam of light as she tried to pierce me through the chest.

Rather than move myself, I beat my wings hard enough to toss her back, breathing a narrow spray of fire at her. I had to keep my blasts limited, making sure I didn't catch Morgana's tree on fire. When we'd discussed even using my fire near the tree, Morgana had lost it.

Helena dodged back, and I felt Scarlett knock on my back and whisper. "We're off to do our part."

I didn't react as I felt Scarlett and Jadelyn slide off my back, other than smile, as I was now able to maneuver without fear that Jadelyn would fall off.

Morgana and Kelly were slowly moving behind Helena, creeping toward the portal to the celestial plane.

I did my best not to look and call attention to them.

"You'll need to do better than that to take me down," I taunted Helena, trying to make sure I kept her attention and helped cover any noise as the girls moved.

"Pervert." She came again, but this time, my front claw surprised her with its force and speed, coming up at the last second to bat her to the side.

The nephilim took the full brunt of my claw, which would have been comparable to getting hit by a truck. But she bounced and skidded through the rubble of the building. Still, she popped back to her feet. Her clothing was torn, but her body was otherwise fine.

I stared, trying to figure out how she was so durable.

She looked down at her torn clothing and her exposed panties, her face darkening dangerously.

"Now you've done it." Helena wiped at her mouth before the white light coalesced around her, wrapping her in silver armor. "I'm going to roast you over a spit."

I chuckled nervously. I'd planned to distract her more than anything, but I would have felt more comfortable if my hit had done more to her.

She blurred forward, moving far faster than before. I hadn't expected her spear to go for the soft spot under my jaw. In my surprise, I didn't have enough time to move my enormous body out of the way.

Thinking quickly, I worked to collapse myself, shifting into a winged dragon knight to avoid the hit.

"Careful, you could poke someone's eye out," I taunted her, flapping my wings and leading her away from the portal.

Helena screamed, throwing herself into the air after me.

I ducked, dove and sprayed fire to keep enough distance between us. Without a weapon, I had no intention of testing my hands against that spear.

Using the tactics I had, I focused on my breath and my magic to harass the nephilim. But once again, she came out of each attack with nothing more than soot on her silver armor.

"Envokus!" I yelled, hurling a fireball at her reckless charge.

The fireball exploded, sending her flying backward in an arc. As her body flew backward, she once again spread her wings, flapping them to stabilize her body.

As we fought in the sky, I knew we would have been spotted. And my gold scales and fire would no doubt give away my identity.

Sure enough, it wasn't long before a green dragon rose into the air to join me.

"Zach." Yev sounded surprised.

"Not now, Yev. Kind of busy."

Helena had stalled in the air, staring at the two of us as she weighed her next actions.

Down below, the Highaen forces were pushing in. The first of the templars' outer buildings had collapsed under the barrage of magic fire. It was a good sign for their ability to take down the templars, but not so great for Morgana's tree staying sheltered.

Looking back, I saw Helena calculating her next move as well.

"Zach." Yev wanted to get my attention, but I needed to act before Helena either retreated to the portal or joined the fight against the Highaen.

Using Helena's moment of distraction, I caught the shaft of her spear and threw my weight into her, pulling us both out of the sky. As we angled towards the tallest building, the mounted guns on top pivoted and shot at us.

Helena's armor sparked as bullets pinged off of her, and I used her as a shield.

"Let go of me, monster." She struggled in my grip, but I could overpower her now. Even my strength had increased with my size, regardless of which form I was in.

Snorting, I tried to reason with her once again. "Like I said before, you may want to look in the mirror. Your side is kidnapping, torturing, and enslaving. I saw how you were butchering other paranormals in that building. I'm not perfect, but I'm a hell of a lot better than that."

We hit the side of the building, collapsing the wall. I plowed Helena into the floor.

She shouted, "We are angels."

"White wings don't make you inherently good." I punched her in the chest, shattering the floor and sending her down to the next level.

Helena rolled out from under me and twirled up to her feet. "Angels represent the virtues—"

"Does this look virtuous?" I roared. "What the hell did they put in that head of yours?" I gestured to the people dying outside. "You tortured and enslaved the last of the silver dragons, using him as a weapon to kidnap Tyrande. In what sick way can you justify this?"

Helena whirled her spear, but she wasn't pointing it at me. A small frown marred her otherwise pristine face.

Our battle was at a standstill. Neither of us had the force to overpower the other at the moment.

As she paused, I wondered if she might finally be breaking free of whatever misguided principles she'd been operating under. But then she shook her head again, leveling her spear at me.

"We are angels, above mortals. We are virtuous. Impervious to the weaknesses that pull mortals down." She said it with a conviction that dumbfounded me.

"You aren't even an angel," I spat. "I'd bet the real angels only see you as a mutt on a leash. Something to chase pests away."

She flinched, and I could tell I'd hit a soft spot.

Sure enough, she attacked, swinging her spear, and an arc of light that tore through the floor below me. The building groaned dangerously, and creaks echoed through the building.

Helena ran, bursting out a window as the building came toppling down on me.

"Envokus." I threw my anger from talking to Helena at the wall behind me, blowing it out and diving as the ceiling came crashing down.

The collapse displaced enough air that my wings caught, and I tumbled through the air before barely stabilizing myself.

I landed on the ground amid men braced up against a movable concrete barrier. Realizing they were templar forces, I shifted into a dragon just as they recovered from the surprise and turned their guns on me.

As I shifted, I crushed dozens of them. Any that remained were quickly washed with a bright flame as I incinerated them. Scrambling, I got out from the enemy lines, taking to the air once again, realizing there were now small holes filling the webbing of my wings.

Luckily, they didn't do too much but annoy me as I regained altitude to determine my next move.

The Highaen forces saw the hole I'd made crashing into the templar line and were using it, rushing in to wedge themselves between the templar forces and get access further in.

I continued scanning, wanting to find Helena. But I came up short, unable to figure out where she had gone.

My instincts called to me, so I ducked low, shifting back to my dragon knight form just as Helena came hurling down like a meteor.

I moved to the side, but she continued her dive, moving straight into the Highaen forces. She landed amid them, sending dozens flying.

Yev was there in her green dragon form, trying to stop Helena, but she was having the same problem I'd had. Helena was too durable, and her weapon was too effective at slicing into us.

I paused, watching them fight and realizing I could help even their odds while Helena was distracted.

Diving at the fighting nephilim, I swooped low just as she was trying to hit Yev so that I could snag her spear, jerking it up and out of her grasp. My claws tingled painfully as I clutched the spear and the magic faded out of it.

"Yev, focus on the templars," I shouted as I flapped hard, escaping with Helena's spear.

The spear started to dissolve into light, but I clenched it tightly and forced it to stay in my hand.

"Give that back." Helena ignored everything else and flew up after me, wanting her weapon back.

I beat my wings hard, working my way around the compound and back towards Morgana's tree and the portal.

I hoped my distraction had been long enough. I was fairly sure it was, but in the heat of battle, time seemed to move a bit differently. And the next part was what I'd been nervous about.

I needed a sign that everything was done.

As I moved toward the tree, Morgana raced out of the portal, followed by a big werewolf. I expected they'd be hurrying, but they looked like they were running for their lives. My heart rate picked up as I beat my wings just a little harder.

I saw a body over Kelly's shoulder, and I hoped they'd gotten to her soon enough.

It was time for the next part of the plan, but before it could happen, the ground outside the portal rippled.

Something was forcing its way into our world.

A man with six wings pulled himself out of the portal, the ground shaking with his first step. Behind him, angels poured out of the portal in his wake.

Helena gasped behind me. "No," she screamed. "You can't come through. The celestial plane!"

The archangel looked up at Helena with a snort. "Some sacrifices must be made." His voice rang out through the whole compound. "Kill the intruders and capture our target."

The angels that had followed him out fanned out in every direction.

I realized some angels had four wings, different from the normal two I'd seen so far.

Morgana and Kelly could handle themselves. I had bigger fish to fry.

A roar of flames exploded from my maw as I passed over the newly arrived angels. More than a few of them baked under my fire, but there were dozens still racing to join the fight against the Highaen forces.

The archangel turned, looking up and meeting my eyes. I felt a chill wash over me as he rose into the sky with a flap of his wings. It was like he'd teleported. He moved so seamlessly.

"I thought we'd killed the golds long ago. Seems some of you roaches survived."

Slowly circling the archangel, I clutched Helena's spear tightly in my hand.

Helena flew over, hovering before him submissively. "Raguel." She dipped her head.

I snorted, talking to buy myself and my women time. He wasn't part of the plan. "The archangel of justice, come to commit atrocities? How fitting."

CHAPTER 28

"I am justice. Whatever I declare is right is just. Perks of being the archon of justice," the archangel sneered. "I don't need some two-bit dragon that just ate the last silver dragon telling me about right and wrong."

I growled, angry at him for spinning the truth. "You made sure he was alive only in name. What you did to him was disgusting."

Raguel shrugged. "He was a useful tool. I'm truly sad to see him gone."

Everything about the archangel, from his tone to his eyes, was icy cold. I shuddered.

The concept of angels I'd had growing up was dead wrong. They were cold, calculating beings that had likely lived too long perched up in the celestial plane. Anything that I'd describe as humanity and empathy was gone from the being in front of me.

"What about this one? How is this tool working? Wasn't even able to stop me." I motioned to Helena.

Raguel's appearance had put a wrinkle in our plan, but we still had more we needed to do. The best thing I could do was keep him from personally acting for as long as I could. And if I could drive a small wedge between him and Helena, I'd do it.

He looked at the nephilim with disdain. "She's not bad for a half-breed. Certainly has her uses—in the mortal realm at least."

Helena's face darkened, but she looked away from him to hide it.

Raguel smirked, and I wondered if he thought she was blushing. He was cocky enough to think that.

I knew better, though. Helena's jaw was clenched in anger. If I saw somebody look that way at a bar, I'd expect a jaw-crushing punch to be coming next.

I waited, seeing if she'd attack him, but she didn't. She cooled off and turned back.

Raguel looked down below, sighing. "I have some justice to serve to some very naughty elves. Helena, don't let the dragon get away; he'll make a wonderful mount, even if he is a gaudy gold. One day, he might even be big enough to displace your mother."

Raguel disappeared, only to reappear amid the Highaen forces and carve a swath through them.

Still holding Helena's spear, I chased after him, trying to catch up.

Helena's body appeared in my way as she made a barrier of light to stop me. "I have my orders."

I laughed, confusion spreading across her face.

"Helena, I don't want to fight you. Don't you understand you're just a tool? You're just like the silver dragon to him. It's just worse because you are willingly following his orders. If you stopped obeying him, what do you think he'd do? Accept it or put you in chains?" I waited for her to think about that.

Even if I couldn't physically hurt her, I wondered if I could make her hesitate enough to get around her.

Once again, she shook her head, muttering, "Shut up." Then a white wall of magic flew towards me.

I twirled her spear and slammed the blade into the wall of magic, curious about what would happen.

It exploded in a shower of sparkles.

"This is pretty nice. Maybe I'll keep it." I hefted the spear and flew past Helena, who hovered angrily in the sky.

She didn't make any movement towards me this time, though.

"You'll never win," she said without turning around. "You can't defeat him, and there are six more. If you even killed one, another archangel will rise to take its place."

I paused, but only for a moment. "What's the point of living if you don't go after what is right? Those people down there he's going to slaughter? They deserve to live. Tyrande deserves freedom." Done talking, I kept moving.

I found Raguel amid the Highaen forces, taking blasts of magic to his body without flinching. He was moving so quickly through their ranks that I wondered if he was teleporting.

The six wings on his back swayed discordantly. It was like they were feathered tentacles rather than wings.

I used my dragon sight on him, noticing as he repositioned himself that there was a small tether connecting him back to the portal to the celestial plane. Throwing myself down on top of him, I hoped my new spear would be enough.

Raguel dodged my attack, staring at me in disappointment. "Did that useless thing let you go?" He looked up to see Helena slowly following after me. "I suppose we'll have to retrain her."

Even from a distance, I could see her flinch. I didn't know what 'retraining' entailed, but I knew enough to know it likely had some sort of torturous brainwashing.

My instincts flared in my body, and I followed them, swinging the spear in front of me. There was a clang as it stopped a blade that hit it.

Raguel had used my moment of distraction to attack. I was extra thankful to Morgana in that moment for training me to always be ready. It had just saved my life.

My jaw cracked open, spewing fire out around the spear.

Raguel disappeared, those six wings of his flowing behind him as he reappeared a hundred feet back.

I did a quick glance at the battle, my heart sinking. Despite distracting Raguel, the four-winged angels were powerful and made their way through the ranks of the Highaen army. They weren't nearly as fast as Raguel; nonetheless, their blades were finding elven throats with every swing.

The odds were quickly shifting in the Church's favor.

I spotted my alpha wolf as she jumped, catching one of the more powerful angels by surprise and bringing it down in a tussle. The Highaen collapsed on them, killing the angel swiftly.

If Kelly had joined the fight, that meant she and Morgana had finished their part. And if that was true, Morgana was out of the fight.

I clicked my tongue, spotting her tree through the wreckage of the circular building. We had one more part of the plan left to execute, and that was up to me.

Breaking from my fight with Raguel, I flew away, up over Morgana's tree. He followed me, and I could barely get the spear between us every time he attacked. His speed made it hard as he flitted around me, his blade stretching and shrinking with his attacks.

Flying up above him with a large flick of my wings, I readied my magic. "Evokus."

This time, I didn't focus the magic on coming out of my hand. I gathered it in my mouth.

For what was coming, I knew I'd need more emotion. I let my mind drift back to the Silver Slave's body, carved up with runes, his eyes gouged out. I remembered how defeated he had looked as they'd shuffled him out of the back of the shop, and the flicker of hope I'd brought.

My mind flitted to Helena, brainwashed into following them, despite being nothing more than a pawn. I grew angry, deeply angry at their sick sense of justice and right. They were monsters, a threat to dragons, and I wouldn't let them destroy all I loved.

Growing brighter, my emotions became a powerful fireball in my mouth, and I breathed out, releasing it down towards Raguel.

As I expected, he dodged it, shifting to the side with speed that I couldn't hope to hit. But he hadn't been the target.

My fireball continued down until it hit Morgana's tree. It exploded, swallowing the tree, along with the portal to the celestial plane.

Raguel did a double take. "NO!" he screamed, ignoring me and disappearing into the fires of the explosion.

I calmly waited up above, knowing exactly what he'd find.

Helena hovered a small distance from me, but she wasn't attacking. She seemed unsure, watching and waiting to see the result once the explosion cleared.

As the fire died down, the smoke began to waft away. I stared after it, keeping my senses open for any sign of attack.

An angry scream sounded within the smoke, and Raguel walked out from it, rage on his face. The smoke continued to clear behind him, revealing an empty pit. The tree and the portal were gone.

Raguel turned his head slowly to face me. His wings were coated in a thin layer of char and still burning at the tips from his trip into the fire, but he didn't seem to care.

"What have you done?" he demanded.

"I believe you were the one who dodged my attack," I replied casually. "So, I'd say you were my partner in crime to destroying the portal to the celestial plane. Thanks for the help."

He raged in silence before his blade sparked against my spear in a quick attack. I used his force to rebound and glide down to the ground.

As much as I was enjoying flying, I knew I didn't stand a chance against an archangel. I waited on the ground for him to join.

He descended, hovering just above as Helena landed near us.

"Is the portal really gone?" She stared into the space where it had been.

"It is. I can't feel it," Raguel confirmed.

"Give me my spear." Helena turned to me, holding out her hand.

I could tell she was angry, and I had no reason to trust her, but something told me that she needed to see this through.

Tossing the spear to her, she caught it, whirling the weapon and pointing it at Raguel.

"I am not your tool anymore. There will be no one to replace you if you die." Her voice shook with rage, but her arm holding the spear quivered slightly. She'd been trained to fear him, but she was trying to fight it.

I smiled, still not sure quite what had prompted the final shift, but it seemed to be tied to the portal. Whatever sat on the other side seemed to have been enough to keep her from toeing the line.

Raguel narrowed his eyes on Helena. "Careful, you might poke your eye out with that thing. Even if the portal is gone, another will be made eventually."

"I would rather live free for a few hundred years than be your *tool* for eternity." She spat the word like a nasty bit of bile that had rested in her throat for too long.

Hearing shouts, I noticed that the four-winged angels still had an edge on the elves, even with Kelly's help.

I took off as Helena and Raguel clashed.

Glancing as I flew away, I watched Raguel take Helena by surprise, but her silver armor held up. And her spear was holding off his blade, but she was fighting recklessly.

She wasn't fighting to live; she was fighting to kill Raguel, regardless of the cost.

I wanted to help her, but I couldn't do that and also help the Highaen and Kelly. Making the choice, I headed towards the battle, shifting into a dragon as I moved.

I swooped low over the templar forces, blowing out flames and melting through an entire swath. As I expected, the angels around took note.

They swarmed up to me as I pulled out of the dive. Like a hungry swarm of mosquitoes, the angels flew to me, trying to grab me and smother me until I went down. They stabbed into me, using their blades to weaken me as they climbed on me like insects.

I did my best to shake them off, my claws and teeth finding a few unlucky angels, but there were too many of them. And they were dodging my attempts.

While I wasn't loving the new wounds in my side, I was glad they hadn't gone for my wings. I doubted it hadn't occurred to them; they must have had orders to take me alive. They clearly hadn't noticed that their portal was gone.

"Zach," Yev roared, joining me in the sky.

"Yev, hit me with all you've got," I told her, praying that it would work. The cuts hadn't done any meaningful damage yet, but it was only a matter of time.

"I—" She hesitated for a moment before she puffed acrid smoke from her nostrils and breathed deep. Then she hit me with her green fire.

With the time I'd spent looking into my own dragon situation, I'd learned about the five breeds of chromatic dragons. Copper dragons should have the same breath as her and be resistant to her corrosive breath.

I waited, gambling on a hunch I'd started having. Now I just had to see if I could be copper as well as gold and silver.

Her breath hit me and stung for just a moment before all the pain went away. The few living angels on me scattered, most of them turning into bubbly goo and melting away into the green mist that her breath left behind.

Yev was staring at me, her eyes wide. I lifted up my claw.

I had been expecting them to look copper, but instead, my scales were a deep emerald green. I was a few shades darker than Yev.

As I flew out of the green cloud, they rippled and turned gold again. I smiled, pleased with myself.

"W-what was that?" Yev stammered.

"Later. Help me with the remaining angels." Although, I wasn't sure I could explain what had just happened. I had a little information, but it wasn't nearly enough to understand my own situation.

Soaring through the sky as the angels ran, I finally felt like an apex predator. My dragon preened inside of me, happy to finally be in its rightful place. The angels were quick, but with my increase in size, I was much faster.

I swooped over a cluster of angels, catching one of the four-wing bastards in my teeth, shaking him and swallowing the mana-rich creature down my throat.

Others came at me in small numbers, trying to fight, but every time they did so, Yev was there. She'd blast me with her corrosive fire and scatter them. Swarming seemed to be their only technique, and we had stopped it.

Also, the angels were delicious.

I had to work to maintain control as my beast delighted in the chase. But my time flying in the Sentarshaden tree had taught me the need to control some of those primal instincts.

Yev was quiet, flying behind me, supporting me with blasts of green fire when I needed it.

We worked as partners, clearing them from the area.

Eventually, there were no more angels in sight. They'd all either fled or died.

I turned, looking at Yev and giving her a nod of thanks for her support. I hadn't realized until that moment how much more powerful dragons were in groups. If they were resistant to each other, they could easily take down foes.

With the angels taken care of, the battle between the Highaen and the Church was coming to a close. The Highaen had the templar forces entirely circled and were slowly tightening their ranks as they cut them down.

Over in the pit where Morgana's tree had once been, Helena and Raguel fought viciously.

I swooped low over their fight, landing on the edge of the pit as they backed off, cautious at my presence.

Yev had stayed behind, sweeping over the remaining templar forces and making sure that the Highaen came out victorious.

Shifting back to my dragon knight form, I moved in, my mouth watering at the idea of eating an archangel. If they were anything like the angels, they'd be delicious.

I licked my lips subconsciously.

"Excuse me." An elf ran to my side. "I was told to give you this by one of your mates." He held out the silver sword that I had taken from Jared.

I took it with a huge grin on my face. Jadelyn had my spatial artifact, but Scarlett was the one with this sort of humor. Later, I'd do something nice for her, because it truly rang of justice to kill Raguel with this.

The sword burst into a bright white blaze as I held it, making the air around me blur.

"Your sword has taken a liking to me," I said.

Raguel's brow pressed down in confusion from seeing me hold one of his swords. "That's not possible."

Pointing it at him, I proved that it was not only possible, but happening before his very eyes.

"I don't see why I can't both be a monster and serve true justice." I paused, keeping my eyes on Raguel as I asked, "Helena, are you with me?"

She tossed her head, her short, white hair of hers in disarray. She winced slightly, and I realized for the first time that her arm was bleeding.

"If you truly are more attuned to justice than him, prove it and kill him. I'm on your side until he is dead, then I hope to never see you again," she said.

Her arrogant tone rankled the beast, but I was fine to have an ally for the battle.

I could use backup, and Morgana would be out of commission, Scarlett busy protecting Jadelyn, and Kelly with the Highaen. So it was up to Helena and I to deal with the archangel.

"Both of you together? Good. Anything else would be below me." Raguel put one arm behind his back and held his sword with a single hand. "Come."

I charged, the sword leaving a wake of white fire behind my attack.

As we clashed, it was like hitting a brick wall. He casually blocked my sword, parrying it off to the side and into Helena's spear in a single swift stroke. Then he kicked where our two weapons met, forcing both of us back.

"Stay out of my way," Helena hissed, twirling her spear and charging back in at Raguel.

The archangel blocked each of her attacks, warping the space between their weapons constantly. It almost looked like her spear was magnetically attracted to his sword. I studied his movements.

He was using magic, much like Morgana did, but he wasn't doing it as well. His arrogance made him do big, bold magic, not using it efficiently like she would in a fight.

Curious, I decided to try a bit of magic of my own.

"Evokus." I raised a hand, red and blue magic swirling in my hand. Pointing it, I launched it from my palm.

Raguel turned, parrying my magic with his sword, which was for show as he shifted it using his own magic. My fireball shifted around him to the side, but he hadn't been expecting the power in the explosion that came right after.

The smug look on his face was wiped away as he and Helena were blasted into the air.

I took the opportunity, lunging forward and using all my strength to leap. I only had a moment to skewer him before he'd recover.

Seeing me coming, he shifted midair with his wings, but he didn't get entirely out of the way. My blade, one he had made and blessed, tore through his side.

Twisting, I slashed at him, but he'd regained his bearings. He maneuvered away, floating in the air beyond my reach. I couldn't help but notice that he wasn't teleporting anymore now that the portal was gone.

Raguel touched his side and came away with a red, bloodstained hand. His face twisted into a rage before he calmed down dangerously quickly.

As he surveyed the area strategically, realizing that the templars and angels were

gone. He was alone, surrounded by enemies.

"You all think you've won. But archangels
aren't known for their ability to destroy
armies; they are known for being where
you least want them." He glanced over at the
Highaen forces. "I wonder who's protecting
Sentarshaden, hmm?"

The sinister grin on his face was the last
thing I saw before he shot backwards.

As he moved, Helena's spear appeared
right where he'd been, and I almost
punched the ground in frustration at the
miss. But that was when I noticed that her
spear was covered in blood, one of Raguel's
wings falling to the ground next to her.

A hundred yards away, Raguel fell, skidding on the ground and cursing up a storm.

My predator instincts kicked in and I
shifted, leaping the hundred yards in a
dragonwing-powered leap. Still clutching
the silver sword, I pounced on him, shifting
back and nailing one of his other wings to
the ground.

"You sick bastard." My fist caught his jaw
and snapped his head sharply to the side
before I grabbed the sword again and twisted it, destroying another of his wings.

Raguel yelled, hitting me hard enough to
fling me off of him as his wings swept him
up off the ground.

That was all the time it took for Helena to
descend on him.

He backpedaled, blocking her spear with far more effort than he'd needed before. His magic was wearing out.

I smiled, wishing Morgana was there to see it. She would have loved that his arrogant use of magic was part of his downfall. Now was no time to gloat, though. I got back on my feet and attacked him from the side.

His sword was blurring back and forth between Helena and me as he struggled to keep up. Two of his wings bled freely and the other four twitched painfully, slowing down his ability to move around.

Helena opened herself wide, and Raguel took the bait, plunging his sword into her shoulder. She wrapped her spear around his back, crushing his wings to him and holding them still.

"Kill him!" she screamed.

Her words had no effect on my decision. My sword was already sinking in through his side and up through his chest.

I ripped my sword back out, taking another of his remaining wings with it. I avoided cutting through him to where I'd hit Helena. Despite my dislike for the nephilim, she was my ally at least for the time being.

Raguel sagged, his blood burning on the silver sword, staining it a darker color. Blood bubbled up through his throat as Helena released him and stepped back, pulling his sword out of her shoulder.

His voice was garbled as he said, "It might take time, but the others will come, eventually. When that happens, you both will wish you were dead."

Raguel coughed several times, and I wasn't about to let a good meal go to waste.

Shifting into a dragon, I devoured him, feeling my skin itch with fresh growth.

Archangels were delicious.

Helena wrinkled her nose at me, clutching her shoulder. She shook her head, staring at me for a moment before she took several steps backwards and flew away. I had a feeling there was a lot she needed to process.

"Should we go after her?" Yev stomped up behind me.

"No." After fighting with her against Raguel, I wasn't going to chase after her or even fight her. She may not be a friend, but at least she didn't seem like an enemy any longer. And her enemies were now my enemies as well. We may need to fight side by side again one day.

"Let's get cleaned up." I turned, looking for my mates.

CHAPTER 22

T he Highaen parted for me with awe in their eyes.

"You lied," Yev said, following me. "You lied to my mother and me. Why?"

"The Highaen forces are compromised," I said simply. "The angels were ready and waiting for you when you fled the magic range. Even if they had guessed that we had some sort of extraction plan, they wouldn't have known enough to focus all the key resources of their attack. You have a mole."

Yev's jaw clenched, but she didn't refute me.

"There was a lot riding on this," I reminded her, spotting Kelly.

She was still shifted, standing over Jadelyn, Scarlett, and Morgana. Morgana was sitting on the ground, clutching her arm closely. Her left arm was wrapped in woody vines that popped out of her skin, like something was living in it.

She had told me it would take her out of the fight, but I had no idea it would look like that.

Yev gasped behind me. "Your tree! But I thought you destroyed it."

Morgana pointed at Scarlett. "Kitsune. What Zach destroyed was an illusion."

Scarlett did a small salute. "At your service." She turned to Yev. "Your father has Tyrande."

"You got her?" Yev gasped. "How?"

I pointed to Morgana and Kelly. "They ran into the celestial plane and got her out. You two cut it a little close." I turned to them, concerned at what had happened on the other side of the portal.

"Hey, we did pretty good, all things considered." Kelly put her hands on her hips.

The sight of a massive werewolf making such a feminine motion made the edges of my lips curl up in a half-smile.

"It was the furball's fault; she should not do a stealth mission again," Morgana stated weakly, still clutching at her arm.

"My fault? It was the blueberry who was busy slurping down angel blood like it was a buffet."

Morgana shrugged. "I needed to be on the top of my game to carry my tree."

Yev nodded, agreeing with Morgana. "Carrying a tree is a heavy burden."

"There you are," the matriarch of the Highaen family's sharp voice cut through the crowd.

She paused, seeing our group. But as her eyes scanned us, they zeroed in on Morgana and her arm.

Kelly's hair stood on end, and Morgana looked ready to fight.

"Calm down." Yev's mother glanced at me for a moment before looking back at Morgana. "I think you'll be safe from any aggression from elves for a long time. After all, you are now the only elven connection to the new king of the dragons."

She actually did a slight bow to me. "May I take my daughter away?"

"Please, don't stand on ceremony." I felt uncomfortable with her change in demeanor.

It seemed that my help to save her daughter's life had put me in the better graces of the Highaen matriarch. That, and she was no longer on edge, fearing for her daughter.

"Actually, I'd like to see Tyrande. I assume that's where you are going?" I asked.

"Yes, please come." Yev's mother dipped her head to me and pulled Yev with her.

I scooped up Morgana, who grumbled at me.

"I'm not going to let you walk with that arm," I replied.

She rolled her eyes but didn't argue. Morgana was looking pale from the effort it had taken for her to move her tree.

The rest fell in behind me as we walked deeper into the Highaen forces.

The army hadn't taken any prisoners, and were taking care of their own wounded and collecting the dead.

It would be days before the mess of the battle was all cleaned up. I was glad Morgana had gotten her tree. All of these elves moving around near her tree would have put her on edge.

I couldn't wait to see how the paranormals would cover up the mess of a battle site. But I'd let the Highaen family figure that out. I didn't need the headache.

We walked a bit further through the group, coming up to Tyrande, who was sitting up in the bed of a truck while an older man wearing leather armor talked to her.

The man said something that made her laugh before she doubled over in pain. He was quick to dodge forward, helping her sit again, his face torn in angst at her pain.

"Mom, Yev." Tyrande seemed in good enough spirits. Her eyes then shifted behind them to the rest of us. "Thank you."

"No problem." Kelly bowed her lupine head.

It was only fair for Kelly to take some of the credit, given that she had carried Tyrande out.

"What happened to the archangel?" Tyrande asked.

"Dead. I ate him." I grinned. Bugger had been tasty too. If he hadn't been so difficult to kill, I could go for round two with another one,

Tyrande looked me over. "You were big out there, bigger than I remember."

"You missed a few things," I replied. It was a poor explanation, but I wasn't about to get into the details in front of all the soldiers around us. "Glad you are okay."

"A little banged up, but I'll be all right." Tyrande gave me a big thumbs up. Her eyes shifted to Morgana's arm. "I see you have your tree. With your new mate, I'm guessing it is going to go somewhere very secure."

Morgana grinned from my arms. "I've been told I can pick anywhere in the world."

"Damn right. I'll build a fortress around it," Jadelyn agreed.

"I don't want to know." Tyrande held up her hands. "I'm just glad to be back on this plane, and I'll be thrilled to be back home in boring Sentarshaden."

The man that had been in front of her stepped up to me and clasped my shoulder. "Thank you for bringing back my daughter and protecting my clan during the battle. But I would ask for a moment of your time... alone?"

I looked at Morgana in my hands, then over to Kelly, who seemed most able to hold her.

"Don't give me that look. I won't bruise your precious blueberry." Kelly held out her arms.

I rested Morgana in her arms before following the man who appeared to be Tyrande's father.

He walked a short distance away, enough to give us some privacy.

"First off, I'm Styvan. I'm those two troublemakers' father." He smiled in good humor at the two girls.

"An honor to meet you." I was respectful; he'd been nothing but good natured since I'd met him.

He appraised me again. "You seem like a good lad. Maybe a decent leader. But I can't help but worry about my little girl, even if she could crush me under her heel."

I waited, curious about what was worrying him.

He looked up at me. "Everyone has seen the newsreel of the Bronze King…"

I nodded, realizing he must be concerned about me as the leader of a group of dragons, which may soon include his daughter. But I waited to let him finish.

"Anyway, my daughter will be drawn into the conclave and for the first time, I know no one to look after her." He scratched the side of his head. "So, what I guess I'm getting at is: will you look after my daughter at this conclave? Given your status, I'd expect you to be able to deal with any troubles she has."

I nodded, not sure that I needed even more responsibility on my shoulders.

Then it hit me why his phrasing bothered me. "It almost sounds like you are giving her away to me," I tried to make a joke.

But he didn't laugh. Styvan's face was set in an impassive expression for an awkwardly long moment, but then he smirked. "Just look out for her. Yev has her own mind, and I know better than to insert myself into her affairs. I like my head on my shoulders." He turned it around and made a joke of his own.

I smirked, imagining a furious Yev if she was told who she had to marry. She was headstrong. But I had already been expecting that the Highaen and others would try to push their girls onto me. I just hadn't expected it so soon.

"You haven't answered my question." He prodded.

Looking up at the sky for answers, none came. But I knew that, in the end, if Yev was in danger and needed me, I would help her.

"Sure. I'll do my best. But I have no idea what we are about to walk into."

"You'll land on your feet. I can see that much." He patted me on the shoulder.

"Now, let's go rejoin the girls before they cause more trouble."

I liked him. He seemed very fatherly, nurturing.

An elf in Highaen colors jogged up to me, carrying two bundles before we could rejoin the girls. "We have something for you." He looked proud of the two bundles.

I took a peek under the cloths, one was several dragon bones, likely those that had been stabilizing the portal along with Morgana's tree. The other bundle were two angelic blades.

"Styvan, take these, they are for Yev." I grabbed the bundle of bones and gave it to her father. Given that I just ate the entire silver slave, I ought to share.

He smiled. "She'll love your gift."

"It wasn't—never mind." I grabbed the second bundle, holding it under my arms, thinking two more blades for my hoard. Maybe I'll make an entire section for the weapons I take from the angels.

After the minor distraction, we continued to the girls.

"Is everything okay?" Tyrande's mother asked.

"Perfect, dear." Styvan nodded happily. "Now, what do you all say we start heading home?" He pat his bundle with a smile.

There were murmurs of agreement from everyone.

"I'll tell the jet to head back to Lucerne." Jadelyn pulled out her phone.

Styvan nodded. "I wondered how you got here. We were watching reports of flights to the area for other reasons. You jumped?"

"Off a dragon's back!" Kelly said excitedly.

"I want to hear every detail," he encouraged her, listening as we started walking back to the bank of cars.

Kelly was more than happy to tell a slightly embellished version of the story.

I smiled as I watched everybody head to the cars, exhausted but safe. I was glad that we had won that battle, but I wondered how much we'd done to shut down the war.

Morgana had described this base as an R&D facility. Something told me this wasn't their only stronghold.

"Morgana, do I want to know how many bases like this the templar have?" I asked as we got into the car.

"No. There are dozens," she said with a sigh. "Maybe more. I only really know about this site. I haven't spent time learning about the others."

I realized that we might have cut the head off the hydra, but others would pop up in its place given enough time. They would open up another portal, too.

While we'd won, the Highaen forces had taken a heavy hit, and the city would go into mourning. Hundreds, if not thousands, of elves had lost their lives fighting the angels that had come out through the portal.

With the portal closed, it would hopefully take hundreds of years for them to pour through, but I knew I'd likely live long enough to face off against them again one day.

"What's next?" Jadelyn asked me, seeming to notice me lost in my thoughts.

"We head home. And then we need to get ready for this conclave. Although, I'd much rather be heading off on a real honeymoon. I need a vacation." I settled into the seat. It had been a long day.

A now human Kelly was squirming into clothes behind me. "I'm glad we are going back to the city. We need to pick up my barrel of potion from Hestia."

"Ah, yes. Would hate it if the furballs couldn't make more furballs," Morgana teased, but as she talked about little ones, there was a bit of light in her eyes. Something told me she wouldn't hate having them around, although she might grumble about it.

"I liked you better when you weren't so pathetic, blueberry. It's hard to tease something so weak." As Kelly said it, she moved over and helped Morgana get situated and comfortable. The two of them confused me, but they seemed to be growing on each other in their own ways.

Jadelyn sighed, looking at her phone. "It looks like we will have a fan club when we arrive. The picketers are still outside." She held up her phone for me to see.

Sure enough, the crowd seemed to have grown since I'd last seen it, despite us not being at the house.

"Will they leave?" I asked.

"Probably not for weeks." Scarlett grabbed the phone to see for herself. "Damn. You are popular."

"Yeah, he is. Look at this." Kelly held her phone between the seats for the three of us to see.

It was a paranormal news broadcast. The reel behind the presenter had several angles of me flying away from Jadelyn's home. Then it shifted to a big picture of my face, with my name written across the bottom.

"Oh, fuck," I cursed and crushed the armrest. "That's my name."

"Duh." Kelly rolled her eyes and withdrew the phone. "It's out. You are famous."

I groaned. "Not helpful."

"Look at it this way: you don't have to hide anymore," Jadelyn tried to spin it for me.

All of them were encouraging, but I couldn't help but feel like everything had turned my life upside down. And now all the marbles were falling out.

"Buck up, alpha. Remember what we talked about? You once pushed me to be the world's first female alpha. You can be the world's golden boy now."

Scarlett snorted. "You had me for the first half."

"No, I'm serious," Kelly grumped. "He's about to become the leader of the mother fucking dragon race. He's going to be the world's golden boy."

"Let's not keep saying that. I'd hate for that to catch on and see 'Golden Boy' plastered under my name on some news channel." I did an over-exaggerated shudder.

Kelly just laughed, and I wasn't sure how seriously she'd taken me. I'd meant it. But she just went back to scrolling on her phone.

***

"Here it is." Hestia led us inside to a large, blue plastic chemical barrel. "I thought about getting one of those lifts, but then I realized that a gold dragon was coming to pick it up. So, it shouldn't be a problem."

She stared dead at me, ignoring Morgana and Kelly who were with me.

"So, the semen. Yours, I assume?" She watched me.

"Uh." I wasn't prepared for that question. "Yes."

She let out a soft whistle and protectively covered her pocket. "Gold dragon semen. This stuff might pack more of a kick than I expected." She smiled, seeming more pleased with the deal she had struck.

Then Hestia turned to Kelly. "Remember, only let them have one drop about ten minutes prior to sex." From there, Hestia went into other instructions on the proper administration and storage of the potion.

I was more concerned with other things. I walked over and grabbed the drum, lifting it and carrying it out to the black SUV.

"Is that sealed tight, boss?" one of Scarlett's men asked, watching me place it in the back.

"No idea," I answered honestly.

The man quickly came back to check it and strap it in. "Can't be too careful. I was told this stuff was worth more than its weight in gold."

I nodded. It probably was, and while making the ingredients Hestia had needed had been pleasant enough, I didn't love the idea of having to go re-negotiate for more with her now that she knew I was a gold dragon.

Knowing the guards would protect the potion, I went back inside. It looked like the instructions had stopped, and Morgana was passionately speaking to Hestia.

"The Highaen have agreed that, as long as your father doesn't start raising an army, you are completely off any lists except surveillance." Morgana sounded like she was saying it for the second time.

"No, I'm hidden here."

"You aren't hidden," I corrected her. "The Highaen know exactly where you live and what you do every day."

Hestia blinked. "No. That's not possible. I move every three months. I jump from different work fields, picking up odd jobs."

"Tyrande knew your address off hand," Morgana clarified.

"Shit." Hestia bit her nail, looking a bit panicked. She started moving around, like she was going to grab items and run. "Shit. Okay. I can handle this. I've prepared for this."

Morgana placed a slow hand on her friend's shoulder, helping her breathe.

"You're okay, Hestia," Morgana replied. "You don't have to run. You don't have to hide anymore. You can live your life freely."

Hestia looked like she was lost somewhere between hyperventilating and crying tears of joy. I could only imagine what all those years staying under the radar and keeping herself isolated had done to her.

"So, what do I do, Morgy?" Hestia asked.

Kelly snorted at the nickname, but I shot her a look, letting her know to leave it. Last thing I needed was them starting another spat.

Morgana ignored Kelly, focusing on her friend. "I want you to come back to Philly. Your father misses you."

I cursed the mention of her father re-
minding me of my failed task. I reached
inside the spatial artifact and pulled out the
forgotten letter. "He really does. He sent
this with me."

She eyed it skeptically "You only bring
this out now?"

Scratching the back of my head, I went
with the truth. "There was a lot going on. I
forgot about it."

Morgana snorted. "He is the new king of
dragons. Give him a little slack and maybe
he'll owe you a favor."

I rolled my eyes. We did not know I was
king of the dragons yet. But the fact that
Hestia didn't question it made me realize
that everybody had interpreted the Bronze
King's statement the same.

"Either way, there's the letter. And you can
catch a ride back to Philly with us if you
want."

Kelly coughed into her hand and shook
her head. "Mile high club," she grunted.

"When do you leave?" She waved the letter, not yet opening it.

"Tomorrow," I told her.

Jadelyn's plane had flown back the night
before. The pilots were doing a thorough
inspection, making sure our emergency
exit stunt hadn't caused any damage before
we flew back over the ocean. We were told
it would take most of the day.

"I'll have an answer by tomorrow morning," Hestia promised Morgana. "You go have fun with your dragon. If I don't talk to you before you head off, tell my dad that I love him. And I want him to live his best life."

I nodded, accepting the cue to leave. I ducked out of her home, seeing the driver close the trunk and get in the front seat before we all piled in.

"Where to?"

"Back home." I was ready to get back to Jadelyn and Scarlett.

He nodded as he strapped in, putting it in drive and pulling out into traffic.

We wound through the city, reaching Jadelyn's house and the crowds that awaited us.

It took a small army of her guards to part the crowd enough for our car to get through. And even then, people were slamming up against it with their cameras, trying to capture a photo inside.

After we passed through, the guards were using all their strength to hold back the crowd, pushing them back as the gates tried to close.

Scarlett had said they had upgraded the gate with a motor four times the recommended size for just that reason.

People were insane.

"So, how's fame?" Morgana gave a throaty chuckle, watching the people outside act like zombies hunting for the last survivors.

"I'm just trying to tune all of them out," I admitted. "Otherwise, it will drive me insane."

"You could just... you know." Kelly blew out a big breath. "Smoke them."

I was unamused. "Yes, Kelly. That definitely would not have any blowback."

But she just snickered.

Jadelyn met me as I stepped out of the car. "Everything went okay?"

"Yeah, though Morgana tried to convince Hestia to come back with us."

"I assumed that failed?"

"We got a maybe," I explained.

Jadelyn nodded, less surprised at Morgana's invitation than I was.

She turned, leading me into the home. "We have the Highaen sisters over. They wanted to say thank you one last time before we left."

"They've said thank you enough." The two dozen gifts that had been sent over were plenty.

She gave me a look that told me to just go with it. And I understand her point. Having the heirs to a powerful paranormal city owe you a favor could come in handy down the line.

But we'd also been flooded with invitations from all the other powerful families in the area wanting to meet us before we headed out.

Jadelyn had weeded through those and said none of them were enough to delay our flight plans. But if we visited again, we'd have to politely accept more than a few of them.

"Zach." The two sisters turned to me, their purple eyes boring into me.

I noticed that they'd gotten a bit more dressed up than usual. I wondered if they had some party or function to attend. Yev had her hair artfully done up in a bun with bangs framing her face, while Tyrande had her hair braided in a crown.

"Good to see you again." Tyrande blushed.

"She's been going on about the hero and his heroic harem," Yev teased Tyrande, who elbowed her hard in the gut. Not that the dragon seemed to care one bit.

Tyrande shook her head, and I was amazed at how the braid didn't even budge. "She's making things up. Besides, she can't get over the bones you gave her."

"Girls, my mate is amazing. We don't have to fight over that." Jadelyn hung off my shoulder. "I'm married to a gold dragon." She grinned from ear to ear. "It's so fun to get to say it!"

"You are a very lucky woman," Tyrande settled down and agreed. "But we didn't come here just to poke at Zach. We came to see our friend before she leaves. Who knows when you'll come back now that you are attached to that thing." She swirled her finger in the air as she pointed at me.

"Wherever the winds take us." Jadelyn shrugged. "Apparently, we are going to a dragon conclave soon."

Scarlett squinted her eyes, but saved that conversation for later. I couldn't wait for the 'what to do when a dragon attacks you' drills.

"Spring," Yev said. "Spring equinox is what my messenger told me."

I turned to her, surprised. "You already got your message from the Bronze King?"

"Yep. First thing this morning." She fished around in her purse and brought out a golden card. "It says I can bring my mates or a guest. I'll probably just bring Tyrande."

The high elf heiress bounced excitedly. "I get to meet all the big dragons. It will be fun. I convinced our parents it makes sense from a diplomatic standpoint."

"Yes, I'm sure being in a room full of the most dangerous paranormals on the planet will be 'fun.'" Morgana was less amused. "I bet at least one of the male dragons will try to get handsy with Yev."

The high elf sisters wrinkled their noses in unison.

Morgana took on her trainer's voice as she continued. "These are old creatures, and you need to remember that. The idea of sexism and sexual harassment might have only come up during their latest nap."

"Will we be safe?" Scarlett asked, taking a quick glance at Jadelyn.

"Zach marked us. We will be fine." Jadelyn pushed back her shoulders, clearly ready to dig in her heels if Scarlett tried to stop her from coming.

I tried to ease everyone's mind. "We will figure out all our protocols and safety plans."

Scarlett nodded profusely as I said the word protocols, and I had to bite the inside of my cheek not to laugh. Sometimes, she was easy to please.

I continued on. "I'll keep all of you safe and make an example of any dragons that need to learn their place."

"Aww. I love my dragon." Jadelyn cuddled in, and the Highaen sisters looked away. I wondered why they were more uncomfortable with us touching than they were before, but it wasn't worth raising.

I sat back, enjoying some easy conversation with the sisters until they finally left, and we packed up for our flight in the morning.

CHAPTER 50

As we headed out to fly back to the states, I started to get an understanding of what a mess my life had become.

As we made our way out of Jadelyn's home, we were swarmed the second the cars made their way out of the gates. There was one point when the bodies pressing up against it nearly tipped the car.

Luckily, Scarlett had protocols for everything. Men popped out of the two escort cars and pulled people away so that we could exit. Once we made it past the mass of people, our driver floored it, getting us out of the chaos.

But as we neared the train platform, it wasn't any better. Stepping out of the car, I had to shield my eyes from all the cameras flashing around us.

"How did they know we would be here?" I grumbled, trying not to go blind.

"Someone has probably been watching Jadelyn's jet. This is the only way out of the city. Unless, of course, we want to fly Air Dragon, but that has its own problems." Scarlett's tails twirled and brought up an illusionary wall that lasted all of two seconds before someone poked it and popped her illusion.

Jadelyn put a hand on my shoulder. "Don't eat the reporters." Her voice was like a calming balm. "We'll get on the train and close the blinds."

I grumbled. "Can't I just use the fear aura again?"

"No," Scarlett was quick to answer. "Please don't. You are lucky you didn't kill anyone the first time."

We continued to push through the crowd, and I tried to keep my eyes on the train and not get lost in the flashes. Pushing our way through, we finally made it to the train. But as I stepped on, I could see the reporters lining up to get on as well.

Moving quickly, I found a booth, and we all piled inside. I moved to close all the blinds before leaning back into the seat with a heavy sigh.

"Now that we have a moment alone, I have a gift for you." Morgana pulled a jewelry box about the size of her hand out of her bra.

"You didn't have to." I felt bad that I hadn't gotten her a gift.

"No, she did," Jadelyn disagreed. "We all put something into this."

Morgana smirked as she handed me the box, and I opened it up. She was feeling better, but still not quite back to normal. She still carried her tree, rooted in her arm.

Inside the jewelry box, set in black foam, was a bracer. It was similar to the one that Jadelyn had given me before my duel with Simon, but the design was slightly different. The one in the duel hadn't been able to hold up to my dragon breath. Who knew what this one would surprise me with.

It was a dark gunmetal black bracer that radiated enchantments.

"What does it do?" I asked, assuming it was like the other. But the moment it left my mouth, I realized it would be awkward if it was just decorative.

"I enchanted it to function like your lovely spatial artifact," Morgana snickered.

Jadelyn bobbed her head excitedly. "We had one of the Highaen enchanters look at those manacles and copy the size-changing aspect of them. So it'll shift with you."

I looked at the bracer in a new light.

"We also inscribed the inside." Scarlett pointed at the inside of the bracer. "But we left plenty of room for others."

I raised an eyebrow at her.

"What? As your first mate, I understand there will be more. Making room for them is important, too." Scarlett grinned. "We just have to make sure you slow down."

I nodded, glad that she was becoming more comfortable.

"The metal is a tungsten carbide something something," Kelly so aptly explained. "It's supposedly just below diamond in hardness, super heat resistant, and now that you have green scales too, it is corrosive resistant."

"If that isn't enough, it is enchanted for durability against all the dragon breaths," Jadelyn added.

"I don't know what to say. This is amazing." I slipped the bracer on, feeling stronger as I wore it. Not just because it was tough, but because it let me carry a piece of my mates with me. "Thank you so much."

But now that it was brought up, I figured we should talk about what had happened in battle. "I was surprised when I was able to become a green dragon. I thought I might only be metallic; that was unexpected."

"We'll check my library when we get back," Morgana said. "But I doubt I'll have much in there to provide any information. Dragon history stretches far back, before man could write or even talk. This conclave could be a really good resource. You can rub elbows with the oldest dragons in existence. If they don't know, then we'll just figure it out through some experimentation. We are here for you, Zach."

I looked around at my mates, who were all staring back at me. Caring love rested in their gazes.

"Thanks. I love all of you too."

"Even if you are some freakish alien dragon, we'll still love you," Kelly confirmed. "If you could have tentacles, that would be awesome, though." She let out a soft sigh.

"Do you have a new fetish we need to be aware of?" Jadelyn laughed.

"No." Kelly's face turned red. She totally had some strange sexual ideas up in her head.

Unfortunately, now wasn't the time to explore them.

"I don't think I'm some strange alien dragon, Kelly. So no tentacles, but we can play with my tail some if that would help satisfy an urge."

"I said there wasn't any weird fantasy," she grumbled, crossing her arms and looking away. "But what do you think you are?"

Everything in Morgana's books had described Pendragon as a type of chief of the dragon tribe. The Bronze King was definitely pushing me that way.

But the shifting scales and how the Silver Slave had instantly recognized me as more told me that there was some bigger destiny riding before me.

"I'm not sure, Kelly. But it's big, bigger than I imagined. I just hope that the Bronze

King will have some answers and be willing to share them."

"We'll shake him down for answers if we have to," Morgana reassured me.

"Or buy them. I hear dragons like gold." Jadelyn grinned, throwing her weight behind me.

"Holy crap." Kelly was looking at her phone. "Look at this." She held it up for me.

It was a paranormal app… about me. It had statistics on it like a baseball card. There was even a place to insert profiles to date me.

"What is that?"

"I have no idea, but it is hilarious." Kelly pulled her phone back and Jadelyn leaned over to see it.

"We can get our lawyers to take that down. We can say they are impersonating you." She shook her head, a distasteful frown on her lips.

Morgana was pulling out her phone and snickering. "It's like a dating app, but it only has one male. And it's already number three on free apps."

I groaned, putting my head in my hands. "Of course it is."

"Oh, this looks pretty nice," Kelly said.

"Please tell me you didn't download the app." I glared at her.

When she didn't respond, I knew she had and was using it.

"They have a lot of your pictures. This is like stalker level," she murmured as she scrolled through the app. I didn't want to know.

Gazing out the window, I watched the snowy landscape fly by, hoping that, once we were out of the paranormal circle of influence, it would get better. They couldn't swarm me so openly when there were normals around.

The platform at Lucerne was still chaos, but as I stepped into the normal part of the train station, it did calm down.

Letting out a heavy breath, I thanked my lucky stars.

"Scalewright?" a man in a suit asked our group as we walked out. He didn't seem to need confirmation as he opened the door to the black SUV.

"License." Kelly held out her hand, squaring up her shoulders almost like she was ready for a fight.

The man obliged, clearly ready for the check.

Kelly glanced at it and at his face before handing it back. "He's our driver. Pile in."

We all got in, and I noticed that the driver was staring at me through the rear-view mirror.

"I can't believe the gold dragon king is in my car," he gushed.

I sighed hard.

"Yep. I'm married to him." Jadelyn claimed me by wrapping her arms around me.

"I hear dragons have large harems. My daughter is quite fetching if you are looking for more," the driver half-joked, half-offered his daughter up to me on a silver platter.

I didn't respond, letting his offer elapse as politely as I could. It made the rest of the drive rather awkward. I wasn't sure what to say to him after that. But he drove all the way out to the rented private hangar.

"Welcome back." The pilot was out front to greet us. "I'm afraid we have a minor problem."

"What now?" I growled.

The pilot shrank back and nervously itched at his arm. "You see, there's a lady here that we can't seem to get to leave. She says she was invited. She also caused a slight issue with the reporters that showed up."

Sighing, I strode purposefully into the hangar to see Hestia waiting with an enormous suitcase, little stalks of herbs poking out of the zipper that looked like it was holding on for dear life.

"Hi, I decided to take you up on your offer," she said.

I was relieved that it wasn't anything more. I turned back towards the pilot. "It's okay. She's with us. What happened to the reporters?"

The pilot pointed to a pile of people in the corner of the hangar. A dozen men and women were collapsed on each other, their cameras hanging around their necks.

"They kept trying to take pictures of me, so I put them to sleep." Hestia pulled out a small vial with a big smile on her face.

The pilot leaned over to whisper to me. "She threw one of those, and some gas came out and knocked them all out."

"You know what, Hestia? I think I like you more already. Knock as many of them out as you want." I walked over, grabbing her bags and bringing them over to the plane.

Scarlett was busy running around the plane, completing all her security checks while Jadelyn waited at the bottom of the stairs.

I moved past Jadelyn, starting to climb the stairs.

She reached out and stopped me. "You have to wait for the check."

I pointed to myself. "Dragon. I'm both fire and explosive resistant."

Crossing her arms, Jadelyn looked at Scarlett, impatiently tapping her foot.

"Not yet, Jade. You can't get on there until I'm finished, even if you have a gold dragon husband." She didn't even look up from the landing gear.

Jadelyn stomped her foot like a spoiled princess. "That's not fair."

"He's the king of dragons, Jadelyn. He basically gets to make the rules," Kelly reminded her and stepped up on the plane behind me.

"Not you too."

"Maybe the dragons can get you some powerful enchantment so that you can tag along with your mate," Scarlett suggested, standing up and tugging at a cord before coming back to the gangway. "Please head on up."

The rest of my mates joined me in the cabin as Hestia sat down in one of the egg-shaped swivel chairs, a little awe on her face.

"This is... nice," she said.

Jadelyn's jet was nice, all suede leather, none of that fake stuff.

"Welcome to traveling with the Scalewrights." Scarlett took her own seat casually. "There are some drinks in the cabinet there if flying makes you nervous."

"Nah, I'm good. I have potions for that sort of thing." Hestia pulled back her frilly skirt to show a bandolier of potions strapped to her thigh.

Morgana took her own seat. "Please, don't use any potions in the cabin. This space is far too enclosed."

"It was one time, Morgy. Are you ever going to let me live that down?" Hestia glared. "You've never trusted my potions since."

"You made my skin green for a week, and I nearly went blind."

"But it helped, really. Since you were blind, you couldn't see all the people mocking your green skin."

"Wait, blueberry was a green bean?" Kelly started laughing.

Morgana glared at Hestia. "You said that potion would help me get a date to the Tredelas party that year."

"We were kids!" Hestia threw her hands up in the air. "I barely knew what I was doing."

Morgana put a hand to her face. "I don't think you know that much more now."

Hestia let out an enormous sigh and looked at me. "Careful with that one. She'll never let you live down an honest mistake."

"Oh, I'm aware. I wrecked one of her cars, and she barely lets me drive anymore," I replied, laughing.

"See, that one is completely understandable, though," Hestia replied, siding with Morgana and giving me conversational whiplash.

The engines on the jet whirred up, and we all quieted down during takeoff.

As soon as the seatbelt light went out, Kelly was unbuckling herself.

"Sorry Hestia." Then she turned to me. "I want my mile high badge. Come on back, big guy."

She undid my belt and pulled me back toward the bed.

"Wait, what's happening?" Hestia looked back at the bed, and her eyes went wide. "I'm right here."

Kelly grabbed the divider curtain and swung it closed with a metallic swish. "All better."

"That does absolutely nothing," Hestia complained from the other side of the curtain.

"Take one of your sleeping potions," Morgana chuckled as she also walked around the curtain. "Because I'm about to be loud."

"Gross. Is this payback for that one time?" Hestia complained.

Morgana paused halfway to the bed. "Yes, now that I think about it, this is payback. Now knock yourself out. Literally."

***

Hestia was passed out, drooling on herself and had been since we got going on the bed.

We landed back in Philly, and I let out a sigh of relief as I ran my hands through my hair in an attempt to get the wet mop back into a presentable state. I really needed a haircut, and I wasn't going to T for it.

"You look fine," Jadelyn replied. She looked immaculate as always, her hair and clothing perfectly charming.

"Yeah, but I'm coming home a very different person than I left," I replied. "And apparently, my every move is now going to be documented."

As the cabin door opened, I took a deep breath and walked out.

Cameras flashed in the distance, but thankfully, they were held back by Scalewright's security.

I froze at our welcome party. The paranormal council was arrayed out before me in their entirety.

Even the Summer Queen was in attendance. And next to her was a pale blue-skinned younger fae wrapped in furs that accentuated rather than hid her curves. She stood near enough to the Summer Queen that they might have been talking, but far enough away that she clearly was separate.

"Lady of Fall," Jadelyn commented.

The Lady was beautiful, like the other noble fae I'd seen. It was an eerie sort of beauty; it was hypnotic, but it also gave me pause. Like something about it just wasn't quite right, but I couldn't put my finger on it.

"Son!" Rupert shouted, coming up and grabbing my arm, wrapping one of his arms around my shoulders as he turned with me to the council. "Welcome home. Everyone, I know most of you know him, but let me introduce Zach Pendragon, the gold dragon, and my son-in-law."

He was so boisterous and excited to show me off.

"This is unnecessary." I squirmed under his arm.

"Nonsense, son. You'll need to put on a show for all of them, make yourself known. I know! Come golfing with me tomorrow." He said it so casually, it almost seemed like he'd just thought of it, but something told me that wasn't the case.

He squeezed my shoulders for a moment before letting me go and introducing me to the council once again.

When I got to Sebastian, he narrowed his eyes only for a moment before sighing. "Welcome. You've been named an ally of the elves. The Highaen have ensured that no elf will bother you. If only you had made yourself known when you had first come to town, things might have been different."

He only seemed slightly bitter that I had killed his nephew, which was progress. A resigned sigh was the best he could give me. He was smarter than to continue a vendetta against a gold dragon that had friends within the elves.

The Highaen's attitude towards me was another layer of protection he hadn't been expecting. But I wasn't about to feel any sympathy. His nephew had come after me, and he'd encouraged it. But in doing so, they'd bitten off more than they could chew.

Moving down the line, I met some of the less important members and ended up at the Fae.

"Pleasure to meet you again." The Summer Queen stared at me with her entrancing golden eyes. "The power I felt from you now makes sense. And it has blossomed even further." She made a small bow of her head. "My offer of a lovely retreat in the summer realm is still open to you and your mates."

There was something about the fae that was intoxicating. Every move and every word was filled with subtle temptations.

"I believe a gold dragon would enjoy the beauty of winter just as much." The Fall Lady stepped forward.

The Fall Lady had cool silver eyes and skin so pale it was slightly blue. And that blue was accented by the blue makeup she wore and the frosty hint in her hair. The furs were wrapped perfectly around her body to accentuate her curves.

"Pleasure to meet you. Thank you for your mother's help with Nat'alet."

Fall smirked. "When she discovered what you are, she was furious that she had been barred from watching. What a sight it must have been to see the two of you battle."

"Not as impressive as you might think." I grinned, trying to downplay it. A power had come out of me during that battle that I didn't want anyone knowing about.

"My mother sends her most sincere apologies that she didn't do more to assist you during that conflict."

It was everything I could do not to snort in her face. Her mother had done as little as possible to recover a piece of her power and walk away.

"All is well that ends well." Jadelyn gripped my arm tightly, no doubt sensing my annoyance.

But I didn't growl or eat her, so I was clapping myself on the back in my head. I was making progress. However, my annoyance must have been clear, because the Summer Queen smirked in victory over the Fall Lady.

Jadelyn pulled me past all of them to the crowd that waited beyond. A caravan of black SUVs waited, and the middle one had its doors opened as we approached. My mates and I piled into it.

"Where to?" the driver asked.

I looked at Morgana, who was currently wearing a big coat that was far too much for the new climate, but kept the roots wrapped around her arm hidden.

"Let's get you to the Atrium," I said to her, before turning to the driver. "Bumps in the Night. Do you know the club?"

"Of course. I go there often enough." The driver put the SUV into gear and pulled away from the airport.

CHAPTER 31

"Morgana," a blonde vampire greeted her as we stepped into her club. "I thought you wouldn't be coming back for a while." The way she said it sounded more like never.

"Plans changed." Morgana's eyes landed on me.

Only then did the blonde vampire notice me. Her eyes went as wide as saucers.

"My mate dared run from me. Don't worry, I dragged her back," I said with extreme satisfaction.

"Of course." The vampire kept staring at me, but then seemed to replay what I'd said, her head snapping towards Morgana. "Mate?"

Morgana patted her shoulder. "Yes, I'm his mate, and he's claimed me. So that means he's not on tap for any of the vampires, understand?" She leveled a hard stare at her employee. "And I would appreciate it if you could pass that around; he smells quite good."

"Yes, of course." The vampire nodded a little too quickly, accidentally tapping into some of her vampirism speed as she did so. "Oh, also, a truck with a bunch of barrels came in today."

"Just unload them into my area; they are blood for me." Morgana waved away the issue. "Keep running things as you have. I might be a little busier than I was in the past. Happy to have you still manage the place."

At that, the vampire seemed happy. "Yes, will do." At least she wasn't getting demoted with Morgana back.

We walked past her, but the vampire's eyes lingered on my neck.

"Am I going to have a problem with the vampires in your establishment?" I asked Morgana.

"They might have a problem, but I assure you that you won't be the one with a problem. Your sweet dragon blood is for me alone." She said it a little more loudly than seemed necessary. And there was a drip of menace to it that I knew were for the prying ears around us.

The rest of my mates were quietly trailing behind us as Morgana led us through the maze that was the spatial dimension she called home. As we reached the Atrium and made our way through the halls, we wound up in front of an unassuming door.

Morgana was emotional as she spoke. "Long ago, I had hoped that one day I'd be able to retrieve my tree."

She clicked the door open, and we were transported to a small space with green pasture. I poked a nearby bush, confirming it was real.

Hanging above us was a glowing sphere that mimicked the sun.

"That's a sun stone," Jadelyn said, looking up at it. "Very expensive."

For Jadelyn to call something 'very expensive', I translated that to exorbitantly or even prohibitively expensive for the rest of us.

"Nothing is too much for my tree," Morgana said. "There's even a shell enchanted by a nymph buried here to keep the soil the perfect moisture."

She knelt down in the center of the space. Pulling out one of her knives, she slit her wrist just below where the center of the roots came out of her arm.

After making the cut, she punched her arm into the soft soil.

The root retracted from her arm and slithered off of her, growing rapidly in the soil. A tree came to life, growing what would have taken a dozen years in the span of several breaths.

And as it grew, something rippled at the edge of the branches.

"Fuck," Morgana cursed.

We all came to the same conclusion of what was about to happen. The portal to the celestial plane reappeared, attached to Morgana's tree.

She grunted as she got to her feet and rapidly moved to the edge of the space, her hands swirling with magic. I wasn't sure what she was doing, but I hoped it would be enough.

A hooded figure came to the edge of the portal, too blurry to make out.

Morgana looked back over her shoulder at the figure. "If you step one foot out of there, I have rigged this space to collapse."

"Morgana," Aziel said, now easier to see as he stood a hair's breadth from the portal. "Something can be worked out, I'm sure."

"No," Morgana finished what she was doing. "You may as well close that portal on your side. It is now nothing but a death trap should one of you step out."

"So be it. We'll wait." Aziel stepped back, fading from view.

"Sorry," Jadelyn tried to comfort Morgana. "I know. We all hoped it would separate from the portal."

Morgana shook her head. "I'll set a trap. If something crosses the threshold, the space around the portal will collapse, along with anybody within it. But my tree will remain safe."

"Powerful shit. Why didn't we use that earlier?" Kelly put her hands on her hips.

"This is a space I created. I can uncreate a piece of it, no problem." Morgana rolled her eyes. "I can't do something like that in the natural world."

"Let's get out of here." I grabbed Morgana's hand. Her wrist had already healed after planting the tree, and she was looking better. "Put your amulet on. I'd like to go back to my apartment."

Morgana put the amulet on. She looked strange to me without her blue skin, but she was just as beautiful.

"Frank is going to die when he sees all of us," Scarlett laughed.

I could already imagine the minor heart attack he'd have at seeing me with four women. And it was going to be satisfying.

We headed down to Morgana's garage, jumping into a silver BMW and heading to my apartment.

As we neared my apartment, I saw a number of people 'casually' gathered around. Their phones were out, and they seemed ready to snap photos.

I cursed. I'd hoped they'd be forced to stay more undercover.

As soon as Morgana pulled up, they were not so subtly using their phones to take picture after picture of my mates and me. It was still annoying, but I was glad that they weren't as pushy as they were in Sentar-shaden.

We pushed past, and I wondered how long it would take before they were plastered on some website or maybe even that new app.

I pulled my key out of my new spatial artifact and unlocked the door. We hadn't been gone too long, but it still felt odd coming back to the apartment. So much had changed.

As I entered, I found Frank and Maddie snuggling on the couch. I smiled, glad somethings hadn't changed.

"You're back," Frank said, looking over at us. His eyes went wide as he took in the four stunning women surrounding me.

'Holy shit,' he mouthed where Maddie couldn't see.

"Welcome back." Maddie smiled at us. "I think I know all of you, except you." She pointed to Morgana.

"Morgana," the vampire drow politely introduced herself. "Nice to meet you."

The badass mercenary was gone, replaced by a normal woman. Not to mention the amulet hid her blue skin from my roommate and his girlfriend.

"Uh, we were gonna go out to eat if you want to join us." Frank gave me a big grin.

As much as going out to eat with Frank sounded like a pleasant break from everything, staying in sounded better and would have fewer flashes.

But I also loved that it was the same with Frank. Nothing had changed like it had in the paranormal world. His relationship with me was the same as since before I became a dragon.

"Can we just stay in? We've been eating out a lot," I fibbed.

"There's not much to work with in the fridge," Maddie hesitated.

Jadelyn was already opening said fridge and looking through it. "You live like..."

"... a college dude?" Frank defended me.

"No, I can work with this," Jadelyn corrected herself. "Just give me a minute to get set up."

Scarlett pointed out to Jadelyn where the cooking essentials were and helped her navigate the kitchen.

"You should make those muffins again. I'm afraid Frank ate all the ones you had left in there." Maddie prodded Scarlett.

My little muffin-loving fox grinned ear to ear. "That's okay. I'm glad you enjoyed them. They would have gone bad by now."

"That's what I said!" Frank pulled up a chair to our small table. "See?"

Clearly, Scarlett had unknowingly provided an answer to some minor argument between the two of them.

"It still isn't right to eat someone else's food." Maddie held her ground.

"Just get some ingredients, and I'm sure Scar will be happy to make more," I tried to settle it before the two of them got upset with each other.

"Already done," Frank said proudly. "So, are you guys excited about next semester? Picked your classes out? Oh shit, that reminds me. Some transfer girl was around looking for you."

Maddie helpfully picked up a scrap piece of paper and handed it to Frank.

"She said to call her when you got back. I think her name was Sabrina."

I took the paper with her number. "When did she come by?"

The succubus discipled under one of the magi's famous wizards was a friend and had said she'd be transferring over here. Apparently, after Jared had outed her, things had gotten a little dicey, and she was looking for a more paranormal-accepting place to finish college.

"Uh, around the time you left?" Frank guessed.

That meant she came to find me before finding out I was a dragon. I hoped she hadn't freaked out at the news. She was a demon after all. It's not like they weren't also known for being scary.

I realized Frank was staring at me, and it took me a moment to figure out that he was still waiting for me to answer his questions.

"No, I haven't signed up for classes yet. We need to do that."

I'd decided at that moment that I wanted to continue with school. Even if it wasn't going to be how I made my income, it brought a normalcy I enjoyed. And I could certainly still use the skills and knowledge.

Even better, it was now an excuse to stay out of the purely paranormal circles where people would fawn over me and my new status.

Until the conclave, I'd take all the normalcy I could get. From what Yev's invite had said, I still had a few months before I'd have to meet the conclave of dragons.

"Did anything else come in the mail?" I wondered if I'd gotten my messenger from the Bronze King.

"Nope, nothing but the usual garbage and bills." Frank shrugged while also managing to push the bills a little closer towards me.

I stared at them, a little less excited about anything that would pull from my hoard. I picked up the stack and sifted through them, putting those that weren't on autopay to the side so that I could deal with them.

"You know..." Jadelyn started.

"Don't." I put a hand up. "I can deal with my own bills."

She raised her hands in surrender while Kelly snickered. I shot her a glare, and she turned to Jadelyn.

"Want help in the kitchen?" Kelly asked.

"Yes, please." Jadelyn had set out several cutting boards and a mixing bowl. Scarlett was already getting to work on another round of muffins.

Maddie got up from the table and joined my mates in cooking.

Morgana, oddly enough since she owned a bar, just sort of hung out in the kitchen. I wondered how long it had been since she had eaten normal food.

Frank leaned over conspiratorially. "Scarlett and Jadelyn know about each other? I knew you were dating both, but that's a bold move."

I laughed, realizing just how much I'd missed him. "Actually, I'm dating all four of them. And yes, they all know."

Frank's face fell into shock, and I wondered for a moment if he was about to stroke out. "Four? Four! Man, please teach me your secrets."

"There's no secret, I swear."

He deadpanned, glaring at me. "Tell. Me. The. Secret."

"I guess there's just a certain kind of girl that accepts it." What I couldn't say was that it was a paranormal girl who also happened to understand that I was a dragon.

He nodded very seriously. "I see. It starts at the women. Think I could convince Maddie?"

"Not a chance in hell," I told him honestly.

She had practically wrangled him out of his womanizing phase. Somehow, I doubted that she was going to let him pull in another girl.

"No, what you said makes perfect sense." Frank scratched his chin. "I'll just have to work on Maddie." He was determined to try, anyway.

I patted him on the back, glad that he wasn't going to let her go. She was good for him.

"Good luck, man," I laughed to myself, grabbing a seat and watching my women as they chatted and laughed with each other, finally letting myself relax for the first time in a long time.

***

At Jadelyn's place a few days later, we were all hanging out just before dinner was going to be served.

"Rachel, I said to keep it to one drop. Holy hell, do you need me to come over?" Kelly had stepped away to have a conversation, but she was loud enough for us all to hear.

"Dear god. No, I don't need details. Just tell the betas to keep it to one drop. No, put him down in a cellar for a couple of days, and then make him clean up his mess. He needs to cool down."

She hung up the phone and walked back to the table as we all stared at her with raised eyebrows. There was no way she was going to get out of telling us what that call was all about.

Kelly scratched the back of her neck. "Ha. Sorry, that was a surprising call."

"Sounds like someone decided to double up on the potion?"

"Triple up." She swore. "Don't worry, the pack is chaining him down. Apparently, his girl locked him in the bathroom and called for help. She needed a break, and he just couldn't calm down."

None of us liked the sound of that situation, but it also meant that Kelly and the girls of the pack were going to lay the smack down on those poor betas.

"This is the fertility potion?" Claire, Jadelyn's mother, tried to tactfully ask.

"Yeah." Kelly's wolf ears wilted.

Claire threw her head back and laughed. "Oh, that's grand. Werewolf-strength Viagra. You better not let word get out about that stuff."

Rupert shook his head. "Not that we need it, of course," he defended his manhood.

"No, but I can imagine some of the old farts wanting a pinch of the stuff to help themselves," Claire joked.

The laughter was cut short as the silverware on the table jumped and clattered, a few of the tall wine glasses spilling.

"What the hell was that?" Detective Fox was on his feet instantly, just as a guard ran in panicking.

Scarlett had Jadelyn under the table, standing over her, ready for an assault.

The guard began reporting immediately. "Dragons. Dragons just landed in the back of the house. Sorry, sir, we didn't even see them until they were on us."

I put my hand up. "Let me handle this. I suspect they are here for me."

The guard nodded to me almost reverently. I still wasn't used to everyone's change in attitude towards me.

"I want to see the dragons!" Jadelyn stuck her head out from under the table.

"Absolutely not," Scarlett replied, but Jadelyn crawled out and stood up anyway.

"Let's go!" She bounced over to me, and I looked over at Scarlett for permission.

Scarlett frowned, but Jadelyn just grabbed my arm and stuck her tongue out at her head bodyguard.

"Safest place is with my big, gold hubby. Remember?"

Scarlett grumbled, but finally she nodded that it was okay.

"You know, we really should get to work with the formal wedding." Rupert picked at his beard. "Make it the event of the century."

He got up, and that was the signal for the whole table to follow me out.

Claire clapped her hands together. "That's it. We are all heading out to see the dragons. Later, though, let's talk about a formal wedding. I think we should let all the girls participate."

"Do dragons have formal wedding traditions?" Ruby asked me.

"I have no idea," I answered. "Maybe we could look it up or ask some dragons."

"Good idea." Claire nodded excitedly.

I'd been joking. I didn't exactly have other dragons on speed dial yet.

I walked with a small entourage behind me as we exited the Scalewright house and entered their gardens. Four dragons were in their backyard, and two of them appeared to be arguing.

"No, this one was mine," the massive blue dragon growled at the only slightly smaller white dragon.

Beside each of the two large dragons were smaller dragons that looked just like each of them.

"He gave me the message for the gold. See?" The white held something in her massive claw.

"There isn't even a name on it. There are no names on any of them! We were just given them and sent out to deliver. But I was given the gold to deliver his message," the blue growled back. "Besides, I outrank you. Get lost."

I didn't think they were going to work this out themselves, so I cleared my throat and stepped forward.

That got their attention as I spoke. "Excuse me, but I believe one or both of you have a message for me?"

The blue gasped on seeing me, her nostrils flaring like two massive caves. "You... you aren't a gold." Her neck craned and swooped down just inches from plowing a trench in the backyard. "Pendragon, I... I see."

However, the white bounded forward, shifting into a naked and startlingly beautiful woman. She pulled along the smaller white dragon, who transformed into a younger version of the woman.

"Hello, nice to meet you, King," she said.

She bowed low, while still naked, pushing her daughter to bow as well. They had long beautiful white hair that touched the ground with their bow before she straightened back up.

My eyes strained to look lower, but I forced them up on her face. Even without looking directly at them, I knew her body was practically gravity defying, and her daughter was just as beautiful.

"Lisa," the blue grumbled, shifting as well, while remaining in the bow. "It is proper to bow as dragons."

"He wasn't raised as a dragon," Lisa, the older white dragon, argued before turning quickly back to me.

"This is my daughter, Larisa." Lisa pushed her daughter forward with a bright smile. "I'm so glad someone like you has taken up the mantle, but to see a Pendragon in the flesh is incredible. You'll need someone well versed in dragon politics to guide you."

She not so subtly nudged her daughter further forward.

My eyes betrayed me as they dipped down before I wrenched them back up to focus on her eyes. "Lovely to meet you."

"You can already tell by her crass actions that she's no expert diplomat, which you do, in fact, need." The blue shifted into another lovely lady, her skin retaining flecks of scales that worked to at least keep her modest.

Her daughter was similar to her, but her skin was a shade darker. Both of them had electric blue eyes and black hair that shone blue where the light caught it.

If Frank were here, he'd be drooling. All of them were elevens on a ten-point scale. I wondered if all female dragons were this hot, or if they had some extra shape shifting skills that I had yet to learn.

"I'm Ricca, and this is my daughter, Chloe. I'm third among the Bronze King's wives. Lisa here is the eighth and last. Please

accept his message for the conclave of dragons that will meet this spring equinox."

"Thank you." I took the gold card she gave
me, and the gold card from Lisa, not wanting either to feel slighted.

I stared at them, not quite sure what to do
next. Both of my 'messengers' had brought
their daughters and were clearly waiting for
me to say more.

"I have no idea what I'm going in to. Some
advice would be welcome," I tried.

"Please, join us in our home. We'd love to
host you. And I heard you mentioned Pendragon? What's a Pendragon?" Claire asked,
her hostess skills kicking in.

Both of the older dragons shut their
mouths immediately, looking between
them. They'd clearly not intended for other
ears to hear what they'd said.

"A dragon thing," Chloe suggested, filling
the awkward silence.

"Ah, dragon things. I guess we'll have
to get used to that, dear," Rupert laughed
good-naturedly. "Do dragons dine in the
nude?"

Scarlett interjected herself. "They'll be
putting clothes on. I'm sure we have something that could fit them."

The two elder dragons' faces shifted as
they took in my kitsune mate. They looked
downright chilly, and I was not allowing
that to happen.

"Ladies, this"—I clapped my hands on Scarlett's shoulders—"is my first mate. Not only was she the one that helped introduce me to the paranormal world, but she's the woman that has been with me the longest and knows me best."

I smiled, realizing the opportunity to pawn off their attention. "So, I've asked for her help. We all know I'm going to end up with a few dragon mates, and she's the best person in the world to help me figure out which ones will work with our family."

I cheered inside as their attention suddenly flipped to Scarlett, their faces much warmer.

Lisa wrapped her arm around Scarlett like an old friend. I had a feeling I'd have to apologize later to Scar for putting her in their sights, but it felt so good to not be the focus.

I was prepared for diving into the dragon dating pool, but I had most definitely not prepared myself for dragon mothers.

Claire led the group back inside for the dragons to find suitable clothing. Because, otherwise, I wasn't going to be able to eat anything without spilling tonight.

I walked behind them, flipping the gold card in my hand. The fine print allowed me to bring my harem. I double checked, breathing a sigh of relief. I'd need each and every one of them to bring me through whatever was to come.

There was no way I was going to navigate a conclave of dragons successfully without them by my side.

AFTERWORD

Thanks for joining me in Dragon Justice 3. We saw Zach get more than a few powerful upgrades. He's flying, he can cast a lovely single spell, and we even got green scales.

I'm loving Dragon and hope to make it a long series. There's the dragon conclave obviously coming up, along with the group behind Nat'alet and the church won't take things laying down. So much of the world yet to be explored, not to mention the fae and hell. For now, I'm moving onto the next series in the rotation.

Saving Supervillains is a new series, a super hero world, but I've done my best to make heroes and villains more complex than a cardboard cutout. Not all heroes are perfect little angels and not all villains do it for the wrong reasons. Our main character is a cynic, seeing past 'hero' and 'villain' to the person underneath the powers. That's how he ends up saving a wayward villain who can't control her power.

After that, it is back to the conclusion of Mana. I might leave an open end should I ever want to return to it. But for now, I'm ready to end the series. Dao is heading towards its own conclusion and I'm mulling up another series to replace it as well.

As always, if you can, drop me a review. It greases the gears in Amazon's system and helps a ton. It is also how you get longer series. I want to make Dragon as long as I can, so leave a rating or review to help.

Leave a Review

Also By

Legendary Rule:
Ajax Demos finds himself lost in society.
Graduating shortly after artificial intelli-
gence is allowed to enter the workforce;
he can't get his career off the ground.
But when one opportunity closes, another
opens. Ajax gets a chance to play a brand
new Immersive Reality game. Things aren't
as they seem. Mega Corps hover over what
appears to be a simple game. However,
what he does in the game seems to effect
his body outside.
But that isn't going to make Ajax pause
when he finally might just get that shot at
becoming a professional gamer. Join Ajax
and Company as they enter the world of
Legendary Rule.

Series Page

A Mage's Cultivation:

In a world where mages and monster grow
from cultivating mana. Isaac joins the class
of humans known as mages who absorb
mana to grow more powerful. To become
a mage he must bind a mana beast to himself to access and control mana. But when
his mana beast is far more human than he
expected; Isaac struggles with the budding
relationship between the two of them as he
prepares to enter his first dungeon.
Unfortunately for Isaac, he doesn't have
time to ponder the questions of his relationship with Aurora. Because his sleepy
town of Locksprings is in for a rude awakening, and he has to decide which side of
the war he is going to stand on.

Series Page

Dao Divinity: The First Immortal
Darius Yigg was a wanderer, someone
who's never quite found his place in the
world, but maybe he's not supposed to be
here...Ripped from our world, Dar finds
himself in his past life's world, where his
destiny was cut short. Reignited, the wick of
Dar's destiny burns again with the hope of
him saving Grandterra.
To do that, he'll have to do something no
other human of Grandterra has done before, walk the dao path. That path requires
mastering and controlling attributes of the
world and merging them to greater and

greater entities. In theory, if he progressed far enough, he could control all of reality and rival a god.

He won't be in this alone. As a beacon of hope for the world, those from the ancient races will rally around Dar to stave off the growing Devil horde.

Series Page

There are of course a number of communities where you can find similar books.

https://www.facebook.com/groups/harem-lit

https://www.facebook.com/groups/HaremGamelit
And other non-harem specific communities for Cultivation and LitRPG.

https://www.facebook.com/groups/WesternWuxia

https://www.facebook.com/groups/LitRPGsociety

https://www.facebook.com/groups/cultivationnovels

Made in the USA
Monee, IL
12 January 2024

51638254R00305